MW00622595

THE (

Clint Mayer is a big m
thinks. When Clint leaves Beaverkill for the rough and
tumble dock town of Wilton, he hooks up with Charlie
Fletcher, good time saloon owner and businessman.
One of the businesses Charlie runs out of the bar
involves a string of working girls, but he has to pay off
Detective Red Brandon and it's wearing him down.
He's had enough. Clint agrees to buy him out, but then
he meets Charlie's wife, Debbie. Clint thinks he can
find a way to keep the bar, manage the girls and stay
away from Brandon. He may even come away with
Debbie. But Debbie has her own ideas—deadly ones!

DIAL "M" FOR MAN

Hob Sampson knows the blonde will be trouble—pure
poison. It starts when she calls him up to fix her TV
set. But she has a lot more on her mind than reception.
Doris is all woman, and she makes sure that he knows
it. She's married to one of the richest men in town,
Ferris Condon, a man with a grudge against Hob a mile
wide. Hob knows his repair business will never get
ahead while Ferris plots against him, but does he want
to get involved with the man's wife? Shouldn't he be
with Kathy? He's comfortable with her. But Hob can't
resist Doris. And before he knows what's good for him,
he's plotting with her to do something he knows is so
wrong—and so necessary. Because Ferris Condon is all
that stands between desire and Doris, and that's a fatal
place to be.

DIAL "M" FOR MAN

THE CHEATERS

TWO NOVELS BY
Orrie Hitt
Afterword by
Michael Hemmingson

STARK HOUSE

Stark House Press • Eureka California

THE CHEATERS / DIAL "M" FOR MAN

Published by Stark House Press
4720 Herron Road, Eureka, CA 95503, USA
griffinskye3@sbcglobal.net
www.starkhousepress.com

THE CHEATERS
Originally published by Midwood and copyright © 1960
by Tower Publications.
Reprinted by permission of the Orrie Hitt Estate

DIAL "M" FOR MAN
Originally published by Beacon Books and copyright © 1962
by Universal Publishing.
Reprinted by permission of the Orrie Hitt Estate

Introduction copyright © 2011 by Joyce Gordon
The Sleazy Side of the Street copyright © 2009 by Brian Ritt
as published on James Reasoner's Rough Edges website; revised 2011
Themes and Motifs in Orrie Hitt's Fiction copyright © 2011
by Michael Hemmingson

ISBN: 1-933586-35-4
ISBN-13: 978-1-933586-35-9

Special thanks to Frank Loose for all his help and encouragement with this project.

Cover design and book layout by Mark Shepard, SHEPGRAPHICS.COM
Cover from the model collection of Robert A. Maguire
Proofreading by Rick Ollerman

PUBLISHER'S NOTE

First Stark House Press Edition: October 2011

REPRINT EDITION

An Introduction to the Real Orrie Hitt

Growing up with these types of books being worked on at our kitchen table? And at all hours? Who knew??? We really didn't. It was never discussed until we were older and more mature. And then we realized that Dad was writing about real-life events and people that became even more exciting in his creative mind! By today's standards, these books are mild but in order to protect us, Dad kept these books from being marketed in our small town.

The only thing that we knew about Dad's writing was that if we were out and a thought came to his mind it didn't matter if the only available paper was a placemat, a napkin or even toilet paper; it was written down and went home with us that night.

At the time the only "hot" thing we knew about our Dad was his love of spicy foods and an occasional spurt of a hot temper when one of us did something foolish. What we recall is a kind, brilliant man who loved to listen to people and participate in conversations that would last for hours!

Dad provided for us in the best way he could—as a husband, and a father. His prolific writing was an art, as well as his livelihood. His family, however, was his LIFE!

Is this reprint of two of our dad's books a new place in time for Orrie E. Hitt? If so, he would be thrilled!

NANCY HITT GOODING
MARGARET HITT SQUIRES
JOYCE HITT GORDON

The Sleazy Side of the Street
by Brian Ritt

Orrie Hitt wrote about low-rent people in low-rent places.

His men were rotten to the core, as bad as they come: lust prowlers, promoters, cheaters, suckers, pushovers, and Peeping Toms. Their names were Dutch, Arch, Rip, Brick, Buck, Shad, Slade, Big Mike, Clint Crown, Johnny Vandal, and Jerry Slink. They dreamed and schemed, manipulated and manhandled.

Meet one of Hitt's men: "He was a big man, a couple of inches over 6 feet, and he weighed 180 pounds. He was all raw muscle and bone with broad shoulders and close cut sandy hair. As for being handsome he didn't know... Most of the women thought he was pretty much of a man at the age of 26 and that, to Dutch, was what counted."

–*Naked Flesh*, Kozy Books, 1962

His women were too hot to handle: ex-virgins, frigid wives, sin dolls, wayward girls, torrid cheats, easy women, frustrated females, inflamed dames and, most often, trapped. Their names were Sheba, Sherry, Honey, Candy, Cherry, Betty French, and Lola Champ. They used what they had to use to make a buck–limited opportunities left few other choices. They were duped and deceived, approached and abandoned.

Meet one of Hitt's women: "As soon as she was in the room she stood in front of the mirror and slowly stripped. Men would pay to see this, would they? Well, she would give them their money's worth and have them begging for more. Two hundred a week was a lot of money, a hell of a lot. She could push her pride aside and do whatever was necessary to make that much money."

–*Sin Doll*, Beacon, 1959

His places were shabby streets, strip alleys, pleasure grounds, private clubs, passion pools, girls dormitories, dirt farms, nudist camps, and sexurbia counties.

Visit one of Hitt's places—The Hotel Shelly: "By my watch, every night in this creep joint was too long. The rugs in the lobby were faded and the seats of the chairs sagged worse than the knees in my pants. The manager had a lousy disposition and a couple of ulcers as big as watermelons. One of the bellhops was always chasing strange-acting guys. After almost a month in this racket I was ready to get out of the hotel business for good."

—*Shabby Street*, Beacon Books, 1958

You might even say Hitt wrote about low-rent emotions: unnatural urges, warped desires, untamed lusts, tormented passions, taboo thrills, and strange longings. Once he even wrote a book about panda bear passions.

Feel one of Hitt's emotions: "His hands roamed her body as a savage roams the darkness of an unknown jungle. He filled his hands with her, sensing the rich beauty of her flesh, and he bore down on her mouth, crushing her lips. She twisted nearer to him, moaning with longing and anticipation, her restraint shattered, her fingernails clawing at his skin, bringing pain, turning the desire that he felt into raw, reckless lust."

—*Naked Flesh*, Kozy Books, 1962

But there was nothing low-rent about Orrie Hitt. Behind the tawdry and lurid titles, covers, and subject matter of his books, there was a beloved and faithful family man who worked ten to fourteen hours a day.

He was born Orrie Edwin Hitt in Colchester (now Roscoe), New York, on October 27, 1916. Died in a VA hospital in Montrose, New York, from cancer, on December 7, 1975. He married Charlotte Tucker in Port Jervis, New York (a small town upstate where he became a lifelong resident), on Valentine's Day, 1943. Orrie and Charlotte Hitt had four children—Joyce, Margaret, David, and Nancy. In contrast to his macho male protagonists, Orrie was slightly under 5'5", and his pants' length was 27", which his wife had to alter because stores didn't sell pants that short. But make no mistake: as will become clear later in this article, Orrie Hitt was a hell of a tough old bird, with more grit and backbone than any number of his fictional he-men combined.

Hitt wrote approximately 150 books. In his prime, he wrote a novel every two weeks, typing over 90 words per minute. "His fastest and best works were produced when he was allowed to type whatever he wanted," said Hitt's children. "His slowest works were produced when publishers insisted on a certain kind of novel, extra spicy, etc."

(Note: A large part of the information in this article comes from a lengthy interview with Orrie Hitt's four children, conducted in 1993 by R. C. Holland for his fanzine *Books Are Everything!* Holland conducted the interviews by mail and combined the answers into single blocks, rather than quoting each individual. I'll do the same for this article and when quoting will simply refer to "Hitt's children.")

Most of Hitt's books were paperback originals. He wrote a few hard-covers, as well. Pseudonyms include Kay Addams, Joe Black, Roger Normandie, Charles Verne, and Nicky Weaver. Publishers include Avon, Beacon (later Softcover Library), Chariot, Domino (Lancer), Ember Library, Gaslight, Key Publishing, Kozy, MacFadden, Midwood, Novel, P.E.C, Red Lantern, Sabre, Uni-books, Valentine Books, Vantage Press, Vest-Pocket, and Wisdom House.

He wrote in what is known as the "sleaze" or "adults only" genre. Many of the writers in this genre were hacks, using the thinnest of plots merely as an excuse to throw some "tits and ass" (to borrow a phrase from a famous Lenny Bruce stand-up bit) between two covers to make a quick buck. Other writers used the genre as a stepping stone to more "legitimate" writing, later unwilling to discuss this part of their career. But for Orrie Hitt, writing for the "sleaze" publishers allowed him to portray a side of American life not dealt with in the mainstream media during the 1950's and early 60's. While the culture-at-large touted a too-perfect world where father knew best and where a woman's life was made complete by the latest-model Frigidaire, Hitt's men were desperately trying to wring another buck out of their latest scam and his women were trying to provide for their fatherless babies without having to resort to posing nude for "girlie" photos or to prostitution. While life was writ large and presented in 3-D, VistaVision, and SuperCinecolor, the lives of Hitt's characters were as glamorous as the dirt under a wino's fingernails.

Hitt's work for sleaze publishers like Beacon and Midwood benefited due to the fact that he actually observed and investigated the people and places he wrote about. When he wanted to write about a nudist camp, he went to a nudist camp–though, his children were quick to respond, "he would not disrobe."

His research allowed him to write convincingly enough so that author Susan Stryker, in her book *Queer Pulp: Perverted Passions from the Golden Age of the Paperback*, writes, "Only one actual lesbian, Kay Addams, writing as Orrie Hitt, is known to have churned out semi-pornographic sleaze novels for a predominantly male audience." Stryker thinks "Orrie Hitt" is a pseudonym, and "Kay Addams" is a real lesbian author! I'm sure Orrie'd be laughing his ass off about that one.

Of course, Orrie wrote about the subject most everyone was interested in, but that few talked about openly during the repressive, button-down 1950's: S-E-X.

"[My agent] was obviously under the impression that women didn't have breasts", Hitt wrote in an autobiographical article for *Men's Digest* magazine, "and that you didn't write about them if they did–or that men and women slept together."

But it wasn't just about sex for Orrie Hitt. It was also about guts.

"The characters," a Hitt protagonist (a movie producer) says, "were very real, red blooded people who tore at the guts of life. That's what I'm after. Guts."

And if there was one person who knew about guts, it was Orrie Hitt.

Life started out tough for Hitt. His father committed suicide when Orrie was 11 years old. Afterward, Orrie and his mother moved to Forest-burgh, New York, where they worked for a private hunting and fishing club. Orrie was paid 25 cents an hour–good money during those Depres-sion-era years.

Tragedy struck Hitt again during his years at the private club. Hitt's children explain: "[Orrie's] mom died at her sister's house on the club property during an ice storm, so [Orrie] walked to the house to get his mother and carried her back to his car in order to get her body into town."

During his high school years, Hitt decided he wanted to be a writer. Ini-tially, his ambition was greeted with something less than cheers and applause.

"I guess I was in my second year in high school when the teacher gave me the bad news," Hitt wrote in *Men's Digest*. "I'd never make it as a writer. To begin with, I didn't know up from down about the English language and, secondly, I was too much of a dreamer."

Hitt continued. "What the teacher told me hurt, especially because those were the years of the Great Depression and I knew, since my wid-owed mother was only making $50 a month as a hotel chambermaid, that there would never be enough money for college… It seemed to me that the teacher had taken that hope away from me, the only real hope I'd ever had since I can remember."

But the lack of encouragement from Orrie's "educator" didn't stop him. He soon started writing articles for outdoor magazines–and selling them.

Hitt's senior year in high school produced an amusing irony between student and teacher.

"During that last year in high school I was told that an educational book published once a year in Albany would consider articles on school subjects from students and teachers," wrote Hitt. "I wrote about our rifle club…The teacher who told me I couldn't write selected some other sub-ject. My article was published and the teacher's article was rejected. After that I was pretty sure that, right or wrong, the guy I saw in the mirror when I shaved was the man whose advice I'd follow."

Then came World War II, and the 24-year-old Orrie Hitt enlisted in the Army, going in as a private and coming out as a first lieutenant. Upon his release, Orrie had a wife and first child to support, so he curtailed his writing career for the next 6-8 years, taking a variety of odd jobs which barely paid the bills. He sold life insurance, roofing and siding, and frozen foods to stores. He worked for a local radio station as a DJ and ad salesman. Altogether, Hitt worked between 15 to 17 jobs, all the while pining to pursue the passion he felt he was born for.

"Oh, I might've done a few short stories which didn't sell but I'm not counting them," Hitt wrote. "A book was in the back of my mind and I was unable to shake it."

And then the Iceland cometh.

Iceland???

"My next stop was Keflavik, Iceland, working at the airport hotel and, again, the pay could've been better," Orrie wrote. "However, I found in Iceland what I wanted. Once I had learned my duties there was plenty of time to write. And this time it was a book."

Hitt worked at the airport hotel for a year. When he got back to New York he "made the rounds of publishers myself, receiving encouragement but no contracts." Hitt did find one taker–a "vanity" publisher who wanted Hitt to pay them to publish the book. (He turned them down flatly.) Finally, he found a legitimate publisher who wanted his book and, "A few days later I had a royalty contract."

That was 1953, and Hitt's first book was titled *I'll Call Every Monday*, published in hardcover by Red Lantern books (later re-issued as a paperback by Avon).

From that point, according to Hitt's children, Orrie's work schedule was "continuous and incredible. From morning to dinner time he was at the kitchen table with his typewriter, and his iced coffee and ash tray full of half-smoked Winstons were at his side... Ideas flowed out at 90 words a minute on his old Remington Royal...There he would sit, amidst all the comings and goings of a busy family of four children, and write to his heart's content...The only days I remember him not typing were Christmas, New Year's, and Easter."

During the evening Hitt watched comedy shows on TV–Red Skelton, Jackie Gleason, Sgt. Bilko. Or a buddy stopped by and they'd throw back a few cold ones and watch wrestling. Makes sense when you consider the dark, violent, emotionally harrowing lives he wrote about all day.

As a man-about-town in small, blue-collar Port Jervis, Orrie "was a loquacious man, anxious to talk to anyone who would listen...especially when he had a few too many beers," Hitt's children remembered. One night while Mr. and Mrs. Hitt were at a bar, a woman tried to "pick-up" Orrie, curious if he was anything like the characters in his books. Orrie saw quite a bit of humor in the situation. Mrs. Hitt, however, did not. POW! Right in the kisser, Orrie!

As a father, Hitt's children characterized him as, "sensitive and loving and stopping at nothing to provide for his family. He wasn't interested in 'keeping up with the Joneses,' just in doing well enough so his family didn't have to want for anything... Every one of our friends liked dad. He would listen or help when needed and they could always use his shoulder to lean or cry on... He was nothing like the characters he portrayed in his books."

As a breadwinner whose income depended on free-lance writing, Hitt and his family experienced both feast and famine:

"There was a time when we owned a beautifully remodeled home, we had beautiful new cars, one daughter was in college, and we had plenty to eat," said Hitt's children. "But when the chips were down and the money was gone, things got pretty bad. Once we lived from hotel room to hotel room, leaving when the rent came due... We went from eating out every Wednesday night to eating from garbage cans in the city!"

As a writer for the "adults only" market, life in a small town was not always easy for the Hitts:

"We knew that [Orrie] attempted to have his books marketed in places other than our small home town due to the nature of the books," Hitt's children recalled. "As children, we encountered a fair amount of prejudice from other families as the news of dad's source for our livelihood spread... When we read his books, however, we could see the events that occurred in his life and the people that lived in our small home town that provided the inspiration for his characters."

Shades of Peyton Place!

Hitt earned between $250 and $1000 in advances for his PBO's. He earned additional money from reprints and royalties, though not all his publishers were on the up-and-up, a situation not unusual for many of the fly-by-night (some should have been called "lie-by-night") publishers serving the "adults only" market at the time.

The Hitt children: "Some [of Hitt's books] had words and phrases added without his consent... Some reprints were done without prior authorization and some appeared to have been pirated. In the latter case, the titles, authors, and names were changed, but it could never be proven."

Hitt's books also contain the common mistakes (typos, misspellings, words printed twice, words left out, etc.) that characterized the slim-to-none editing style of the sleaze publishers.

As for the content of Hitt's books, it wasn't all angst and anguish. Orrie wrote some wonderfully loopy metaphors and similes, as well.

"If she bore his child it was an obligation that he'd have to face. To run or to ignore it was to deny that he was a man. Onions? Why was he thinking of them? Onions were so much a pound, depending on the season. Well, the pleasures of the flesh cost money, too... Yes the price of onions and the price of desire. So totally unrelated and, yet, in cost so much the same."
–*Naked Flesh*, Kozy Books, 1962, pgs. 94-95

"Her nipples could stay hard longer than a bear could hibernate."
–*Wilma's Wants*, Novel Books, 1964, pg. 62

Intentionally funny, or not? Personally, as I sit back and chuckle, wondering how Hitt's mind made the connection between the responsibilities of parenthood and onions, I really don't give a damn. I just enjoy it.

Toward the latter part of his career, Hitt's writing took an unexpected turn. In 1961 he started writing for a publisher called Novel Books. In contrast to some of the other sleaze publishers, where the story was just a frame around a sometimes mind-numbing succession of softcore sexual liaisons, Hitt's books for Novel turned this concept inside-out. Although the titles, cover art, and blurbs were as sensationalistic as ever (A NOVEL BOOK IS A MAN'S BOOK!), between the covers, Hitt filled his pages with points-of-view addressing current social and political issues.

Some examples:

On writing about sexually provocative subjects: "Of course I wrote about loose wives, wandering husbands, girls who were too willing, men who were anxious, but I considered these things as a part of life and I wrote about life."
–*Wilma's Wants*, 1964, Novel Books, pg. 82

On censorship: "As a writer, and as an American, I dread any form of censorship. Of course I agree that discretion should be exercised...but I do not think that the right of expression should rest in the hands of any particular group."
–Ibid, 1964, Novel Books, pg. 94

On a free society vs. a dictatorship: "Damn! How could I be so blind! The minute you take from one man to give to another, even if the first man is a millionaire and the other man is broke with ten mouths to feed–you're taking away man's inalienable right to freedom and ownership of his own property like Jefferson and Paine talked about. The minute you tell a man he owes his life or his money to another man, you've got a dictatorship, a

socialist police state where character, ability, and ambition are just words that don't mean a damn thing. Brave New World, that's what it is."
   —*Shocking Mistress!*, 1961, Novel Books, pg. 153

Orrie took one hell of a leap from onions and nipples to Jefferson and Paine, eh? And though I wouldn't put his writing in quite the same league as the Founding Fathers', I don't think I'm reaching too far to dub Orrie "the thinking man's" sleaze writer.

Orrie Hitt died at a too-young 59 years of age. Quite possibly, his steady regimen of coffee, cigarettes, and 10-14 hour workdays contributed to the cancer that caused his early death, although this is speculation on my part. Besides his fairly young age, there was another tragic element to Hitt's death. "Our dad died in debt in a veterans hospital," said Hitt's children, "although he had helped others all his life. But, when we needed help, the same people were nowhere to be found."

Hitt's children summed him up this way: "We're proud of both our parents. When we lost our dad, we also lost our best friend. Dad taught us many things in life: hard work, love, honesty, respect, caring, and never giving up."

Doesn't sound like a sleazy guy to me.

References

Hitt, Orrie. "My 'Sex' Books", Part 1. *Men's Digest*, #31, 1962. Pages 37-39.

Holland, R.C. *Books Are Everything!* Vol. 5, No. 1, Whole Number 21. 1993. Pages 28-48.

Stryker, Susan. *Queer Pulp: Perverted Passions from the Golden Age of the Paperback*, Chronicle Books, 2001. Pages 61,66.

Various novels of Orrie Hitt.

The Cheaters
By Orrie Hitt

Chapter One

I wanted a job tending bar about as much as I wanted three legs in my pants but when you've got ten bucks in your pocket and a girl waiting for you in a rented room you don't argue with anything that comes your way.

"Seventy-five a week," the girl in the employment office said. "And a day off. It could be worse."

"Oh, sure."

The girl was rather attractive, probably in her middle twenties, and when she smiled her teeth were very white.

"And you won't have to pay any fee," she assured me. "Mr. Fletcher will do that. He only asked us to get somebody big and strong—I guess there's trouble in the bar off and on—and he told me he would take care of the rest."

"It must be some dump."

"Well, it's in The Dells—on the corner of Fourth Street and Main—and when you're in The Dells you're in the slums." Her eyes brightened. "But it isn't bad pay, Mr. Mayer. The uptown bars wouldn't pay more than sixty a week for a bartender."

This was my second day in Wilton and although I had been to a lot of places this was my first real chance for a job. Ann and I had left the Catskills, around Monticello, because there hadn't been anything doing, not even table work for her or odd jobs for me, and I had to take whatever was thrown in my direction.

"Okay," I said. "You give me a note or something and I'll hop down there." The address she had mentioned was only a couple of blocks from the room Ann and I had taken on Clay Street in a run-down rooming house where the woman hadn't cared whether we were married or not. "I have to have something, don't I?"

"No, I'll call him while you're on your way and he'll be expecting you. We've done business with Mr. Fletcher before."

"I see."

"He gets a bartender and the man stays a while and then the man leaves." She favored me with another smile. "Perhaps you'll be different. Perhaps you'll stick." She glanced at the card I had filled out. "Not that you've stuck very long at anything before. You haven't. But then the most you ever made was sixty-five a week and the added ten may make a difference."

"Time will tell."

"If you're hired we'll get our fee, anyway."

"Naturally."

About five minutes later I got out of there, the girl promising to phone this Fletcher that I was coming, and I walked down the street, smoking as I walked.

Wilton is a city of about twenty thousand and most of the men in it work on the railroad, in the factories or along the docks. I had tried some of the factories but they hadn't been hiring, nearly all of them telling me they were going to lay off help, and the same thing had been true of the docks and the railroad.

"We can't live long on ten bucks," I had said to Ann that morning. "Something has to break and break fast."

"I'll try the restaurants and diners today."

"You do that and I'll hit the employment agencies. One of us is bound to come up with a little work."

She had beamed and the slash of her lips, curving upward at the corners, had been as red as her red hair.

"Maybe if we both get jobs we can get married, Clint."

I hadn't made any direct reply to this but I had kissed her—she had been naked and warm there in the double bed—and she had apparently taken my action to mean I felt the same way about it as she did. The only hitch was that after sleeping with her for almost two years I still wasn't sold on the idea of spending the rest of my life with her.

I walked along, thinking that I might be a heel, but I decided that if it hadn't been me it would have been somebody else. We had both been born and brought up in Beaverkill—that isn't very far from Roscoe, also in the Catskills—and our farms had been side by side. The first time I had been with her, four years before, she had been sixteen and I had been twenty. She hadn't had any previous experience with a boy and I had hurt her, making her cry out in the back of the car.

"You could have given me a baby," she had said afterward. "A girl in school did it once and got a baby."

"Rest easy. I took care of that."

"How?"

"Don't tell me you're that dumb."

Nights that I could get the family car, following this, we parked and made love. This went on for two years and then after her father, Arch Stempert, got my oldest sister Olive in a family way we pulled out and left the mess behind us. For the next two years we had worked the resort hotels, doing all right during the summer months but practically starving to death during the winter. This past winter had been worse than ever and we had decided to try our luck in Wilton.

"I worry every month," she kept saying. "Some night we're going to get drunk and careless and I'm going to end up with something growing inside of me."

"My sister got rid of hers."

"And it cost my father three hundred dollars. I'd never have an abortion, Clint. Never. If you give me a baby it's going to live."

I continued walking down Main Street, thinking of these things and wondering where it would all stop. At the age of twenty-four I didn't have an actual trade that I could follow except farming, if you can call that a trade, and I had no desire to go to work on a farm. I had had all of a farm that I wanted back in Beaverkill. You worked six or seven days a week and if you figured the hours you put in you made peanuts for every hour that you broke your neck. If you owned the farm it was a different story—my father and Arch Stempert did okay—but you don't buy a farm with ten bucks.

The further I got down Main Street the more ugly the buildings looked, every one of them in need of some sort of repair. Kids, ragged and dirty, played in the street, jumping to the sidewalk to avoid the passing cars, and a drunk lay sleeping in a doorway. There was an empty wine bottle near the drunk and a package of unopened cigarettes.

I couldn't figure out why anybody would pay seventy-five dollars a week for a bartender in this miserable neighborhood but if it was what the man paid it was what he paid. Seventy-five was a lot better than fifty or sixty.

I crossed Clay Street, thought about going down to the rooming house to tell Ann, and decided that she would be out. Besides that, I didn't have the job yet. It could be just a bum lead and I'd be right back where I had started from.

I saw the bar long before I got to it. It was on the corner, in a brick building, and there were several neon beer signs burning in the windows. From where I was I could look to the end of Main Street and see the start of the docks with the river in the background. A freighter was moving slowly up the river and overhead the sky was a pale blue. Even if I didn't get the job, I thought, the guy might give me a free drink. And I needed a drink. This business of jumping from job to job isn't any good and you're always on edge. I had thought of getting a bottle the night before but food comes first and you can't stretch money.

The only person in the bar when I entered was a fat man sitting at a table and he glanced at me.

"You must be from the employment agency," he said. "The girl said you were a big guy and, if you're the one, she wasn't lying about it."

I walked over to the table.

"That's me," I said.

He got up and held out his hand. He was short, bald as a board and he had a red face. I judged him to be fifty and maybe a few years older.

"Just call me Charlie."

I shook his hand. It was fat and flabby.

"I'm Clint."

He looked up at me.

"How tall are you?"

"Six-four."

"Weigh about two hundred?"

"One ninety, give or take a pound one way or the other."

"Ever tend bar before?"

"A couple of times."

He walked toward me with the beer and I noticed that he had a slight limp but I couldn't tell whether it was his right leg or his left leg that was doing it.

"Care for a drink?"

"A beer would be fine." I would have rather had a shot but I didn't want him to think I was a whiskey hound.

While he drew the beers, I looked the place over. The bar was quite long and there were some booths in the back, bordering a small area that could be used for dancing. The walls and ceiling didn't appear to have been done over in a long while but there was a good back bar, well stocked, and two large mirrors. Between the mirrors stood a tank containing tropical fish.

"Not much doing this time of the day," he said, putting a glass of beer in front of me. "We don't hit our stride until the people get out of work and then we boom along until closing time at three."

"You always stay open until three?"

He nodded and reached for a cigar.

"Every night of the week. While we may not do much after midnight— mostly uptown guys looking for girls—our customers expect it and we have to please them. About two you get the girls—they're usually finished for the night then—and they're heavy drinkers."

"Girls?"

"That's what I said. There are four of them who work out of here and they have rooms up the street. It may not be legal but it's good for business. We get some big spenders who make dates with the girls. If the girl they want is busy they hang around and wait and the cash register rings."

It followed. He didn't have a dive in the slums for nothing. The girls probably gave him a cut and that could amount to a considerable sum of money. I had worked one place in Sullivan County where they could have given the booze away free and still cleaned up plenty on the prostitutes. But the police had caught up with the owners and I'd been out of a job in less than a month.

"What about the cops?" I asked, taking a drink of the beer. "You pay off to stay out of trouble?"

"I do and the girls do. The detective, Red Brandon, who works this section, knocks the girls down for all they can afford. I even heard that last year he knocked one of them up but you can't prove it by me. She don't come around no more. Some say she went to Florida with a salesman and that she stuck him with the kid."

"Nice people," I said, lighting a cigarette.

"None of them that come in here are nice. You get a husband at one end of the bar and a wife at the other end and they're both playing around with somebody else. If you ask me, half the kids in The Dells are bastards."

"Any of them yours?"

"Have another beer," he said without answering.

He drew a couple of more and he was very good at it. There was just the right amount of head. If there's anything that burns me up, even though I'm not paying for it, is to have a beer that's half foam.

"I need a big guy," he said, resting his weight on his elbows. "Some of those dockers are nuts and they can get out of hand. They don't bother me none because I own the joint but if a bartender can't take his own part they've got no respect for him. I don't allow no fighting in here. If they want to fight they've got the street." He shrugged. "You know how some people get when they're tanked up. They either want to pick up some dame or they want to mix it with the rough stuff. The dames I don't mind. Half of the single girls and wives in The Dells are nothing but whores. You'll see what I mean if I take you on. There isn't a form of creep in the world who hasn't been in here at one time or another."

I assured him that I wasn't afraid of anybody and that I could take care of myself. I remembered a guy in Roscoe who would be willing to attest to that fact. I had busted his jaw in three places with one smash.

"You honest?" Charlie Fletcher asked me.

"All I want is my seventy-five a week."

"That was what the last fellow, Barney, said, but he clipped me right and left." He paused. "My wife, Debbie, takes care of the cash in the morning and she discovered it. Let me tell you you don't fool Debbie none. She's got an eye out for the buck and what she misses isn't worth finding." He laughed, obviously pleased that he had such a competent wife. "You try knocking down and she'll catch you every time."

"She won't catch me because I won't do it."

"I just told you that's what Barney said. So did a couple of others."

"And I said what I said. You have to take it or leave it."

He seemed to accept my statement and he began telling me a few things about himself. Debbie was his second wife—his first one had died of cancer of the breast—and he had a daughter who was twenty-eight.

"But Ruth don't want no part of this business," he explained. "She's got a nice house and nice kids—four of 'em—and her husband has a big garage. Of course," he added, "I own part of the garage. When you get right down to it I own parts of lots of things. I even got an interest in a housing development—middle class homes—and they are just some of the reasons I have to have somebody take over nights for me. Days we aren't very busy and I can get along but the nights are hell. It starts at five o'clock and goes for about seven hours and I've had enough of it—close to twenty years suffering through people's remarks." He leaned forward. "The right kind of a guy can feather his nest here, Clint. You get a fair pay for doing your job and if you show me that you've got the right sort of interest in it I'd consider selling out."

"With ten dollars in my pocket I'm not a likely prospect."

"Oh, it wouldn't have to be cash. We could work out some kind of an arrangement where you could pay me off by the month. That works out better from a tax standpoint for me. You could earn a nice living by working part of the shift yourself and hiring somebody else to work the other part."

We seemed to hit it off right away but it was more on his side than it was on mine. I never had much use for any man who sold female flesh, or had anything to do with it, and I didn't draw the line with him. To me, a girl was somebody to be pursued, conquered and enjoyed. You buy fish by the pound on Friday, or any other day of the week, but that, in my book, didn't go for a girl. I had been with several girls who sold their favors for money but it wasn't quite the same as getting it for nothing. When you get it for nothing it's because the girl wants to and it's better that way. That was one thing about Ann—she had a bed for a mind and that's where she put her body.

"You married?" he asked me.

"No."

"Girl?"

"Yeah, I've got a girl."

"She with you?"

"We've got a room on Clay Street."

"You might call her and tell her you've got a job."

I was slightly surprised.

"So soon?"

"I make up my mind fast. You've got the build to command respect and I might as well take a chance on you—if you prove out—as take a chance on somebody else. Right now you don't know much about me and I don't know much about you so that makes us even."

I listened to him while he resumed talking about himself. He was fifty-two—I had come close to guessing his age—and he lived with his wife in the apartment over the bar. His wife didn't have much to do with the business, only took care of the money, and once in a while she came down to have a drink before closing time. When he was free at night—my hours would be from six until three the next morning—he went to meetings uptown and took care of his other affairs. I was to have Tuesday off—Tuesday, he said, was slow in The Dells—and if he had me work any extra time I would get paid for it.

"When can you start?" he asked me.

"Right now."

He smiled.

"Well, that's what I like to hear. I don't go for guys who have excuses. If you need a job you need a job and there's no two ways about that."

"True."

"I can work with you tonight for a few hours and show you the ropes. There isn't much to learn, only where I keep the money to cash pay checks and like that. Beer is ten cents and shots are thirty. So is gin. We sell a lot of gin. You won't get asked for any fancy drinks because most of our customers—I don't mean the guys from uptown—never heard of them."

"Sounds easy."

"It is and there's money to be made here. Some of the drunks leave their change on the bar and that belongs to you. There was a time that I tried to keep it separated for them but I gave up on that fast."

My glass was empty and he drew me another beer, more head than it had been the last time but it was still all right. I noticed the taps were all one brand and I asked him about that.

"These people will drink anything," he said. "Why put up with three or four salesmen when you can get all you need from one?"

"Sounds logical."

He didn't draw a beer for himself.

"I've got sugar," he said. "I shouldn't touch the stuff. All I have to do is get high and I suffer the next day."

"The beer isn't the best brand," I observed. "You must save about two dollars on each half that you buy."

He grinned.

"You catch on fast, but at ten cents a glass you have to cut corners."

"Naturally."

"There's a phone under the bar if you want to call your girl."

"Thanks, but I don't remember the name of the woman who has the rooming house. And my girl won't worry. She'll know that I got something or I would have been back."

"Trusting soul, huh?"

"Not so trusting but what can she do about it?"

I broke the ten to get change for cigarettes and he kept on talking about himself. It was true that I had only met the man a short time before but there was something about him that I didn't like. It may have been because he made money from girls or it may have been that he seemed so sure of himself. I didn't know just what it was but for the chance of a job I would have gone to work for the devil and not thought twice about it.

"We'll get along," he said finally.

"Sure."

I wondered if we would and for how long.

Chapter Two

The girl in the employment office had been right about The Dells being a slum area. After the day shift on the docks and in the factories ended they started coming into the bar, most of them in their working clothes and all of them drinking fast and hard. A lot of them hit the wine—that was twenty-five cents a glass—a few went for whiskey but a large majority stuck to beer or gin.

"It's a long bar," Charlie Fletcher said.

"Long enough."

"But you cover it fast. And you don't let the empty glasses set. That's important. They come in here to drink and you can't make any money from an empty glass."

It took me a while to get used to the cash register—it wasn't a new one—and he showed me where he kept the money for cashing checks. He had the money in a fishing tackle box in one of the cabinets under the back bar, all sorted out in singles and fives and tens and twenties.

"No personal checks," he said. "You cash a personal check down here and you might as well throw the paper away."

At seven one of the taps ran out and I had to go down cellar with him to prove that I could tap a half.

"Slick," he said when I had finished with the job.

"I told you I could, didn't I?"

"So did some of the others but when it came right down to it they didn't know what they were doing."

He stayed with me about half an hour longer and before he left he gave me a combination to the safe.

"Before you close put all of the bills from the register and that check cashing box in the safe. I don't care about the change in the drawer. If anybody breaks in here they can have the god-damned change."

I hit a lull about eight but a few minutes after that it began to pick up again. Some of the men who had been in earlier had been home for supper and now they were back. Most of them hadn't changed their clothes and they talked about their work on the railroad or on the docks or how they were getting pushed around in the factories.

"You gotta have a union," one man said. "You work in a shop without no union and you might as well go out and hang yourself."

"The unions are a lotta crap," his companion said. "The guys in charge get you a ten-cent raise, boost your dues a buck a month and ride around in Caddys."

There were a few women at the bar—apparently they had come in with their husbands—but they were playing the field and nobody seemed to care.

"You couldn't be no worse than my old man," one woman said to the elderly male sitting beside her. "He ain't been with me that way in over six months. You'd think I had something wrong with me."

It kept me busy bouncing up and down the bar but it was good to be working again. The ten wouldn't last us long, or what was left of the ten, and I'd have to ask Charlie Fletcher for an advance in the next day or so. I didn't think that he would refuse me. Almost anybody who starts on a new job needs some help in the beginning. Of course, there was plenty of chances to knock down—the people at the bar weren't paying any attention to what I was doing—and I won't say that I didn't think about it. But I quickly pushed the idea aside. I needed this job, needed it badly, and I couldn't run any risk of being caught. I didn't know his wife but she was probably a prying old bitch with the mind of a hawk and the suspicions of a female dog with a new litter of pups. For all I knew she might be one of the women at the bar. I hadn't met her and I didn't know her from a bale of straw.

By eleven I had a full house, both the bar and the booths in back, and I had to put on all the steam I had to keep up with the demands of the customers. It was easy to understand how he had made money in such a dump and it was just as easy to understand why he wanted to get out of it.

"You don't know me," one girl at the bar said as I poured her a shot of rye.

"How would I? I just started here."

"I'm Martha Foster."

"So okay."

"Didn't Charlie tell you about the girls?"

"He told me."

"Well, I'm one of them." She smiled at me. "You help steer some men my way and I could be very nice to you."

She didn't look older than eighteen and she had a tight little body that was probably very good. Her dress was low in front and she had a nice cleavage, not the deep kind that you sometimes see but the wide cleavage of breasts that were far apart.

"I'll do what I can," I said.

She was still smiling at me.

"I'll bet there's one thing that you can do—and do well."

I left her alone and it wasn't long before she left with a man. I didn't want to have anything to do with her. I had all I could take care of in the rooming house on Clay Street.

For the rest of the night, or a part of it, anyway, girls kept coming in and going out with men, but by midnight most of the working people had left. There was only one argument, something about baseball, but it didn't amount to anything. I just told the guys to shut up and they shut up.

By midnight there were only two men at the bar and I had a couple of drinks, whiskey this time, and talked to them. They were from uptown and they wanted a little fun before they went home. I mentioned Martha Foster and the one man said he had been with her once.

"She's good," he said. "She don't rush you and if you want something out of the ordinary she's willing."

About half an hour later Martha returned, joining the two men, and they soon went out together. It wasn't long after this that three girls came in and ordered shots, two rye and one scotch over the rocks.

I had seen all of the girls during the evening, going and coming from the bar, but now that we were alone they introduced themselves. One was Gloria Forbes, another Jennie Corby and the third said she was Kathy Nelson. Of the three Kathy was the best and she didn't look much older than Martha, possibly a year or, at the most, two. They made no excuses about what they did for a living and they got a big kick out of comparing the men they had been with that night.

"He got in bed with me and then he couldn't," Kathy said. "I told him he should take some of those pep pills they advertise. But he paid me and said he would be back again. Can you make ten bucks any easier?"

They stayed about an hour and they drank steadily. A few men stopped in at the bar but all they were after were quick drinks and they didn't bother with the girls. When the girls said goodnight they went out alone.

For the next half-hour I sat at the end of the bar, belting the booze, and thinking about what good luck I had had! Maybe Charlie's place left a lot to be desired but it was a job and you don't start out at seventy-five a week on many jobs. I hadn't found any change on top of the bar, not as he had said I might, but most of the people hadn't been loaded enough to forget what belonged to them.

I was on a double shot of rye, still thinking, when the door opened and this girl came in. With the red sweater that she was wearing and the way she filled it out I didn't pay much notice to her face. Ann was thirty-six at the bust but this girl was a hell of a lot bigger. My guess was that if she wasn't forty she wasn't anything at all. And the bounce to them as she came toward the bar sort of took my breath away. They were tilted and high, sticking straight out, but there was a fullness to them like I had never seen before. I swallowed hard and looked at the rest of her. She had a flat stomach, hardly anything to it at all, but when I glanced at her hips under a gray skirt I saw that they were alive and moving, the kind of generous hips that could drive you out of your mind if you stared at them long enough.

"Hello," she said, sitting on a stool that was close to me.

I got up and moved behind the bar. "Hi."

She was blonde, her hair long and almost down to her shoulders. She shook her head, fluffing out her hair, and those blue eyes of hers were deep pools of mystery. She had full lips and as she smiled I saw that her teeth were very white and even. I guess I could say she had the face of a movie doll and not miss the target by much.

"Scotch and soda," she said. "And make it light on the soda."

"Okay."

I took the best scotch in the house—Charlie hadn't told me how much to charge for scotch so I had been charging only thirty cents—and fixed the drink. My hand trembled slightly but I didn't think anything about that. Any guy was apt to be unsteady when a dame like this walked in on him. You took one look at her and you saw a bedroom. In fact, you saw more than that. You saw her in the bedroom, naked and waiting for you, her voice low and soft as you went to her.

"You must be Clint," she said as she stirred the drink.

I didn't know how she knew my name.

"I'm Clint."

She sat there for a moment, thoughtful and silent. I was looking down into those blue eyes again and that bedroom didn't seem to be very far away at all. She lowered her eyes briefly, picking up the drink, and my glance wandered to her breasts. My throat was dry and hot. The sweater was tight, probably about two sizes too small for her, and the weave in the material parted just enough so that I could tell that she wasn't wearing any bra underneath. She was a woman up there, all woman, and she needed support for them like I needed a second head.

"I'm Debbie," she said, putting the glass down and looking up at me once more. "Debbie Fletcher. Did my husband tell you about me?"

I had to have a drink and I reached for the rye. Hell, she wasn't half his age and all along I'd been thinking that she was some old slob. Suddenly, and for a reason I didn't understand, I felt a burning dislike for him, even worse than it had been before. He had this beautiful number all to himself in the apartment over the bar and when he got the urge he took her to bed. Somehow it didn't seem right.

"I see," I said.

Her laughter was filled with music.

"You act surprised. Why?"

"Well, there's a big difference in ages."

"Thirty years, almost to the day. His birthday is one week and mine is the next." She toyed with the glass. "Is it a crime to marry somebody old enough to be your father?"

"No, I guess not." The rye went down easily and quickly. "If you love somebody the age doesn't have much to do with it."

"My parents didn't think so."

"You can't always satisfy parents. They get something into their heads and you can't get it out short of cutting their heads off."

She had another drink and lit a cigarette, taking the cigarette from a pack I had lying on the bar.

"How did it go tonight?" she asked.

"All right."

"Any trouble?"

"Not to speak of."

"The girls in?"

"They were here."

"What do you think of the girls?"

"It isn't my job to think. They spend their money and they bring business to the bar. What they do is their business. I don't have anything to say about the matter."

"I wish he would get out of it."

"Then talk to him."

"I have but it doesn't do any good. He figures he makes forty or fifty dollars a night from them and that's good money."

"It won't do him any good if they put him in jail because of it."

"That's what I've said but he won't listen to me. Charlie is a funny man. The more he makes the more he wants. Every night he's out on some sort of a deal and I sit upstairs by myself. A girl gets tired of that. You turn on the television and all you see are westerns. You read magazines and it's the same old junk. A girl—any girl—wants more out of marriage than that."

I got the impression that he wasn't living up to his physical obligations with her and that interested me. I poured another slug of rye for myself and decided that if I was married to her she would have to beg me to stop—and then I wouldn't stop.

"What does a girl want out of marriage?" I inquired.

Her eyes were very frank.

"Pretty much the same as a man should want."

"Oh?"

"If she's young and healthy—and I'm both, I think—she wants to be loved and have a family. But he says he's too old for children. He's already got a daughter older than I am. Can you tie that? I'm a stepmother and my stepdaughter was born six years before I was."

"Novel, to say the least."

"And don't think Ruth hasn't reminded me of it." She didn't stop drinking and I poured the shots for her.

After the fifth or sixth one she didn't want any soda and that made it easy. I wasn't doing so badly on the rye and it wasn't long before I began to feel what I had consumed. Even a bartender can't belt the bottle and stay sober forever.

"Wonder where he could be at this hour," she said at one point.

"Beats me."

"I could make a guess and be a hundred percent right."

"Which puts you a hundred percent ahead of me."

"You met that Kathy Nelson, didn't you?"

"I met her."

"Well, he's got a yen for that. Don't ask me why. You'd think he had enough at home to keep him satisfied."

"I'd say so."

I stayed until three but not many people came in. One guy was so drunk I wouldn't serve him and he called me a dirty bastard. Most of the time we just drank and talked. She said that she would be glad when he sold the bar, if he ever did, and that she had the desire to travel.

"Florida," she added. "Have you ever been there?"

"No."

"Neither have I but from what I've heard it's for me. Give me a sandy beach and a bathing suit and I wouldn't ask for anything else."

I figured that she wouldn't have to ask for anything once she put on a bathing suit. Somebody would give it to her and give it to her good. While her old man was chasing some whore a guy would be giving her what came natural. I just wished that I was that guy and the more I talked to her and the more I saw of her the more I wished that I could have just ten minutes with her.

She helped me with the money, putting rubber bands around the bills, and when we walked to the safe, me carrying the check cashing money, we bumped together. A strange sensation crawled up and down my spine at the contact and I had all I could do to keep myself from going after her right then and there.

As soon as we had the money locked up we had another drink before turning out the lights.

"I hope you stay," she said.

"Why?"

She was slow in replying.

"Because I kind of like you. Charlie said you were big but I didn't think you were as big as you are. We've had some big bartenders before—none as big as you—but they didn't last."

"How come?"

"They had light fingers."

"You won't have to worry about that with me."

"I hope not."

I switched off the lights—she said to leave the small one over the cash register burning—and I snapped the lock into position as we went outside. The entrance to the apartment upstairs was at one end of the building and I parted from her there. I'd have given all of my left arm and half of my right to have gone up there with her. If I knew anything about girls she was in the mood to be loved and I was in the mood to make love, endless love that would come to a climax in a world all of its own.

"See you," I said as I started down the street.

"You can count on that."

I should have been tired but I didn't feel like going to the room. It would be a bigger thrill to just walk the streets and think about that Debbie Fletcher. She would be good and I knew she would be good. She would be the best that a man could have—and then some. She would drain a man of all need, all fury, and then she would cry for more and more.

I wiped the sweat from my forehead and walked toward Clay Street. I decided that I must be going nuts. We had had a nice talk together but she hadn't said anything really out of the way. She hadn't acted like a girl on the make—and, yet, there had been that look in her eyes, a look that had held something between a promise and a challenge.

When I got to Clay Street I turned left and I had a little difficulty finding the rooming house. The only way I could distinguish it—there were several houses that all looked alike—was because half of the railing for the front porch was lying on the ground.

It was getting late, probably close to four o'clock, and I didn't think Ann would be up but she was. She was sitting on the bed, wearing a thin yellow negligee that contrasted well with her red hair, and she smiled at me when I came in. I walked over to her, bent down and kissed her, feeling her quick response and her arms that crept up around my neck.

"I thought you left me," she said.

I sat down beside her.

"What made you think that?"

"Because I knew how little money you had left and you were very depressed. People do funny things sometimes."

"I got a job."

"So did I. In a diner uptown. And I worked."

"The hell."

"I made almost ten dollars in tips."

"Not bad."

"But on the way down I wasted some of it. I thought you would want a drink and I was fairly sure that you wouldn't use any of the ten to buy it. I got a pint of rye."

"I've already had plenty to drink."

"I know. I can smell it. And I could taste it when you kissed me."

I told her about the job, about the seventy-five dollars a week, and she was pleased. The diner where she had hired out, she said, was modern and the tips excellent. Some of the girls working there had told her they knocked out a hundred dollars or more a week.

"We made a wise move coming down here," I said.

"Didn't we though?"

"You can starve to death in that god-damned Sullivan County at this time of the year. Your only chance is to get a job in a hotel that doesn't close and those jobs are hard to come by."

"We had one once," she reminded me.

"So we did."

"Until the man who owned it tried to take me to bed and I slapped his face for getting fresh."

I remembered the place and I remembered the man. It had been a fairly large hotel and the man who made the mortgage payments had, at one time or another, slept with nearly all of the waitresses. He had been attracted to Ann right from the start—I had been helping in the kitchen and I had been able to see him follow her around, patting her fanny and things like that—and we had only lasted a month. He had followed her into the storeroom one night as we were getting ready to close, shutting the door behind him—there hadn't been any lock on the door—and I had heard her hollering at him. She had already been fired by the time I busted in and I had lost my own job by clipping him one on the jaw. The only good thing about it had been the fact that he had paid us that morning and that we didn't have any pay coming.

"We can get an apartment," she was saying.

"Huh?"

"Well, with what you're making and what I make we can swing it. How much do you have to pay for a furnished apartment?"

"I don't know."

"It wouldn't be much more than sixty or seventy dollars a month, would it?"

"I wouldn't think so."

"You'll be getting seventy-five a week and I'll make at least that. We can even put a little away." She yawned and lay back on the bed. "Gee, isn't it wonderful? This morning we were almost broke and now we've got the best break we've ever had. It just goes to show you that if you keep on trying you're bound to make out." She laughed. "What if the folks could see us now? They wouldn't say we were nuts, would they?"

"It's more than they make on the farms, for all of their hard work."

I got up from the bed and found the bottle of rye, still wrapped in brown paper, standing on the dresser. I unwrapped the bottle and twisted the cap loose. There weren't any glasses around but the bottle was fine with me.

"This room is a dump," she said, sitting up, her breasts rising and falling beneath the thin material.

It was a dump but for five dollars a week we couldn't expect much more than that. The walls hadn't been papered in years and there were big cracks in the ceiling. Some of the plaster from the ceiling had dropped down onto the faded carpet and nobody had bothered to clean it up. The furniture was old—what there was of it—and the bed had a big hollow in the center that made two people sleep very close together.

We sat on the bed and drank from the bottle, smoking cigarettes and talking. I should have been paying attention to her but I wasn't. I was thinking of that Debbie Fletcher, those big breasts of hers, and those blue eyes that had held some meaning that I hadn't understood. While I was sitting in a rented room on Clay Street she was in her apartment, either alone or with Charlie. I had more or less indicated to her that I didn't think there was anything strange about a young girl being married to an older man but this marriage I didn't quite figure. She had so much to offer a man that it didn't make sense that he should stray so far away from the nest.

"We could even get married," Ann said.

I tried to clear my mind and focus it on the present. She had been on that kick ever since we had left Beaverkill but I couldn't really blame her for it. I was getting mine and she wanted a ring on her finger. But what girl doesn't? You give her the business a few times and she thinks she's got you for life.

"It's better to wait," I told her. "Things look good right now but you don't know how they'll look next week. A couple of times before we thought we had it solid and then it blew apart."

She was silent for a moment.

"I'm tired of putting it off, Clint."

"Let's see how things turn out."

"It wouldn't cost us any more to live together married than it costs us now."

"I suppose not."

"And every month I'm scared to death that I'm going to turn up pregnant. I wouldn't mind getting pregnant if I was married to you but I don't want to get pregnant while I'm single. It just doesn't seem right."

"I never gave you any reason to worry about getting pregnant, have I?"

"No, I guess not but how do you know that we won't get to drinking and go too far some night? Other couples have done it and we aren't any different. All it takes is once at the right time."

"Or the wrong time."

We killed the bottle and I wasn't feeling any pain by the time it was done. You might even say that I had a heavy load on and that I was pulling the whole works uphill.

A few minutes later I turned out the light, undressed and went to bed. But I didn't touch her that night. All I did was kiss her and wish her sweet dreams. I couldn't touch her.

All I could do was think of that Debbie Fletcher and wish that she were there in that bed with me.

Some day, I promised myself as I drifted off to sleep, my wish would come true. The big question was when.

Chapter Three

It went along pretty good for the next week. I got to know most of the people who came into the bar and none of them gave me any trouble. The register was usually right—once or twice it was off a few cents, one way or the other—and Charlie was pleased.

"You're honest," Charlie told me one day. "I'm sold on that."

"All I want is my pay."

"I might even give you an extra ten. It's worth it to me to know that the joint is running smoothly."

It wasn't necessary for me to get an advance from him. Ann made from ten to fifteen dollars a day in tips at the diner and she gave me what little money I needed. I saw very little of her, since she was working days and I was working nights, and most of the time she was asleep when I got to the room. One night, about the third night, she came down to the bar for a while but she didn't stay long.

"I've been waiting for you," she said when I crawled into bed beside her. "How do you stand it down there, Clint? It's obvious that most of the girls just hang around the bar to pick up men."

"All I do is work there. I don't ask any questions and nobody gives me any answers."

"They need a short order cook in the diner. You've done that work before. It would be almost as much money and we could be on the same shift."

"I'm doing okay where I am."

"Maybe you like the place."

"Maybe I do."

I didn't like the place. What I liked was the hour before closing when Debbie always came down from the apartment to have a few drinks. She usually wore a skirt and sweater but one night she had on a white blouse and it was very easy to tell that she didn't have a bra on underneath it. I could look right through the material and see the dark centers of her breasts and when she took a deep breath they pushed out hard and full against the blouse.

"Free show?" she asked me.

"I don't know what you mean."

"You know what I mean. If I girl doesn't have it up here you men just aren't interested."

I poured the scotch for her.

"Charlie's lucky," I said.

"Only he doesn't take advantage of his luck. He's out every night. You know that. He takes a shot for his sugar, changes his clothes and disappears. Sometimes I think I'm losing my appeal."

"You haven't lost anything."

We got to know each other fairly well during these talks and she told me how she had met Charlie. She had won a beauty contest—no big money in it—and because she could sing one of the uptown clubs had put her on the bill.

"They wanted more than singing. They wanted me to do a dance and then they wanted a breast show. I was just a dumb kid and I went along with it. I sang a couple of numbers, stripped out of my gown, did a dance and then took off my bra, not just down to a flesh colored bra but all the way to the skin. Charlie caught the show one night and he asked me over to his table. It was a rule of the management that the girls had to accept invitations from men who wanted to meet them—they made a neat profit off the drinks they sold—and I met Charlie. The others who had met me only wanted to take me to bed but Charlie played it very cool. Nights that he couldn't be at the club he sent roses and the nights he came he brought me presents. When the police raided the club and picked me up for indecent exposure Charlie hired a lawyer for me and the lawyer got me off. I was out of work at the time—I didn't know what I wanted to do—and I just drifted into marriage with him."

This was all very interesting, of course, but it wasn't getting me what I was after. I tried to hide my desires but she was smart enough to recognize them.

"I know what you'd like to do," she said one night.

"What?"

She put it straight on the line.

"You'd like me to take you to bed."

"Well, you're a very beautiful girl."

"Think so?"

"I know so."

"What about your girl?"

"She's just a girl."

"And I'd merely be another one?"

"I doubt that very much."

"Why do you doubt it?"

"Because there's something special about you."

But I didn't get up to her apartment and once when I tried to kiss her before I left for the night she put me off.

"Maybe I'd like for you to do it," she said, smiling up at me. "But I'm married and I have to remember that."

"Yeah, I guess you're right."

That was one night when I woke Ann up when I got into bed. I had to have her, had to have somebody, and if I couldn't have Debbie Fletcher I would take the next best thing.

"Don't," she said after I had crushed my mouth down over her lips. "Don't, Clint."

"Don't tell me you don't want to."

She returned my kiss and her lips were blazing, her naked body coming in against me.

"Oh, I want to. It isn't that." She kissed me again. "I've missed you so damned much and now I want all of you. You know what that means, don't you? I don't want you to be careful. I want you time after time, hour after hour, until you no longer can give me what we both have to have."

She got her wish, got it with all of the violence of the male hungry for the female, and when we woke up we were locked in each other's arms.

"You may have done it," she said.

"Time will tell."

"Don't ever leave me if you did. I could stand a lot of things alone but not that."

I attempted to cheer her up.

"Just because there's lightning in the sky doesn't mean that a tree is going to be struck."

"I hope you're right. I was a little beside myself last night."

"I wasn't far behind you."

"But I've got no complaint. I asked for it."

Some afternoons when there wasn't anything to do—I hated staying in the room alone—I went down to the bar and hung around. Almost every other afternoon Debbie went to the hairdresser—it didn't seem to me that it was necessary for her to go so often—and sometimes when she was away from the apartment Charlie took one of the prostitutes upstairs. While this was going on I took over the bar or helped myself to a few slugs of whiskey.

"You've gotta get it out of your system," Charlie explained. "Man was made for woman and woman was made for man."

"Seems to me your wife is all the woman that you need."

"Outwardly, yes, but when you tangle in the sheets with her she's like a block of ice."

I couldn't believe that but I didn't argue with him about it. He was married to her and he should know more than I knew. There are plenty of girls who look like sex pots and who are frigid. To my way of thinking it would take a man to wake her up and Charlie wasn't the man.

It was a funny thing but this possibility, that she was frigid, only served to make my desire for her deeper and deeper. I simply had to look at her, or think about her, and I wanted to see all that she was, all that she could offer. I wanted to make love to her as no other man had ever made love to her, to feel her body respond in a wild and glorious passion.

I was behind the bar one afternoon—Charlie was upstairs with Martha Foster—when this redheaded man came in and sat down on one of the stools. He was big, not as big as I was, but big, and he ordered a beer. I made change from a dollar and he stood a quarter on end.

"You the new bartender around here?"

"That's right."

"How do you like it?"

"It's okay."

"He pay you all right?"

"I've got no word against that." I took a quarter out of my pocket and matched his effort. "But I don't think it's anybody's business how he treats me except mine."

His eyes, gray and pale, drilled my face.

"I make it my business," he said.

I shrugged my shoulders.

"Go ahead. It won't get you far."

"You'd be surprised how far I can get."

"Well, I can't stop you from trying."

"Got some salt for the beer?"

"Why not?"

I got him the salt. A lot of the people who came into the bar used salt in their beer. Personally, I could never go for it.

"Guess you don't know me," he said, lighting a cigar.

"No reason why I should. You haven't been in here while I've been working."

He gave me the same kind of a look again.

"I'm Red Brandon."

I knew who he was then. I had heard a lot about Brandon from some of the customers. The Dells was his territory and he was a tough cop. He was also dishonest. And he was brutal. If a guy gave him any trouble he lumped him with his billy and then hauled him in for assaulting an officer. The victim could bury himself in lawyers and it wouldn't do him any good. The Dells was the slum of the city and anybody who came from the slum wasn't any good at all.

"Okay," I said. "You're Red Brandon."

The tone of my voice, edged with a sneer, didn't bother him a bit.

"They say your name is Clint."

"That's right."

"And you live with a dame in a rooming house on Clay Street."

I decided that Charlie had been talking to him.

"We've got a room," I admitted.

He finished his beer but when I went to draw another one he said he didn't want any.

"She put out?" he asked.

I rinsed out the glass and took my time about replying to him.

"You're off base," I said, turning the glass upside down underneath the bar so it would drain. "You just hit a ball over the foul line in left field."

"Don't get smart with me."

"Who's getting smart?"

"You are. I don't care if she sleeps with you or not. What would a guy live with a dame for if she didn't sleep with him? All I care about is whether or not she sells it."

"She doesn't."

"Sure about that?"

It was one of the things that I was sure of.

"Ask her yourself and find out," I suggested.

"I'm asking you."

"And I told you she doesn't."

He told me he wanted another beer and I drew it. People like that burn you up. They dirty one glass, you wash it and then they dirty a second one.

"I get a cut out of every dame working The Dells, fellow, and don't forget it. If she's on the make and you try to count me out it'll go rough for you. I get fifty bucks a week from each girl for her protection and there's no fooling about it."

"You're a hell of a police officer," I said. "The people hire you to enforce the laws and you turn around and break them."

"Don't blame me. Blame the people who set the pay scale. I get five thousand a year to go out and risk getting a bullet in my guts. And don't think it hasn't been close a couple of times. It has. If I didn't take the money from the girls somebody else would. Take this bar away from them and they'd have to have a pimp. A pimp costs money. I might as well get my share and be happy with it."

"It's no affair of mine."

"And don't make it one. Guys come in here, strangers, and they want to make a connection. It's all right for you to tell them about the girls but don't try getting a slice of the dough. If everybody gets their finger in the pie they'll be driven out and I don't want that to happen."

"I won't."

"You hadn't better."

He left shortly after that and I washed out the second glass. The way I added it up he wasn't doing badly. There were four regular girls and if he got fifty a week from each one of them that was two hundred dollars. I had already found out that there were other girls on the street—some of them came into the bar—and they were all available for a price. They were all afraid of Red Brandon, though, afraid of getting pinched, and they had to be careful. They usually spent the whole evening with the same man and they took what they could get for their favors. Many of them just did it for drinks and they didn't charge. A few of them were married but most of them were single and about twenty and they worked days in the factories.

When Charlie came down from upstairs I told him that Brandon had been in. He wasn't very happy about it.

"He doesn't trust anybody," Charlie said. "The girls pay him off every week and so do I. What's he worrying about?"

"I don't know."

"I own the house where the girls take the men and they pay me so much a trick. Out of that I have to pay him. Christ, does he want it all?"

"He wouldn't refuse it and that's for sure."

"Gimme a shot, Clint."

"What about your sugar?"

"The hell with my sugar."

I gave him the best rye in the house and he swallowed it in a hurry.

"You mind taking over right now?"

"Not at all."

"I'll pay you for it."

"Thanks."

"I got a million things to do uptown. There's a man who wants to buy most of my property and I've got a good notion to sell it to him. I don't mean the bar. The bar could become something between you and me."

"Whatever you say."

"Just watch out for that Red Brandon. He could frame you faster than you could down a glass of beer."

I watched him go. I wasn't worried about Brandon any. What could he do to me? And why would he do it? I was only a fool who worked for a living and I didn't have anything that anybody wanted.

Up to a certain point, it was a normal night in the bar. The girls arrived about nine and they made dates right away. From then until after midnight they kept coming and going, picking up the men who were waiting for them. The longer the men waited the better it was for business. They were from uptown, salesmen and guys like that, and they drank the hard stuff. A few of them went out and forgot to take their change with them. I made two or three dollars that way.

At two o'clock I was alone in the bar and I dug into the rye, watching the door and waiting for Debbie, promising myself that she wasn't going to get away from me that night. I had my pay—Charlie had given it to me when I had arrived, plus an additional ten—and she had the time. For a whirl with that hunk of flesh I was willing to spend my last dime. She might be cold to Charlie but she didn't look cold to me. She looked like a furnace fire to me, a fire that only needed to have the draft turned on.

At two-thirty the door swung open but it wasn't Debbie. It was Kathy Nelson and she gave me a full smile, just as she had been giving me a full smile ever since I had been working there.

"You alone?" she asked.

"See anybody else?"

She was wearing a close-fitting white dress, low enough to be inviting in front, and she had a good shape. Of all of the girls I had found it more difficult to understand how she could sell herself.

"Gin," she said, sitting down at the bar. "Nothing else. Just gin."

I gave her the gin and she put a five on the bar. I didn't pick up the five.

"On the house," I said.

"Thanks."

"You girls spend enough here."

"Does Charlie think so?"

"I don't know what he thinks but I would guess that he's happy about it."

"He's a pig."

"Suit yourself." I looked down the front of her dress and saw what I wanted to see.

"And his wife is a bitch."

"Those are harsh words."

She favored me with another smile.

"You'll find out. Give yourself enough time and I won't have to draw you a picture. She's the biggest whore on the street and—"

"Shut up!"

She laughed at me.

"You must like those big bubbies of hers."

"I said to shut up."

She drank the gin and left without saying another word. After she had gone I noticed the five was still on the bar. I picked it up and put it in my pocket. She could go to hell.

At three o'clock I put the money in the safe, turned off the lights and put the lock into position on the way out.

I walked up the street, as lonely as a man on a deserted island.

This, I concluded, just wasn't my night.

But, I further concluded, I would have my night.

And it would be something out of this world.

Chapter Four

During the following month one day was about the same as another day. I got up at one o'clock, sometimes two, and had coffee and a couple of rolls in a diner up the street. There was a liquor store near the diner and I frequently bought a bottle and took it back to the room, drinking the liquor straight, and wondered why Debbie Fletcher was obviously avoiding me. She had stopped coming into the bar prior to closing and I missed her. Once in a while she came in during the evening, taking a few bucks from the cash register, but I didn't have any chance to talk to her then and that hurt. Nights when I returned to the room I was slopped and when I had a day off I found a nice quiet bar uptown and knocked myself out.

"You're drinking too much," Ann told me. "You drink on the job and you drink off the job and you throw your money away like water."

"So whose money is it?"

"I thought it was ours. I thought we agreed to put half of our pay in the bank every week and save for an apartment. I'm doing my share. There isn't a week that goes by that I don't go to the bank with fifty dollars."

But nothing she said did any good. I'd get up, promise myself that I wouldn't touch a drop that day and then, even before I realized it, I would be back at the stuff worse than ever. It got so that I thought Charlie would bawl me out for being half lit most of the time but he never said a word. He was busy with his property and any of the prostitutes who would go to bed with him and he didn't seem to care what shape I was in as long as I could do the work.

A few nights, drunk and disgusted, I took Kathy Nelson to her room and she wasn't bad. She didn't charge me anything.

"You do it for money but there comes a time when you want to do it because you want to do it," she explained after our first session. "I kind of like you and you're certainly as much as a girl could ask for."

"Well, thanks."

"These other men don't mean anything. It's purely mechanical. You go to bed with them and they give you money for it. They buy you like they would buy a tank of gas for their cars."

Red Brandon didn't bother me any but he worked over one of the girls who had spent her money one week and couldn't pay him. He gave her a black eye and cut her lower lip to such an extent that she had to have a couple of stitches taken in it. Not many of the men would have anything to do with her, not when she was looking like that, and before her next payment was due to Brandon she dropped out of sight.

"Gloria was about at the end of her string," Kathy told me. "She was thirty-one and that's old in this business. She started when she was sixteen and being a whore has its price. You're good for about eight or ten years, getting as much sex as most girls get in a lifetime, and then your price drifts down to two dollars. Usually you're on the booze and if you can't get two dollars you'll do it for drinks. You're used merchandise and nobody wants you."

"It ought to be something for you to think about."

"I have thought about it and one of these days I'm going to break loose. All I need is the guts to go out and make an honest living."

When she told me that Red Brandon often went up to the apartment over the bar to visit Debbie Fletcher I didn't believe her. In my liquor-twisted mind Debbie had become some sort of a goddess to me and I couldn't imagine her having a relationship with a man like Brandon. Brandon was no better than the lowest scum in The Dells—lower, perhaps, because of the way he abused his position—and I didn't figure her to be the type who would go for just any man.

One night, however, after I had locked up—Kathy hadn't shown and I was alone—I almost ran into him as he was coming out of the door leading to the stairs to the apartment.

"Don't get any ideas," he said, picking at his teeth with a toothpick. He had a habit of doing that, of chewing on the toothpick and then spitting it out. "I just came from some very private property."

"Charlie's private property," I corrected him.

He spit out the toothpick and he didn't try to miss my feet.

"Nuts to Charlie. He's got so many dames to play with he don't know where to stop or where to start."

I was off the next day and I killed a fifth of rye before Ann got home from work. It was true about Brandon and I had to accept it. He was getting what I wanted and I hated him for it. It was strange that my hate didn't reach as far as Debbie. He was probably forcing himself on her, standing behind his shield and using it as a lever.

Ann was late getting in and I didn't have to look twice at her eyes to see that she had been crying.

"We've got to get married," she said, pulling the white uniform over her head. She threw the uniform on a chair, standing there in a half slip and bra. "That is, if you ever stay sober enough to stand up in front of a justice of the peace."

"Tell me why."

"Because I think I'm that way."

"Oh, Jesus!"

"I stopped and saw a doctor and he said there's a good chance that I am.

I have to go back in about a month and then he can tell me for sure."

"So we'll wait and see what you find out."

"But I don't want to wait." There were fresh tears in her eyes. "Why should we wait? I've got enough saved so that we can rent an apartment and get most of the things that we'll need."

I waved the suggestion aside.

"There's pills you can take to get rid of it," I said. "I don't know anybody in a drug store but some of the girls who come to the bar use them off and on and they seem to work. I could get some for you."

"I'd never do that."

"Why not?"

She let the half slip fall to the floor. She had on a new pair of panties, very brief, and they didn't hide much.

"You don't realize that I want your baby," she said slowly. "We keep talking about getting married but we never do anything about it. Now it's time that we did. A baby would be good for both of us. We've been growing apart, Clint, and nobody has to tell me that. Mornings when you don't come home until five or six o'clock I know you've been with somebody else. What you need is some responsibility and another job."

"Where could I get paid as much?"

"It isn't what you get paid, it's what you spend that counts. They still need somebody in the diner, the same as I told you before. You wouldn't be paid as much, that's true, but you'd be away from the liquor and you need that. It's pulling you down but you don't seem to know it. I like a drink, too—as much as the next one—but there is a limit to it."

"It relaxes me."

"That's just an excuse. If we had a regular home you'd get interested in other things. And after the baby comes you'll have something to work for. Other men have done it. Why can't you?"

We argued for a long time that night. She wanted marriage and she wasn't willing to settle for anything short of it. As for myself I didn't know. She would make a good wife, a fine mother, but things had changed for me since we had arrived in Wilton. I couldn't think without thinking about Debbie Fletcher and when I was taking Kathy or Ann physically I still thought about her. Yet I knew that I was reaching for a straw in the wind. Debbie wasn't interested in me or she wouldn't have quit coming down to the bar and having a few drinks before I closed up.

"Things will work out," I assured Ann.

"They will if we make them work. All it takes is a few dollars and a ring. We could even stay here in this room for a while, much as I dislike it. That would give us a chance to save some more money."

I don't know what time I fell asleep but she was still talking when I did.

When I got up the next day about noon she had long since left for work.

I didn't stop at the diner for coffee or anything to eat—I was worried about her condition—and I went straight down to the bar. Charlie was glad to see me.

"Got to go to New York," Charlie said. "I won't be back until late tomorrow afternoon and I'm wondering if you'd take over for me today and open up the joint about noon tomorrow."

"Okay."

"It's extra pay for you."

"Thanks."

He poured a shot of scotch for himself.

"Remember I was telling you that I was dickering to sell my other properties?"

"I remember."

"Well, I think it's going through. I'm going to New York with this guy and he's going to raise the down payment from a brother." One shot of scotch wasn't enough for him so he had a second one. "After I get back we can talk about the bar. You've been here long enough to know the score and you can see that there's money to be made. I wouldn't be living in the apartment and you could use that for the girls. You'd pay off Brandon the same as I have and before you know it you'll be rolling in dough. Give yourself a year and you can buy some dame a mink and think nothing of it."

"Sounds great."

I wasn't busy that afternoon and I stayed away from the liquor. I had plenty of time to ponder the situation and the more I thought about it the better it seemed to be. The only hitch was that I would have to do business with Red Brandon but if Charlie had gotten along with him I guessed that I could. The other problem was Ann. She would kick up a storm if I took over the bar, no matter how much money it meant, but that didn't change my mind in the least. There was a good possibility that she wasn't pregnant, that nature was just fooling her, and there was also a good possibility that I wouldn't marry her if she was. I didn't know. I had an opportunity here to make a fat killing and I was going to take advantage of it.

It was a slow night, slower than usual, and the girls didn't get many tricks. They sat at the bar, drinking and talking, but when Brandon came in for a short beer they were silent and resentful. There was hate in their silence, a deadly hate that could have plunged a knife straight into his belly.

By two I was alone—Kathy had picked up a late date—and I sat at the bar drinking, going over in my mind how I would work it if I owned the bar. Three girls weren't enough to handle the normal traffic and there were plenty of good-looking ones in The Dells who might be in line to earn a good income. There was no reason why I couldn't get a five for giving a guy a good address and if it was done with any degree of sense Brandon didn't have to be cut in. I wasn't frightened of him. He made his nut from the girls who used the bar and I couldn't see that he had any more than that coming. If Charlie and his wife weren't living in the apartment upstairs the whole operation could be easier and faster. Maybe I would get a couple of girls to work on the same basis, just to make Brandon feel good, and the others could do their stuff on the quiet. From what I had seen of the girls in The Dells they were all putting out and they might as well get paid for their services.

I don't know what time she came in—I guess it was about two-thirty—but she was wearing shorts and her legs were bare and the halter made only a feeble attempt at concealing her breasts. She looked better this way than she did in a dress or a skirt and sweater and when I stood up I could see right down inside the front of her halter.

"You think I died?" Debbie asked me, sitting down on a stool.

"No, but I thought I had the crud or something."

She laughed and smiled up at me.

"How about some scotch? A double."

"Anything you want."

I got her the drink, pouring it over ice, and a dull ache began pounding over my eyes. Her husband was in New York and he wouldn't be home that night. She was lonely, or she wouldn't have been there with me, and if she got an edge on there was no telling how far we could go.

"He's away for tonight," she said.

"Yeah."

"He's selling out everything he owns."

The first drink didn't last her any time at all and I poured her another one, adding half a shot for good luck.

"So I understand."

She lit one of my cigarettes and inhaled the smoke. What she didn't do to that halter when she inhaled isn't anything to write about. They got bigger than ever and they pushed up and out. I had a crying need inside of me to reach across the bar and grab them and hurt them, to drive the pain so far into her that it would never leave.

"He told me about the bar."

"It's a good deal for me."

"If you go for this sort of thing."

I didn't measure the rye when I slopped it into a glass.

"Well, somebody is going to run it, aren't they? That somebody might as well be me. I've worked for peanuts long enough."

"So have I."

"You're doing all right."

"You call twenty-five dollars a week all right?"

I was surprised.

"Is that what he gives you?"

The halter had slid down some but she didn't bother to adjust it. The space between her breasts was deep and dark, the sort of thing you see in the girlie magazines.

"That's what he gives me," she said. "Out of that I have to pay the hairdresser and for anything else that I need. You'd think I was married to a man who was broke instead of a man who is up to his shoulders in money."

We were both dry and we had a couple of more drinks. When she reached for another cigarette I flicked my lighter and leaned over the bar to give her a light. I got a good peek that time and the pound in my head increased. I didn't know what I had to do but I had to have this girl, had to have her as much as the air that kept me alive. Her husband had said that she was frigid but if I was any judge of a girl she could come alive and savage if she was treated right.

"Did he say anything about me?" she inquired.

"No."

"Not that he's going to divorce me?"

I couldn't believe it.

"Divorce you?"

"Yes. He said the marriage was a mistake, that everything about us was a mistake. He wants to be free and live his own life."

"That's a hell of a thing to do."

Her shoulders lifted and fell and the halter went lower and from where I stood I could see the side swells of full and rounded breasts.

"I guess I came down here tonight because I had to have somebody to tell my troubles to."

"That's all right."

"Before we were married there wasn't anything that he wouldn't buy, nothing that he wouldn't do. The week after we were married he named me on all of his insurance policies. They come to hundred and fifty thousand."

"That's a lot of insurance."

"I know it is but in a month he changed. He was out with other women and I was left alone every night. It's been the same way since. One night he even brought a girl home with him and he took her in the spare bedroom. How do you think I felt?"

"The bastard."

"I called him that, too, but he didn't care. He just laughed at me. He said

I married him for what I could get and that I wouldn't get very much. I haven't. A girl needs love and affection and what's left in him has been for other girls." She finished her drink. "Thanks for listening to my tale of woe."

"You're welcome."

We drank until three and then I turned off all of the lights, all except the one over the cash register. I didn't even bother to put the money in the safe. This hunk of flesh was for me and I had to make her understand that.

We sat at the bar, a bottle in front of each one of us, and we continued to drink. We talked about her husband, how he treated her and the things he did, and she asked me about the girl I was living with.

"It's nothing serious," I said. "We left home together and we've traveled that way. You know how those things are. You just get into a situation but because you're in it, it doesn't mean that it's important."

"Have you any plans for getting married to her?"

"None at all."

I don't know how long we sat there but I finally suggested that we move back to one of the booths. Anybody outside could look in and see us at the bar and some of the drunks might try to come in and have a drink. The law says that you close at three and the law means just that. If you get caught serving booze after that hour you can lose your license. I knew that Red Brandon wouldn't bother us but the state has snoops out and they don't play mumbo jumbo with you.

Once we were in the booth, one of those way in the back, we were close together and when I was half-way through my drink I dropped my right hand down and let it rest on her bare leg. She didn't object and the contact with her skin charged me up as though I had just grabbed hold of a thousand volt wire.

"I like you more than I should," she said.

"Do you?"

"That's one reason I've stayed away from the bar as much as I could. I know my marriage is shot but I knew what you were thinking about me and I don't want a cheap affair."

"Love isn't cheap."

"It is if it's just physical."

My hand moved over to feel the inside of her thigh. Only then did she put a hand down to restrain me.

"It doesn't have to be cheap," I said, bringing my hand up to fumble for a cigarette.

"What do you call it when you live with a girl who isn't your wife?"

I lit two cigarettes, one for each of us.

"And what do you call it when Red Brandon sneaks up to your apartment?" I countered.

"So you know about that?"

"I hear things."

She smoked in silence and then she took a long drink of the scotch.

"He's been after something that he'll never get," she said, taking my hand and putting it right back where it had been, maybe an inch or so higher. "He tried to force himself on me but he didn't get very far. All we did was talk."

"What about?"

"How he has a wife and he wants to leave her. He's made a lot of money, saved most of it—so he claims—and he promised me the other side of the world. It didn't make sense and I didn't believe him. He's nothing but a crooked cop and he's making so much money down here that he would never give it up. I told him to get what he was after from one of the other girls and to leave me alone."

I believed her and I felt better. Brandon had never done anything to this girl and she wasn't the kind to permit him to enjoy her favors. She was lonely and lost, more than a little confused, and all she needed was a man to love her.

It was only natural that I would eventually kiss her, that I would mash my mouth down over her lips and crush her in my arms. She hesitated for a second and then she let out a little cry, deep from within. Her mouth opened up, filling my blood with excitement, and her arms came up around my neck, pulling me in close and warm. I brought one of my hands to the front, pushing it between us, my fingers seeking the glorious treasures that were now only partially covered by the halter.

"Don't untie it," she whispered as we broke apart, both of us breathing heavily.

"There are two good reasons why I want to."

She kissed me, laughing some. It was only a short kiss but while it was going on my fingers found what they wanted to find. She was round and full and the centers were hard and swollen.

"You can do it upstairs," she promised me.

"What about Brandon?"

"He's off tonight."

"He was in the bar earlier."

"I know. He came up to the apartment but he went home." She kissed me on one cheek and it was a wet kiss. "He tried to get what you're going to get."

"The hell with him."

"The hell with him is right."

She had to remind me to snap the lock on the way outside. I had waited for her so long, wanted her so much, that there was only one thing I could think about. In a matter of minutes I would hold her naked and alive and she would be mine.

We rounded the building and I saw a figure lurking in the shadows on the other side of the street. It looked very much like Red Brandon but in that instant a dozen Red Brandons couldn't have stopped me short of my goal. She might be another man's wife but her husband was away and he was probably burning out his clutch with some other dame. What was right for one was right for the other and tonight, the wonderful hours of it, would be mine.

The apartment was modern—I hadn't been in it before—but I didn't pay much attention to anything. I just followed her into the bedroom, waited for her to turn on the light, and then I was kissing her again. This time I untied the halter, almost ripping it loose when I had trouble with the bow, and, listening to her cry out, I kissed her where every girl wants to be kissed.

"You like?" she wanted to know, teasing me.

"They drive me insane."

"And you're driving me that way."

Jesus, they were big, big and ripe, ripe as fresh fruit on a tree. I went from one to the other and a long moan came from her. She dug her fingers into my hair as I pushed her toward the bed and the pain almost blinded me.

"Don't keep me waiting," she begged. "Please don't!"

I didn't keep her waiting. I helped her with her shorts, stripping her naked, and then she was down there on the bed. She was a blonde all right, blonde and lovely, and I didn't even take the time to get out of my clothes. I did what I had to do, did what I should have done that one night with Ann, and then I was after her, after her with a need that was greater than all else.

Charlie had told me that she was cold but she was far from being that. She responded to me as no other girl had ever responded, time after time, again and again, lifting herself to me in a frenzy of passion that left me weak and nearly helpless.

"I love you," I said long after, lying beside her.

"How much, Clint?"

"All the way."

"Enough to do anything for me?"

"Anything. Anything at all."

I didn't know what she meant by that but I didn't give it a second thought. All I could think of was that I was with her, that she had been mine and that this moment would never end.

And it didn't end.

Not until noon the next day.

It was great.

Chapter Five

Charlie got back from New York about the middle of the afternoon and he was in a terrible mood. The man's relative had been unwilling to put up the necessary cash and the deal had fallen through.

"And to think of the time I wasted with that bastard," Charlie said, downing a drink. "Not to mention the booze I bought him in some of the best joints in town."

"You'll find somebody else." I drew a beer and it was running wild. "If you don't land one sucker you can always find another one."

"I don't know. Most of the stuff I want to sell is here in The Dells and a lot of people don't want to invest in the slums. There's been talk of urban renewal—lots of towns are doing it—and that would mean that the buildings down here, or most of them, would be destroyed. That's one of the big reasons that nobody makes any improvements. They figure to sit it out and see what happens."

We were alone in the bar and as far as I knew he hadn't been upstairs yet. I drank some of the beer and decided that he didn't have anything to go up there for. His wife had gotten her sex the night before and that morning and she had gotten plenty of it. She had been like a bomb exploding the last time and if I hadn't been afraid to have stayed longer I wouldn't have left her, not even to open up the place. He had told me that she was cold but I had found her to be a bundle of fire that had risen to me in the flames of passion.

"How many buildings have you got?" I asked him.

"There's nine and all of them are rented full."

"That's a lot."

"It is when I think about what I had when I started. Did I ever tell you about that?"

He hadn't and I didn't give a damn.

"No," I said.

He waved for another drink and I poured him one. He was going to do some talking and I couldn't stop him. Of course, I could have told him that I wasn't interested but you don't offend a man who is in a position to help you. He could set fire to all of the buildings that he owned for all I cared. What I was interested in was the bar.

"I was born here, Clint. In The Dells. I grew up on the streets and I saw all the poverty there was to see. I saw guys gutted and girls raped and all of the other things that went with it. I made up my mind that I would do better than the others were doing and when I was eighteen I was working nights in a factory, running a stubborn machine and busting my back for a few dollars a week. One night I was coming home—I got finished at two in the morning—and this cab came out of a side street and ran me down. Both of my legs were broken but the right one was pretty bad, the bone shattered and sticking right out through the skin. That's why I limp today. Well, I was in the hospital a long time, several months, and while I was there I got to thinking. I wasn't going to go on working for peanuts. I'd sue the god-damned cab company and I would use the money I got to go into business. It was there that I met my first wife. She was a nurse, a cute little number, and she felt the same way about me that I felt about her. I had a private room and she was working nights. Before I left the hospital she used to come into the room, close and lock the door and we made our time together. A couple of months after I got out of the hospital she was knocked up and I married her. I didn't do much for quite a while—my legs were all right but I could-n't stand on them very long—and she kept on with her job. Finally she got so big she got in her own way and she had to give it up. A month before Ruth was born the insurance company came across with a twenty-thou-sand-dollar settlement and I bought a little store that sold magazines and newspapers and candy and that kind of junk. I did all right but not with the junk that the previous owner had been selling. One day a guy came through selling dirty books, the kind with pictures in them that you keep under the counter, and the money began piling up in the bank. There were some young girls who hung around the joint and I fixed them up with guys from uptown—for a fee. I was going strong when I met Brandon and he started milking me. The son-of-a-bitch has been doing it ever since."

"You did all right for yourself," I said, thinking of the money he had received for his busted legs.

He motioned for another drink and I gave it to him.

"Maybe, but I played it smart. As soon as I had enough saved I bought a building, took out a mortgage on it, and jacked up the rents so that it would show a profit. This was before the war and you couldn't have done it then but I already had my rents established and what could they do to me? Later, I sold the store for a good profit and took over this dive. The war brought business to the docks, business all over town, and at one time I had twelve girls working out of here. Money didn't mean anything and I cleaned up. My wife didn't approve of what I did but she never said much. She put up with it and then she got that cancer. I took her all over, spending a young fortune, but it didn't do any good. The cancer just wasn't in her breast, but in a gland in back of the breast—I don't know what they called the gland now—and it was only a matter of time. She put on weight after Ruth was born but when she died I don't think she weighed more than eighty pounds. Jesus, what a way to die, I tell you. If the crazy bastards in Washington spent half as much doing something about cancer as they do in getting rockets into the air they'd be able to pat themselves on the back."

I left him at the end of the bar to wait on a customer who had just come in but all the guy wanted was for me to cash a personal check. I told him I couldn't. He came in almost the same time every day and I always told him the same thing.

"It's good," he protested.

"Then take it to a bank."

"But my bank is uptown."

"So you should be uptown."

I left him and drew a beer for myself and the guy left.

"A paperhanger," Charlie said when I joined him. "I've got a check of his somewheres in the safe. I should burn it up and just watch the smoke." He pushed his glass toward me. "Load it up, huh?"

"What about your sugar? Isn't this bad?"

"To hell with the sugar. I got problems enough without worrying about any sugar. Most people who work in these places get it sooner or later. That's why life insurance rates are so high for us. Doesn't seem fair to me. Some of the guys on the other side of the bar drink more than we do."

"Yeah, but not steady."

He shook his head.

"You're wrong. I know plenty of guys in The Dells who just live for the bottle. In a way, you can't blame some of them. They have slobs for wives and their kids are always dirty. They go home and they find nothing but dumps. Coming down here is a way of getting away from it. If it's payday and they're flush they may take on one of the girls or they may make out with something young for free."

"I guess you're right."

"I know I'm right. This world is made up of sex, Clint, and don't let anybody tell you differently. A guy marries a woman but he still wants a change. And so does the woman. They both get tired of the same old approach, the same love, the same satisfaction. Just being beautiful doesn't mean much. A girl can be like a living doll to look at and she can be like a dead person in bed. I ought to know. I married one of them."

I lit a cigarette and watched the smoke curl upward toward the ceiling, a buff-colored ceiling that had been stained by the smoke of thousands of cigarettes. He didn't know what he was talking about. That wife of his was so hungry for sex that she was like an animal caught in a trap. I could still feel where her fingernails had raked me along the back, where her lips, demanding and hot, had crushed against my mouth.

"I'm going to divorce her," Charlie said. His eyes found my face. "Did she say anything to you about that?"

"No," I lied.

He lifted his drink and put it down again.

"You don't know what it was like after my wife died. I finished bringing Ruth up, sent her to college—God only knows what she did with her education—and after she was married I put her husband in business."

"You own part of it, don't you?"

"Yes, but I don't take anything from it, if that's what you mean. They're young and they need the money and I don't need it. I own the building but someday it will belong to them."

"What about the bar?" I asked.

"I started to tell you about Debbie."

"So you did."

"After I was all alone I used to wander from place to place, picking up a girl here and there and paying her for what she did for me. I guess it didn't make much sense. I could have had anything I wanted down here then—and now—and some of them aren't so bad. But I caught her strip act one night—a customer who came in here said how good she was—and I went breast happy. I didn't use my head. I did everything I could for her, even to getting her out of a jam with the law. I tried to make time with her—I won't say that I didn't—but she put me off. I thought she was a nice girl and the next thing I thought was that I was in love with her. The only way I could get her was to marry her and I did. I married her and we went to Atlantic City for a week to tear a bed apart."

I hated to think of him having been with her, of anybody having been with her. I wanted to think that I had been the first, that it had been real between us, that what we had shared together was the kind of love that you read about.

"I didn't have sugar then," he went on. "Or, anyway, nobody knew it if I did. It bothered me because I was so much older than she was, that I had to protect her in case I died, so I took out some big insurance. The insurance man who sold it to me said it was better if she owned the insurance on my life and that she paid the premiums. He explained that in this way the insurance money would go to her tax free and that only the rest of my holdings would be taxed, giving her cash when she needed it and not forcing her to sell anything else I had at a loss. The idea was good at the time—I won't say that it wasn't—but right now it isn't any good. I can't get additional insurance because of my sugar and she refuses to give up the ownership of the policy. She says that it belongs to her and that she's going to keep it. What do you do with a dame like that?"

"I don't know."

"What I want is to be free of her and leave Ruth everything." He hadn't had much to drink but he probably hadn't eaten and he was feeling them.

"She's a bitch, Clint. She's all bitch. I've lived with her long enough to know and she's all bitch. If she was what she seems to be I wouldn't be running around with other dames, not the way I do. I'd cut down on the booze and I'd give her a jolt every time she turned over in bed."

I decided that he was stupid, for all of his money-making and the financial success he had made of himself. She had enough woman in her for two men and that was no fooling.

"What about the bar?" I asked him again.

"I don't think you've listened to a thing that I've said."

"I've listened."

He watched the flow of liquor as I poured it into his glass.

"You like it here, Clint?"

"It's okay."

"What about the girls?"

"I didn't like that much at first but it seems to be a part of the business. If they don't make their contacts here they'll make them someplace else."

"You'd have to pay off Brandon."

"That's understood."

I thought he was going to drink the drink when he lifted the glass but he didn't. He threw it against the back bar and it smashed in a million pieces.

"I hate Brandon's guts," he said, his face red. "I hated him at the start and I hate him now. He's no cop. He puts me in mind of the sewage you see along the docks. Ever been down there?"

"Not all the way, no."

"You see garbage and all that goes with it. Brandon is garbage. He stinks."

"He's got a lot of power in The Dells."

"Sure, because of his shield. If he wasn't a cop he wouldn't be anybody at all. He'd be lucky to get forty dollars a week for scrubbing somebody's floors."

I had my own idea about how I could handle Brandon. He wasn't in the bar all of the time and he didn't know everything that went on. If I owned the dump I could line up some new girls and he wouldn't have to know a thing about it. Some of them who came into the bar were young and pretty and it was a cinch they put out.

"How much do you want for this place, Charlie?"

He thought about it for a moment.

"I'd only sell you the business," he said finally. "But I'd rent you the building. That would make it easier for you to buy."

"Sounds fair enough."

"I was offered forty thousand for it once."

"That's a lot of money. You should have taken it."

"Maybe. But I wasn't ready to sell then. Now I am ready. I would rather take less and get away from it."

I leaned across the bar.

"How much less?"

He rubbed the side of his face with his hand.

"Say, thirty thousand, for the stock and fixtures."

"There'd have to be a down payment," I said. "Where the hell would I get it?"

"Forget the down payment. The more I take in in a year the more I have to pay in taxes and it's better to spread it out over a longer period of time." He gave it some more thought. "What if you paid me two hundred dollars a month for the building, including the use of the apartment upstairs, and five hundred a month toward the purchase of the business?"

He was talking money, big money, but I knew that it was there and that I could make it. Even if I couldn't find somebody to help me right away I could get along. It would mean fifteen hours a day, if I opened up at noon, but I was young and I could stand it. All I had to do was stay away from the liquor and I would be all right.

"It's a hell of a good chance for me," I said.

"I think so."

I should have felt kindly toward him because he was making it easy for me but I didn't. I couldn't look at him, or think about him, and find one thing that I liked. He was a big, fat hunk of flesh and I didn't have any use for him.

"My lawyer can draw up the papers," he went on. "If you're serious about this you can take over right away, right this minute. The sooner I'm done with this god-damned business the better I'll be satisfied. Let somebody else worry about Brandon and the girls. I've had enough of it. As soon as I've gotten rid of my other properties—and I will—I'll sink my cash in that housing development and that'll be my retirement. That and what you pay me. If I don't end up pulling in three grand a month I'll hang myself just to see what it feels like." He considered the remark he had made and laughed. "No, I won't either. If I hang myself that bitch will get a hundred and fifty thousand bucks and I don't intend to give her anything. Once I'm away from her she won't be able to pay the premiums—I'm sure I won't pay them—and the insurance will go to pot. She'll be right back where she started, stripping in some cheap club and showing the boys how big her bubbies are. By the time she's thirty she'll be taking them on for two bucks a throw."

I walked to the tap and drew a beer for myself and it still had more head than I liked. If he divorced her it would be a good thing and then we would be able to find something real together. She could take care of the money and the bills and I would operate the business. In a year we would be in clover and he could go to hell. During those few moments I thought of Ann only vaguely. We had practically grown up together, ran away together, but there wasn't any more to it than that. If she was going to have a kid she was going to have a kid but it didn't have to ruin my life. Here was a chance to add up the chips in a big way and nobody was going to stop me. She was a pretty girl, a nice girl, and she would eventually find somebody else. If she had a kid she could tell the guy that she was divorced and he wouldn't know the difference.

"I'll take you up on that deal," I said, returning to stand in front of him. "You want out and I want in. You made your nut here and I can do the same. What do I care what kind of a dump it is?"

We shook hands, my big hand closing over his thick fingers, and he said he had to go uptown to take care of some business. He knew a man who had money who was buying a lot of properties around town and he thought he might be able to interest the man in what he had.

"Luck," I said as he went out.

I didn't care whether he had any luck or not. All I knew was that I was in line to make some big money and I was all for it. Give me a year and I would be driving a Caddy instead of walking. Who could ask for more?

I thought of having a belt of rye, just one to celebrate, but I stuck to the beer. If I once got into the whiskey I would stay on it and I had a long night ahead of me. Just what I was going to say to Ann when I returned to the room on Clay Street wasn't clear in my mind but I knew that it was all over between us. What I had felt for her hadn't been love, just the need for sex, and I no longer had that need. I could get all I had to have in that direction from Debbie Fletcher and I wouldn't have to worry about her husband. They were as far apart as a tax collector and a tax-payer and all I had to do was to take what I wanted to take when I wanted to take it.

I watched people moving along the street outside and I wondered how I could increase the afternoon business. There didn't seem to be much way of doing it except by using girls. I doubted if the girls who worked nights would want to work during the day but if I could get some others, girls who lived along the street, I might be able to attract businessmen from uptown who would spend a few bucks with me and get a little play on the side. I knew that a lot of executives did that in other places. They had to be home at night but they could get away during the day and they had their fun then. Not long before that there had been an article in a magazine about the call girls who worked the afternoon shift in New York and there was no reason why I couldn't do the same thing. I would have to start out on a small scale, building it up, but I felt that it would only be a short time before I had money pouring in from that sort of a pitch. Brandon wasn't around The Dells in the afternoon, just at night, and if I sent the men to the girls, for a five-dollar fee, he wouldn't have to know anything about it.

I left the bar and walked around the place, looking it over. As soon as I had the money I would have it painted and the lights changed. The lights weren't dim enough, not for the kind of operation I had in mind. If a guy was at a booth with one of the girls and he had wandering hands he didn't want everybody to be able to see what he was doing. The same went for the girls. If a girl was on the make she would do things for a guy in the shadows that she wouldn't do in the light. Even if she was selling herself she had to have some privacy.

Not long after this Debbie came in and she was wearing those shorts and that halter again.

"The fat slob got back," she said, sitting down at the bar.

"Yeah." I moved behind the bar, reaching for a shot glass and a bottle.

"He didn't even come upstairs. Not that I give a damn. But I wouldn't have known that he was here if I hadn't seen his car parked at the curb. I was at the window, wearing nothing, and I got into this stuff fast."

I decided to have a shot myself.

"His deal fell through," I said.

Her eyes lifted to my face.

"Maybe I should cry, huh?" She swallowed the liquor and I poured her another one. "Did he say anything about me?"

"Well, he talked of a divorce."

"What else?"

"He said you owned the insurance on his life."

"True."

"And that you wouldn't be able to pay the premium after he left you, that it would all go for nothing."

She shook her head and the ends of her blonde hair rubbed across her bare shoulders. She was wearing the halter tighter than she had the day before, up higher, and I couldn't see much of anything.

"I'll pay it," she said. "And if I don't pay it I'll still be protected. I talked to an insurance man about that and he looked at the policy. There's something about an extended insurance clause in it and if the premium isn't paid he'd still be insured for almost another three years. My guess is that he won't live much longer than that at the rate he's going."

"Forget about him," I said.

"Why should I? He married me and I'm his wife. When he put this gold wedding band on my finger he bought me for keeps. He never gave me anything, only a few bucks every week, and he isn't getting rid of me so easily. Maybe he doesn't love me and I don't love him but that hasn't got anything to do with it. Part of what he has belongs to me and that's the way it's going to stay."

I had three drinks, one after the other, and rinsed out the shot glass.

"Give him his divorce," I said.

The bottle was in front of her and she helped herself to it.

"Tell me why, Clint."

"Because I'm taking over the bar and I can make more than enough for both of us. You don't need him. If he wants to be free let him be free."

"It's a good break for you," she said.

"And for you, too. He made a bundle here and we can do the same thing." I shouldn't have been hitting the liquor so hard, not that early in the day, but I found another shot glass. "I wish you would divorce him. I wish to hell that you would, baby. I'd put a ring on your finger that would mean something for both of us."

"Do you have any idea how much he's worth?"

"Not in the least."

"Close to three hundred thousand. Add to that a hundred and fifty thousand of insurance and it's close to half a million. A good bit of that could be mine—the insurance would be mine, anyway—if he suddenly turned up dead."

"He didn't look like he was going to die when he left here."

"How can you tell? How can you be sure? It happens every day to people who are in better health than he is. All you have to do is to read the papers and you know that it's so. And what if he had an accident? That policy would pay double. You have to think of those things, Clint."

"I'm trying to think about us."

"I know you are but we don't have to hurry. We have lots of time. We can always take a room in some hotel and do what we want to do. It doesn't mean that we can't be together. It just means that I have something that I don't want to let go of."

I talked to her, trying to make her see it my way, but it was no use. He was a guy with money and she was determined to get her share of it. I didn't exactly blame her. She'd never had anything, no more than I had had, and she wasn't willing to give up without getting what was coming to her.

I was as lonely as hell after she had gone, saying that she was going to get her hair fixed, and I did a job on the bottle. I wanted that girl and I wanted her bad. I wanted her in a room, all naked and yielding, and if I gave her something that would grow inside of her it wouldn't bother me in the least.

About five the customers began drifting in and I was busy.

It was good to be busy.

I had so much on my mind I was going nuts.

Chapter Six

We had a big night in the bar. The men came down from uptown and the girls were kept busy, grabbing a drink here and there and taking the suckers to their rooms up the street, staying just long enough to earn their money and then returning for new prospects.

"You oughta get more than that for twenty bucks," one man told me. "She was out of her clothes in six seconds and in bed in ten. Five minutes later I was out of the room and it was all over with."

"Well, they have to catch the traffic while it's moving."

There were three girls at the end of the bar, drinking beer, and they had been coming in almost every night since I had been working for Charlie. You could tell that they were stuff and once in a while one of them picked up a man, drinking heavily when the man was paying and then going off someplace with him. They didn't look to be more than eighteen or nineteen but I didn't care as long as they were of legal age. I was pretty sure that they didn't work, or if they worked they didn't make much at it, and that a few easy dollars would come in handy for them.

It was midnight before I got a chance to talk to them. There weren't many people in the bar by that time, a couple of drunks arguing about whether or not the wrestling matches on television were fixed, and a woman of about fifty, heavily painted, who was trying to get some young dock worker to go home with her.

"You won't be sorry none," she told the dock worker. "I may have lost most of my youth but there's one thing I haven't lost and that's for god-damn sure."

"What about your old man?"

"Oh, him. Who cares about him? He gets his from some sixteen-year-old girl on the second floor and he don't care what I do."

"What about the girl's folks?"

"They both work nights."

"Convenient."

That was The Dells for you—sex, poverty and booze. If you didn't feel like sleeping with your own wife you slept with somebody else. And if you didn't have a wife you slept with somebody else, anyway.

I bought the girls a beer and they thanked me.

"How about a shot?" I asked them.

The one with a pert little nose gave me a wet smile.

"That on the house, too?" she asked.

"Sure."

"Say, you're all right. Old Charlie would never give a shot away. He said you either paid or you didn't drink."

"Well, I'm not Charlie."

I gave them all shots and took one myself.

"You girls come in here a lot," I said.

The one with the nose shrugged. She didn't have a lot to offer in the way of a body but some of those without a dream shape can be very good. There was nothing to stop her from wearing falsies and after she got a guy into a room it would be too late for him to back out.

"So what else is there to do?" she wanted to know. "We live together, the three of us, and you get tired of looking at the crummy walls in the flat."

"What do you do for a living? The three of you?"

"Sweater factory," the girl in the middle answered. "That's up on Eighth Street."

"Do good at it?"

She frowned and even with the frown she was rather pretty. So was the third girl, but especially the third girl. Whenever she took a breath her breasts pushed out against her thin white blouse and I could see where the tips were.

"If you call thirty a week good," the girl in the middle replied. "They pay you forty, a dollar an hour, but after everything is taken out you have thirty or thirty-one left. That's why we live together. We couldn't get along if we didn't."

"You've seen the girls that work out of here?"

"We've seen them. Who hasn't?"

"They do very well—two or three hundred a week."

"That is a lot," the third girl said.

"Sure, it's a lot." I gave each one of them a second shot.

"You kids don't fool me any. You drink beer while you're paying but after you pick up a sucker you drink something else, like this. I'm not stupid. A man buys you a few drinks and he takes you home. Don't tell me that he doesn't score. I know better than that. You could be eating steak but you're willing to settle for crackers and cheese. Does that make sense? If you're going to go the limit with a man you might as well do it for money."

It wasn't hard to convince them. They were existing on the edge of nothing and you could have put the three of them together and they wouldn't have had enough morals for one girl. I told them that they could get fifteen and twenty dollars a shot and that I would get my cut from the men I sent to them. It wasn't what I wanted, not an afternoon fix, but if I could steer enough men their way they wouldn't stay in the factory very long and I would be able to build up an afternoon business.

"Don't tell Brandon," I cautioned them. "And don't tell anybody who might tell him. If this operation is very quiet it can be highly successful."

They agreed and we had a drink on it. I wrote down the address, the number of the fiat, and they said they would stay in the following night and that they would take on anybody I sent them. As they departed I watched them go and I didn't feel sorry for what I had done. They would have drifted into prostitution anyway and I had only made the road easier for them.

The bar was empty by one and I sat down on a stool, smoking and drinking. I wished that Debbie would come in so that we could be together. I hadn't gone to the room to stay with Ann the night before and I didn't care whether I ever went there again. If I didn't show up she would come to know that we were finished. The few clothes I had there weren't important. I could always get more clothes and none of the things were much good.

I thought a little bit about my folks back on the farm but I didn't waste too much time on it. It was almost as though I had never been a part of the family, that I hadn't grown up milking cows and pitching hay and walking a quarter of a mile to the school bus stop. They had their lives and I had mine and I doubted very much if we would ever cross again. My folks were satisfied with what they had but I had never been satisfied on the farm. I wanted a fast car and a fast woman and a fast way of life. Running the bar would make all of this possible. Running the bar would buy the car and it would buy all of the best things for Debbie, things that she had never had before.

"You're like a bull," she had told me that morning. "You must have your batteries overcharged or something."

"Is that bad?"

"Bad?" she had demanded. "It's good, you crazy fool."

"I'll have to go down to the drug store," I had said.

"For what?"

"You know what."

"Try the dresser. You'll find what you want in there. The top drawer on the left-hand side."

I lit another cigarette and wished that she were with me, that I could take her in my arms and mash my mouth down over her lips, to run my hands over her glorious body, to give to her a moment of pain and a moment of living.

I was still thinking about her, sweating all over, the sweat of a man on fire, when the door opened and somebody came in. I glanced up expectantly and then let out a groan. It was Red Brandon.

"Dead," he said as he sat down on a stool beside me.

"We had a busy night but it all came in a few hours."

"That's the way it goes."

"I guess so."

He got out a toothpick and began chewing on the end of it.

"I want a hundred bucks," he said.

"For what?"

"Because I want it."

"Hell, you must have a reason."

He spit out the toothpick and it hit me right in the face, just under one eye.

"Sorry," he said.

"I'll bet, you bastard."

His eyes grew hard and deadly.

"How about the hundred?"

"Get it from Charlie."

He laughed at me.

"But I want it from you."

"Why?"

"Because I saw Charlie and he said you were taking over, that's all." He dug for another toothpick but apparently he didn't have one.

"This is payday, fellow. I get twenty-five dollars a week for each girl."

"There are only three right now."

"Is that my fault? She cheated on me and I gave her a going over. She had it coming to her. The other girls shell out and she's no different. But because she isn't here it doesn't mean that your rate goes down. It stays the same, winter and summer, twelve months out of the year. If you don't like paying a hundred for three girls go out and get another girl."

"Maybe I will. You know how much liquor you have to sell to clear a hundred bucks? For Christ sakes, it doesn't make sense. I break my rear in here and you come around and grab the profits."

"Don't tell me your troubles," he said. "I've got no time to listen to troubles. I got enough of my own. And, just to set the record straight, I don't think you're operating with three girls. I was standing outside a while ago, looking in, and I saw you talking to three more. I know them. They're out for money and they don't care how they make it. My guess is that you're going to line them up and when you do that I want more dough."

I sighed and went to the register to get the hundred. You couldn't fool this guy, not for a second. He was all over The Dells and he knew every pitch that could be made.

"You're nuts," I said, giving him the money. "We were just talking and having a couple of drinks."

He put the bills in his pocket.

"Time will tell," he said, getting up from the stool. "You try and cheat me and you'll be so sorry you won't know what's going on." He turned and stopped as he started for the door. "I want to see you after you close, in the alley in the back."

"What for?"

"You'll find out when you get there." He forced a smile. "It'll only take a couple of minutes and we may understand each other better afterward."

If he hadn't been a cop I'd have gone for him then but he was a cop and the law was on his side. I could yell until the end of next week that I had given him dough and nobody would believe me.

"I'll make it if I can," I said, thinking that I wouldn't make it.

He went out without saying another word and I tilted the bottle to pour a shot. He had been on Charlie's back all these years and now he was on mine. I decided that he wouldn't get off until he dropped dead or somebody killed him.

I tried to think of something that I could do but there wasn't anything that I could do. The girls brought a lot of business into the bar and I had to have them. To exist on the local trade and to pay off Charlie would be impossible. Most of the people who lived in The Dells drank beer and you can't make a fortune from that. You have to get rid of whiskey and most of the whiskey drinkers came from uptown, guys on the prowl for a dame and a moment of pleasure between the sheets. While they were waiting at the bar they tore into the booze and that was good profit. If I could pick up a few extra fives each night to send men to the new girls I would do all right but I would have to be careful. It might even work out if I had to pay Brandon twenty-five a week for each one. Once I got things rolling I would be working for nothing one night but the rest of it would be mine. The girls would probably want one night off and that would leave me five nights when I could clean up.

I tried to make up my mind what Brandon wanted to see me about but I couldn't. He was a difficult man to understand, difficult and dangerous, and I had to play along with him if I wanted to make a go of what I was doing. You may hate a guy's guts, just as I hated his, but if he can hurt you you have to follow the rules of the game that he puts down for you.

Martha Foster came in just before closing and had a double scotch over ice. She was wearing a knit wool suit that didn't pretend to hide much of her shape.

"That bastard is outside," she said.

"Who?"

"Brandon. Who else is a bastard in The Dells?" She lifted her drink. "He's the biggest bastard in the world." It was obvious that she was close to being drunk. "The whole stinking world," she said. "You can look the whole stinking world over and you won't find a bigger bastard."

"I agree."

"He comes to get his money and then he wants your flesh. Isn't the money enough for him? Why does a man have to be such a hog?"

"I don't know."

"It's my turn tomorrow and I don't look forward to it. He'll show up about four, right after he goes on duty, and he'll go to bed with me until five. I'll have to swallow a pint of scotch before I can bear him."

"Tough."

She nodded.

"It's worse than tough. He doesn't have any respect for a girl. He doesn't have any respect for anybody. I may be a prostitute but most men treat me decently."

"They should."

"You do." She paused. "There's something nice about you, Clint, that makes a girl feel wanted."

I knew what she was after. She was after a few free drinks and then she would be willing for me to take her to her room. But I couldn't do it that night. There was that business with Brandon—why couldn't he have taken care of it when he had been at the bar?—and it was only right that I see Ann. We had been together a long time and if I was going to walk out on her she was entitled to know why. You may not love somebody but that doesn't mean that you leave them hanging on a limb. You put the facts on the line and you let the future take care of itself.

I bought her a couple of drinks and told her that I couldn't go with her, that I had something else that I had to do.

"I know what it is," she said.

"What?"

"Debbie Fletcher."

"You're wrong."

"And you're wrong if you think she's your kind, Clint. She isn't. She's in a class all by herself and don't let anybody tell you differently."

She walked out as I began turning off the lights and I dismissed her remarks as simply the remarks of a girl who was jealous. Debbie had so much in so many ways and Martha only had one thing in one way.

I didn't add up the cash but bundled up the bills, keeping the fives and tens and twenties separated, and put elastic bands around them. Then I took the check cashing box and everything to the rear of the building and put it in the safe. I didn't know how much money was there but even with giving Brandon his hundred there was enough.

I left the light burning over the cash register and left the bar, snapping the night lock on the door behind me as I stepped out onto the sidewalk.

It was a nice night, hardly any cars moving, and once in a while a whistle sounded as a freighter made its way up the river, the crew seeking a place where it could be anchored until morning and finally unloaded at one of the docks.

I walked around the building and started up the street. I didn't have any intention of seeing Brandon. What the hell did he want from me that I hadn't already given him? As for the new girls I was putting on I had half decided that I would have to cut him in, that it could bring me trouble if I didn't and that it could also bring the girls trouble. At first, they might object to paying for protection but if they wanted to be safe it was about the only way that it could be done.

"Hey, you."

I had passed the mouth of the alley and I swung about, feeling tense inside.

"Yeah?" I said.

"You forget about our date?"

"Sort of," I lied.

I could see him standing there, just a figure in the shadows of the building.

"That's bad," he said. "Very bad." His voice was hard and there was a knife-like edge to it. "When I want to see somebody I want to see them."

"Okay."

I walked over to where he was leaning against the building. He must have found a toothpick somewhere because he was chewing one.

"You could have had a shack up with that number who just came out of the bar a little while ago."

"Maybe I didn't want it."

"Maybe there's something else that you want worse."

"Maybe I want to be left alone."

He spit out the toothpick and it hit me on one shoe. I didn't like that. He had the attitude that he was spitting on a bum, that I was just a tramp out of nowhere. If it had been anybody else I would have slammed him, driving my fist into him fast and following it up with a fast blow to the belly, but he was a cop and you don't hit cops. They can be good or bad but you still don't hit them. They've got the law book in their pocket and you can rot in jail if they make up their mind to shove you in there.

"You want something else," he said.

"Such as?"

"Such as what's upstairs. You went up there with her last night and you'd like to be with her again, wouldn't you?"

"I think that's my business."

"You're like a lot of guys," he said. "You take a look at those knockers she's got and after that you've only got one thing on your mind. Don't lie to me, fellow. You want to jazz her. You want to jazz her bad. You want to rip those god-damned clothes off of her and take her down naked onto a bed."

"Leave her out of it."

"Why should I?" he demanded. "I like her, too. I may be forty-five but that don't stop me from knowing what I can do with a girl like her. If you'd ever seen my wife you'd know. She's a fat tub of lard—won't take care of herself the way other women do—and when I see her without her clothes on I want to puke."

"Fine thing to say about your wife."

He spit again, not with any toothpick in his mouth, and he hit the other shoe.

"I ain't been with her in months," he said. "She thinks there's something wrong with me, that I ought to get some pills to take, but it ain't that at all. I would rather take on these pros down here in The Dells than I would my wife. They may not like me much—I don't give a god-damn whether they do or not—but they put out and that's what a woman is for, isn't she? She's built the way she is to take on a man and give him his fun, isn't she?"

"If you say it's true it must be true."

"Don't be wise."

"I'm not wise. I'm only agreeing with you." I reached into my pocket and found a cigarette. "What the hell is this all about, Brandon? You asked for money and you got your money. What goes on between your wife and you doesn't concern me in the least."

"No, but something else does."

"You tell me what."

"Let's go back into the alley."

The alley was dark, like a hole in the ground.

"I'd rather stay out here."

He laughed at me.

"You got no choice, fellow. I call the shots. People do as I say in The Dells or they end up in trouble. Consider something, will you? I could put a bullet into your guts and just say that you were resisting arrest. Who is to deny it?"

I had to do as he said and there were no two ways about that. If he told me to climb the side of the building in my bare feet there wouldn't be very much that I could do about it.

"Okay," I said.

I followed him into the alley, nearly tripping over a board or some piece of junk. He was being very cozy about this, very mysterious, and it didn't please me a bit.

"Far enough," he said at last.

I filled my lungs from the smoke of the cigarette and then ground the butt out under one heel.

"Now that we're here what do we do?"

There was a light in a flat on the second floor of the building next door and it spilled down into the alley. I could see some of him, not all of him, but I could see his face. It was a brutal face, far from being pleasant. All I had to do was look into it and my spine got cold, the way your spine gets cold when you know that anything you do is bound to be wrong.

"Leave her alone," he said.

"Who?"

"Debbie."

So that was it. He had been trying to make time with her and he was sore at me because I had. She had told me the night before that he had tried to force her, using every trick that he had, but she had resisted him.

"Why not let her decide that?" I asked.

His face twisted in anger.

"Because she's not capable, fellow. You come along—a big guy with a good-looking face—and she's just waiting for some guy to make time with her. You give her enough to drink, get her high, and she don't know what she's doing."

"You've got me all wrong."

"The hell I have. I've got you figured right. You're out for any dame that won't say no and you take what you can get where you can get it. I know you spent the night with her last night. I was right across the street and I stayed there until morning, just waiting for you to come out. But you didn't come out. You got her up there and you made your play and you went for it. The only thing is that it's the last time, fellow. You hit the sheets with her again and you're finished in The Dells. If anybody shacks with her it's gonna be me. I've been playing for that number a long time now and there ain't anybody who's going to cut me out."

"Maybe you've already been cut out," I suggested.

"A wise bastard, huh?"

"No, not wise. I'm just telling you the truth. If a girl doesn't want to have anything to do with a man she isn't going to do it no matter what you say to her."

"I'm ready to retire from the force," he said.

"What's that got to do with it?"

"Plenty. I can divorce my wife and Charlie will divorce her. I'm not a poor man, guy. I can take her to the best places and we can live it up."

"What will you do when your money runs out?"

He sneered.

"Who worries about that? There's always ways. The main thing is that you leave her alone. Got me? You stay far away from her, like she's got a disease or something."

I thought about that, of not bothering with her any more, and I knew I couldn't do it. She had become a part of my life, ripping through my blood whenever I thought of her, and I wasn't going to make any promise that I couldn't keep.

"Why not let her decide that?" I said. "She's old enough to know who she wants and what she wants."

"I figured you'd be stubborn." This time he spit at my face and I backed away just in time. "You're nothing but a dumb rabbit and you've got no sense. You think because you've got a good looking face that that is all that matters. Well, I'm going to show you. I'm going to teach you a god-damned lesson. I'm going to make you so pretty that no dame will ever look at you again."

I saw what he held in his hand, a chain with a bunch of keys on it, but I didn't realize until he struck me, full in the face, that the keys had been filed down until they were razor sharp. I don't know how many cuts I got that first time but I knew there were several and I could feel the blood running down into one eye, taste the salt where one of my lips had been slashed.

"You crazy son-of-a-bitch!" I breathed.

I went for him, wanting to kill him, but he was fast and those keys on the end of that chain were deadly. Twice they got me on the arms, drawing blood—I couldn't see the blood but I knew there was blood—and now the blood was in both eyes. Jesus, I couldn't find him, couldn't see him, and again and again I felt new cuts being opened up all over my face. I was helpless, like a bull being beaten down with a hammer, and after I fell over a box, unable to tell where I was, I just continued to lay there.

It may have been ten minutes and it may have been half an hour before I was able to wipe the blood out of my eyes with my handkerchief and leave the alley. I looked for him as best I could—it was difficult for me to see very far—but the street was deserted and there was nobody in sight.

Still working at my eyes with the handkerchief I stumbled along the sidewalk, going from side to side as though I was drunk. The cuts hadn't hurt at first but now they did and it was difficult for me to move my lips without pain.

When I was near Clay Street I met some woman who asked me what time it was and I told her I didn't know.

"Nuts to you," she said.

I was sober now, dead sober, and inside of me my hate for Red Brandon was a terrible thing. He was a cop, true enough, but he had done a job on me and someday I would pay him back. I didn't know how it would be or when it would be but I knew that it would happen. He was scum, dirt off the street, and somebody had to take care of him.

That somebody, I told myself, would be me.

Chapter Seven

I made my way up the stairs of the rooming house and down the hall toward the room. There was a dim light in the hall and I saw that the handkerchief was red with blood. So was the front of my shirt, as red as though I had been stabbed by a thousand knives. Some of the pain had left my face but had been replaced by a dull ache and a burning sensation.

There was a light under the door and I hesitated before I opened it. She would be angry about the night before—of that much I was sure—but I didn't have anyplace else to go. I doubted if I could get into a hotel, looking as I looked, and all I wanted to do was go to sleep and forget everything that had happened. He had marked me, marked me for life, and the face that had once been handsome would no longer be handsome.

She was sitting up in bed, reading some sort of a magazine, when I went in. She didn't look up.

"The wanderer returns," she said.

I tried to ignore the coldness to her tone.

"So I have."

"The least you could have done was to have called. There is a phone in the lower hall, you know."

I walked to the dresser and looked at myself in the mirror, leaning close for a careful inspection. God, I was a mess. One eye was badly swollen and my upper lip had started to puff out. Most of the cuts didn't seem to be too bad but there was one along my right cheek that was deep and ugly looking. When I wiped the blood away I thought I could see the white of my cheekbone. I shrugged and turned away from the mirror. Maybe I had been lucky. I could have lost an eye.

"I had an accident," I said.

She looked at me then, her face white and tense, and she let out a low scream. In a matter of seconds, wearing just bra and panties, she came to me. Forgotten seemed to be the fact that I hadn't returned to the room the night before.

"Clint, what happened?"

"A fight," I replied.

"You've had fights before but you never came out of one all cut up."

"The guy had a broken bottle," I lied. "There's nothing worse than a broken bottle."

"And your arms!"

I examined my arms. The cuts in my arms weren't deep but there were several of them and there was one that ran all the way from my elbow to my wrist. Those keys had been a deadly weapon, a weapon that could cut a man to ribbons in a matter of moments.

"I'll get the stinker," I said softly.

She stood before me, as nearly naked as she could be and still be wearing anything at all. I hadn't seen the bra or panties before and they were very thin, just a double thickness of material covering the nipples of her breasts and another double thickness you know where.

"You should go to a hospital," she said.

"To hell with a hospital."

There were tears in her eyes.

"Well, if you won't do that you should at least have a doctor."

"I don't want any doctor."

Her uniform was lying over the foot of the bed and she picked it up and put it on, scuffing into a pair of loafers as soon as she had done so.

"I don't care what you want," she said. "I'm going down and I'm going to phone for a doctor and you can like it or lump it."

She went out, slamming the door behind her, and I sat down on the edge of the bed. She was kind, thoughtful about me, but there wasn't much room in my thoughts for her. There was just that hate for Brandon, getting bigger every second, a hate that was both savage and unreasonable. I couldn't kill a cop and get away with it. Nobody could. You killed a cop and every cop in the country was after you and they kept after you until you were caught.

I thought of going to the police, to someone higher up, and of laying the facts on the line. But that, I reasoned, wasn't any good. All he had to do was to deny that he had touched me and I had no way of proving that he had. Then there was that business about the girls. Cripes, I was in trouble, deeper trouble than I had ever been into in my life before, and I had to admit it.

I was on my second cigarette when Ann came back into the room.

"I had to call three doctors before I could finally get one," she said. "But he'll be here in ten or fifteen minutes. Even he wouldn't consent to come until I told him that we could pay him. What are you supposed to do if you don't have any money? Bleed to death?"

"I'm not bleeding very much now."

"No, but those cuts should be treated. If you don't get something onto them you could get an infection." She sat down beside me on the bed and our thighs touched. "I knew something like this would happen," she went on. "All I had to do was see that bar once and I knew there would be trouble. Perhaps now you'll listen to me. That short order cooking job is still open and you could step right in there. It would be better than being around the booze all the time."

"And for a lot less money." I wasn't yet ready to tell her that I had taken over the bar; that could come later. "And, anyway, I don't like to cook."

We were still arguing about it when the doctor arrived. He was a little man with a big case and he wanted his money, twenty bucks, before he would even look at me.

"It's not my fault," he said as I gave him the money. "You get hung up down here more times than you get paid. And it doesn't do you any good to send bills. Half of the time the people move and they don't leave a forwarding address. All you do is waste four cents and get nothing."

He had me lie down on the bed and he washed out the cuts with some kind of solution in a brown bottle. When he came to the big gash he frowned and went over it carefully.

"We'll have to take a few stitches," he said. "But that won't stop you from having a scar. Some of the other cuts are going to leave scars, too."

"I guess it can't be helped."

"Not after it's done you can't. The thing to do is not to get into fights." He got something out of his kit. "I'll freeze that for you and you won't feel it when I sew you up. All you have to do is tell me when your face is numb."

The needle hurt when he shoved it into my skin but one more hurt didn't matter much. I was thinking of that long scar, that it would always be there, and as big as I was I could have cried.

I told him when the side of my face was numb and it didn't take him long to sew me up. After he had that job done he put some bandages over the long cut and some of the other ones.

"I must look like the devil," I said.

"Well, you look like somebody who bit off more than he could chew."

"I guess I did."

He began putting his things into the bag.

"You come up and see me in a week, will you?" He mentioned the address of his office on Pike Street. "I think you'll heal pretty fast." He laughed. "And don't tangle with the same man again. You may not be so lucky the next time. That one slash in particular could have slit your throat and you'd be a dead man by now."

"Thanks for the advice."

After he had gone, reminding me again to visit him, Ann kicked off her shoes and got out of her uniform. My face was still numb and what wasn't numb felt stiff and sore.

"I wish I had a drink," I said.

"If I know you you've already had enough to drink tonight."

"Could be."

"Is that where you were last night?"

"Yeah, I tied one on."

"With some other girl?"

"No," I lied. "No other girl."

"I wish I could believe that."

I was sitting on the edge of the bed and she was standing in front of me.

"You'll have to believe what you want to believe," I said.

She reached behind her and unhooked the bra. I watched her as she got out of it. She was medium size where Debbie was big but she did have nice breasts. I remembered the first time that I had seen them this way, back in Beaverkill, and she had been slightly ashamed of being nearly nude. But I had pleased her, pleased her in the back seat of the car, and the shame had left her, the shame being replaced by a passion that had flamed like a rocket out of control.

"I might as well be a stick of wood," she complained. "You don't even know that I'm here."

"I know you're here all right."

"Can't you say anything else?"

"Thanks for getting the doctor. I guess I needed one."

"You still haven't told me what it was all about."

I walked over and looked at myself in the mirror. I was patched up pretty good, looking like somebody who had had his head smashed through the windshield of a car.

"Just a misunderstanding," I said. "This guy saw things one way and I saw them another. It didn't turn out to be much of a fight. The blood got in my eyes and I couldn't see him. You've heard of the fellow who couldn't punch his way out of a paper bag, haven't you? Well, that was me. He had me solid before I knew it and it was over with in a matter of seconds."

I swung away from the mirror and she turned her back to me as she got out of her panties. She didn't face me again until she had put on a shortie nightgown that didn't hardly hide anything at all.

"You've got to give it up," she said.

"Give what up?"

"Working at that bar. I doubt if my boss would hire you the way you look now but I'll tell him I've got somebody and keep the job open for you. Give yourself a week or ten days and most of those cuts will be healed."

I had to give it to her and I had to give it to her straight. There was no point of leading her on. I might not be in love with her but that didn't mean that I didn't have to be honest with her.

"I'm taking over the bar," I said. "I took it over today."

Her eyes were serious.

"What are you talking about, Clint?"

I told her about Charlie's offer and that I was going to grab it.

"I'm tired of working for somebody else," I said. "This is a chance, a big chance. I don't want to go on making sixty or seventy-five dollars a week for the rest of my life. How far can you go on that?"

"Other people do."

"Well, I'm not other people. I'm me. I'm the guy who washed pots and pans for peanuts and who took all the slop that anybody could hand out. So I took it because I had to. I didn't have any choice. But now I've got a choice and I know which way I'm going."

She sat down on the bed and that shortie was really short. I could see what you went to a carney girlie show to see but just at that moment I wasn't interested in anything that she had.

"I hope you get rid of those girls," she said.

"Fat chance. The girls bring business into the bar and they're part of it. You can draw beer all night long and wind up broke. It's the guys who come into the bar to wait for the girls that makes the cash register ring."

She shook her head in dismay.

"Haven't you got any pride?"

"What's pride got to do with it?"

"Girls selling themselves and you making money from it."

"Only indirectly. I don't ask the men to come down and see the girls and I don't pimp for them. If they didn't work out of that bar they would work out of another one. What they do is their business and not mine."

"It still isn't right."

"Is it right for us to live together? Has it been right from the start?"

"Not the way we do, no."

"Then we can't judge other people. The law says it's wrong for a girl to sell herself to a man but if she gives herself for nothing the act is the same."

"Are you calling me a prostitute?"

"Far from it. I'm just saying, that's all."

She lay back, closing her eyes, and now she was all exposed.

"Have you forgotten what you said the day we left home?"

"We said a lot of things." I felt uncomfortable. "I don't remember all that we said."

"You said you would love me and love me and that you would never let me go." She smiled faintly at the memory and took a deep breath. "And that first night we stayed together in Liberty. The man didn't think we were married and he didn't want to give us a room but you talked him out of it."

"With five dollars."

"Is that how you did it?"

"Sure. Money talks. It screams right out loud, louder than a pig getting stabbed."

While I stood there looking at her it all came back to me—the terrible yearning to be with her, the longing to press my body to hers, the fears and the doubts that she had shared with me after leaving home. It was like seeing a movie, a movie I had seen before, a movie that no longer impressed me. I looked at her but I wasn't seeing her. I was seeing that Debbie Fletcher, alive and needing me, needing me with all of the completeness that a woman needs a man. I glanced at her breasts and I was in that apartment over the bar, all of her loveliness revealed for me to see.

"Money isn't everything," Ann said.

"Just the biggest half."

"Not even that." She sat up and forced a smile. "We've had it tough, Clint. We've had it very tough. Nobody has to tell me that. We knew what it was like to be hungry and then there was that one night when we didn't have a place to sleep. That was last year, just before the fishing season opened, and we were between jobs."

"We stayed in the bus station," I recalled.

"And it was cold."

"Yes, it was cold."

All of these things should have brought me closer to her but they didn't. She was like someone I had known a million years before, in another time, another life, a life that had slipped away from me the way sand slips between your fingers.

"I wish I could make you see things as you should see them, Clint—I don't blame you for not wanting to struggle with money but most people have to do it. Even if you had a million dollars you'd still have problems, money problems."

"Maybe."

"You would. Others do. If you weren't worrying how to make money you'd be worrying about how you could keep it." She leaned forward and the top of the shortie dipped away from her breasts. "Honest you would. There's no such thing of having everything just the way you want it."

"But there's such a thing as trying."

"In a bar that caters to—whores?"

"That may be one way."

"No, it isn't. Nothing you could get through that could ever do you any good. What if the police should get wise to you and close you up?"

"They won't."

"How can you be sure?"

"Because I am sure. The detective who works The Dells gets paid off."

"That's rotten."

"And expensive."

She got up and moved to the dresser to pick up a package of cigarettes.

Any other time I might have gone for her, gone for her because I wasn't with Debbie, but my face hurt quite a bit and the urge to know her again had died somewhere inside of me.

"There's something we have to talk about," she said through the smoke. "I'm pregnant, Clint, as pregnant as they come, and it's up to you to do the right thing."

I thought of being married to her and it wasn't what I wanted.

"We can take care of that," I said.

Her face brightened.

"When can we get married?"

"I'm not talking of getting married," I replied slowly. "There are ways of getting rid of it."

The brightness left her face and eyes.

"You can't possibly mean that, Clint."

"But I do mean it. Who wants a kid? All you have to do is have a kid and we'll be in a fix that we'll never get out of. A kid is for people who know where they're going."

"You should have thought of that when you gave it to me," she said bitterly.

"Yeah, I should have thought but I didn't. You didn't think either so that makes two of us." I moved to the dresser to get a cigarette for myself. "I'll pay the freight on it," I told her. "They get about six hundred bucks in the city but up here it ought to be cheaper. My guess is that three hundred would do the trick."

"I'm not having any abortion," she said firmly. "To begin with, I don't think it's right and, secondly, there's always the danger of getting an infection afterward. Lots of girls lose their lives every year having abortions."

"I think I could get you some of those pills I mentioned before."

"The pills are out, too. You put something inside of me, Clint, and whether it turns out to be a boy or a girl it has a right to live."

"There may be some mistake."

"There isn't any mistake. It's too late for that now. The mistake was in what we did but we did it and I'll pay for it alone if I have to."

"I'll help you out with money," I said.

Her chin tilted.

"I don't want your money if you don't want me."

"Well—"

"Don't lie to me, Clint. There's somebody else. There has to be somebody else. You said you got drunk last night and while I believe that I don't think it's the whole truth. If it's one of the girls who work the bar—"

"It isn't one of them."

"Then it's somebody else."

"Yes," I admitted. "It's somebody else."

Her face fell apart.

"I can't fight that," she said. "No girl can fight it. I heard that if you gave yourself to a man enough times you soon didn't count with him. I didn't believe that and I should have believed it. I was always ready, always willing, and you only had to show me a bed, to put your arms around me and kiss me. It was all of the world that I wanted, all of the world that I cared about. I lived for those moments with you, died when you were so tired that you didn't make love to me."

She kept on talking and I began to pack. What was the use? We had reached the end of the string. She wanted to go one way and I wanted to go another. The same thing happens to lots of people and my only regret was that she was in a family way. If I knew her she would refuse any help that I might offer and she'd go on working. What, I asked myself, would happen if she couldn't work? She'd probably go crawling back to Beaverkill and move in with her parents, bringing up a kid that other kids would call a bastard. It wasn't much of a future for a girl twenty years old.

"I won't cause you any trouble," she said. She was sitting on the bed again. "You can be sure of that."

"Thanks."

"I could go to the authorities, Clint. You know that, don't you?"

"Yes, I know it."

"And I could make you marry me."

"You could sure try."

"But I don't want you that way. I'd want you because you wanted me and that's the only way I'd ever want you. I wouldn't make you do something that you didn't want to do. What good would that do me? I'd have your name and that's all I'd have. Later there would be a divorce and I'd only lose anyway."

I closed my suitcase.

"At least you're being sensible about it," I said.

Her eyes were wet as she looked up at me and she swallowed a sob.

"Can I be anything other than that? Do I have a choice? I'm like one of the girls in the diner—she's expecting, too. She was going out with a married man and they went too far and now she's going to have his baby. She'll have hers before I have mine—you can see that she's carrying it—and maybe we can work something out. I can help her when she needs me and she can help me when I need her. We'll get along. I thought something was happening to us, that it would happen, and I've talked to her about us rooming together. She can't go home—her parents won't have anything to do with her—and she's all for it."

I thought of kissing her on the way out but I guessed that a guy didn't do it when he walked out on a girl. All you did was grab your things and run like a thief.

"You know where the bar is," I said. "If you need anything I'll be there."

"What I need right now is a husband."

"Except that." I lingered by the door. "Think it over, Ann. You aren't doing the kid any favor by bringing it into the world without a father. What are you going to tell it when it gets older?"

"For God sakes, stop torturing me!" she cried out. "Haven't you done enough already? How do I know what I'm going to say? How do I know anything, other than that I'm going to have your baby and that you don't love me? What else can I know? You tell me that, can you?"

She was stretched out on the bed and sobbing when I left her, closing the door as quietly as I could. As I walked down the hall I heard a man and woman fighting in one of the rooms, the man yelling at the woman that she was a slut and the woman yelling right back that he was a drunken bum.

Clay Street was like a tomb at that time of the morning and I walked to the corner in the hopes that I would catch a cab. I didn't know where I was going. I just knew that I was going somewhere, that I wanted to lay down and sleep the sleep of the dead. Inside of me there was hate and love and the feeling that I had done the wrong thing to a girl who hadn't deserved it.

Love for Debbie Fletcher....

Oh, Jesus, how I wanted her, wanted that naked body of hers next to me, wanted all the love that she could give, wanted to give her all of the love that she could receive. The next time I was with her I would show her what a real man was like, make her beg for more and more, make her cry out in the painful wonders of the flesh. And the next time I wouldn't be careful with her. I would give her all of me, all of me, and if she got caught I wouldn't care. I would marry her the next day if I could and if Charlie kept his word that day might not be far off.

But there was hate inside of me, too, a raging hate for Brandon that would someday have to seek its price. Cop or no cop I didn't get cut up for the hell of it. Some of the scars I would carry with me to my grave but he would carry a bigger one. The alleys of The Dells were dark, little islands of violence, and a knife could do the job. As long as I wasn't seen nobody could prove anything. Death came suddenly in The Dells and his name would merely be added to a long list of unsolved crimes.

I reached the corner and waited patiently for a cab. Dawn was beginning to break and there was a slight chill in the air. I remembered then that I hadn't changed my shirt but it only took me a couple of seconds to get a fresh one out of the suitcase. I changed there on the corner and dropped the bloody shirt into an ash can with a heavy iron lid on it.

It was fully thirty minutes before a cab came along and I hailed it.

"Uptown," I told the driver as I got in. "The first hotel you find."

"Got you."

I leaned back as the car growled forward and closed my eyes.

For better or worse I was starting a new life.

I grinned.

For better or worse....

Chapter Eight

It didn't take the cuts on my face too long to heal and nobody who came into the bar, not even the girls, said anything to me about them, except to mention the fact that my face looked terrible after the bandage came off. It did and that one cut was red and ugly appearing.

On the night that I left Ann I stayed at a hotel but the next morning I rented a two-room apartment, complete with bath, on Bruce Street. Bruce Street was within walking distance of the bar—it only took me about fifteen minutes to get there—and it was in a decent neighborhood. The rent was sixty a month, which wasn't bad, and the way things were going for me I could afford it.

I opened up every day at twelve and sometimes Charlie came in to have a drink or two. He had had his lawyer draw up the papers for the sale of the business and the rental of the property but there were a lot of forms I had to fill out to arrange for the transfer of the liquor license.

"You're all right if you've never been in trouble," Charlie said one afternoon. "They look into everything that you've ever done and if you've ever been convicted of a crime they won't go along with it."

"The only thing that I ever did was to get arrested in Roscoe for speeding in my old man's car."

"No. I mean something serious."

"Nothing serious."

"Then there hadn't ought to be any difficulty."

Afternoons he spent running around trying to sell his other property, or checking on the housing development, and most of the time Debbie went with him. That didn't click with me, her going out with him so much. He wanted a divorce and she wanted his money and I couldn't see what they had in common. Sometimes he would take her arm as they walked to his car and I knew that he wasn't going out much at night. I didn't see her at all, not the way I had been seeing her just before closing, and there was nothing for me to believe but that she was taking care of him up in the apartment. I'd be working, running back and forth with drinks, and then I would think about it, of the two of them together, and something sharp would stab me in the guts. There was something going on that I didn't know about and I wanted to know.

"You should have learned a lesson," Brandon said when he collected his money. "If you haven't learned one by this time you're apt to wind up in a casket."

He had the hots for her, had them bad, but with Charlie around most of the time there wasn't much that he could do about it. Often I saw him across the street, just standing there and watching the apartment and the bar, and the hate that was inside of me would be something terrible.

"I don't see why we have to pay him," one of the new girls said to me. "We do all of the work and he takes fifty dollars a week from each one of us. And that isn't all he takes. You have to go to bed with the bastard and he's like a pig."

After taking that beating from Brandon I knew that I couldn't cheat on him, that if I tried it he would only catch me and he would do something else, something worse, that I didn't want done. Often I thought of getting him after work, of doing away with him and of dumping his body in the river, but I knew that I had to have something better than that. I had to wait, like a snake waits for a rat, and when the moment was right I had to strike fast.

The new girls did good right from the start. Within a week they had quit their jobs in the factory and I was getting plenty of customers for them during the afternoons from uptown. Mornings I left the apartment early and I circulated with the cab drivers near the hotel and the railroad station, letting them know that flesh could be had for the asking. Most of them got five dollars for giving a guy a tip, plus the fare of running him down to the bar, and I got another five for putting a man next to a girl. A lot of afternoons I picked up seventy-five bucks on the side and I also did a good whiskey business. Nearly all of the men were executives or professionals of one type or another and they had money to spend. At night the three girls didn't do very much and they would sit at one end of the bar and hit up the hard stuff. I was getting money from both directions and it wasn't difficult to take. There were lots of days that I cleared two or three hundred, all told, and the money I had to give Brandon didn't bother me any financially. It only bothered me because I didn't want to pay him. With whatever else he had going for him in The Dells he was knocking down plenty every week and I resented it. He was a cop but a crooked one and I resented that, too. Once I heard that he might be moved to another section of the city but nothing came of it and he continued to prowl the alleys and the streets. There was dope to be had in The Dells, any kind you wanted, and it was said that Brandon got his share out of this racket, too. As far as I could figure it he was good for about five hundred a week, plus his pay.

Nights after the place cleared out I'd sit at one of the stools, staring at myself in the mirror, and drink more than I should drink. Maybe I had been handsome once but that one big scar took all of it away. The doctor had said that it wouldn't be so noticeable in time but that when he said "time" he meant years.

"You could have a plastic job done on it," he had added. "I don't think there's anybody in Wilton who could do it but there are lots of good men in New York. It would cost you some money but it would be worth it."

"We'll see."

Whenever I was sitting there drinking and the door opened up I hoped that it was Debbie but it never was. One night I tried calling the upstairs apartment on the phone but Charlie answered and I hung up without saying anything. I couldn't understand her, couldn't understand—anything at all.

Some nights I took one of the girls home, mostly Martha Foster, but I never took any of them to the apartment. I was very careful about how I went to the apartment, making sure that nobody followed me. I still had dreams that I would have Debbie up there some night and I didn't want Red Brandon to know where I lived. If our affair resumed, and it didn't seem as though it would, our meetings would have to be in secret.

"You're a funny guy," Martha said to me one night.

We were in her room and we were having a drink from a bottle that I had brought along from the bar. She was sitting on the bed, her dress dipping down between her legs, and I was standing there, a glass in my hand, looking down at her.

"What makes me so funny?"

"Because you aren't the way you used to be. You're too serious and you seem to be thinking about something else when somebody is talking to you."

"Maybe I am."

"Others have mentioned it to me."

"Have they?"

"Charlie was inclined to be sour but he usually had a laugh for a joke. You don't laugh. You seem to be carrying the burdens of the world on your shoulders. What the hell is it all about?"

"Sometimes I wonder."

She got up from the bed and came toward me, her hips swaying.

"I know what you need," she said.

"I wouldn't be here if I didn't."

"Something for free, huh?"

"Well, I sure as hell don't expect to pay."

She stood close to me and reached up with one hand and touched the scar with the tips of her fingers.

"Anybody ask you about that?"

"Not so far."

"Not even Charlie?"

"No. He just said I must have run into a bigger man than I am."

"Mind if I ask you?"

"Go ahead."

The palm of her hand was hot against the side of my face.

"How did you get it, Clint?"

"Some guy with a broken bottle."

"What did Debbie Fletcher say?"

"She hasn't seen me since."

She lifted her drink and watched me over the rim of the glass.

"You've got a yen for that, haven't you?"

"I wouldn't turn it down."

"You'd be smart if you did."

"I guess I'm not that smart."

"She and Charlie seem to be hitting it off."

"So they do."

"If you ask me, he isn't going to divorce her, not the way I heard. She's playing some sort of a game but what it is is beyond me."

She was talking sense, a lot of sense, and yet, in a way, it didn't make sense. He had been running with anything on the street, or uptown, and now he had settled down. It was a long cry from being what I wanted. I wanted her free of him and I wanted her for myself. When I thought of her in these terms I didn't think of Brandon. Somehow I would pay Brandon back for what he had done to me.

I walked to the dresser and poured another drink, a big one that would sock the lining of my stomach like a ball of fire.

"You don't know much about me," she said as she unzipped her dress.

"No."

"And I don't know much about you."

"It's better that way."

"Why?" The dress came up over her head. She wore only bra and panties underneath, no slip. "Why is it better?"

"Because people can know too much about each other."

"Such as me being a prostitute?"

"I didn't say that."

"I've been one since I was sixteen but it wasn't all my fault. I had a step-father, a little skunk of a man, and one day when my mother was at work and I had just got home from school he raped me."

"He should've been put in jail."

"Sure, but what could I do? My mother worked herself silly to support him and there wasn't anything that he could do, even to drinking, that was wrong. Then she got put on the night shift in the factory and he really had his run. He told me that he would go to my mother with all sorts of lies about me and he made me sleep with him. I knew enough to be careful but he wouldn't be careful and in a few months he had me in a family way.

I kept going to school and living at home until I began to show and then my mother kicked me out. I didn't have any place to go but an aunt took me in and I lost the baby during the sixth month. My aunt lived on a farm and the doctor said I lifted something that I shouldn't have lifted and that was the cause of it. I was as sick as a dog for a few days and then I was okay."

"Why didn't you stay with your aunt?"

"Because I hated the farm and there was a hired man who tried his best to do something to me in the barn after I was all right. I told my aunt about it but she didn't believe me and I left. When I got here to Wilton—my aunt only lives twenty-five miles away—I couldn't afford anything but the room rent in The Dells and before I hardly knew it I drifted into this racket."

"You've made money, haven't you?"

Her eyes were sad.

"With my body, yes. I bring the men up here to the room and they all get the same thing. But it isn't what I want. It isn't what any girl wants. A girl wants a home and a husband and a family. If she wants anything less than that she's a fool—or she's dishonest with herself. And she wants to be loved by somebody. She wants to be needed. We were created to give life and love and not just physical pleasure."

I had never heard her talk this way before and I had another drink. She wasn't bad, not bad at all. She wasn't any raving beauty as far as her face was concerned but she had a nice shape and I knew that she could give all that a girl was expected to give.

"I kind of like you," she said.

"I don't exactly hate you."

"I kind of like you a lot, Clint. You're big and strong and you know how to make a girl live. These other men don't mean anything to me. Some of them try to be nice but I hate them all. They buy me like they would buy a pound of hamburger and if I don't show them all of the passion they expect they get sore. It's only when you want a man and need a man that sex is important."

I put my glass on the dresser. I was getting drunk, tired of this talking, and I went over to her and took her in my arms. She came to me without any restraint, pressing in close, her lips crying out for the love she was unable to find with the men who came to her. It was a savage kiss, a brutal kiss, and while we were kissing I found the snap on her bra and unhooked it, letting it hang loose and getting at her with one of my hands in front, shoving the bra up out of the way and finding her naked flesh.

"Help me," she whispered.

"How?"

"I don't know. But help me. Give me something to live for, Clint."

I gave her something to live for, the only thing that I could give her. She was like a raging storm on the bed, lifting to me in a torrent of desire, all of her inhibitions gone, all of her demands the demands of the ages, demands that surged through both of us in an almost unending wave of mutual satisfaction.

For all of my good fortune, if you could call it that, I should have been happy but I wasn't. Sometimes I thought of Ann, thought of her growing big with my child, of her making her own way alone. One night, the guilt of what I had done deep within me, I went to the rooming house on Clay Street but the bedroom door, in answer to my knock, was answered by a sleepy-eyed man and he said he didn't know where she had gone and, furthermore, he didn't give a damn.

One morning, feeling flush, I sent my mother a hundred dollars, enclosing a short note, and three days later I received a reply. My mother wrote that my father hadn't been feeling very well for a long time, that they had sold the cows and that my sister, Olive, had left home, getting a job in Liberty where nobody knew her. The disgrace of what had happened to her had been too much for her to face and in a small community the story of her pregnancy had been well known. My mother wished me well and said she appreciated the hundred dollars. The next week I sent her another hundred.

For the first time in my life money wasn't any problem but I didn't enjoy my situation. I would be behind the bar, looking out at the street, and I would see Debbie walking toward the car with Charlie. The sweat would gather all over me then and my hate for him was almost as much as it was for Red Brandon. She belonged to me and no matter how I argued with myself I couldn't see it any differently. She belonged in my arms, my lips upon her lips, my body knowing her body, all of the fury that was within us belonging to each other.

"Hot," Charlie said one day when he came in shortly after I had opened. "Hotter than the blue blazes of hell."

"Ought to be good beer weather."

"But not so good for the girls."

"Oh, no? How come?"

"Because a lot of the free stuff goes swimming down at the docks and if a man knows where he can pick them up he can score without spending a dime. Some of them may be under age but what difference does that make to a man who is on the prowl? Sixteen or twenty, it's all the same."

He had a brandy and soda—somebody had told him that this wouldn't bother his sugar so much—but he didn't offer to pay for it. He never paid. I guess he thought I got the stuff for nothing.

"Miserable day to go to New York," he said. "There's no place in the world worse than New York on a hot day. You go into an office that's air-conditioned and then you come out onto the street and cook."

"More deals?" I inquired.

"Just some stock to sell. What the hell good is stock? It goes up one day and down the next. If I put the dough into the housing development I know where I stand."

I drew a beer for myself and tried to sound casual.

"Anything more on the divorce?"

"Give me another drink."

"Sure."

I gave him a double and a fly landed on his forehead. He didn't seem to notice the fly.

"I'm not so keen on the divorce right now."

"Change your mind?"

"I guess you could say so. I must have been nuts, running around with those other dames and raising hell." He gave me a wink and a slight grin. "Remember, I told you she was cold? Hell, it must have been me or my approach or something." He licked his fat lips. "She's a hungry one, that girl is. She puts out and puts out and there ain't no stopping her. I take care of her and go to sleep and then she wakes me up and she wants me again."

He said some other things about her, things that hardly any husband would say about his wife—what she did and how she did it—and I drew a beer, not caring if I got a big head on it or not. I only knew one thing. She had gone back to him, or he had gone back to her, and they had found something together and I was on the outside looking in. I didn't like it. Hell, I didn't like it one little bit but I couldn't change anything by being bitter about it.

"What about your property?" I asked him.

"I think I've got it sold but to hell with the god-damned junk if it isn't. I'd get maybe seventy or eighty thousand, all told, and it's a good invest-ment the way it is. If we ever get urban renewal it may be worth more then than it is now. I understand the plans are drawn up and that the federal government will pay the biggest load of the shot. Can you tell me why the federal government would pay out money to help a city?"

"I don't know." I had heard something in regard to urban renewal, or maybe I had read about it in the paper, but my knowledge on the subject was limited. "Maybe they've got so much money they don't know what to do with it except give it away."

He finished his drink.

"Well, I should care. If you ask me, half of those politicians are a bunch of crooks. Me, I'm interested in Charlie Fletcher and not some son-of-a-bitch who goes around kissing babies and handing out cigars. And I'm just the guy who can take care of Charlie. Once I get rid of that stock I can dump another bundle into that housing development and I know it'll pay off. People are moving from the city to the country and they want homes they can afford. They don't give a damn if you put them together with tacks as long as the roof doesn't leak and the furnace runs."

I didn't know how much stock he had and he didn't tell me but I decided that it must be quite a lot. If he carried the mortgages on the houses after he sold them he would get six percent interest and that wasn't bad.

"Another jolt," he said. "Another little jolt and I'll head for the city."

I gave it to him, not a double but the kind I would usually serve for thirty cents, just up to the white line on the shot glass and not a drop more.

"Besides what I get from the houses I'll have the dough coming from you and I'll be well fixed."

"When do I get the use of the apartment?"

"Relax. Rest easy, will you?"

"I could relax a lot easier if I wasn't paying rent on it."

He scowled.

"How do you arrive at that? I just charge you rent for the bar and when the time comes I'll throw the apartment in for free."

"I didn't know that."

"You do now." He motioned for another drink. "Give me some time, will you, Clint? I don't know just what I'm going to do. Once my investments are set up we may take a long trip. I've never been to California and they say it's nice. I always had the urge to travel but never had the time until now."

He didn't stay too long and I watched him go out and round the building toward the alley where he kept his car. A few more customers like him and I'd be in business for nothing.

It was a busy afternoon and the bar got a good play from the uptown crowd. I had it arranged with the three girls that none of the men could see them without a card from me so I got my five bucks from each one. Most of them had three or four drinks before they left and on the way back from their fun they stopped for some more. Once in a while you got a customer who felt the need twice, each time with a different girl.

"Hell of a thing," one man said. "I knock on a door and she meets me stark naked. I'd rather have them dressed and take off their clothes myself."

"Me, too," his companion agreed. "It takes a terrific girl to look good without anything on. Take my wife, for instance. She gets a girdle around her belly, a couple of falsies in her brassiere and she looks like a million dollars. But after you've got her stripped she puts you in mind of a girl who never grew up all the way."

About four it began to taper off—the executives had to get back to their offices or go home—and I began hitting a jug of rye for all that it was worth, sitting at the bar and feeling in a blue funk. Sure, I was making money, almost rolling in it, but that didn't count. Charlie was keeping her, not going through with a divorce, and that was the worst news I had received since Ann had told me that she was going to have my kid. What, I asked myself, could she see in him? He was just a fat slob with half of his brains dragging in the gutter. She had everything that a man could want, everything, and he owned her the way he owned the stocks that he was going to sell. It wasn't right. I was nuts about her, crazy nuts, and there wasn't a girl I had known who could compare with her. All I had to do was close my eyes and I could see her coming into the bar, wearing shorts and a halter, really asking for it. Then I opened my eyes and I saw myself in the mirror over the back bar. I wasn't the same guy I had been then. Brandon had taken care of that. The scar looked worse than it had ever looked. It wasn't a straight scar, but long and jagged, the kind of a scar that I was sure would mar me forever.

The phone began to ring in back and I figured it was some salesman. Most of the people in The Dells didn't call for lost husbands or wives until around nine or after but some of the salesmen did their business by phone. I had told all of the salesmen that I wanted them to call on me but it hadn't done much good. They continued to phone and I continued to order from them because they had the stuff that I needed.

I got fooled.

I got fooled a hell of a lot.

It was Debbie.

"Is he gone?" she asked.

The blood pounded through my veins.

"Yeah, he's gone. A long time ago. But I thought you had gone with him."

"I told him I had a headache."

"Do you have one?"

"No. I had to see you."

The pound was all through my body.

"Where are you now?"

"Uptown."

"You could have seen me before," I said.

"How could I?" She sounded annoyed. "He's been chasing me like a dog on the loose and Red Brandon told me what he did to you, that you weren't to see me."

"I get it. There just wasn't the time or the chance for everything, was there?"

"Something of the sort."

"Charlie didn't tell me whether or not he was coming back today," I said.

"He isn't. He hates to drive on the open highway at night and he's staying over."

"Perfect."

"I'm at the Wilson Hotel and nobody can find us here. You come up after work. It's room four-fourteen." She laughed. "The door won't be locked."

We talked some more but I don't remember all that we said. One side of me said that she was just cheating on her husband and the other side said that she meant it. I asked her if I should bring a bottle and she said that a bottle wouldn't hurt, that we would get a little high and talk and she left no doubt about where it would end.

I don't know why I continued to drink after I had finished talking to her but I did. I didn't know if she would laugh at me because of the scar, or cry, or what she might do. I would get what I wanted and I would get it good and yet, that wasn't the most important thing. There was, I felt, something big here, something that I didn't understand, a strange something that was far larger than anything I had ever faced before.

At five the dock workers began drifting in, most of them beer drinkers, and by six I was as busy as a mother dog with ten pups to nurse. But I didn't mind being busy. It was a good thing for me. I didn't have a chance to think and thinking isn't any good for you when you're not sure what you're thinking about.

And I wasn't sure.

That much was for certain.

Chapter Nine

I thought the night would never end, that three o'clock in the morning was something on the end of nothing. There were a couple of arguments, one between two dockers who disagreed about how to unload a ship, and I threw them both outside. They turned on me, spitting abuse, and they said they never would be back. But I knew they would. That kind always comes back and you would be better off without them if they didn't.

The night girls were busy, running back and forth to their rooms with men, and the day girls sat at the end of the bar drinking. Once when I was down there, fixing a gin for a guy who could hardly stand, I heard one of them bitching about having to pay Brandon protection money.

"I don't mind the money," the girl in the middle said. "You figure out what we're making now and what we were making in the factory before and we're four or five times better off. I'll pay him every week, just as he says, but he better not try anything else with me. I never liked that guy and I don't like him now. He may get his dough but he won't get me."

The other girl had had a sexual experience with Brandon and she said that it had been awful, worse than any man who came to her with the necessary fee for her services in his hand. She described in detail what he had made her do for him, something that even a whore would seldom do, not if she had any sense of being decent, and the girl in the middle cursed bitterly.

I can't say that the day girls and the night girls got along very well but they each knew what they had to do, what was expected of them, and there weren't any fights. They were polite and cold to each other, never drinking together, and they didn't cut into territory that didn't belong to them. It was a satisfactory arrangement all the way around and they were all earning a good income. The men who came to the place at night didn't come during the day and the reverse was true.

About one it was dead—the girls had left sometime before that—and I sat at the bar drinking, not drinking fast but just enough to take the edge off of my nerves. In a couple of hours I would be with her, both of us secure behind the locked door of a hotel room, and I'd make up for all that I had missed since I had last been with her. But there was a nagging doubt in my mind, something that the liquor couldn't kill, and I couldn't answer it. She had been avoiding me for a long time, playing up to her husband, and now she wanted to see me. She must have her reason for that and while I tried to determine what it was I couldn't. A guy, I decided, who tried to understand a woman was licked before he started. A woman had her own reasons for doing something, reasons that differed from those of the male, and all I could do was to wait and see what it was she wanted. I grinned and slopped some more liquor into the glass. I knew what she wanted. She wanted the same thing that most girls wanted. Hell, she wanted it bad and she would get it, get it so many times that neither one of us would be able to keep count.

I watched the fish swimming around in the tank and told myself again that I would get rid of them. Nobody in the bar ever paid any attention to the fish and I always forgot to feed them. In addition to this, the motor that pumped air into the tank didn't run half of the time and some of them had died, anyway. I reminded myself to tell Charlie that he could have the things or that I would throw them out. The tank took up a lot of room and it stuck out over the edge of the counter and it was in the way. If I came down the bar from the right side to the cash register and I didn't think about the tank I'd bump into it. My right elbow was sore from not remembering this and that, to me, made it necessary to chuck the fish. I could load up the space I would get with wine and put a light behind the bottles. We had a few wine drinkers and it was unhandy to reach under the counter for the stuff.

I expected Martha to come in and I wasn't wrong about that, though she was later than usual.

"That stinking Brandon," she said, sitting down beside me.

"He after you again?"

"He's across the street, just standing there. I'm coming down the street and minding my own business when he jumps out and scares me half to death. Why doesn't he ever go home?"

"I don't know."

"I'd rather be dead than be married to a man like that."

"I'd rather be dead than be a man like that."

I knew she wanted a drink and I got up and poured one for her. She put her money on the bar—she never failed to do that—but I pushed it toward her.

"On the house," I said.

"Thanks, Clint."

"You're welcome."

The drink didn't last her very long.

"He wants to sleep with me," she said. "He said for me to get my booze, go to my room and that he would show up when he got ready."

"Which doesn't give you much choice, does it?"

I had set the bottle on the bar and this time she helped herself to it.

"I'm sick of this, Clint," she said. "It's bad enough to have to pay him every week but it's worse when you have to sleep with him." She made a face. "Not that you get much sleep with him. You don't. I often wonder where a man his age gets that much energy."

"Beats me."

"Someday I'm going to get out of here. Someday I'm going to wise up to myself and make a break for it. I've got some money saved—not a lot—but two or three thousand. There are jobs I can get and I can make a living."

At one time or another all of the girls said the same thing, or very nearly the same thing. They knew what they were doing was wrong but it was doubtful if they could change going from man to man. They made big money, bought nice clothes—the dress Martha was wearing, low and square in front, had probably cost forty or fifty dollars—and they couldn't face a future with just an average income. They might leave the business for a while, for a few weeks or a few months, but sooner or later they would be back into it again. They were too used to selling their bodies to change. The only thing that would change them was death and after that it would be too late.

"I just need somebody to go with me," she was saying. "You could do that, Clint. You could go with me. My money would be yours and we'd share it together."

"And where would we go?"

"I don't know. I haven't thought about that. Just anyplace. Just so that we get away from here."

"What would I do?"

"There must be something that you'd be able to get."

"And you?"

"I'd help out. I'd do anything that I had to do."

There was something to what she suggested, something honest and right. I was making big money in The Dells but I was just as bad as the prostitutes who worked out of the bar. Charlie had made his doing the same thing and I felt that I could do as well as Charlie had done but that wouldn't take the slime off of the money that I put into the bank. Yet the slime wouldn't show when I wrote out a check that didn't bounce or bought a five-thousand-dollar car and paid cash for it.

"I can't," I said thoughtfully. "I'm tied up here and you know it. I can't just walk out and let it go to pot."

"You haven't got any guts."

"Maybe that's some of the trouble. I've been knocking around too long to let this opportunity slip through my fingers. Call it guts or what you want to call it and it all comes out the same. The only work I really know is farm work and you don't get much for that."

"Probably two or three hundred dollars a month."

"Big deal."

"And your house. You have to count that. You get a house and your electric and your heat. All you have to do is buy your food."

We had a few more drinks and we argued about it. Once she said that she was in love with me but I discounted that. I didn't think that a girl who had known so many men was capable of love and I made up my mind that I wouldn't go to her room again. She was out for a man, a man she could cling to, and I wasn't the man. What I wanted was uptown in a hotel room waiting for me. It was, I told myself, all that I would ever want, all that I would ever have to have.

She was crying a little when she left, saying that she wished things were different between us, but I couldn't help that. A man doesn't fall in love with a prostitute if he knows she's a prostitute. Oh, some men might—I've heard of it happening—but such instances are few and far between. When a man falls in love with a girl he wants somebody who seems to be better than he is, somebody he can look up to and love with all of the meaning of love. And I don't mean just physical love. That's part of it, true, but it's just one part and there is so much more to it. A girl doesn't have to be pretty to encourage a man's love. All she has to be is truly female, all female, and the rest will take care of itself.

I put the money away in the safe and closed a little early, picking up a bottle of vodka on the way out. Vodka is a potent drink and I wanted Debbie to blast her brains loose and let herself go. I wanted to see her naked body, to touch it and learn its secrets again, to force her down onto the bed and make her cry out in a storm of need.

I met Red Brandon just outside of the bar.

"Going someplace?" he asked me.

"Home."

"And where is home?"

"That's for me to know and for you to find out."

"Don't get smart with me, chum."

"Who's getting smart? It happens to be my business and none of yours."

He stepped close to me and I could smell that he had been drinking.

"Remember what happened to you before?"

"I haven't seen her since," I said.

"I know you haven't. Her old man has been giving her the works and I've had trouble seeing her myself. Just don't get any idea of cutting yourself a piece of her cake. If anybody scores I'm going to score and that's for goddamned sure."

"Help yourself."

"Don't worry. I will. I'll get all of the goodies that she's got."

A cab came along, moving slowly, and I hailed it. I was glad to get away from Brandon. Just being around him made me nervous. I couldn't imagine what he might try next and I knew if he tried anything at all I would be out to nail him. I also knew that I had to be very careful. There isn't anything worse than a crooked cop—unless it's two crooked cops.

It was a ten-minute ride up to the Wilson Hotel and I relaxed. I should worry about Brandon. I would be having a ball with Debbie and he would be getting his from Martha. If I was any judge of it he would get cheated. Martha had to feel passion before she came alive in a man's arms—not with fake moans but with real moans—and I knew that she didn't feel any of this for him.

I don't know why but I thought of Ann just then. I ought to go and see her and give her some money. She was in a bad spot and she didn't have anybody to lean on, only a job that she wouldn't be able to keep after the burden inside of her got to the point that she would have to stop working. I had given her the kid—of that I was convinced—and the fact that I didn't love her, or was pretty sure that I didn't love her, had nothing to do with it. She couldn't shoulder all of the responsibility and it was up to me to help her. I had the money, more than I had ever had before, and I wouldn't miss it. She couldn't very well go back home and expect to be welcomed with open arms. She was on her own, carrying my child, and I couldn't let her down.

I tipped the driver a buck when we got to the hotel and he thanked me. It was, I could tell, far more than he had hoped for from somebody he had picked up in The Dells.

The Wilson Hotel wasn't the biggest hotel in the city but it was modern and clean and even at that time of the morning you didn't have to wait five or ten minutes for somebody to give you a lift in the elevator.

"Party?" the man wanted to know, noticing the bottle in my hand as we started up to the fourth floor.

"Just a friendly drink."

"Well, keep it quiet. You make any noise and the management blows the roof off the place."

"There won't be any noise."

And there wouldn't, not unless the springs on the bed squeaked.

I didn't have any difficulty finding the room and the door was unlocked, just as she had said it would be. I went in and she turned from the window and smiled at me.

"I was watching for your cab," she said.

She was wearing a blue robe of some soft material and it hugged every curve and swell of her body. She had it belted in the middle but the V was deep and wide and I could see the hollow between her breasts.

"Did you see it?"

"Yes. And I wanted to know if anybody followed you."

I hadn't thought of that.

"Did they?"

"No. There was another cab right after yours but it was some woman and she was drunk."

"Good."

I began tearing the seal off of the bottle.

"Aren't you going to kiss me?" she demanded.

I walked over to the desk and dropped the pieces of the seal into the wastebasket, twisting the cap loose on the bottle as I did so.

"There's time for that," I said, wanting to kiss her but wanting her to come to me first. "Where the hell have you been keeping yourself?"

"With Charlie. You know that without asking."

"I hope you had fun."

"Don't be silly. How could any girl have fun with him?" She came over and examined the bottle in my hand. "Vodka," she said. "I like it but, Jesus, it makes me drunk."

There wasn't any ice but I found two glasses in the bathroom and I poured a couple of drinks, real strong ones. I handed her the fullest glass and looked down inside of that V again. The swells of her breasts rose up on either side of her cleavage and something told me that this would be a night that I wouldn't soon forget. We'd kill the bottle and then we would do the thing that we both wanted to do, but before we did that there were a few things that I had to know.

"What about the divorce?" I asked.

"I think he's changed his mind."

I gave her a grin.

"Because you sexed him into it?"

She drank part of her drink and I kept staring at the way those melons of hers stuck straight out and up.

"Well, I had to do something, didn't I? He was all set to change his will and that would have cut me off from everything but the insurance. I even went to Charlie's doctor and he said that Charlie's sugar isn't so bad. If I had to give up the policy I might not ever collect on it. Where would that leave me? His daughter would have everything and I would have nothing."

"So how did you get him to change his mind?"

"Simple. I got him into bed one night and I gave him more sex than he'd gotten from any six of the tramps that he'd been seeing. After that he was a different man. All he wants to do is see me naked and make love. I can't say I get a charge out of it, not the way I did with you. But he's my husband and I have to put up with it. The main thing is that we don't separate, that I keep what's mine."

"Where does that leave us?"

She laughed.

"It leaves us right here in this hotel room—with a bottle to drink from and time on our hands."

"Hell, I'm talking about later, about the years ahead."

Her face sobered.

"I don't know, Clint. I honestly don't. On one hand I want you, want you more than I've ever wanted any man, but on the other hand I want to get what's coming to me."

I didn't hold her desires against her and it was good to know that I meant something to her. No girl walks out on a fortune if she can help herself, and he had a fortune. If she could hang on and he died someday, most of it would be hers.

"Where does his daughter fit in?" I asked. "What if he died tomorrow? What would she get?"

"Just the garage, free and clear. She and her husband would have the garage free and clear and they shouldn't ask for more than that."

I had heard something about the law, how a child could claim part of an estate, but I didn't know anything about it. Maybe that only went for minors, those under age, and not for older children. But even if she got half of everything except the insurance—she wouldn't be able to touch that— Debbie would still have a whale of a lot of money.

"That Brandon did a job on your face," she said, examining the scar.

"Indeed he did."

"And because of me."

"That's what he said."

"He'd cut you again if he knew we were together."

"He'd try it all right. Or worse."

"What could you do?"

Our glasses were dry and I fixed each of us another drink.

"I've been thinking about it," I said. "You don't get cut up this way and not think about it. I used to have a pretty good looking face and now it's ugly."

"Don't say that."

"Well, it is. I look at myself in the mirror when I shave and I feel like screaming. Then I think of Brandon and I know that someday I have to fix him for it. I don't know when or how but the time will come."

"You'll only get in trouble if you try it."

"Which wouldn't be the first time."

"But he could get you into trouble in a lot of ways. There are any number of charges he could frame you on and get away with it. You could talk your head off and it wouldn't do you any good. And what could you say?

You're mixed up with those girls and that's a violation of the law. When you took over the bar you put yourself right in the middle of everything."

I thought about it for a moment.

"I guess I did," I admitted. "No matter where you turn he has you cold. I could yell my head off about paying him protection and nobody would believe me. Even if they looked into his bank account he probably has it under another name."

"Charlie says he does."

"And Charlie ought to know."

We drank and talked and I looked her over. I didn't feel like talking. There was just one thing that I wanted to do with her.

"He's still getting money from Charlie," she said.

That was news to me.

"How come?"

"Because Charlie owns the house where the girls stay. It isn't much, only fifty dollars a week, but Charlie hates his guts because of it. Believe me, there isn't anything that Brandon won't do for money."

"Or to get at you," I said.

She nodded and lit a cigarette.

"Yes, and me, too. You don't know how many times he's called me on the phone lately. He knows that Charlie doesn't get up until almost noon and all of his calls are in the morning. Some of the things he says to me are positively filthy. Just yesterday he said he was going to do something terrible to Charlie and that I would be sorry. And he told me not to see you again. He said if I ever saw you again it would be the last of you, that the river would swallow you up and that nobody would ever see you after that."

"The river might be a good place for him," I said. "If it was timed for the hour that the tide went out he'd be washed into the sea. There's a good chance that he'd never be found. And even if he was there are other people in The Dells who hate him besides me."

She gave me a long look.

"You've been thinking about it," she said.

"I've been thinking about something. I think of it when I look at my face and I think of it when I've been drinking. I don't mind so much him sucking money from me—if it wasn't him it would probably be somebody else—but he carries things too far." I paused. "How does Charlie pay him?"

"By check."

"I wouldn't think Brandon would take one."

"He didn't want to—he insisted on cash—but Charlie wouldn't have it any other way and Brandon is just hungry enough for money that he's been taking them."

"That's stupid."

"Why is it stupid? Brandon thinks he's safe. He's been with the department a long time and nobody has ever questioned him. He's been in The Dells so long he thinks he owns it and everybody in it." She tossed her blonde hair, fluffing it out. "Well, I've got news for him. Here's one girl who will never belong to him."

I walked over to her and grabbed her roughly by the shoulders. Under the robe I could feel the smoothness of her skin, could look down into that wonderful well of flesh that separated her breasts.

"You're mine," I told her harshly. "God damnit, none of these things can change that."

Her mouth was waiting, expectant, and I didn't keep her waiting. She spilled some of her drink on one of my arms as I pulled her to me but I didn't care about that. I drove my mouth down there over her lips, forcing the breath out of her lungs, so starved for her love, just a little of her love, that everything turned black for a second.

"You know how to kiss," she said as I let her go.

"There's something else I can do even better."

She pulled my head down and kissed me greedily.

"And don't think I don't want you to."

Even in that instant, of feeling her lips moving against my mouth, I knew that something had to be done about Charlie and Brandon but I wasn't sure just what it was. The checks Brandon had received from Charlie figured in somehow but it wasn't quite clear in my mind as to what extent.

"I'm loaded," she said, pulling away from me.

"You don't act it."

"Maybe I don't but I always get loaded when I drink vodka. Five or six drinks—we've had more than that—and I don't care whether school keeps or not."

She drifted away from me, turning on the radio and getting some hot music. She didn't turn it up too loud but just enough for the sound of it to fill the room.

"You've never seen the dance I used to do," she said. "That may not be the music for it but I'm going to show you my way."

I had been to girlie shows in carnivals, to a few stag affairs, but I had never seen anything quite like her. She moved round the room like a giant cat stalking a victim and when she swung about that robe seemed to lift from her legs and come up around her hips, letting me see just about everything there was to see.

I sat on the bed, the palms of my hands wet, and I didn't pay any attention to the music. She was like something that you dream about, pray for—something that never quite seems to happen to you.

"You aren't just a breast man," she said as she came over me. "You're a woman's man, every inch of you." Standing before me she removed the robe, giving meaning to every movement that she went through, and her nude body was even better than I had remembered it. Maybe I wasn't a breast man but I liked them and she had them. Oh, cripes, she had them and as she moved away from me, moving into a torrid dance, they lifted and fell just the way they should. I sat there fascinated, unable to move, only able to think of one thing. Here was sex and here was love and here was the girl who had both.

When she ended the dance she fell on the bed beside me, breathing heavily, her arms reaching up to claim me.

"Give me what I cry for," she said. She got her wish and she got it again and again and again. She got it all the rest of the night, even after the light of day filled the room.

I left her at eleven, just in time to go down and open up the bar.

I didn't think I would want another girl for as long as I lived.

Chapter Ten

My liquor license came through all right but a man from the Liquor Authority who stopped to see me said I wasn't selling enough food.

"We know that half of the places don't sell enough food," he told me. "But they keep a supply of stuff on hand and instead of ringing up everything in beer or liquor they ring up some for food."

"What happens to the food if it spoils?"

"They throw it out and buy more. The main thing to do is to cover yourself and license. If you get an accountant who knows this racket he can help you."

I got an accountant by replying to an ad in the paper but he wasn't much help. He had worked several years for some slipper factory but they had fired him and he was on his own. He wanted everything just so, figures for everything, and he nearly drove me nuts whenever he came around to go over the tape from the register. I didn't think that he was worth the money I had to pay him—ten dollars a week for an hour's work in one of the back booths—but he was better than nobody at all and I put up with him. I paid Brandon out of the money I got from the men who were looking for girls so the accountant didn't know anything about that. One night he stopped in for a drink and he asked about the girls but I told him they just hung around and he didn't ask again after that.

The food was an expense—Charlie laughed at me because he had never bothered with it—but I spent about ten or fifteen dollars every day at the nearest grocery and meat market and I gave it away to some of the poor people who lived in The Dells. I found out right quick that there were a lot of poor people and they would send their kids into the bar to ask me to give them what I could. I tried to divide it up but that was almost impossible and some of the kids got sore at me. Outside the kids would fight over the food, like rats in a dump, and sometimes it got so banged up that it wasn't good for anything at all.

"God damn foolishness," Charlie said. "You figure out how much beer you have to sell to clear ten or fifteen bucks? There's no sense to it, Clint."

"Well, I want to keep my license. One day some snoop is going to demand to look at my books and I want to be in the clear."

"They used to look at mine and they never said anything."

"Maybe you paid them off."

"Maybe I did."

"Then it comes out to almost the same thing. What's the difference if I give the money to the grocery or to some jerk who is only trying to shake me down?"

He began drinking more than usual, showing up at the bar as soon as I opened, and staying for a couple of hours. You'd have thought that after he had been in the business for so long that he would have been conditioned to drinking but it didn't take much to make him drunk and staggering. How he was able to take care of his business uptown, when he said he had something to do, I don't know. Some days it was a wonder that he didn't give away everything that he had.

"I don't figure my wife," he would say. "Every morning she goes out and she says she's looking for an apartment. Jesus Christ, if she'd only leave it up to me I could find an apartment in a day. Or, if she was willing, we could take one of those new houses in the development. I can't understand having all that money invested and then having to rent."

I understood and I had her figured. She wasn't looking for any apartment. She left The Dells about nine in the morning and she met me at a place we had decided on the previous day. There were about a dozen hotels in Wilton, counting the small ones, and we shifted around from place to place. I don't have to tell you what we did during the little time that we had together. I always rented the room and as soon as she entered it she got out of her clothes. She was wild, good as they come, better than any girl in The Dells, and she gave just as much as she took.

"I think I ought to have a baby," she said one morning when we were lying exhausted on the bed.

"You nuts or something?"

"No. I've been reading up on the rights of a kid in sharing a father's estate and there's a lot to it. If he died and I was going to have a baby that would be another share that I would be able to control. But I wouldn't want it to be his baby. I'd want it to be yours."

"Nobody would know."

"That's what I mean."

Sometimes we talked about what we would do if he should die, where we would go and how we would handle all of that money. She was rather set on going to Florida and it didn't sound like a bad idea to me. I was getting sick of the long hours I had to work in the bar, of putting up with the girls and with paying Brandon off. The only trouble was that Charlie wasn't dead and it didn't look as though he was going to die right away. I had heard that people who had sugar couldn't drink but he was drinking and he was getting away with it. If it didn't bother him now, I reasoned, there was a good chance that he would go on living for years.

She couldn't get out at night. After I finished work there was Brandon to worry about and Charlie was usually home—and we had to get our loving during the day.

"He's getting wise," she told me one morning. "He can't see why it's taking me so long to find an apartment and he says he doesn't think I'm looking for one. He says he's going out and look for one himself this afternoon."

"That's bad."

"Of course it is. Once we move I won't have any excuse to get away from him and then what will we do?"

"I'm not sure."

Her naked body was pressed against mine, all naked and hot, and when I kissed her I knew that this had to go on and on for us and that it couldn't stop.

"I love you, Clint," she whispered.

"And I love you."

"So where does that leave us?"

"Here in bed in a cheap hotel room."

"Don't joke."

"I'm not joking. It's true. We have to sneak around corners and steal what we want from each other. It isn't the way it should be. We should be together all of the time, just making love and doing what we want to do."

Our lips were welded together for a second and we sought each other with our hands.

"Tell me what to do," she pleaded, moving away from me. "You tell me what to do, Clint."

"Divorce him."

"That's what Brandon keeps telling me."

"Nuts to Brandon. What's he got to do with this?"

"Go on. I'm listening."

She was stretched out beside me, her breasts lifting up full and round.

"There are lots of places where you can get a divorce," I said. "Let's not kid ourselves. We talk about him dying, how it would be for us with all of that money, but he isn't going to die, not right away. Hell, he may outlive both of us. You don't love him and you never did so why go on with it? What if you never get his insurance or any of the other stuff that he has? I'm making good money, big money, and I can take care of you. Give me just a few years and we won't have anything to worry about. You can have your own car and I'll have mine. There won't be much that we can't have."

I talked to her, trying to show her, but she was stubborn. She had set out to change his mind about divorcing her and she had. She hadn't done that for nothing and she wasn't going to throw it all away.

"You don't know what it's like to have to go to bed with him," she said. "You don't know what it's like to do what I have to do and even feel a little bit clean inside. It's almost as though I'm a prostitute who isn't getting paid for what she gives."

"Then break it off."

"Would you give up a fortune for a few years of passion?"

I had to think about that.

"I don't know," I said honestly. "Maybe. Maybe not."

There wasn't a day that we didn't talk about it and the more we talked about it the more I wanted her to be mine forever. It got so that I hated Charlie as much as I hated Brandon and that was a lot of hate. Even when he came into the bar to drink I didn't feel like discussing anything with him. He never paid for his drinks, which burned me, and as far as I could see he was nothing but a fat slob who kept standing in my way.

"Got an apartment," he said one day. "Nice place in a nice section but we won't be able to get into it for a month. Hope you don't mind us sticking it out upstairs a while longer."

"Why should I mind? You've been there, haven't you? One month isn't going to change the world."

"You could be using it for the girls."

"And then Brandon would stick me for more."

"Possibly, but you can always get it out of the girls. Be smart, Clint. Remember that with a whore you make her pay. Anybody who doesn't make a whore pay is out of his mind."

Debbie didn't keep our appointment the next morning and I didn't see her for a week. I nearly went nuts. I would go to the apartment half drunk and fall asleep but in a matter of minutes I would be wide awake, sitting up, sweating, remembering the wonders of her body and the way that she responded to me. Days I just banged around the bar, doing what I had to do, the making of money something that seemed to have lost its meaning. Several times I tried calling the apartment but when I did he answered and I hung up, my hands shaking and my guts tense and tight. All I had to do was think about her and I was a wreck, a hopeless ghost of a man who was blinded by all of the love that was being lost. More and more I turned to the bottle, seeking from the bottle the answers to the thousands and thousands of questions that kept churning around inside of me. I didn't find any answers. I got drunk and stumbling and I didn't care whether I worked the bar or not.

"Straighten out and fly straight," Martha Foster told me. "You act like a guy who's been beaten over the head with a club and kicked in the belly."

"That's the way I feel."

She laughed at me.

"Aw, nothing's that bad," she said. "If anybody should want to cry about their life it should be me."

"Good. We'll cry together."

But we didn't. We just drank and when I closed up I went to her room with her. She was extremely competent that night and I decided that if she was half as good with her customers they didn't have anything to complain about. Long after she went to sleep I lay beside her and thought about the two of us running away together. I had a little money, she had some, and it might be better than this. I was in love with a girl who couldn't be had, not all the way, not so that we could make a life together, and I would be better off if I forgot her. Yet I knew there was more to it than that, that I would never forget her, that she was in my blood as much as the red and white cells that kept me alive.

I left her the next morning before she was awake and took a cab uptown. I had thought of seeing Ann for quite a while but I hadn't gotten around to it and there was nothing else to do. I had three or four hundred in my pocket that would help her out. It would also make me feel better if I tried to do the right thing.

She was in the diner, working behind the counter—or I should say she was reading the paper—and there was only one other customer in the place. I sat down in front of her.

"Coffee," I said.

She glanced at me, said nothing, and put the paper aside. She went to get the coffee and I thought her hips were a little wider than they had been. After she had drawn the coffee and began moving toward me I saw that she had a little bulge to her tummy.

"Aren't you talking?" I asked as she put the coffee in front of me.

She looked me straight in the eyes.

"What is there to say, Clint?"

I poured sugar into the coffee and stirred it.

"There might be a lot to say."

"I doubt it."

"Look—"

"No, you look. You left me and I've been on my own. I'm getting along. The other waitress and I are living together and we're saving our money. I'll manage."

She was putting up a bold front but there were tears in her eyes.

"Here," I said, digging into my pocket. "You can use three or four hundred, can't you?"

"Not the kind of money you have."

"Why not, for Christ sakes?"

"Because I know how you earn it and I wouldn't touch it if I had gloves on. Besides, I told you I was getting along. I'm not fooling. I've found out that you can do what you have to do if you have to do it."

"You're being pretty silly about this whole thing."

"No, I'm not. I was silly before but I'm not silly now. I made a mistake and I'm willing to pay for it. What more do you want from me, Clint?"

"I don't want anything from you."

"No, but you think you can make yourself decent by giving me a few dollars."

"It's more than a few."

"A few or a lot it's all the same. What you could have given me you weren't willing to give."

"Such as?"

"A ring on my finger. Well, all right. If you don't love me I don't want you. I'll have the baby, boy or girl, and I'll bring it up. I won't cause you any trouble and I won't ask you for any money. I'd rather have just a little money and know that it's honest."

I drank my coffee and smoked a cigarette. What did you do with a dame like that? Half of the money in the world is dishonest and if everybody stayed away from it most of us would be half broke. Shrugging my shoulders, I picked up the money and returned it to my pocket.

"I've got it if you ever need it," I said.

"Thanks for nothing."

"What are you going to do?"

"What do you care?"

"Just wondering."

"Stay around here, I guess. I can't go home and we both know that. If I have an easy birth I won't be out of work very long. When the baby gets older I'll move to some other town and tell people that my husband died. Lots of girls do that. The baby never has to know that he was an unwanted child."

It took plenty of nerve to do what she was planning on doing but I felt pretty sure that she was capable of doing it. She would pay all of her life for one careless moment and I was to blame. It made me feel badly, like a skunk that has been sprayed by his own odor.

"You keep the money," she was saying. "You may need it to get yourself out of trouble. Or didn't you read the paper this morning?"

"No, I didn't read it."

She gave me the paper and I saw right away what she was talking about. The police had raided an uptown apartment the evening before and had arrested three girls for prostitution. An official of the police department stated that the drive was just getting under way and that the cops were going to rid the city of every last prostitute.

"That doesn't bother me any," I said, pushing the paper aside.

"But it could."

"I don't think so. If the cop down there nails me he's in it, too, and no cop is going to arrest himself."

However, I won't say that I wasn't worried about it when I left the diner. I was. Why the hell did they have to go and do a thing like that? Women had been selling themselves since the beginning of time and no matter what they did they wouldn't be able to stop it. The girls would get fined fifty or a hundred bucks and as soon as they were free they would get another apartment and pick up where they had left off. As long as there were guys who were willing to buy there would be girls who were willing to sell. To put a stop to that was in the same class as moving the world with one hand.

I got a cab near the bus station and rode down to The Dells. What was I worried about? I was paying for protection and so were the girls and it was up to Brandon to see that we got it. He had a good thing coming his way and he wasn't going to give it up just because of a little scare.

"Gonna be a hot day," the cab driver said.

"So it would seem."

"Hot days are fine for me. People don't like to walk when it's hot and they hitch a ride in a cab."

"Sounds reasonable."

I got off at the corner, tipped him a buck, and walked over to open the door. It was hot, a close heat that brought the smell of the river with it. By the middle of the afternoon the kids would be down to any of the docks that were vacant, diving off into the scum and filth that spewed out of the sewer further up the river. It was a wonder they didn't catch some sort of a disease. Not only the boys went there, but the girls also, and from what I knew the boys made time with most of the girls. Sex started young in The Dells and since both parents worked in nearly all of the families it gave the kids plenty of opportunity to iron out the sheets in private.

I spent about half an hour going over the cash from the day before, not counting what I had taken in from the men who had visited the girls, and tried to figure out how I could manage to get along without the girls. That was almost impossible to do but I divided the take in half, judging that the men had spent that much or more, and it wasn't hard to see that I couldn't meet my obligations from the local trade. I was running a lot of beer through the taps but at ten cents a glass you don't make much from beer and you have to have a liquor trade to keep you going. Or heavy wine drinkers. There's a good profit in wine but I wasn't doing enough in that direction to take up the slack.

Charlie came in as I was cleaning down the bar and he smelled of sweat, a smell so strong that I knew he hadn't taken a bath in several days.

"Have to go to New York again," he announced, sitting down on a stool. The stool squeaked beneath his weight. "You need anything?"

"Not that I know of."

"Always buy your glasses in New York. They're cheaper."

"I'll remember that."

I poured him his usual drink and resented the fact that he didn't put any money on the bar. Where else could he drink for nothing?

"Read the paper?" he inquired.

"I saw it."

"Don't worry about it. They put on these drives every once in a while but they don't mean anything."

"I hope not."

"Well, they don't. Somebody gets the bright idea of getting his name in the paper and it's the only way he can do it. Ten to one the same guy has paid some dame for a roll in the hay."

I couldn't wait for him to get started for New York. I had no way of knowing whether or not Debbie was going with him but if she didn't she would be all alone in the apartment. If I had to lock up the place and throw the key away I'd do it to be with her again. Brandon didn't show up until later in the day and therefore he didn't concern me. He was on duty from four until midnight, during the hours that most of the girls worked, and after twelve he prowled around on his own. Sometimes I tried to determine how much he made in a week but it was wasted effort. It was certain that he hit the dope pushers hard and there were probably other methods that he employed.

"You driving back tonight?" I inquired casually.

"No. Staying over."

"You and Debbie ought to have a time of it."

He gave me an evil grin.

"I didn't even ask her. I just said I was going. She's good and all that but a man wants a change once in a while. Some of those dames in New York are hot babies and for a hundred bucks you get yourself fixed up like a king."

"You can get the same thing in The Dells for nothing."

"Not the same. It's never the same. You just think that it's the same. I know a girl off Lexington Avenue who could set fire to a bed just by looking at it."

I drew a beer for myself.

"Your wife wouldn't like it if she knew."

"Probably not." He frowned. "Funny how she's changed. She was hot when we got married but then she turned cold all of a sudden. Now she's hot again. I don't follow it unless she's afraid of losing my money. If I thought that I'd skip out on her so fast that it would take her an hour to pick her rear up off of the sidewalk."

I drew another beer and swallowed it down in nothing flat. He wasn't sold on her—I could tell that—and maybe he would divorce her anyway. All she had to do was to make one false move and he'd be finished with her. It was even better news than his going to New York. If he ever cut away from her I would be in solid and steady and that was what I wanted. She was the kind of a girl you could starve to death with and not mind it at all.

He had a couple more drinks and left. As soon as he was gone I poured a healthy shot for myself and stared at the phone on the wall. She was so near and yet she was so far away. She was right upstairs—maybe she hadn't dressed yet—and I was down there in the bar wanting her so much that my legs ached with the want.

I had three shots before I went to the phone. My heart was making the noises of a shotgun going off inside of me and the sweat was running down my forehead and into my eyes. Jesus, it would be wonderful to be with her again, to know the glory of her love and the hungry force of her lips.

She must have been waiting for me to call because she answered the phone right away.

"He's gone," I said.

"I know. I heard the car go out."

I clutched the phone tight.

"Baby, I've missed you!"

She blew a kiss into the phone and laughed.

"Don't think I haven't missed you, honey, but I couldn't get away." She paused. "Or I mean I didn't dare risk it."

"Why?"

She was silent for a moment.

"I'd rather not talk about it over the phone. We can talk about it when we're together."

It was my turn to blow her a kiss.

"I'll lock up right now," I said. "What do I care if I lose an afternoon's business? I haven't had a day off in so long that I can't remember when it was."

"You'd better look across the street before you do that."

I looked out of the window and groaned. Brandon was standing on the opposite side of the street, watching the bar.

"Hell," I said. "Damnit it to hell."

"He doesn't miss a trick."

"I guess he doesn't."

"You don't know how little he hasn't missed."

"Probably not."

"He's got me in a hell of a spot."

"He's got a lot of people in spots."

"But not like this one."

I asked her what it was all about but she wouldn't tell me more. She told me to work the bar as usual, to close up as usual, to go to my apartment and to return to the building about six in the morning. By that time, she said, Brandon would be home and we wouldn't have to worry about him. I agreed, not wanting to agree, but there wasn't anything else that I could do.

It was still too early for the afternoon trade so I returned to the bar and had a couple of belts from the best bottle in the house. Brandon was still across the street, just standing there, hardly moving. I only had to look at the guy and I felt nervous. What kind of a pitch was he cooking up now? You never knew with a guy like Brandon. All you could be sure of was that he was out to get you and to get you good, to use the power of his shield to bend you to his will.

I expected him to come in long before he did and I was chewing on the end of my cigarette rather than smoking it.

"Beer," he said, sitting down on a stool.

I went around the bar, picked up a glass and drew him a beer. I had to slop foam off the beer three times before I got a good head on it.

"Salt," he said as I placed the beer in front of him.

I gave him the salt. The salt was damp inside of the shaker and he had to pound on it before he could get any of the stuff to come out.

"See the papers?" he asked me.

"I saw one paper."

"Which one? There happens to be two."

"Does it make a difference?"

"Well, the one has got a big editorial in it about gambling and prostitution and vice. It calls for a shake-up in the department if the city can't be made clean." He sipped some of the beer. "The people read that crap and what they print has a big influence on what goes on in the department. You take a guy who is chief and he wants to hang onto his job. The only way he can do it is to get out and raise hell."

"Go on."

"That's why I'm down here early today. I figured I had to talk to you and make you see how this thing is going. If they closed in on you they could take your liquor license and you could draw a rap for supplying girls."

"I'm paying you for protection," I reminded him.

He laughed at me.

"Can you prove that?"

"No, I can't prove it but we both know that it's true. You get yours every week from every direction. It's your job to see that we're left alone and that nobody bothers us."

He stared at me thoughtfully.

"That's a big order," he said.

"So you've been making big money, haven't you? Christ, you add it up and you're probably making more than I am. I've got the headaches and the expenses and all you do is walk around and collect."

"Another beer."

I drew it for him. He was as bad as Charlie, never putting any money on the bar. Of course he only drank beer and he didn't drink very much of that. But it was just the idea of the thing that annoyed me. You stand behind a bar and you expect to get paid for what you serve.

"It's going to cost you more," he said finally. "When the top brass was sleeping what you gave me was all right but now I'm going to have to spread a little money around."

He held up his hand. "Don't look so excited. It won't last long. These things come and go and you have to expect them. I can take the heat off of you but I have to come across with the bucks in order to do it. Sometimes I think it's a good thing that cops aren't paid enough money. If they were paid enough money you wouldn't be able to touch them."

I had an idea that he wouldn't do anything, that he would simply take all that he could get from me, but I wasn't in any position to argue with him. Without the girls the business was lost—how could I ever pay Charlie what I had to pay him?—and I had to go along with what he said.

"How much?" I asked.

"Double what it is now."

"Jesus!"

"And five hundred to get the ball rolling."

I reached for a bottle. I had to have a drink.

"I don't know if I can afford it."

His eyes showed no feelings at all.

"You can afford it. You've been making a nut for yourself and if you haven't blown the cash you've got it. If you have blown it then it's your tough luck. I could run you in right now, easy as hell, and I could make out a case against you. All I need is a couple of the girls and one of them would talk and put the finger on you. They always talk when they think they're going to be sent away and they'll do anything to get out of it. I know. I've been in this racket so long that I know. You put a dame in a jam and she tells you her life story."

It seemed to me that he was in a bad spot, too, but he had ways of getting out of it and I didn't. All he had to do was promise the girls that they would only be questioned and I was pretty sure they wouldn't say anything about having paid him money. They would get a lecture from the judge or a little fine and they would go free. But where would that leave me? It would leave me holding the well-known bag and there would be a hole in the bottom of the bag. I could just see myself doing from two to five years, or whatever it was they gave you, and the money wasn't important.

"I wish Charlie had this bar back," I said.

"That's why he sold it to you. He saw this trouble coming and he wanted out from under. He's a big boy now and he belongs to a lot of big clubs. He couldn't afford a scandal and, anyway, he had his clover made. Then you came along and you were hungry for a buck. You were a natural for him and you fell into the garbage heap like somebody had thrown you out."

Silently I cursed Charlie and I cursed myself for having been so stupid. But I was in it now, in it up to my head, and once you've started down the road you can't turn back. Oh, you can turn back but you can't ever wipe out the smell that you leave behind you. And if I tried to quit now, if I tried to change, I knew that Brandon would put the prongs to me, driving them in deep and sharp and not caring what part of me got hurt.

"Okay," I said and walked to the safe. "You hold all of the cards and I'll just have to watch you play the game."

"Well, at least you aren't dumb."

"I wouldn't say that."

I got the money out of the envelope where I had been keeping most of the take from the men and as I removed each bill it was like parting with an old friend. I couldn't make it up, that much I knew, and if I had to pay double for the girls it was going to cut heavily into my business. I'd be doing a lot of work for nothing, taking chances for nothing, but no matter how I looked at it I couldn't see how I could help myself. He was calling the shots and I was running the bases. The trouble was that the bases were getting pretty full and after a while I wouldn't have any place to run.

"I hope you choke on it," I said when I gave him the money.

He counted the bills twice, coming up short the first time and coming out all right the second time. He stuffed them in his pocket and got up from the stool.

"Don't worry," he said. "You'll be safe all the way down the line."

I watched him go.

I didn't know whether I'd be safe or not.

I was willing to bet that I wouldn't be.

Chapter Eleven

Business was slow that afternoon, not the way it usually was with the uptown crowd coming in, and it hardly paid me to stay open. At four the day girls came up and they were crying the blues. They each had had a trick and that had been all.

"It's just a scare," I explained to them. "Three girls got knocked off last night and the men probably don't want to take any chances. Give it another week or ten days and they'll be coming at you faster than ever."

But this didn't satisfy them. They had been making good money but they had been spending it as fast as they made it. They were all broke, or close to it, and they didn't know how they could exist until the storm had passed by. On top of this Brandon had been after them for more money, not saying why, and this didn't help matters any.

I set up a few free drinks for them while they talked it over and I even offered to support them until the tide turned in our favor.

"Don't be so god-damned generous," the one girl told me. "I should hang around this stinking hole for crackers and soup? Not me, mister. The girls in New York get a lot more than we get and that's where I'm going. How about it, kids?"

The other two agreed and I tried to convince them that they didn't know what they were doing, that New York was a big place and that they didn't know anything about it. It was no use. They were used to the big money and they couldn't stand doing without it. On the last round of drinks I charged them. It was only ninety cents but it was better than giving the stuff away. Ninety cents was as good to me as it was to them.

After they left, making all sorts of plans about how they would work in New York, I walked along the bar and kicked at things in disgust. I had brought them into the racket and now they were taking off on me. That left me without any girls for the afternoon trade and this had been where I had been making most of my money. The night girls brought in the heavier drinkers but the five dollars from each man had been what had counted.

I got the same old crowd about five, workers and like that, and they drove me nuts running back and forth to the beer taps. A few drank wine, a couple whiskey, but most of it was beer. Each time I dropped a dime into the register I wondered how much profit I was making but I knew that it wasn't enough. I had a lot of expenses, all of them closing in on me at once, and the loss of the girls was critical. Then I told myself that I would be able to get other girls easily and the future didn't seem so black. I had enough dough in the bank and in the safe to hang on until the cops got interested in something else and that was some sort of comfort.

"Loan me ten dollars," one man said.

"Like hell."

"Just until tomorrow."

"No."

While you aren't supposed to run charge accounts in a bar, Charlie had done it for some people but I didn't know. They were all the same to me. They worked on the docks or in the factories and they got drunk and they made a lot of noise. There was a television set in the bar but there was no use turning it on because you couldn't hear it. If there was a time that you could hear it some jerk put money in the juke box and all you could follow was the picture.

There was a young girl at the bar—she had the body of a woman but I didn't think she was of age—and she was making a play for a man old enough to be her father. The man came in every night—he was married to some woman who didn't care what he did—and it was my guess that he would take her into one of the alleys, or to her place if nobody was home, and show her that he was man enough to warrant her interest. The girl had been coming into the bar during the last week or so and she was after a different man every night. Once she had suggested that a little play between us might be in order but I had only laughed at her, not because she wasn't attractive but because messing around with her just didn't make sense to me.

The rush only lasted until a little after seven and then I hit a lull. It took me a while to get the glasses washed and the bar cleaned up but after that there wasn't anything to do. Nothing to do but think. She was upstairs, all alone, and I couldn't even get to her. I had to wait until a crazy hour of the morning before I could go to her and give her the love that she needed.

I sat at the bar, not drinking anything at all, and thought of Brandon. Brandon was like a doctor who was cutting me up into a thousand pieces and throwing the pieces in any direction that suited him. I had been paying through the nose before but now I was paying in blood. To add to my discomfort, I had no assurance that he could keep the other cops away from me. He might pay off some but it only took one honest guy to push the cart all the way down the hill—a cart that would have me in it.

There were a lot of things I thought about as I sat there, such as growing up on the farm and smelling the sweet, clear air of the country. At this time of the year it would be hot during the day but at night it would be cool and sometimes you would have to use a blanket to keep warm. In the morning there would be a big breakfast, eggs cooked just right and steaming coffee, and after that you would go out in the fields and work until noon. If it was too hot to work after lunch you hung around in the shade or took a swim in the Beaverkill, banging your feet and legs on the rocks but having fun anyway. In the evening you would take the family car, pick up your girl and perhaps park on a lonely road. You would have the windows of the car down, smoking and talking, but after you ran out of talk you made your move. Generally, the move was to the back seat and if the girl was willing she didn't deny you. She would come into your arms, all soft and alive, and the love that you would find would be the wonderful physical love of a man for a girl. If you had forgotten to go to the drug store, or you left what you needed at home, you took a chance—you both took a chance—and in the days that followed there would be a secret worry that you would share that something might have gone wrong. If it went wrong you married her and in four or five years you had more kids than you knew what to do with. If the home of your parents was large enough you moved in with them but if it was too small you threw up a shack, using a dug well for water, and you sat up at night wondering how you could keep your bills current. You never had anything, never anything at all, but you had each other and maybe that was enough. Or maybe it wasn't. You slept together, leaving your bedroom door open in case one of the kids got up, and you were seldom careful about your sexual relationship. You had three or four kids already and one more wouldn't matter. If you hit the switch and an additional member of the family was on the way you built another room onto the shack, promising each other that you wouldn't do the same thing again, that you were already deeply in hock and that you would be months paying off the hospital. But it didn't stop there and you were only kidding yourself The family got bigger and the shack got bigger and the bills got bigger. You saved enough money to pay off some of what you owed but then a cow died and it was the same thing all over again. You never got ahead. You kept going behind every day of your life. You could save money for Christmas, maybe in one of those clubs that they have, but the day after you got your check something came up and the money didn't go for Christmas after all. You bought the toys and the other things that you needed on credit, if you had any credit, and you had twelve payments that you had to make and no fooling about it.

It's funny the things a man thinks about when he's alone and discouraged. You see the mistakes that you have made but you're the one who made them and you're stuck with them and you can't do anything about it. You tell yourself that you'll be more careful in the future but you know that's a lot of crap and that you won't do it. All it takes is somebody to show you how you can get something for next to nothing—the way Charlie did to me with the bar—and you're sucked in. You reach for the sky but you can't even find the clouds that are just over your head and you wind up with two hands that are as empty as the night itself.

I was glad when somebody came in and ordered a beer. It stopped me from thinking. I was thinking too much and the main trouble was that I didn't know what I was thinking about. One second I saw Ann pregnant, pregnant with my child, her stomach getting bigger every day, and the next second I saw the naked body of Debbie lying on a bed and waiting for me. I saw Ann, proud and unafraid, and I saw Debbie, needing me as much as I needed her, needing me in that special way that a woman needs a man.

"Everybody die?" the man asked me, glancing along the empty stools.

"Seems so."

"Probably because of the talk of a strike."

"A strike?" I hadn't heard anything about a strike.

"On the docks. There's a vote tomorrow and we may all walk out. I don't blame the fellows none. The pay scale is lower here than it should be. We work just as hard as anybody else and we get less money for it."

I drew a beer for myself. A strike was all I needed. The dockers drank heavily on payday but they couldn't drink if they didn't have any money coming in. I couldn't understand why they might want to go out on strike. I cashed quite a few checks every week and most of them represented a fairly decent income.

"Nobody wins in a strike," I said.

"Only the unions but we have them just the same. If it's a short strike it's okay but if it's a long strike you never get back what you lose. Three years ago we were out for three months and the docks lost a lot of business. When we went back there was only jobs for eighty percent of us and if we have another long one it'll be even less than that."

He only had three beers, saying that he had to save his money, and I was alone again. The news about a possible strike was bad news and I wasn't discounting any of it. The way things were going I'd be broke before I knew what was going on.

The girls came in at nine and they were in an unhappy frame of mind. They had heard about the arrests uptown and Brandon had put the arm on them for another twenty-five dollars a week each.

"I don't know what to do," Kathy Nelson said. "We'll be shelling out more to him than we should."

"You'll do it and like it," Jennie Corby advised her. "If you don't pay him he'll do to you what he did to Gloria Forbes. You want to take a beating like that? And if he didn't beat you he'd frame you. A cop can always get even and a crooked cop knows more ways than an honest one."

"Well, I'll pay it but I won't like it. How do I know that he won't frame me anyway? If he gets the heat put on him he'll put it on somebody else."

The night was almost as bad as the afternoon had been. Only six men from uptown came in and each of the girls got two tricks. The men didn't drink much, acting nervous, like they were being chased by somebody and that they wanted to get their business finished with. I couldn't blame them, not the way things were, but it didn't do the cash register any good. By midnight, when I checked the tape, I had less than a hundred and fifty dollars and it was a cinch that I couldn't go very far on that.

I was hoping that Martha would leave me alone, that she wouldn't show up, but she came in around one. She had changed from a red dress to a black dress and it looked very good on her. It had a low front, just low enough to disclose part of the hollow between her breasts, and it clung to her body like she had been born in it.

"This can't go on," she said as I poured a drink for her.

"Well, what can you do about it? You can't work the street corners or force the men to come down here. We just have to sit it out."

"Who can afford that?"

"You can. You've got some money saved."

"So have the other girls."

"Then there's no problem. A store may open up one day and make a lot of sales and the next day make hardly any. You have to expect it."

She downed her drink straight.

"Don't try to make it sound so simple, Clint. It isn't simple. We don't make any money, you don't make any money, nobody makes any money. But we still have to pay Brandon. We pay Brandon or we go to jail. For my part I've had enough of it."

"Are you serious?"

"Very serious. I told you before that I wanted to break away and now is as good a time as any."

"Luck," I said.

Her eyes searched my face.

"You could go with me, Clint."

I won't say that I didn't consider it briefly. She wasn't much, not the kind of a girl a man would want to marry, but I wouldn't have to marry her to be with her. I had some money—I wasn't sure just how much—and I would be rid of Brandon. But there was one thing that told me I couldn't go, that I would find it impossible to do. That one thing was Debbie Fletcher, beautiful Debbie, and I knew that she was the girl for me.

"I couldn't," I said.

"You'll be sorry if you don't."

"Maybe. Maybe not. I've got a bull by the tail here but I've got to hang on. If I let go now there won't be another chance. There'd be just jobs here and jobs there and I'd end up floating from place to place, never earning very much and never being sure what I was going to do the next day."

Her face was sad, almost the face of a child.

"I kind of love you, Clint," she said.

I lit a cigarette and pulled the smoke down into my lungs.

"You only think you do. We've had some good times together and it's been fun and I doubt if you've ever had much of that. But what you think is love is just a way of making an escape. You want to go but you don't want to go alone. I can see that better than you can. If we did do it, it would be all right until our money was gone and then it would be hell. We'd both get to thinking what we had left behind us and whatever it might be that we would find together wouldn't last."

She cried for a long time, saying how she only wanted the better things in life, but there wasn't anything I could tell her that would help her. She was afraid and mixed-up and she had to work out of it by herself. If she had the strength of her convictions she might go on and become a decent girl, a girl who would marry some man and give him a family and forget her past. Yet few are able to do it, to wipe out the stamp of having been a prostitute. They may cast off the cloak for a short while but sooner or later they return to it. I suppose it's only human. They have learned that men will pay to be pleased and they have the goods to command the price.

"I wish you would," she said at last.

"Sorry."

"I wouldn't ask you to marry me or anything like that. There wouldn't be any strings tied to you. If you wanted to leave me you could. All I need is somebody to help me get started right and to stay right. There are things I can do. I can type and I know how to keep files in order. It's just—well, just that I don't want to sink any lower. Every man who comes to my room is a monster, all except you. It's all right for the girls who don't care but I do care. I'm young now but I won't be young for many years if I stay in this business. You saw Gloria. She was old for her age, so old that nobody could ever want her. Her life is finished and when I think that the same thing could happen to me I just shake all over."

Nobody came into the bar and she did her best to convince me that we should make a break for it, that the lid had blown off the pot and that there was nothing left for us in Wilton. As I've said, I considered it but only lightly. If she had been Debbie suggesting the same thing I'd have gone with her without even bothering to lock the door behind me. It's a big country and you can always get along. Or, I should say, you can get along if you love somebody enough to make it worth your while.

She didn't stay until closing and although she asked me to stop by her room I told her I couldn't make it that night. This made her cry some more and I felt sorry for her as she went out. She was just a kid who was trying to find herself and she was having difficulty doing it.

No one else came in and I drank alone, changing over to beer because I didn't want to get a load on. When I saw Debbie I wanted to be sober, dead sober, so sober that I wouldn't miss one exciting movement of her body or one thrill as my hands did to her what they wanted to do.

I stayed until three but it was a waste of time and I closed up. When I got outside I found that it was very warm, warmer than it had been in the bar, and a light rain was falling. However, I decided to walk to the apartment. I wasn't in any hurry and there wasn't time to catch any sleep. Even if I had been dead on my feet I couldn't have slept. In a few hours I would see her and I would know her favors again, know all of the torment of love that was hers to give.

At the corner of Clay Street there was an old house and I saw a couple on the porch. They didn't pay any attention to me or to anything else. I stopped, staring at them. They were right in front of the old-fashioned door, making love on the rough boards.

"I want a boy," the girl was saying. I thought it was the young girl who had been in the bar earlier. "Every time I see a kid in a carriage I go nuts wanting one."

"You must have a loose bearing someplace," the man objected. "You know what would happen if you had a kid by me? Jesus Christ! And you only sixteen."

I walked on. No matter where you looked in The Dells you saw sex and booze. It was a dumping ground for the misfits, the girls and women who were wild and the men who were just as wild. They lived in a little world all of their own, a world of poverty and death and tears and birth. If a man didn't like his wife, if she had begun to sag and she was no longer satisfactory to him, he found a young girl and nobody thought anything of it, including the parents of the girl who were most likely doing the same thing. When a baby came screaming into life it was either put out for adoption—not always by recognized agencies—or the mother went on the welfare. I had read that two-thirds of the welfare paid in the city found its way into The Dells and I had no reason to think that it wasn't so. A lot of times a girl wanted a child so she could pull down a free income from the taxpayers and, if the father was working, she could shake a few bucks out of him on the side.

As soon as I reached the apartment I showered and shaved and put on fresh clothes. There was an all night radio station in Wilton and I flipped the radio on but the music was so terrible that I soon turned it off again. I had recently bought a couple of magazines from a store not far away and I sat down and flipped through them, studying the nudes and making up my mind that none of them had what Debbie had. There was one of a girl stripper in Texas, a girl with long black hair, and she came the closest to having Debbie's shape. Her ample breasts were tilted, probably painted in the centers for effect, and she had a saucy smile on her lips.

It was daylight before I left the apartment and I had trouble getting a cab. The driver was like a lot of them and when I told him I wanted to go down to The Dells he insisted on seeing my money first.

"Not many people around this hour of the morning," he said as we pulled away from the curb.

"I wouldn't think so."

I lit a cigarette and tried to relax but I couldn't relax. I was only minutes away from her and the urge to crush her in my arms, to burn her mouth with my kisses, was like a forest fire sweeping through dry timber, boiling up in a wave of flames and smoke that was beyond all control.

"Thanks," he said when he let me out and I gave him an extra dollar. "I'll frame it. It's the only tip I ever got for a run down to The Dells."

"Here's another one to go with it."

"Say, fellow, you're generous."

I wasn't generous. I was feeling good, feeling high. We'd be alone, just the two of us, and what we wouldn't do for each other wouldn't be worth doing.

The street was deserted as I pushed open the door that led up to the apartment. A small light burned at the top of the stairs and a couple of the steps squeaked as I climbed them two at a time.

I didn't knock. I just went in. The door opened into the living room and there was a light on, not that it was needed because there was plenty of light coming in from outside. She was on the davenport, sound asleep, and the split in her robe revealed the inside of one perfectly formed leg. The top was open, too, and one of her breasts was fully exposed. I closed the door, not making a sound, and walked over to stand looking down at her.

She was the beauty of woman, full and lovely, the beauty that no painter can paint. Even in sleep her breast was lifting and ripe, her lips the lips of love, lips that could move to the invitation of love and could speak of love.

I bent and kissed her, thinking of the nights that I had wanted her, of the nights that I had needed her, thinking of all of the nights I wanted to share with her in all of the nights that were to come.

She stirred, first moving her head from side to side, and then as her eyes opened she began kissing me back, her arms moving up to encircle my neck.

"Let's not talk now," she said, pulling me down beside her. "There are so many things to say but this has to come first." Her lips moved against my mouth. "This always has to come first."

"Always."

And it did.
Don't say that it wasn't good.
It was.
The best.

Chapter Twelve

About nine that morning we moved out to the kitchen and she fixed coffee.

"Eggs?" she inquired.

"Hell, no. Not after that. I'm stunned."

She laughed and got cream from the refrigerator.

"You're quite a man," she said. "I'll bet you've pleased a lot of girls."

"A couple."

"Well, count me amongst them. Charlie is a five-minute lover but your five minutes go on forever."

She was wearing the robe and she had it belted in the middle but I knew what was underneath it. Her.

"You complaining?" I wanted to know.

She was close to the table and she came over and gave me a kiss.

"No complaints," she assured me. "Most girls have more sex drive than a man and if a girl can find a man who can keep up with her she's lucky."

"You found one."

"So I did."

I was out of cigarettes and I took a package from a carton lying on the table. I didn't care for the brand, they were too mild, but anything was better than not having any at all.

I sat there watching her as she moved around the kitchen, drained of almost all emotion, and I thought about how it would be to be with her for the rest of my life. The sex part of it was big—I won't deny that—but there was more to it than just sex. Here was a girl who could bear my children and look up smiling at me from a hospital bed, a smile that would hold all of her heart, all of her love, all of her life. A pang shot through me as I remembered Ann. She would be bearing my child, too, but it wasn't quite the same. With Ann it had been a mistake, a moment of heedless passion, but with this girl it would be different. With Debbie it would be deliberate, a driving force inside of me that sought to assert itself.

"Did anybody follow you down here?" she asked me.

"There was nobody on the street." The robe dipped open as she bent over to pour the coffee. "Or, if there was, I didn't see them."

"We didn't see Brandon before either."

"Huh?"

She sat down opposite me and dropped sugar into her coffee. I noticed that she used three spoons of it and I could not understand how she could drink it after making it so sweet. Then I remembered that my father used four, sometimes five, and it didn't seem so unusual.

"But he saw us," she said. "The places we went before weren't as secret as we thought they were. He followed us, first you and then me, and he put two and two together. He says it adds up to four."

"I see."

"And he adds further than that. He adds it up to five thousand dollars."

The coffee was good but I could hardly taste it.

"Tell me more. Not that I want to know more but tell it to me, anyway."

"He wants five thousand dollars to keep from telling Charlie."

The coffee tasted worse.

"Jesus Christ," I said. "Jumping Jesus Christ."

"I told him that I didn't have that kind of money."

"What did he say?"

"He said to get it. He said he didn't care where or how I got it as long as I got it."

"How much time did he give you?"

"Until tonight."

The coffee began to taste better. It wasn't so bad. It could have been worse. What if he did go to Charlie with the truth about us? The business was mine—we had signed the papers and I was buying it—and he would probably divorce her. That would leave her free and we could get married. We'd live in this apartment, up over the bar, and after a few years we wouldn't have to ask a dime from anybody.

"Do you love me?" I asked her.

Her eyes had all of the passion in the world written in them.

"You know I do."

"So beat Brandon to it. Tell Charlie yourself. Tell him how we feel about each other and that you want out. The way things are it's no fun for you to go on staying with him. You stay with a man you don't love and every day you stay with him is a day that we could be together."

"You don't understand," she said. "I want what's mine. I married him to get it and I intend to get it." Her face softened. "Don't you see, Clint? Even if I only got a hundred or a hundred and fifty thousand from him it would mean so much to us. It wouldn't be my money, not just mine alone. It would be yours, too. My God, you can't tell me that you want to go on living here in the slums and doing what you have been doing. You told me about the trouble over the girls, while we were talking, and I knew that it was going to happen. Charlie knew it, too, and that's why he sold you the bar the way he did. He wanted somebody else to take the fall and not himself. You may think that Brandon can keep the other cops away from you but I don't think so. There are honest cops, Clint, and no amount of money can buy them. The way I see it he's trying to make a big haul before his little bubble bursts and he's back on salary again."

"You may be right."

"And it's important that I get the divorce, not Charlie. If Charlie gets a divorce because I've been sleeping with you I won't get anything. But if I get it, if I frame him with a girl, I'm bound to come out of it with a bundle of cash." She leaned forward. "Just think what we could do with a hundred thousand or more. Just think! We could buy a decent business somewhere and have something. There are lots of good places you can get where you don't have to break the law. I don't want to be poor and lay up here nights worrying about you getting picked up for selling girls and having Brandon or somebody else bleeding you to death all of the time. I want a home and I want kids and I want all of the things from my husband that any woman wants."

We talked about it, talked about it a lot, and the more we talked the more I began to see things her way. She would hire a lawyer, somebody who was good, and we'd trap Charlie with one of the girls. He had a yen for that Kathy Nelson so that part wouldn't be hard. All we needed was a raiding party and the stage would be set. I didn't know if she would get as much out of Charlie as she thought she would but I wasn't worried about that. A hundred thousand or more would be fine but if it turned out to be less it would be less. The main thing, as far as I was concerned, was to have the marriage wiped out and to have her for my own.

"These cigarettes are terrible," I said. "You got anything different?"

"You'll find some in his dresser in the bedroom. The top drawer, on the right."

I went to get the cigarettes but I found more than cigarettes. There was a gun in there, probably a thirty-eight, and I checked to see if it was loaded. It was. I asked her about it when I returned to the kitchen and if Charlie had a permit to carry the gun.

"He's got a permit," she said.

"I see." I lit one of the cigarettes and it tasted better. "Now about the money. What can we do about that?"

"How much do you have?"

"Not five thousand."

"How much?" she insisted.

"I'm not sure. Maybe part of that much. I'd have to get my bank book and check the cash downstairs before I really knew."

We each had another cup of coffee—the coffee was getting cold now—and we tried to figure out a way that we could come up with the amount of money that was needed.

"I could try the bank," I said.

"I doubt if they'd give it to you. What security do you have?"

"The bar."

"No, you really don't have that. You're just buying it from Charlie. If you owned it you could put up the stock for security but you don't own it and you can't do that."

"Well, I can try."

"Then try."

"And I know somebody who's got a couple of thousand. I might be able to get that."

"Who?"

"One of the girls."

"I wish you luck but I don't think you'll have any. Those girls hang onto what they get. They earn it the hard way—real hard—and they know where every buck goes."

It was about ten-thirty and if I wanted to get to the bank and open up on time I had to get a move on. I didn't want to leave her, that much was for sure, but I wanted to help her if I could and I couldn't help her by sitting around in the kitchen and talking about it.

"Keep your fingers crossed," I said, standing up.

She got up and came into my arms and her lips were hot and warm.

"You're doing it for us," she said.

"I know."

"For all of the things that we want and that we should have."

"You see a lawyer."

She kissed me again.

"I'll see a lawyer. And you get the money."

"I'll make a stab at it."

"Just don't stab. Get it."

I left a few minutes later, telling myself that it would be more fun for both of us if I took her into the bedroom, and descended the stairs. The steps seemed to squeak more going down than they did coming up and even the door squeaked as I opened it and stepped out into the sunlight.

It was only six or seven blocks to the bank where I did business and I decided to walk. It was hot for so early in the day, burning hot, and already the half-dressed kids were playing in the street. Some of them wore shoes but most of them didn't and their feet were dirty. It was doubtful if any of them had seen water in more than a week, not unless they went down to the docks, and some of the language they were using were words that had been born in the gutter.

They weren't very busy in the bank but I still had to wait several minutes before I could see the man who was in charge of the loan department. He was a tall man with a narrow waist and broad shoulders and I judged him to be in his late forties.

"Now," he said as I sat down, "tell me what we can do for you."

I told him about the bar and how I had bought it from Charlie and that I had an account in the bank but that I was tight for cash.

"Twenty-five hundred would do it," I said. "Twenty-five hundred for two weeks."

"How could you pay it back so soon?"

I couldn't tell him about the girls or how I made most of my money.

"I've got a couple of insurance policies," I lied. "I'm going to cash them in and they'll take care of it."

"May I see the policies?"

"I don't have them with me. They're with my folks up in Beaverkill and I have to send for them."

"I think you have an account with us, don't you?"

"Yes."

"Well, we could loan against that."

"But I need that, too."

"I see."

"If I had the insurance policies now I wouldn't bother you."

He thought about it but even before he gave me his answer I knew what it was.

"We couldn't," he said. Then, trying to soften the blow, "It isn't that I don't trust you. Don't think that. You probably need the money just as you say and you probably have the insurance policies that you mentioned. It's just that we have rules and we have to go by them. Even if I did okay your loan, which I can't do, it would have to go before a committee and they don't meet again for another three days."

In the end I drew my money out of the account—it wasn't as much as I had thought, only twenty-one hundred—and got out of there. You can't fool bankers and a lie doesn't do you any good. You tell one lie and you have to tell another one but when you have to produce the stuff that you've been talking about you can't do it. Just the same it made me a little sore and added to my frustration. Where the hell was I going to get twenty-nine hundred dollars? My only hope was Martha and if I could get what she had, plus what I could dig up in the bar, I might be able to make it. It would leave me short, even worse than I had started out, but I couldn't think of anything else.

I didn't have any trouble finding the house where she lived—I'd been there enough times—but when I reached the second floor I wasn't quite sure which room she slept in. I took a chance and beat the hell out of one door with my fist. There was no answer.

I cursed, trying the knob, and found the door unlocked. I pushed the door in, expecting to find the room empty, but it wasn't empty. She was sitting up in bed, her face white, the sheet pulled up around her shoulders.

"Thank God," she said huskily. "I thought it might be the police."

I laughed and closed the door, leaning up against it and lighting a cigarette.

"I'm some cop," I said.

She let the sheet fall down, reaching for a package of cigarettes on the stand near the bed, and she was all naked up above. She didn't have the breasts that Debbie had but she wasn't bad and she was all woman. I thought of the nights that I had been with her, how she had pleased me, and if I hadn't been in a hurry I would have gone for her again.

"It isn't very funny," she said, blowing the smoke out of her lungs. "I didn't sleep at all last night. Everytime a door opened or closed I thought it was the cops." She shook her head. "It's no way to live, Clint. You're afraid every second of every minute. Down inside there's a tight little band that makes you cold all over. How do we know that the men we bring up here aren't cops? It's been done in other places, giving out marked money, and it could be done here."

I didn't waste any time on her. I just came right out and told her what I wanted.

"I'll pay you back in two weeks," I said. "You can count on that. I just got into a little jam and I could use the dough right now. You don't have to worry none. I won't cheat you. You loan me what you've got now and I'll add two hundred to it when I pay you back."

She swung her legs over the bed and sat there in the nude. It didn't bother her any. Hundreds of men had seen her that way, me included, and one more time didn't matter.

"I can't," she said. "I wish I could but I can't."

"Isn't two hundred bucks good interest?"

"Yes, it's good interest. They give you three percent in the bank and they're doing you a favor."

"Then what's the pitch?"

"I'll remember you," she said.

I walked over to an ash tray on the dresser and crushed out the cigarette.

"Say, what is this?" I demanded.

"Only that I'm leaving, Clint. I told you how it was before. I can't go on this way, selling myself and becoming more of a tramp than I already am. I don't know where I'm going—I haven't even thought about it—but I'm getting out of Wilton. I'm packing up and taking my money and I'm getting out today. I don't care if I have to take a job for forty a week running a machine in some factory. It'll be a decent job and I'll be safe and I won't have to worry about the police. My only wish is that you would go with me. There's trouble for you here, Clint—big trouble—and before you know it you're going to find yourself behind bars."

I tried everything, even to promising her that I would go away with her if she would let me use the money for two weeks, but I might as well have been talking to a stick of wood. She had made up her mind and that's all there was to it.

"To hell with you," I said as I went storming out of the room. "Oh, Jesus, to hell with you!"

I walked toward the bar in a daze. There was no place I could go, no place that I could turn. I thought of Ann but she wouldn't have that kind of money and I don't think I could have taken it from her if she had. She had her problems and I had mine. Not only that, but I was sure that she wouldn't give it to me. We were done. Finished.

I would have stolen the money if I had known where to steal it but I wasn't up on that kind of thing. You read of guys holding up banks and stores but most of them got caught and some of them got a bullet in the guts for their trouble. If there had been time to plan I might have done something about it but there wasn't time to plan. She had to have the money that night or her chances of getting a big settlement out of a divorce would be blown apart. It struck me as strange that a man such as Brandon should have so much power but it was a power that you couldn't bend, couldn't sway, couldn't fight. He knew everything that went on with everybody in The Dells and he played for the limit. Most people would have taken a few bucks and been happy but he had to have all or nothing.

As soon as I opened the bar I counted all of the money I had in the place, including the change in the cash register. With what I had in my pockets and the safe I had around four thousand dollars. Would Brandon settle for that? I didn't know. If Debbie could convince him that she couldn't raise anything further he might accept it. Four thousand wasn't five thousand but it was better than nothing.

I had just finished with the money and put it in the safe when a man came in and ordered a beer. He worked on the docks, he said, and the workers had voted to strike. Everybody had walked off the job. It was a savage blow, a blow I would feel in the cash register. Those who were employed on the docks, and there were many of them in The Dells, wouldn't be spending any money until they returned to work or they were out long enough to begin drawing unemployment checks.

"Rough," I said to the man.

"You'll feel it."

"Yeah. Right where it hurts."

The man only spent twenty cents and then I was alone. I walked up and down the bar swearing under my breath. Everything was happening at once. If the cops didn't have a drive on against the girls, the men who came from uptown could lift me from the hole I would be in, but while the girls were being purged the men would be careful. A guy who was married couldn't risk taking a chance and a guy who was single didn't want to get picked up in a possible raid. The men were seldom held, only as a witness for the state, but once in a while the paper got their names and none of them liked that. To make matters worse, there would be only two girls working out of the bar—unless they quit, too—and I couldn't make any fortune off of two girls.

I was on my third drink when Brandon came in. In spite of the heat he wore a coat and I knew there was a gun under the coat.

"I stuck my neck out coming in here," he said, sitting down at the bar. "Four prowl cars have been assigned from the uptown section to work The Dells."

"Then why did you do it?"

"Because I had to see you."

"All right. You see me."

"How about a beer? I've got time for a quick one." I got a glass and drew the beer but I had to throw it out. That tap was running dry and I would have to go down and set up another half. "Five hundred bucks didn't go very far," he said, going around the end of the bar to help himself to the salt. "It didn't go very far at all."

"Don't tell me your troubles."

"I should maybe tell them to my chief?"

"That isn't very funny."

He sat down on the stool again and threw some salt into the beer. The salt just caused the beer to foam all the more and to run down the side of the glass.

"I'm needing another thousand," he said in much the same voice as though he was talking about a dollar bill. "I spread the five hundred as far as it would go but it didn't go far enough. A thousand will turn the trick."

You see what I mean? He was getting it from all directions, dragging down more dough than anybody else in The Dells, more than most of the executives who had charge of the docks.

"I don't know if I can manage it," I said.

"You'll manage it or the roof will fall in on you. One day you'll be in clover and the next day you'll be in a cell."

If I gave him a thousand that would only leave me three and Debbie had to have all that I could raise. Even the four might not be enough for him.

"Give me an hour or two," I said. "This has hit me hard and the girls aren't bringing much in. I lost three of them, the afternoon girls, what with you going up on your protection and all of this stink. On top of that there's the dock strike and you know how that can hit business."

He pushed the empty glass across the bar but I didn't make a move to get him another beer.

"Two hours is what you've got," he said. "If I'm going to button this thing up I've got to button it up fast." His eyes displayed no sympathy, only determination. "You'll get it back in no time at all," he added. "So you lost three girls but you can get more. The Dells is full of them, girls giving it away for nothing, just a cheap thrill, and all you have to do is give them the right deal. This blast against the pros will go on for a week or ten days and then somebody will get raped in the park uptown and all of the cops will be on the hunt for the guy who took what didn't belong to him."

"I hope you're right."

"It's happened before."

"You can't prove that by me."

"And it'll happen again."

"And in the meantime I'm stuck."

"Well, you bought the bar. I didn't. You hired those three girls. I didn't. The other girls were here before but I didn't have anything to do with them. A girl wants to go to bed with a man for money and that's her business. All I do is see that nothing goes wrong."

I had a couple of drinks after he had left and then I went over to the phone. He was pushing his luck, pushing it for all it was worth, and from where I was I didn't think he was doing anything with the money except putting it in his pocket. I had paid him in cash and I didn't have anything to prove that I had done otherwise. He had me in a spot, my back against the wall, and he was hitting me in the guts when my hands were down.

Debbie answered the phone and I told her about the four thousand.

"It won't be enough," she said. "When he sets a price that's it."

I told her about the grand that he wanted from me and this seemed to upset her.

"I'm sorry I got you into this," she said.

"Don't be sorry. We're in it together. He wants dough from you and he wants dough from me. There isn't anything we can do about it. We have to do what we can."

"And what should I do this afternoon?"

"Find yourself a lawyer. Talk the situation over with him. Find out where you stand."

"And then what?"

"Sit tight and wait for something to break. Something has to break and when it breaks it's going to break wide open."

"How do you mean?"

"Let me think about it, will you?"

I told her goodbye, said that I wished I was in bed with her—that made her let out a sexy laugh that made me want her more than anything else—and I hung up.

I returned to the bar, brooding, and drank some whiskey. A thousand here, five thousand there—Jesus, I couldn't do it. I had four thousand, all the money I had in the world, and it wasn't enough. Brandon was like a snake crawling into my bed and biting me in my sleep, a snake that bit time and time again until there was no longer any reason to bite.

I was on my sixth or seventh drink when she came out, standing on the corner, and caught a taxi. She was a dream in a yellow dress and I wanted that dress off of her, wanted her upstairs in the bedroom or on the davenport, wanted her naked and demanding and responsive.

Don't ask me when I hit upon the plan that I was going to follow. It seemed to come to me all of a sudden but I imagine parts of it had been with me for days, vague parts that I couldn't quite piece into a complete picture. I thought of the gun upstairs, registered in Charlie's name, and of the checks that he had given to Brandon. It all tied up into a neat package, a package that would deliver the insurance to Debbie, plus her share of the estate, and which would get me out from under the whole mess that I was in. She didn't have to know, would never have to know, and it would be a secret that I would carry with me to my grave.

Charlie kept a set of keys to the apartment in the cash register, in case he ever forgot his own, and I went around to the bar to get them. The keys were there all right, under the tray used for change, but I stared at them a long time before I picked them up. Once I started I couldn't quit my plan, couldn't trade sanity for insanity, couldn't stop.

It didn't take me long to go upstairs, let myself into the apartment and find the gun. I hid it in my belt, under the sport shirt, and as soon as I reached the bar I put it behind some bottles out of sight.

I was on a long, cool drink when Brandon came in and stood beside me.

"What's the story, Clint?"

"Tonight," I said.

He was thoughtful for a moment.

"That's not so good. I was going to take care of things this afternoon."

"Well, can I help it? You want a grand so you're going to get a grand. But I won't have it until after midnight. I don't have a printing press to turn out money on two hour's notice."

"Where are you getting it?"

"What do you care?"

He was chewing another toothpick and when he spit he spit right at one of my legs. I looked down and saw the wet spot.

"Who cares?" he countered.

"I'm knocking off the girls," I said. "It doesn't pay me to carry them the way things are."

"That's crazy."

"Maybe it is but that's the way I feel about it." I looked him straight in the face. "I know about your squeeze on Debbie. You'll get that, too."

He didn't seem surprised that she had told me.

"Okay," he said.

"But I won't pay off here. The docks aren't working and there'll be nobody down there. I'll meet you at the dock nearest the end of the street. You be there at one o'clock—I'll close up early—and you'll get the money."

He started chewing another toothpick and I moved my leg so that he couldn't spit on me again.

"You'd better not be lying, fellow."

"So who's lying?"

"I'm just telling you."

"And I'm telling you."

It wasn't much of a conversation and I watched him go. He didn't know it but in a few hours he would be dead. So would Charlie Fletcher.

There just didn't seem to be any other way.

Chapter Thirteen

My movements were purely mechanical for the rest of the day. I took care of the few customers that came in, talked to some of them, but when one of them cracked a joke I couldn't even laugh. The hands on the clock over the bar were moving but they weren't moving fast enough for me. Now that I had made up my mind about what I was going to do I wanted it over and done with. And then, suddenly, the clock was moving too fast. Debbie hadn't come back from uptown and Charlie hadn't arrived from the city. Everything had to fit like a glove if it was going to work and I could only do half of the job without Charlie.

At five, or a few minutes after five, Debbie returned in a cab and I phoned her as soon as she got up to the apartment.

"Make yourself scarce," I said. "I'm seeing Brandon on the docks tonight and I'm going to end this thing for once and for all."

"Why should I make myself scarce?"

Somebody came in—I had been alone when I had made the call—and I reduced my voice to a savage whisper.

"Look! For Christ sakes, do as I say, will you? Get out of the apartment right away and go uptown. Sit in a bar and knock yourself out. Stay until one and then come back down here."

She was silent for a moment.

"All right," she said. "I'll do as you say."

I hung up, my hand sticky with sweat and turned to face the bar. Charlie was sitting at the far end of the bar and he had helped himself to a drink. I rubbed my hand over my pants to remove the sweat. If she was out of the apartment he wouldn't stay up there and it was important that I keep him with me.

"See you got back," I said, drawing a beer.

He nodded and poured another drink.

"I had a time," he said. "I didn't see the girl that I usually see but I found another one who was even better." He laughed. "She earned her hundred and don't think that she didn't. I may be an old buck but I know how to take care of a woman."

While he had been talking I saw Debbie pass the place, not looking in, and continue up the street.

"Your wife isn't home," I told him.

"No? Where did she go?"

"I don't know. She said for me to tell you. I guess she had to see somebody or do something."

"Maybe she's getting furniture for the new apartment."

"Maybe."

"She's wanting to get out of The Dells and so am I. You see all of the slobs down here and it's enough to make you puke."

I glanced toward where I had hidden the gun and I knew that he would never live in any new apartment. He talked of slobs but he was one of them himself, probably bigger than most, living off the poverty of other people and getting fat and rich because of it.

"Brandon wants to see us," I said. "At one o'clock. Down on the docks."

"What about?"

"I don't know."

"And why down on the docks?"

"Because he's scared of coming in here, of being seen if he does. There's a drive on against the girls and other cops are working The Dells. He doesn't know where he stands and he isn't anxious to find out."

Of course, the whole pitch would be gone if Brandon came in but I was pretty sure that he wouldn't. And I was equally sure that Charlie would stay at the bar and take a load on. He didn't have anything else to do.

"That Brandon is a bastard," he said. "He's a dirty, stinking bastard. Give you five to one that he wants more money from both of us. Well, he isn't getting any from me. As soon as I get around to it the girls are going out of the house up the street and then I won't owe him a cent. I'd be in money if the rooms stayed empty."

I got a little play at the bar early in the evening but it didn't amount to much. The girls came in about nine—there were only two left now that Martha was gone—and I told them to knock it off for a few days until after the heat died down. They didn't like it, didn't like it a bit, complaining that they had money to pay out and that they had to work in order to do it.

"We don't have anything to worry about," Kathy Nelson said. "We pay for protection so why can't we have it?"

"This is over Brandon's head," I pointed out. "We've paid Brandon but we can't pay every cop in the city. My thought is that you should both move into a hotel until it's safe again."

They stayed about an hour and left, arguing with each other about what they should do. Kathy was inclined to see things my way but Jennie said I was just chicken and that I was trying to frighten them.

"I could go for that Kathy," Charlie said, staring moodily at his drink. "She's hot stuff when she wants to be. Or have you found it out for yourself?"

"I never bothered her any."

"That's silly. These girls expect it. Sure, they go to bed with a man for money but once in a while they like to go to bed just for the hell of it."

"We've got to see Brandon," I reminded him.

"Yeah, I know that. You've told me enough times. Every hour on the hour you've told me. You think I'm dumb or something?"

A couple of men came in and asked about girls. I told them there weren't any that night and they hung around for a while, drinking, and trying to figure out what they should do. About the time they were getting ready to go the young girl who liked older men came in and they made a play for her right away. She was wearing tight slacks, black slacks, and a tight yellow sweater. She dripped sex like a leaky faucet.

"You ain't old enough," the one man told her.

"The hell I'm not. I've been old enough since I was thirteen."

The men had a few more drinks—the girl said she didn't want anything—and when they went out the girl went with them.

"Alley stuff," Charlie said. "A guy can get in a jam fooling around with that kind of a dame. If she finds out who you are and you've got any money she'll blackmail the hell out of you. I went with one once and she cost me a couple of grand before she really got herself knocked up and had to get married. It was a happy day for me when she moved out of The Dells."

I drank some beer but not too much and I stayed sober. Hell, I had to be sober to do what I had to do. All I had to do was to make one mistake and they'd throw me in the chair and pull the switch. Just the thought of such a thing happening made me feel ill. But, I told myself, it wouldn't happen. The cops would go into Brandon's past, digging into every corner, and when they discovered the money he had saved they would know that he couldn't have done it on his salary. The checks Charlie had given to Brandon would wrap the two of them up into a neat package and it would look like Charlie had killed Brandon and then killed himself.

Charlie was fairly drunk by midnight and that suited me fine. He wouldn't be sharp, his senses dulled, and before he knew what was going on it would all be over with. He would be dead and Brandon would be dead and I would have Debbie. I would have her during all of the years that were to come and with the money that she got from the estate we would build a real life together. If we decided to marry right away we could leave Wilton and go someplace where we weren't known.

"Funny my wife staying out so late," he said.

"Maybe she thought you weren't coming back tonight and she stopped off for a drink."

"Maybe. But it isn't like her. Why should she drink in some bar when she can drink here?"

"I don't know."

I glanced at the clock and I thought it had stopped but the second hand was moving and I knew that it hadn't stopped. Each minute seemed to be an hour, an hour of trying to think and not being able to think, an hour that stretched out into the distant and timeless beyond.

At about quarter of one he went to the men's room and I seized the opportunity to get the gun and stick it in my right rear pocket, pulling my sport shirt down to cover it. It wasn't a very big gun but it felt big in my pocket and it felt deadly. I was at the safe, getting out the bills, when he came over and stood beside me.

"That's a lot of money," he said.

"He may want a lot of money."

"Well, that's a lot."

The money, I concluded, wouldn't be on Brandon. The cops would find it on Charlie and they would figure that Charlie had come down to the docks to pay off Brandon and that then, in a drunken rage, he had killed Brandon and, realizing what he had done, finally himself. Hell, it was sweet. Perfect.

I left the lights in the bar burning and we departed from the place a couple of minutes later. Charlie stumbled as we hit the sidewalk and I flipped the lock into position.

"I still don't get it," he said as we started down the street.

"Don't worry. You'll get it."

He missed the implication.

"I can understand him wanting to see you but that's no reason for me to be counted in on it, too. I only own the house where the girls stay. If they were picked up tonight nobody could do a thing to me. Just because you happen to rent rooms to a couple of whores doesn't mean that you know what they're doing. Take a hotel, for instance. They can arrest a girl in a hotel but that doesn't stand that the hotel is in any trouble."

He bitched about it all the way down the street but I didn't pay much attention to him. As we neared the docks my body was wet and hot and cold all at the same time. At one point I wasn't sure that I could go through with it but I knew that if I didn't go through with it my whole life would rip apart at the seams. It wasn't a question of killing a couple of men. They didn't seem to be human to me. Brandon was the scum of the earth and Charlie wasn't much better. I was being driven to do this through no choice of my own, driven into a corner the way a fighter gets hammered to a pulp.

As we neared the river I could smell the smell of the water and the moisture of it filled the night air. There were none of the usual sounds of loading or unloading, none of the laughter and shouts of men working for a living. There was a great big hollow inside of me that just wouldn't fill up. In a few minutes I would be a killer, a wanted and hunted man, a man who would possibly spend the rest of his life trying to run away from himself.

I asked myself as we reached the end of the street and neared the dock if there wasn't another way but I didn't know of any other way. I couldn't afford to pay the money that Brandon asked and I had to have Debbie Fletcher forever. Nothing less would satisfy me. Nothing less would do.

"I don't see anybody," Charlie said quietly.

"He's probably waiting behind some of those boxes."

Boxes lined the dock, big boxes that were piled three or four high. A small hand truck lay on the dock, right where somebody had left it when the strike had been called. I didn't know what was in the boxes but if it was anything that could spoil it would probably spoil. The dock owners couldn't hire non-union help and the help wouldn't come back until their demands had been met. I don't know why I was thinking about this as we approached the dock but I was. I was thinking how poor the people were, how they would nearly starve before they could draw their unemployment checks, but I was also thinking that they were better off than I was, that this thing I was about to do would live with me through every hour of every day and every night. Now that the moment was grinding down on me I began to shake the way a dog shakes when it's cold. I slowed up, letting Charlie get in front of me, and I reached to see if the gun was still in my pocket. It was. It was there, waiting to be used, waiting to kill.

We both saw Brandon about the same time and Charlie said something dirty under his breath. Brandon was in the shadows, leaning up against some of the packing cases, his face a glob of white in the half dark, a dark that was pierced only by the street light on the corner. Again the smell of the river came to me, a thick smell that fought its way down into my lungs, feeling terrible when it went in but feeling good when I let it out. The emptiness was all through me now and my legs were so heavy that I could hardly move them. My whole face was covered with sweat and my shirt was soaked with it.

"I see you brought company," Brandon said, still leaning up against the cases.

"It's Charlie," Charlie said.

Brandon laughed.

"I know it's Charlie, you stupid fool. There's only one fat man in The Dells that walks the way you do and it has to be you."

We were about seven or eight feet from Brandon, just standing there, and I could hear Charlie's heavy breathing. Or I thought I heard him. Maybe it was me that I heard, the air rushing in and out of me like somebody was squeezing me with giant hands.

"I don't know why you're here," Brandon said.

Charlie looked at me and then at Brandon.

"Clint said you wanted to see me."

"If I had wanted to see you I'd have seen you." I got the impression that Brandon was chewing on a toothpick. "What goes on here is between me and the big boy, nobody else."

I saw then, suddenly and terribly, that bringing Charlie had been a mistake, that the whole plan had been a mistake. I wasn't a killer, not the kind of a killer you read about. I hated one almost as much as I hated the other but the hate just wasn't big enough to make me kill. I thought of the four thousand dollars that I had in my pocket, the fact that Charlie would divorce Debbie if he knew the truth about us, but I also thought that four thousand was a lot of money and that it could get us started in something else.

"I want to know what this is all about," Charlie said.

"It ain't none of your business," Brandon told him. "When I've got business with you I'll do it but not until. My business is with your friend and only with your friend."

I wanted a cigarette but I had left them back at the bar and I didn't have one. With the emptiness inside of me getting bigger all of the time I ran my tongue over my lips but it didn't do any good. My mouth was dry and so was my tongue.

"You got the money?" Brandon asked me.

I remained silent. If I gave him the money—if he would accept four thousand instead of five—he would only come back to me for more and more. He would take everything I had, every dime that I owned, and for all of my risk I wouldn't have anything. I wouldn't even have Debbie. She would stick with Charlie, hoping for a big share of an estate that she would probably never get. But if he knew the truth, if he cut her free by divorcing her, we could make a start in some other town and make a go of it.

"I asked you if you had the money," Brandon repeated.

Again I tried to wet my lips with my tongue.

"No," I said.

"Say, what the hell is this?" he demanded.

My hands doubled up into fists and then relaxed. Killing him was the wrong way to do it, the foolish way. Maybe I could make it look like a murder and a self-killing, just as I had planned, but when I went to bed at night the explosions of the gun would still be ringing in my ears. There would be no absolute security for me ever again, not the kind of security that a man has to have in order to live.

"I'm not paying off," I said slowly. "Five thousand is too much money, Brandon."

"In exchange for what I offered you?"

"In exchange for anything. I don't care what you say or what you do. I've paid you and paid you and I've reached my limit. If I give you five thousand now you'll want five thousand later on and this thing will only continue." I turned to Charlie. "I'm going to tell you the truth," I said. "I'm not going to lie. I've been seeing your wife and he wanted five grand to keep it quiet. Well, I'm not paying him five grand. I'm not paying him anything. I'm in love with her and I don't care who knows it."

Charlie was silent for a moment.

"So that's it," he said. "I suspected there was something but I didn't know what it was." He shrugged. "I think I may love her myself but she can have a divorce if she wants one. It won't effect the business any. You can still own it and run it. At my age, I had no right to marry her in the first place but I thought we would find something together."

It was quiet on the dock, very quiet. Down the river a ship blew its whistle but the ship wouldn't be stopping at Wilton. It would go on up the river about twenty miles where it could unload and where there wasn't any strike.

I reached behind me for the gun, hating myself for what I had thought of doing, wanting to be rid of it and to never touch it again.

"There," I said, throwing the gun down on the rough planks. It made a loud noise, bounced a couple of times and then lay still.

"It looks like mine," Charlie said, leaning forward.

"It is."

He stood up straight and faced me.

"What were you going to do with it, Clint?"

"End everything," I said simply.

"I see."

"But I can't do it. It isn't in me to do it."

"You're smart," Charlie said.

"I'm dumb."

Charlie went forward to recover the gun but before he could reach it he was halted by Brandon.

"You touch that and a slug goes right through you," Brandon said. He had his service revolver in his hand, pointed straight at Charlie. "All I have to do is say that you threatened me and that I nailed you."

Charlie rubbed a hand across his face and shook his head.

"What makes you think that would work?" he inquired. "Clint is here and he could tell what went on."

"And what makes you think Clint would be alive to talk?"

"Hell," I said.

I wanted that gun back then, wanted it more than I had ever wanted anything in my life. I had tried to be honest and I had walked into a situation with both eyes open. He could kill us both and get away with it.

"You're both stupid," Brandon said. "You, Charlie, because you think money can buy anything and you, Clint, because you fell in love with the wrong woman."

"We're in love with each other," I protested.

He laughed at me.

"Why do you think you were kept on the job at the bar when the other bartenders were fired in a few days or a week?"

"I did my work."

"No, it wasn't that. She was looking for a sucker and she thought she had found one. You couldn't stop looking at her body and she thought you would get nuts enough about her to go the distance. You almost did. The trouble is you lost your guts in the end."

I didn't know what he was going to do, had no idea, but I did know that I was glad that I hadn't killed either one of them. I had broken enough laws with the girls to last me for the rest of my life and the way it looked to me just then my life might not be very long.

"How many times did your wife used to go to the hairdresser?" Brandon asked Charlie.

"I don't know. Often."

"Did she look any different when she got back?"

"Not that I could tell. I asked her why she bothered and she said it made her feel important. I didn't think it was much of a reason," he added. "As far as I could see she was blowing her allowance on nothing every week."

"Yeah, twenty-five dollars."

"Is that what she told you?"

"She told me many times."

"It was more than that, a lot more than that. Even when I had made up my mind that she didn't love me it was more than that. She took what she wanted out of the cash register and I never said anything."

Brandon laughed again.

"She didn't go to any hairdresser," he said. "She would meet me in some motel and then we would go to bed and afterward we would talk about you. We would talk about your insurance and what we could do with it if we had it. She wanted me to do the job, to put a bullet through your belly, but I told her the risk was too great. We had to get somebody who would fall in love with her and do it on his own, somebody who was just crazy enough over her to want to get rid of you." Brandon motioned the gun at me. "This guy almost did it. He got his lumps from her and he saw the gun in your apartment. After he called her this afternoon and told her to take a walk, saying that it was all going to end tonight, she looked for the gun and saw that it was missing. She phoned me right away, at a place where she always called me every afternoon about that time, and I knew what to expect." He paused and spit out the toothpick. "You were going to kill us both, weren't you, Clint? You were going to make it look like a murder and a self-killing and then you were going to claim the best damned piece of flesh in the city and a big hunk of cash. Isn't that right?"

I didn't know what to say. Brandon was crooked but he was intelligent and he had been ahead of me every step of the way. The thing I couldn't understand was Debbie. She had given me her love, given me her body, and she had led me down a dark road as surely as though she had had a rope around my neck.

"Thanks for bringing the gun," Brandon was saying to me. "All I have to do is kill you and Charlie and it'll be called a crime of passion. They'll put me on the case and nothing can go wrong. I can prove that you slept with Charlie's wife and that's all I have to prove."

I knew that I was facing death and the emptiness inside of me should have lingered but didn't. It began to fade away, like daylight fades into the shadows of evening, and in its place there was an anger that rose up in a constantly mounting fury. I had been in love with her, or I had thought so and she had used me for a pawn. All the time I had thought she belonged to me she had belonged to Brandon.

"It couldn't have worked out better," Brandon said, picking up the gun. "All I have to do is do the job and I'll be in clover for the rest of my life. I'll wait a few months, divorce my wife, and then Debbie and I will go someplace and live like a king and a queen. I've got some money of my own and with what she picks up from you, Charlie, we'll be like a couple of kids at a taffy pull."

"You can't get away with it," Charlie managed to say.

"I can get away with anything."

"But not murder."

"Two murders."

"Or two murders. That's even worse."

"Pray," Brandon said, his voice tight. "Get down on your knees and pray to be forgiven for all of the things that you've done, all of the people that you've cheated. Pray! It's your last chance. You won't get another one on earth."

Charlie, the situation which he faced having sobered him up, began to pray. He didn't get down on his knees. He just stood there mumbling. He didn't want to die. He wanted to live and to die the way a man should.

"I'll give you anything," he told Brandon. "Let me go and anything you want you can have."

"We can't get your insurance unless you're dead."

"But I've got other things. I've got money. I've got property. I'll divorce her so you can have her and I'll start over again."

"I can't go this far and turn back," Brandon said. "There's only one way that it can be and one way that it has to be. If I let the two of you go you could testify against me and ruin the whole plan. If you were alone I might listen but you're not alone and I can't listen. And there's no danger for me. This Clint worked in fine, just fine."

Charlie continued to beg, to plead, but he might as well have saved his breath. Death was staring him in the face and death wasn't going to be cheated. Brandon wasn't going to be cheated. We both had to die there on the dock.

Every muscle in my body became alive with a furious desire to smash this creature down, to destroy him, to give him the kind of a death that he was so intent upon giving to us. I thought of a lot of things just then, of living at home, of growing up, of giving Ann a child who would never know a father. I thought of the hours that I had spent with Debbie, of exploring every curve and swell of her body, of the love which she had said was mine and which hadn't been mine. I thought of the bar, of the girls who had sold their bodies, of the men who had paid me money, of the many, many things I had done and which I shouldn't have done.

"I'm ready," I heard myself saying.

But I wasn't ready. No man, no matter how brave he may be, is ready to die. Life is a precious thing, a fragile thing, fleeting moments in the space of time to which all of us want to cling. There on the dock in the night, death was very real, very close. I couldn't even smell the stench from the river and I found it difficult to breathe.

"Please," Charlie said, taking a step forward. "Oh, Jesus, please!"

Brandon shot him then, the report from the gun blasting the night, the force of the slug striking him, driving Charlie backward.

I don't know why I moved then but I did. Everything inside of me told me that I wasn't going to die without a fight, that I wasn't going to take it and do nothing about it.

I drove into him, hitting him hard, smashing him against the packing cases. I heard something hit the boards near my feet and I knew that he had lost one of the guns. Charlie was behind me, moaning where he had fallen, but there was no time to do anything about Charlie. Brandon's knee came up, driving into my stomach, and I let out a groan but it didn't stop me from grabbing the hand that held the gun, grabbing it with both of my hands and trying to twist the weapon away from him. The gun went off once and the bullet plowed up through the night.

"Bastard," he said.

He was strong, stronger than I had expected, and I found my task a difficult one. Slowly, my superior weight pinning him to the packing cases, I brought his gun hand down, turning his wrist, putting all of my strength into it. Suddenly he gave up fighting me and his gun hand came down, the gun going off again. There was no pain but I knew that I had been hit, hit high on the thigh. I stumbled, almost fell, and I was like a beast fighting for that gun, fighting as only a man who knows he may be killed in the next second can fight. Again and again the gun roared until at last I heard the firing pin click on an empty chamber. By this time I was on my knees, unable to stand, barely able to find the physical power to hang onto him.

A siren sounded in the distance, wailing in the night, and with a mighty effort he broke away from me, kicking me in the face as he did so. Through a haze of pain I saw him run along the dock and across the street.

I crawled to where Charlie was lying, feeling for a pulse beat. It was there but it was feeble and I knew he didn't have long to live if he didn't get help soon.

I tried to stand up but that bullet in the leg had done something to it and I couldn't get to my feet. I felt the pain now, all the way from my hip to my toes, and I could taste the blood where my mouth had been cut on the inside.

"Charlie," I said. "Charlie!"

He said nothing.

The pain was terrible as I crawled along the dock, trying to get to the street. I didn't know where I was going or what I was doing. All I could think of was that I had to get away from there, that I had to get away from everything, that someday and somehow I had to escape from myself.

But I didn't reach the street.

I just lay down and passed out.

It was probably just as well.

Chapter Fourteen

I was in the hospital quite a while and they had to do three operations on the leg before they got it anywhere near right. There's a pin in it someplace, something to do with the bones, but it doesn't bother me any and I only have a slight limp. The doctor says that the limp will go away in time.

The first one who came to see me in the hospital was Martha Foster. She had gotten as far as New York, heard about the shooting on the radio, and taken the next bus back to Wilton.

"You may need some money," she said. "Hospitals cost a lot."

"I've got some."

"But you may have to have more. My two thousand is yours if you run out."

"Thanks but I don't think I will. And there was a policeman in here who said he thought the city was responsible. Brandon was on duty at the time of the shooting."

She bent down and kissed me, her lips lingering over my mouth.

"You should have gone away with me, Clint."

"I guess I should have. You can run your luck out just so far and then the rope breaks."

Her face became sad.

"I wish things were different between us."

"Well, you can't change what can't be changed."

"No, I guess you can't."

"And you'll need the money to make a new beginning. Two thousand may not be much but it can do a lot for you if you'll let it."

She kissed me again.

"I know I'm done being a prostitute," she said. "I never was a very good one. I was looking for the easy way but there is no easy way. I'm going to get a decent job and settle down and if I'm lucky I'll find a man who'll marry me."

"What about the other girls?"

"Jennie can't stop and Kathy doesn't want to stop. If they don't follow their trade here they'll follow it somewhere else. They'll end up getting arrested and going to the workhouse but they won't learn by it. I've seen dozens of them and it all amounts to the same thing. They think that the quick dollars are the best dollars. Me, I just want a home and kids and a normal life."

I don't mind saying that I cried a little after she left, cried for all of the things that we had both been and all of the things that we were going to try to be. I was almost sorry that I wasn't in love with her. She seemed to have found herself and she would make a good wife for somebody. She would give her heart and her soul and all that went with it. It wouldn't just be sex but something deeper and with more meaning.

I had a lot of time to think in the hospital, in between the times the cops came in to talk to me, but I didn't think a great deal about Debbie Fletcher. She was a girl who had played me for a sucker and I was through with that kind of stuff. Marriage to her, even if it had been possible, would have been a mistake. You don't build a house without lumber and you can't build a marriage without love.

"She's a tramp," one of the cops told me. "You can talk to her hour after hour and it makes no impression on her. She just sits and stares and says that she doesn't know anything."

"How's Charlie?"

"As good as you can expect—touch and go. His sugar is against him but the doctors are doing everything they can."

"And Brandon?"

"In jail. This time he's on the inside looking out."

"He was stupid to stay in Wilton."

"Not stupid. He had to stay. He couldn't leave without the money he had in safe deposit boxes and he had no choice but to trust to luck—that you were wounded bad enough to die and that Charlie would die."

"Then you believe me?"

"Everything points to what you said and to the statement that Charlie was able to give us. Brandon's fingerprints were on the gun—he was so sure of himself that he didn't bother wearing gloves—and it all fits. He says that you shot Charlie, then yourself, but you two say differently and we have to believe the majority. Then there's this money that Brandon had put away—about thirty thousand—and no cop could save that much on what he earns. I'm not even married and half of the time I'm paying off a finance company. A cop just can't save a lot of money and be honest."

It was a long stay in the hospital but everybody tried to make me comfortable. A couple of times I wanted to get a wheel chair and go down and see Charlie but I was told that he was too low and that no one could see him. They said that he wasn't responding to treatment, not as he should, and that it was only a matter of time.

On the day I was released from the hospital I had to go down to city hall and talk with the chief of detectives. It was tough getting up the high front steps with a cane but I finally made it.

"We're curious about the large amount of money you had on you when you were found," the chief said. "Where did you get it? We know why you had it, but where did you get it?"

I was past the point of lying and I didn't lie to him. I told him about the deal on the bar with Charlie, of the girls who worked out of it and how I had had to pay Brandon for protection.

"You violated the law," he said when I had finished.

"I know it."

"You could be jailed or fined."

"I know that, too."

He leaned back in his chair.

"But we can't prove anything against you, Clint. The girls have left town and there isn't anybody to testify against you except Brandon and nobody would believe him. On top of that the city is going to pay all of your medical expenses."

"The hospital was asking about that."

"I know. They called me and I told them the same thing. That's why you were able to walk out without paying." He reached into a desk drawer and brought out a bundle of bills. "This is what we took from you," he said. "I don't think you can be proud of the way you made it but you may be able to even things up by the way you spend it."

I picked up the money.

"There's one thing that bothers me," I said. "I haven't asked anybody about it but I'm going to ask you. If Brandon and Debbie wanted me to kill Charlie, why did Brandon cut up my face the way he did?"

"I've thought of that, too."

"He was trying to chase me away from her, not drive me into her arms."

The chief smiled.

"Ever see a child looking at a toy out of reach?"

"Sure. He wants it more than if you stick it in his hands."

"Exactly. That was the game Brandon was playing with you. He told you not to see her and marked you up and that made you want her all the more, didn't it?"

"I guess it did."

"All of it was bait for you, Clint, some of it very clever bait. The demand for five thousand dollars was the final one. They were sure that you couldn't raise that much and that you would be driven to kill Charlie which, by your own admission, you very nearly did. The only hitch was that you included Brandon in your plan—I can't say that I blame you—and when the two of you showed up on the dock Brandon had to do something and do it fast. The same thing that had seemed logical to you seemed logical to him. Once Charlie knew about his wife he would change his will and that wasn't what either one of them wanted. They were playing for big stakes and Brandon was willing to gamble. The fact that you tore into him upset the gamble."

A few minutes later I walked out of there a free man.

The first place I went was to the diner where Ann worked.

I write this on a rented farm in Beaverkill. I can look out of the window and see thirty cows in the distant field. I'm in hock up to my neck—a good cow is expensive—but I do think that I have put the money to good use. I can't work as long outside as many hours as I should because my leg continues to bother me but it's getting better every day.

You may have read in the papers about the trial and, if you did, you know that Brandon was dismissed from the force and drew fifteen to thirty years for attempted murder. Charlie, showing more courage than some men half his age, finally recovered and whenever the mood strikes him he drives up for some fishing. The Beaverkill is very good for trout fishing and you can almost count on him to get the limit. It may sound strange to you but we found something in common that night when death almost cut us down on the dock and I don't mind if he stays a day or so. All of his money is invested in that housing development—he's sold the bar and his other property—and he seems to be doing very good at it.

"I don't know anything about Debbie," he says. "She left town after the divorce and I know that the last premium on the insurance policy wasn't paid. There's extended insurance on it, or whatever you call it, but I'll live so long that she won't get a cent."

The way he looks and acts, all full of life, I'm inclined to agree with him.

I have never heard from Martha Foster but I hope she has found what she was seeking. I know I have.

"I want another child," Ann often tells me when we're in bed together.

I don't know if she'll ever get her wish but I'm doing my best to see that she does. The first baby was a girl, now about a year old, and we're both hoping for a boy.

"Like you," she whispers as her naked arms go around me.

"No, not like me."

"Why not?"

"Let the kid have some brains, won't you?"

"Oh, don't be so silly. Just love me, you big ox."

She doesn't have to ask me twice.

She doesn't even have to ask me once....

The End

Dial "M" for Man

By Orrie Hitt

Chapter 1

Doris Condon's phone call came about five in the afternoon, Wednesday afternoon, just as I was getting ready to close up shop for the day. She did not like it when I told her I could not go out to Neversink Drive until the following afternoon to fix her television set. That's the trouble with the television repair business—everybody wants you yesterday.

"You might try somebody else," I suggested.

"No, I'll wait." She had a low voice, hot and sultry, the kind of a voice that could sell bathing suits in the middle of winter. "They say you're the best around, Mr. Sampson."

"Well, thanks."

"The programs aren't so good tonight, anyway. I guess I'll just curl up with a book and hate myself." She laughed. "If you know a lonelier place than this miserable burg, you might let me know."

I said I would, promised to put her name on my appointment list and hung up.

There was no need to make a note of the name because everybody in Hawley—population a little over fourteen thousand by the last count—knew Ferris Condon, even if they did not know much about his new wife.

Ferris Condon was a tall, heavy man of about sixty, the owner of Condon's Lumber Company. Ruthless in almost everything he did, he had started driving a horse into the woods to snake out logs and he had lied and cheated his way into the beginning of this firm. He had prospered over the years by building houses that would fall apart halfway through the mortgage. The whole town knew that he had been married for a long time, that his wife had left him for a younger man, that he had then acquired his present wife somewhere out of town. Some said she was young and was sexy enough to keep six men happy. But nobody could prove it by me.

I locked up the shop and went upstairs to change. Grand Street was no nice place to live but it was cheaper having my home right over the shop—and more convenient when I worked late. This I did almost every night—except Wednesdays—so I could get repair work done and at the same time keep the shop open for the few people who came in to look at the new sets I sold.

Wednesday nights I always drove over to Kathy Bolton's for dinner. She lived with her father on Fossard Street. Old John Bolton was usually home, but he worked for the railroad and sometimes got a call to work at night. Naturally I liked it better when he was out. Kathy and I had never gone beyond a few passionate kisses, but I kept on hoping.... Not that I would push a thing like that.

I had wanted a real home ever since my folks had left me to go to California. Kathy was the kind of girl a man could build a home with....

I was seventeen when they went to California and left me here to finish high school. I was staying with Aunt Grace then. She died just after graduation but—I don't know why—I just stayed on in Hawley. Ben Stucker and I were working part-time for a fellow who sold and serviced radio and television sets. We got the chance to work full-time after graduation and learned the trade from him—good, too. He was a sharp repairman. Ben and I opened our own shop a couple of years later—with money our families put up.

Thinking about this shop—S&S Television we called it—as I left my own that evening, I looked back and knew we had handled the thing wrong from the first. We had hired Kathy Bolton—to keep books that did not exist—and we had both acted like big shots growing bigger every day. But in three months we had been scratching dirt. When I had found out that Ben wasn't turning in the money from service calls—which I discovered when I sent out a bill—we had split up. We had opened separate shops on Grand Street and still were friends, though I wouldn't give him a connecting wire unless he paid for it.

My place had done pretty well: the year before, I had paid back the family. But Ben had not. He had not given his father a thin dime, and from what he said they didn't even want him coming around the farm any more. He lived in a cheap hotel, drove an old truck, drank when he should have been working and never squared up his bills on time. Besides, he cheated his customers. If a set needed a little adjustment he would pile in a lot of junk and when he took somebody's television to the shop he would keep it for a week instead of a day or two.

Money had not been the only trouble between us. Ben had gone for Kathy as soon as we hired her and two weeks had not gone by before he had tried to make her in the back room. That would have killed it for most girls, but she was the kind that likes guys who need help. She was still seeing him about once a week even though she was out of television and working for a real estate office. I wasn't really jealous but I knew Kathy was too good for him. Ben would sleep with any woman under fifty and he treated them all alike—as sex machines.

"I'll score some night," Ben had once told me over a few beers. "All I need is the chance, and that Kathy Bolton will get what she ought to have. Unless, Hob, you've been there first. I wouldn't know about that."

"Sorry, but it just isn't so."

"And you wouldn't say if it was."

"Probably not."

"You sound serious about her."

"It wouldn't be difficult to feel that way," I admitted. "I could think of worse things happening to a man. Nice girls are hard to find—as you and I both know. You go to some house to make a repair and the woman wants more than her television fixed."

"You turn it down?"

"Not always. A man has his moments."

"Yeah—and the best ones are in bed."

That was Ben. Sometimes you would think they were his only moments.

Upstairs, I got my wallet from a dresser drawer, slid it into my hip pocket and left, locking the apartment behind me.

Grand Street was no top neighborhood: if you did not lock up what you had or nail it down it got away from you.

Out on the street I stopped to look at my window display. There were some television sets there and a few portable radios but the whole place looked like a dump. Then I thought about the bank loan I had applied for and I felt a little better. The bank should give me the money to buy that building and modernize it, I thought. After all, I was careful with my credit customers and the bank knew I did not owe a dime on the Ford. I was not changing the course of the world with my business, but I had both feet firmly on the ground.

Just as I was walking over to my car, Ben Stucker pulled up in his old truck and got out. He was still in his working clothes but I noticed that he had a young girl with him. She seemed one of those girls I had seen wandering the streets at night, especially around the park, who seemed willing to pick up with anybody. But I was not looking at the girl so much. I was looking at Ben. He was a lot shorter than my six feet—maybe five-eight—and drinking so much beer was beginning to make him paunchy. His face had never had a great deal of color, but I thought it was whiter than I had ever seen it before.

"Hob," he said, wiping the sweat from his forehead. "Hob, would you do me a favor?"

"I will if I can." I imagined he wanted to get a tube; he seldom had a good supply on hand.

"I need dough, Hob. Bad."

"Oh, that."

"About three hundreds."

I had it all right but I knew that once I gave it to him I would be an old man before I ever got it back.

"You're out of my reach," I said. "Try the bank or a loan company."

"Hell, I have."

"Then I don't know what else to tell you. I'm thinking of buying this building and I've got every dollar counted and in its place."

He turned and got back into the truck. When the girl asked him something, he shook his head. Moving on down the street to the Ford, I had a strange sense of guilt. In spite of his weakness I rather liked Ben. To ease my guilt about not letting him have the money, I told myself that it was his own fault he did not have the three hundred. If he had worked, the money would be there.

I got into my Ford and drove off.

The car ran fine—it was a station wagon, excellent for my business—and even though Fossard Street was on the other side of town in a good residential section, it took me no time to get there. The Boltons had a nice house. Kathy's father painted it himself every two years. As I walked around to the kitchen door, I noticed he had started again.

It had been a hot day and it did not surprise me that Kathy was in shorts and a halter. Her being dressed that way told me that her father was out on the road, because she had to wear a dress when he was home.

"Steak," she said as I entered. "It's almost ready." She laughed, showing white, even teeth. "Which means hardly cooked."

Her father always kept beer in the refrigerator and I helped myself to one of the cans. While I drank it I watched her moving about the kitchen, and I liked what I saw. She had soft brown hair, a face that could have been used on a magazine cover, and a shape that was both delicate and loaded with curves. Her breasts were not as big as some but because she was so small in the stomach—her waistline was only twenty-three inches—they seemed larger. I often speculated on how a child could grow in such a tiny space but she had the full rounded hips for bearing and I supposed nature would take care of the rest. Birth was the one subject we seldom talked about. That Kathy's mother had died having her may have had something to do with it.

The steak was excellent, rare the way I liked it, and we each had a beer with our dinner. As usual we ate in the kitchen. I had insisted on eating there after the first couple of times. It made no sense for her to run back and forth with a lot of dishes.

After dinner she told me she was getting a raise at the office. Then she smiled, adding that it could have been bigger if she had consented to go out with one of the members of the firm. It was the usual story—the pretty young girl and a flesh-starved husband and father.

"I may have to get another job," she went on. "I don't like having him look over my shoulder to see if I've fastened the top button on my blouse."

"Give him a thrill and take the blouse off."

"Fresh."

The phone rang just as she was clearing the table. While she was answering, I scraped the plates and threw out the garbage. She was on the phone so long that I had another beer and lit a cigarette. Generally we did not do much on Wednesday night except have dinner and talk afterward, but that night I felt like going out and hitting a few spots. I had sold a rather expensive television set to a woman that morning, and while we don't make the profit most people think we do, I had a little extra money.

When Kathy returned to the kitchen, she washed the dishes and I dried. She always told me not to bother but I did not mind. I cooked most of my food in my apartment over the shop and did the dishes myself, so it was a habit with me.

"I don't know what's going on tonight but we can try to find out," I said. "Anyway, we can get out of the house, hit the air and have a few drinks. You wouldn't have to change."

She let the water out of the sink and did not say anything. I thought she had not heard me so I repeated what I had said, throwing in the suggestion that we might stop at that new casino out on the lake and try the music for size. We were both fiends for dancing. Besides, it was a pleasure to hold her tight, to feel the movements of her body as they meshed with mine. There was always the possibility that it would go beyond the dancing and drinking stage, that she would submit, and I would have the thrill of knowing her as a woman. I was not actually considering marriage when I thought of such a thing, but I was not pushing it out of my mind either. People say that you should not have a relationship before marriage but I had seen a couple of marriages go sour because the people had lived up to the established rule and because the husbands learned after the ceremony that their wives were as cold as a January morning. I had just enough blood in my veins to stop me from taking on something that I did not know about.

"Not tonight," Kathy said. "That phone call was from Ben. He wants to see me."

"Aw, forget it. This is my night."

"I'm sorry, Hob. He's got troubles that won't wait."

"He makes his own troubles."

"Don't we all?"

"Sometimes, but it's a disease with him. He isn't satisfied unless he's got a problem that gives him an excuse to go out and drink—if he needs an excuse. Which he doesn't."

"I'm sorry," she said again. "I know you plan on Wednesday night, but I feel I should help him if I can. Listening is about the cheapest thing you can do for a person."

"Your father wouldn't like it. You know what he thinks of Ben."

"He doesn't have to know." She opened a beer for herself. "And you wouldn't do anything for Ben. He said so."

"Of course not. He wanted more from me than talk. He was after money."

"There was nobody else he could ask, Hob. You're different. You can borrow when you're up against it and he can't."

"Give him one dollar and he spends two."

She drank only a little of the beer and poured the rest of it into the sink. "I'm still going to see him, Hob."

"All right."

"But I don't want you to be angry about it."

"I'll send you a card of congratulations."

"Now you're being nasty. What's so wrong about me doing the human thing?"

I did not answer her. I did not say good night and I did not thank her for the dinner. I just got out of there and walked to the car, frustrated and hurt.

There was a little corner bar I went to sometimes, just a quiet place where the men who worked in the factories stopped to have a few beers, and no women, so I drove down there. It was too late to make any service calls and going to that bar was about all there was to do.

I was wrong about the women.

One sat at the bar, which was not filled at this time of night. She was young with long blond hair, and when she glanced toward me briefly, I saw a face that could have gone to Hollywood and made good. But it was not her face or the full, red lips or the blond hair that got me. Her figure left me stunned, as if I had been in a car wreck. Her black dress was cut low in front, revealing breasts that jutted sensually forward, terminating in sharp peaks.

I had a fast beer and I did not look at the girl again.

I was thinking about Kathy Bolton.

Something told me Ben wanted more than talk from her. And might get it before I did.

Chapter 2

I was up early the next morning as usual. Those of us who owned shops and stores along Grand Street had an agreement not to open until ten, but I used the couple of hours before opening to make repairs in the back room. I got a couple of radios ready—I don't like fooling with radios, but they seem to go hand in hand with television—and there was a man waiting for me when I unlocked the front door.

He proved to be one of those customers you sometimes get. He was comparing prices instead of the merits of individual sets.

"I can do better through the mail," he said after a while.

"That's up to you. But think about the service that you can't get through the mail."

"So who cares about service?"

"Nobody does until the set won't work."

After he left, I swept up the floor and wondered where I could display the appliances I had decided to carry. Ten years ago a man didn't have to do that. He could make a nice living from television alone. But now you had to have a companion line. If carrying appliances didn't do anything else, at least it would bring more prospects into the shop. But I had an even more important idea in mind. Television reception in Hawley was pretty good—we were close enough to New York for that—but there were many times during the year when weather conditions caused interference. A sure cure for this would be a cable system, with the picture-power generating from one source. It would not be difficult to get a utility company to rent their poles for a price. A normal home installation of a hundred to a hundred and twenty-five dollars would more than pay for it. Not only that, but your service charge of three or four dollars a month could really make it a worthwhile venture once you got enough customers. Naturally, it took money to get into it and it was a little ahead of me but it was something to think about. One town I knew of had its own television station, located in a garage, and telecast over a closed circuit. In addition to the profit from the cable, the station made money from spot advertising.

There was no reason I could not have called the bank about the loan—the board of directors had met the night before—but I thought it would be better to go down and inquire in person. The bank was not far away and it looked like a dead day. Anyway, I would not be gone long.

I put a sign on the door that said I would be back in ten minutes—who could tell when the ten minutes had started—and I walked down the street. At the bank I had to wait a while before I could see the man who had handled my application.

When I sat down at his desk, he said, "A bank makes money from checking accounts and savings accounts and purchase loans, and we want your business."

"Of course."

He looked at some papers in front of him.

"But the board wouldn't go along with what you had in mind. Frankly, I was quite disappointed and I talked hard for it. However, what I said didn't do any good. They rejected it after a lengthy debate."

I began to wish I had not come to the bank. Being turned down made me feel like a bum.

"My record is clean with you," I said. "It wasn't always easy but I've kept it that way."

"Yes, I know, Mr. Sampson." He smiled. "But these things happen. What can you do?"

"I can't answer that."

"Perhaps if you had a personal talk with Ferris Condon, we'd be in a position to reconsider the application. He's on the board and he objected very strongly."

"Why?"

The man shook his head.

"I don't know. As soon as your name came up he was set against it. I— Mr. Sampson, I hope you'll understand that many things come up at a board meeting and there isn't always time to fight for what you believe in. This was true in your case, to a certain extent, and Mr. Condon is a very important man. As I said...."

I left the bank and walked back to the store. I was not going to talk to Condon on my own. What was the use? He was big. Big and ruthless and hard. How a man like that got on the board of directors of a bank was beyond me. Maybe the more you stole and cheated, the better people liked you. But, no, that was being unfair. And bitter. Bitterness brought you nothing but grief. You could not get the right time of day with it.

Back at the shop I worked right through lunch. I had a set that had more troubles in it than a dictatorship. Finally I put the thing aside. That wasn't like me. Generally I liked a challenge. But today was different. I felt as if I had been kicked in the stomach. I had done everything that a bank could reasonably expect, and the value of the mortgage would have been solid in the building. Even including repairs to the building and taxes, my monthly payments would have been less than rent. And Condon had no cause to stand in my way. I did not know the man, except by sight, and I had done nothing to him. Vaguely, I remembered that my father had had some kind of a run-in with Condon years ago when I was small—but what could that have to do with me now? It made no sense.

Kathy called from her office shortly after three and asked if I were angry with her. I said I was not, but I wondered whether that were true. I did not ask her about Ben. When she suggested a movie for Saturday night, I told her I would let her know. That did not offend her, and we broke off the conversation amicably.

I had several service calls to make and at five I started out on them. In one place I had to pick up a set for shop work, and the kids were up in the air because they would not be able to watch cartoons and they could not go next door for the simple reason that they had had a fight with the neighbor's children. I solved that by leaving the extra set I usually carried in the car for just such a situation, and when I left them they were happy.

One man could not get any picture or sound and he was tickled when I discovered the trouble was simply that the electric wire had become disengaged from inside. He wanted to pay me but I would not take anything for that. The set was an ancient one and he would soon be in the market for another. I was sure that he would think of me when he went out to look. Sometimes you have to give a dollar in order to make one.

With the exception of the call where I had left the replacement, none of them were too difficult. I got rid of a few small tubes and I charged the people only for what I used. I had a policy of making my wages from the profit on the tubes and of not adding anything on, at least when the calls were in town. When I had to go out into the country, that was a different matter. It costs money to run a car, not to mention your time, and you have to figure all that in.

I was almost back to the shop when I remembered the Condon woman's phone call. Slowing the car for the next corner I wondered if I should go out there. Then I decided that I would. Condon had sunk me at the bank but he was not going to get his set fixed for nothing. Of that I was sure. He would pay double and I would not lose any sleep over it.

Neversink Drive is out along the river, and most of the homes are new. A few of the places are large with big lawns, sometimes a swimming pool. But on the average they are houses built by working people who will never see the end of their mortgages without refinancing them once or twice. Condon had put up a lot of the houses and he had stuck the buyers for plenty. Some of the cellars leaked when it rained and walls cracked because of the unseasoned lumber he had used. The people got a lousy deal and yet their friends, even when they were aware of this, still looked up Condon when they were ready to build, confident they would have better luck.

Condon, I concluded as I turned at the driveway, had cut no corners on his own house. He had put together a magnificent pile of stone and steel, along with a swimming pool, in a rumored effort to keep his first wife, but he had lost her, anyway.

There was a Caddy parked off to the side of the driveway and I pulled in next to that. After getting out my kit I walked across the lawn toward the house. I was almost to the front door when I saw this blond approaching from the direction of the pool. I stopped, sucking air into my lungs. One gulp wasn't enough so I tried for some more, the heat rushing down inside of me and coming out in a burst of sweat.

I had seen her before.

In the bar the previous night.

But this time she was not wearing a dress. I don't know what you would call it. Maybe it was a bathing suit or a close relative of a bathing suit. It was black, just as the dress had been black, but there the similarity stopped. This piece of material around her golden-tanned thighs was so high that she hardly needed it at all. The top was strapless, just as low as the bottom was high, and the fullness of her breasts was enough to make a man dive into a pool without any water in it.

"I thought you were Ferris," she said. She laughed and tossed her head so that her golden hair fell in long waves on either side of her face. "But I should have known better. He's having dinner in town tonight." She shrugged and what she had inside of the suit moved provocatively. "Business," she said. "I never saw a man so busy."

I did not want to be Ferris Condon or anybody like him but I did want something that belonged to him. I wanted her, more than I had ever wanted a woman before. It was difficult to explain. For the most part, a woman is a woman, give or take a few curves here and there, but the way she stood there close to me, that tiny pulse beating in her throat, made me feel as if I had been kicked in the belly and wouldn't really mind being kicked again. Nobody, not even Kathy, had ever set me on fire like this.

"You must be the television man," she said when she got tired of my hunting around for some words to use.

I looked down the front of that thing she was wearing. My head began to ache just a little bit. I had a yen to see the whole works.

"That's right."

She regarded me with greater interest, frowning a trifle as she did so, her mouth forming a pout and then opening into a vague, teasing smile. Lots of girls had told me that I was handsome, that my chin and eyes showed strength, but I didn't think that she was arriving at a similar opinion.

"You look familiar," she said. "I've seen you before, haven't I?"

"In that little bar last night."

She must have thought I was getting too much view because she tugged at the material as if to stretch it. She could have saved her time. She was just more woman than could be covered with what she had on.

"Yes," she agreed. "In that bar."

"Not a very nice place for you to go, Mrs. Condon."

"The name is Doris. Of course, I already know yours."

"Okay."

"And nobody bothered me in the bar. Probably I wouldn't have cared if they had. There was no television here and I couldn't find anything to read. I just got tired of being lonely and decided to have a drink. Unlike the wandering wife you hear about, that's all I wanted. A drink."

I sweated some more. I knew what she could have if she wanted something other than a drink. Any day of the week and twice on Thursday.

"What seems to be wrong with your set?" I asked her, reminding myself what I was there for.

"I could look inside of a closet or at the wall and get a better picture."

"Nothing, huh?"

"Nothing. Why should that be? We've only had it a few months. Made me sore. I'm crazy over those programs that come to you in color."

"Could be the picture tube." Not many people had color sets.

"So soon?"

"You can't tell. If a picture tube lasts for a year it may be good forever. Or it could go out the next minute."

"I've heard they cost a lot."

"They do. The regular ones are high enough but they're nothing compared to color. My guess would be about a hundred and twenty-five, depending on what you've got. That's why people with a color set should have another set to use for watching the usual programs. Why put the strain on a color tube when it isn't necessary? Anyhow, we can have a look."

She led me into the house, her hips swaying. I could see that Condon had not spared the money when it came to the interior—the furniture was elegant, and the rug in the living room was so thick that I practically had to crawl through it to get to the television.

It did not take long to find out that it was the picture tube, but I pretended to keep busy so I could look at her. The way she was sprawled out on the sofa it seemed as if all a guy had to do was ask once and he would get a yes. Yes is a very nice word, whether you want to borrow from a bank or experience the favors of a woman. Still, a woman can fool you—just like a bank.

I certainly thought Condon was wrong about the way he built houses but I had to give him credit for his selection of a wife. She could not have been more than twenty-two or twenty-three and she fit that sofa as if it belonged to her, which it probably did. As I worked the chassis of the set loose from its moorings, doing it out of habit, I continued to speculate about her chassis, her full, perfect legs, the near animal lure of her terrific bust and a face that would have made an artist stay up nights.

"Well?" she wanted to know, smiling.

I glanced away from her quickly, knowing she had fooled me. She had been looking at me all the time, stretched out there, and the smile told me she had read my mind.

"It's the picture tube," I said.

My gaze wandered back to her again as she sat up.

"Have you got one with you?"

"No, I haven't. And there isn't one in the shop."

"That's a fine thing." She was annoyed. "People say you're the best man around and I thought you could get it working again right away."

I unhooked the antenna wire and pulled the insides out of the set.

"None of us carry this kind of a tube around here," I explained. "You have to stock the things that are popular, and these aren't, just yet."

She got up, sighing, and walked to the opposite side of the room to a small bar in the corner. There was such a stock of liquor behind that bar that I could not figure out why she had to run out to a corner beer joint.

"So what do we do now?"

"I can get a tube out of New York. That's no great effort."

"When?"

"Pretty soon. If I send the order out tomorrow or call it in I'll have it the first of the week."

"That's going to kill my weekend," she said. "Ferris is leaving on a business trip Saturday morning, and I'll be here by myself. I'd miss not having it."

I began picking up my tools. "I'll do what I can," I promised.

"Why don't you drive in for it?" she suggested. Since it was only eighty miles she was, from her viewpoint, being logical.

"Because I'd have to close up the shop and I don't want to do that."

"All right." She seemed to accept my reason. "But try and take care of me, won't you?"

I wiped the sweat from my forehead. I could take care of her plenty but what I had in mind had nothing to do with her television set.

"Maybe I can fix up a used one for you to have until this one is repaired. You wouldn't get any color but it would be better than nothing."

She reached for a bottle.

"Thanks, but I'd rather have my own."

"Okay."

"I'd pay you extra for your trouble."

"I'll see how it works out."

She set up two glasses. "Would you care for a drink?"

Usually I don't go for anything except beer—oh, maybe a shot at a special party or to celebrate the holidays—but with this Doris Condon I guess I would have tried rat poison mixed with water.

"A small one," I said.

"Ice and soda, or straight?"

"Whatever I get."

She poured out a couple of big ones with nothing added. Either she did not know what small meant, or she assumed that I was merely being polite.

"To that lousy television set," she said as we drank. "May you fix it so that it will last forever."

"We're wasting good liquor," I told her. "Nothing lasts forever."

The bar was high, and since she was close to it, the front of her just lay there on the counter, a front that looked like two big ripe melons that somebody ought to pick. What I saw took my mind off what I was drinking so much that I didn't even feel the stuff as it went down.

"My husband mentioned your name over dinner the other night," she said.

"That must have been when the television quit."

"No, before. He often talks about business—that's almost all he can talk about—and it had something to do with a deal that you had on at the bank."

"I had one on with them but they wouldn't have it with me." I don't know why, but I told her about not getting the loan from the bank. "I wasn't looking for a gift," I said finishing the drink. "He put the queer on the whole thing for no reason at all but he doesn't hesitate about putting up a house that's going to fall down on somebody's skull."

She laughed and started to pour me another drink, but I shook my head and refused. One is about my limit, and with so much woman that near to me, a woman who smelled like a woman, I did not need any booze to pump the red blood cells through my veins. All I had to do was look at her, think about how she would be, and the cells went crazy like two-way traffic on a one-way street.

"He didn't act as if he were very fond of you," she said, and put the bottle aside.

"Hell, I don't even know the guy."

"Maybe you haven't missed much." She smiled. "Or shouldn't I have said that?"

"Look, he's your husband. You can say what you want."

A couple of minutes later, without being asked, she helped me carry the things out to the car.

She stood there on the lawn as I drove away.

I did not look back.

I knew if I did I would go back.

And that could be murder. Once I had started with her, I knew I would never stop. That would be one thing old man Condon could not jinx.

Chapter 3

Ben Stucker came in the next morning before I had a chance to call New York about a tube for Doris Condon's color set. He looked as if he had been up all night. "They took out my phone at the shop," he said. "Yesterday. I didn't even know it until somebody stopped in and told me. The operator gave him the word that the phone had been disconnected."

"There goes your business, Ben. You need a phone to get service calls. People aren't going to drive down to see you just because you didn't pay your bills."

"Things have been rough, Hob. Even the hotel has been yelling. And I can't borrow on the truck. It's two-thirds of the way to the junk pile right now."

I wiped off the top of a display model, thinking that it was funny about where all the dust came from. With a tight, new front on the building, it would not bother me so much.

"I can't help you," I said. "You've got to help yourself."

"Yeah, but how?"

"By cutting out the girls and the helling around."

"That's easy to say, only when you're down as far as I am you don't get up so fast."

"No, I suppose not. People lose confidence in you and it's harder to prove yourself the second time."

He took the cloth from me and went on with the cleaning.

"I'd do anything for a few bucks, Hob. Honest. I don't have a thing on for the day and the lights will go off next. You can't fix television sets without electric current."

I lit a cigarette and turned an idea around in my mind. If I ordered the color tube over the phone, they would ship it when they got good and ready, but if I had Ben pick it up, I would have it before dark. Of course, I would have to pay him for the trip and I wouldn't make any profit from it, but I was not thinking about profit just then. I was thinking about the blond—her eyes and lips and all the rest of her.

When I talked it over with Ben, he was more than willing to run the errand, but he wanted his pay in advance—most likely he did not have enough money for gas—so I gave him some from the drawer and wrote out a check for the tube. He left, feeling better. What I had paid him would not make him rich, but it amounted to a day's wages and he would have money for drinks and to park with some girl in his old truck. For all I knew, the girl might be Kathy Bolton.

The day wore on, and I cleaned up what I had to do in the back room. One set gave me a lot of trouble. I put in several new parts, accomplished nothing, and then, by accident, discovered a loose wire. I soldered the wire into place and got a nice picture. Then I took out the new parts one by one, returning the old parts to the set as I went along, and it developed that the wire had been causing all the trouble. Some men might have left the new parts alone, charging the people for what they did not need, but I did not want to stick anybody. There were enough characters out to do that already.

Somewhat later the phone rang. It was Doris Condon.

"You left a wrench or something on the floor," she said.

"It's nice of you to tell me."

"I'll keep it for you until you come out again."

"Swell."

She hung up before I could give her the good news that I was getting the tube fast. It hardly mattered. I would go out there and surprise her with it. Grinning I kicked a box out of the way. I would surprise her with something else, too, if she were willing and if her husband were out. Then I lost the grin. She was married and they had money and I was just plugging along, an average guy who had nothing to offer a married woman, except trouble.

It was a hot day, very hot. There were only a few people on the street. Those who were not working and who did not have to go out were at home with their fans going at top speed. It was the kind of weather nobody needed unless he sold beer or ice cream.

I don't know when I decided to go down to Condon's office to see him, but I suddenly realized that it was something I owed myself. If I had done anything to hurt my credit, it was only fair that I learn the facts. I had never had any complaints from the suppliers I bought from, so it could not be that. I had to see Condon because the building was important to me and I wanted it. I did not intend to spend the rest of my life trying to operate from a hole in the ground.

Condon's Lumber Company was located near the railroad tracks. Huge piles of building materials were spread out all over the place. A lot of it was green lumber he bought locally. The main office was surprisingly small. Condon wanted to keep his overhead at a minimum.

He wanted to cut our interview short, too. That was obvious the minute I came into his private office. He sat behind a large desk, his face as hard as granite, so I covered the details of my negotiations with the bank as quickly as possible. I could tell from the way he looked at me, with eyes as hard as his face, that I had more chance of getting a bill passed through Congress than I had of convincing him.

"The television business is crap," he said as I concluded.

"I've made a living from it and I've paid my bills. My record at the bank should be proof of my honesty. If I sell a set on time I make sure the folks are good for it."

"Not interested," he said and began looking through a magazine.

"But you must have had something against the deal. You say my business is crap and I could say the same about yours. Or any other business that I didn't understand."

He kept on looking at the magazine, just as if I were not there, and I started to get sore. If I had been in the market for a house he would not have been so rude. He would have kissed the ground I walked on in an effort to close the sale.

"I'm not leaving until I find out," I said. "Make sure of that, Mr. Condon."

His face was red as he threw the magazine aside. "This is my office, Sampson."

"I don't give a damn what it is. You're a big man—I'll grant you that—but you aren't big enough to put me out before I'm ready."

"I threw your old man out of here once."

"Maybe you did."

"After he almost ruined me. But he didn't. Nobody ruins Ferris Condon. I get what I want."

"Lucky, lucky you."

He leaned back in his chair. "I suppose you remember your father, Sampson?"

"Of course I remember. I remember that he worked damned hard. He's still working hard, but he's doing well in California."

"And what about when you were—let's see—four or five? You remember him then?"

"Not much."

"He was selling real estate about that time."

"I think he mentioned it to me once—but all he said was that it hadn't worked out."

"He ever say anything about me?"

"Nothing much, except that you were dishonest. I don't like to tell you that, but it's the truth."

"Dishonest?" he inquired. "I'm just smart."

"That's a matter of opinion, isn't it?"

"You sound like your old man."

"I can't help that."

"He was smart, too," Condon said. "I'm telling you this for your own good, so that you'll know where you stand with me, but I'll say for the record that he was smart. He sold houses when nobody else could, only he wouldn't sell any for me. Then he took a course and he got to be an appraiser. I wasn't on the board at the bank then and the bank hired him to inspect properties. And he inspected mine."

"Most likely he turned them down," I said, catching the meaning behind his words.

Condon nodded, his face savage.

"Every one. I'd get a buyer and he'd look at the place and kill the sale. I had been growing until then but he had me headed for the rocks. I offered him dough to be regular but he wouldn't take it. Finally I worked my way into the board of directors at the bank and I got him fired. We got a new man to take over his job and I unloaded my houses in a hurry. I told you, Sampson, nobody ruins me. He came as close as anybody, but even he couldn't do it."

Everything was clear to me now, very clear.

"So you still hold a grudge, Mr. Condon?"

"Call it what you want."

"And for that crummy reason I didn't get my loan?"

He resumed his former position and picked up the magazine again. "Let's say I guessed you to be a poor gamble."

I tried to talk to him some more but he would not talk, and I was boiling by the time I got out of there. He had been wrong all the way through and now he was still wrong. Because my father had done what was right, I couldn't do anything about the building I was in. Even if I saved and business was good it would be years before I could lay down the cash for it, and by that time it would not be worth buying.

An old lady came into the shop right after I opened up. She was looking for a cheap portable radio to give some youngster as a birthday present. I had a couple of inexpensive imports from Japan which I had been foolish enough to stock, and I sold her one of those. However, I did not take her money until I had made it plain to her that I did not guarantee service or the set.

"That's all right," she said. "He'll probably lose it at the beach anyway. I bought him a good one last year and he had it only a week. The main thing is to give him something."

She went out with her purchase, just as happy as a woman in her right mind.

Then the phone rang. It was Kathy. She said she wanted to see me, asked whether I would be able to stop by at her house after work. I told her I had to make a few calls but that I would get out there as soon as I could.

I waited until quite late before leaving the shop, but Ben did not show up with the tube. I came to the conclusion that he had had trouble with his truck, or had stopped off for a few fast ones. I finally gave up waiting and left a note on the door asking him to bring the tube down in the morning.

I made my delivery and service calls, drove toward Fossard Street. I should have been thinking about Kathy and why she wanted to see me on a Friday night, or why I was going over there at all after the way she had been treating me. Actually, though, I was thinking of that blond out on Neversink Drive, of the promising wildness of her body, of a woman married to the next thing to an animal that thirsted for blood. My blood. I felt that nobody could hold it against me for disliking the man, for wanting to take away from him the blond loveliness that he probably prized more highly than any other single possession he had. It was the only way I had of getting back at him for what he had done to me—and I might have the time of my life, besides.

It was dark when I got to Fossard Street and the only light visible came from the kitchen. I parked the Ford and walked around to the back porch in the dark, stumbling over a milk bottle on the way up the steps. She must have heard me swear because the light came on outside right away and the screen door opened.

"I hope you didn't hurt yourself," she said.

"I'll sue you," I laughed. "How much is a broken leg worth?"

"Hob! I can't come out this way. And you really shouldn't come in. But—oh, well, come on."

I crowded into the kitchen and saw that she had on very little but a look of shame. I realized that she had not expected me this early and that she was not dressed to meet anybody. All she had on were a black bra and black panties and there wasn't an awful lot to either one. I also realized that her father was not home, that he was out on the railroad again, or supposed to be. Most of the railroaders I knew did not work as often as he did, usually every other day, so I figured he had some woman he visited. There was nothing very wrong with that. He had not had a wife for years and he appeared normal enough.

"I'd better get a robe," she said and covered the swells of her breasts with her hands.

"Why bother? You're not showing any more of yourself than you do on the beach." Wearing so little she excited me with the kind of instant tingle a man feels when he thinks he might get something more than a look. "Anyhow, we're friends."

She smiled and color flushed her face. "Just friends, Hob?"

"Let's not get into that," I said and walked to the refrigerator for a can of beer. She already had a can for herself on the table.

"I was only trying to get cool."

"Sure."

"Some girls run around their houses naked when they're alone."

"Call me up when you spot one who hasn't pulled her shades down."

"You'd like that, wouldn't you?" she said, teasing.

There was plenty of beer in the refrigerator, more than her old man ever brought home. She must have been out shopping.

"That would depend on how the girl was stacked," I said, opening a can.

She sat down at the table and lit a cigarette. She inhaled deeply. I knew that the only time she inhaled like that was when she was thinking.

"How am I stacked, Hob?"

I joined her at the table and since she was sitting next to the wall I took the chair beside her. It was plain that she had been drinking plenty of beer and if she slipped into the mood I did not want the top of any table in my way.

"You've got all you need," I assured her. "Your shape will last. When those blimps are trying on new girdles you won't even know how one of them goes on."

She was silent for a long moment.

"Thanks for stopping by, Hob."

"Don't mention it."

"I know I made you angry the other night. I—well, I shouldn't have done it but Ben was so torn apart that I couldn't do anything else. I—I just had to try to help him."

I looked down at her firm thighs that tapered off into long, smooth legs.

"That isn't what you wanted to see me about," I said.

She took a deep breath. "No, it isn't. But let's have another beer first."

I got her a beer, and as she drank it, she came out slowly with what was bothering her. It seemed that at her office she did everything from writing up agreements to paying bills. Of course, she did not sign the checks. The senior partner did that. But he would sign a few in blank to be left in the checkbook to be used as needed—a stupid thing to do—and when they were gone he just signed more. All of this might have been all right, but the junior partner, the man who had his eyes on Kathy's charms, had gotten at the checks, cashed some of them and now was telling Kathy that she had stolen money from the agency. However, he was willing to overlook the lie he had planted if she would permit him certain liberties.

"That isn't so hot," I admitted and got some more beer.

"No, and I can't go to the other partner. Who would he believe? Me or the man who is in the agency with him? The checks were typed, and made out to cash, so they didn't have to be endorsed."

"How much is involved?" I wanted to know.

"About three hundred dollars. I could put it back but I've bought clothes and helped out here at home and I don't have anything."

It seemed to me that everybody I knew needed three hundred dollars. Maybe there was a fever going around that would not disappear until that much money was put up.

We drank and talked it over. She didn't come right out and ask for the cash but why would she have invited me to see her if she had not been hoping I would come across? I told her about the bank and she was shocked.

"But, Hob, I don't understand it."

"There were reasons, personal ones."

Her face grew unhappy. "I was thinking of you getting the loan and that I could...."

"Never mind," I said. "I've got three hundred you can have."

She leaned toward me, smiling. "I'll pay it back. And I'll get another job. There's an opening on the newspaper and I've already called them about it. I go in on Monday to get the details."

With her that close to me there was only one thing I could do. I put my arm around her and got her in closer, our chairs together and her body soft and warm. Her lips were warm, too, and they moved under the pressure of my mouth as I kissed her. There was a fury in her now, a kind of longing and hunger that I had never found in her before. She stopped kissing me for a second when I reached behind her to get at the hook on the bra, but then her mouth came open, a moan gathering and dying in her throat. She moaned again when I brought my hand to the front to get at the nakedness of her breasts.

"This is crazy," she said once, her words husky and thick.

"Don't stop me now," I begged.

She did not. I got up, lifting her from the chair, and we kissed as I carried her into the darkened living room. I knew where the sofa was and I put her on it.

"Hob?" she said as I fumbled with my clothing.

"What is it?"

"I'm—well, scared."

"Don't be."

"You know what happened to my mother. She...."

"There's nothing to worry about. I'll see that you don't get something that neither one of us want right now."

I heard her moving around on the sofa.

"Hob," she said. "Hob, you're wonderful."

She was waiting for me, all naked and anxious, as I went down to her. Her lips spoke silently of her desires, her straining body of her mounting passions.

"Hob," she whispered. "Hob, be gentle with me."
I tried to be.
But still I made her scream.
It was the only time I had ever been first with a girl.

Chapter 4

I was late getting the shop open on Saturday morning. It had been almost daylight when I had reached my apartment. I could not sleep right away, knowing what I had done to Kathy, and when I finally did get to sleep I just could not wake up. When I got the shop open, all I did was stand around, staring out at the street.

I had wanted Kathy a lot of times before, especially when I had been drinking a little, but now that it had happened I suddenly felt I should not see her again. Nobody expects much from the first time, but the last time should have been fine; I had satisfied her, her body coming to full womanhood against mine—but I had felt nothing. Maybe some kind of inner guilt had held me back, the guilt of knowing that you are not going to give a girl the things she really wants—a home, some security and a bank account that won't be overdrawn every two weeks.

There on the sofa, her arms around me, she had said something about marriage, how she supposed it wasn't actually wrong if you married afterward, that a lot of couples enjoyed each other before. All of this was true enough, but I hadn't been too keen on the marriage idea and still I wasn't....

I dug out a cigarette but did not light it. I supposed that I ought to marry her—that we would make out all right if I did. She had lost her fears of sex in the darkness of that room—lost them completely. Her love had been wonderful—but I had been like a stud on a farm, out after any mare that could not jump the fence. Kathy, in truth, had been little more than a convenience.

Well, it all came back to that blond, a woman I hardly knew but who looked good to me. I guess Ferris Condon had something to do with it, too. I wanted to hurt him, no matter what it cost, and the easiest way was through his wife—if she were willing. With a plan like that in my brain I was in no condition to consider marriage and it would not have been fair to Kathy if I did. I had taken the one treasure she would ever have and I sat there living in my own torment because of it; I owed her marriage, my conscience told me, yet the debt was overshadowed by my unfinished business with the Condons.

C.S. Potter, a short, fat man in his late fifties, was the first to come into the shop. I did not know what the initials stood for—everybody just called him C.S.—but he owned my building and several others scattered through the town. He was after his rent.

"I heard the bank wouldn't give you the loan," he said, chewing on his cigar.

"Yeah, it fell flat on its face."

"Then I might as well tell you I've got a buyer who's interested."

"Hell," I said, "it's bad enough building up a location, let alone losing it."

"Sorry, Sampson. Real estate as an investment is for the birds. I'm turning what I've got into cash that I can count."

He took the rent check from me and went out. I sat down again and felt less like working than ever. Moving the shop meant finding another place and probably paying more rent, and since the bank had turned down one application—thanks to Ferris Condon—I could not look to it for help. Whatever I did I would have to do on my own.

It was a hot day, so hot I felt like closing up. When Ben came in, a few minutes later, his shirt already was soaked with sweat. I looked for a box in his hands. He had nothing.

"I haven't much of an excuse," he said and gave me my check for the tube. "I did start for New York, Hob, I was going straight there."

"I should have let you take my car. That truck of yours is falling apart inch by inch."

He leaned against the television set. "The truck had nothing to do with it, Hob. I had the money you gave me and a few miles out I stopped off for a drink. It so happened the television they had wouldn't work and I got my tools and fixed it for them. And after that I didn't feel like going anywhere. I had some drinks on the house—and I met this broad. The broad had a room...."

"Great!" I said in disgust. "I could have done better if I'd mailed the check under a rock. So now what happens to the money I paid you?"

"I'll work it out."

"Next week. I've got nothing now," I said sharply.

"Sure." He started for the door. "Maybe you could find a lonesome ten or twenty around to hold me over?"

"I won't even look."

He went out, mumbling to himself. What was I supposed to do? I didn't have the tube I needed and he had spent my money without earning it. I was tired of playing sucker for him.

The few customers I got in the afternoon I really worked over. One man who put ten dollars down on a portable television asked me to deliver it on that basis. When I told him I would not, he said he would be back the following Wednesday with the balance on the first payment. As I smiled and assured him I could arrange for the outstanding amount to be handled by the bank, I wondered whether I really could. Many small loans do not go before the board of directors, especially if the merchant had a clean record, but now that Condon's attention was focused on me, it was highly probable that he would have me cut off there, too. When that happened I would be slammed against the wall. Of course, there were finance companies, maybe two or three with branches in town, but their contracts were loaded with extra charges.

The day was fair—a buck here and a buck there.

About the middle of the afternoon, Kathy phoned. She did not mention what had happened the previous night but said she was going somewhere with her father for the weekend and that she would not be available. I had the feeling that she was ashamed of what she had done. But when she said she was worried about the partner in the real estate firm and the money, I promised her I would mail her the check so that she could have it on Monday morning.

"You're quite a guy," she said.

"Forget it."

"Wish me the best with the newspaper, will you?"

"Yeah. The best."

I mailed the check to Kathy at the corner box. It was money I could not afford, money that should have gone into stock or something else, but that creep in her office practically had her on her back and I felt obliged to do what I could.

Just before closing I took the finest set I had out to the Ford, dropped the gate in back and put it in there on a blanket. I knew the blond would be peeved because I did not have her tube, but it was not my fault. Or was it? I should not have trusted Ben in the first place.

The house on Neversink Drive was quiet when I got there, and I saw nothing around but the Caddy. I parked next to it and got out. And then, suddenly, I did see somebody.

Her.

Running from the pool into the house as naked as the day she had fought her way out of her mother's womb. She ran fast so I did not see much, but I saw enough to make me hang on to the door of my car, my legs growing weak. I saw a beautiful body, bouncing and dripping wet—a lush body that was meant for more than a nude swim.

I waited about five minutes before I unloaded the television set from the car. Of course I had no way of knowing whether her display had been an accident or deliberate, and I did not care. But I had to cool down a minute before I could walk to that front door.

She met me, her smile somewhat amused. I could tell from the spreading wet spots that she had lost no time getting into a dress. The dress was red, slashed low in front, and the damp fabric clung to her, emphasizing the nudity under it.

"That isn't my set," she said.

"I couldn't get the tube I needed and thought this one would at least give you something. It's not color but you should get some excellent reception."

"All right," she said, following me across the living room.

She showed me where to put the set and was stooping over to plug the wire into an outlet when she said, "You can't think much of my modesty."

I glanced at her. Her breasts were right up close to me. They were rounded and firm, terribly full, and one side was challenging the other to brush through the opening.

"Why not?" I asked, my throat tight.

"For the way I came out of the pool."

"That's your business, not mine."

"It's the best way to swim."

"So they say."

"But Ferris doesn't approve. He claims it's obscene." She stood up. "To hell with him. What he doesn't know won't kick up a fuss. If I have that yen why can't I do it? You can't see the pool from the road."

When I turned on the set the picture was not what I had expected. The low channels jumped and became distorted although the higher ones were clear and sharp. That was the weather, something that nobody could do anything about, and a strong point in favor of a cable system.

"I feel like the devil," she said and yawned, stretching as she did so. For a second I thought she was going to stretch herself out of the dress. "How bored can you get and still live with yourself?" she asked.

"You've got me." In more ways than one, I thought. You've got me fast and solid.

Reaching down and turning off the set, she asked, "Are you in a hurry?"

"I've got nothing much to do but if you don't like this set, there isn't anything else I can do."

She must have realized that she was crawling out of the dress. She fussed with it a little, as if trying to make it cover her better.

"We could have a drink. If you're doing nothing, we might as well do it together. And I've been drinking all day long. It began to throw me and that's why I got into the pool, just to get straightened out and start all over again."

"I'd rather have beer," I said.

"I've got that, too."

While she went for the beer I walked around the living room. No doubt Condon had bought all the fancy furniture for his first wife—but this girl had nothing to complain about. Rooms like this were straight out of the fancy home magazines, the kind women sigh over and men wish had never been printed.

She brought cold beer and started to put together a long drink for herself at the bar. Nothing was said about it when we both sat on the sofa. As she sank into the expensive cushions the hem of her dress pulled up over her knees and, naturally, I began to think about her legs. They were long, lovely and smooth. Thanks to the air-conditioning it was comfortably cool in the room, yet I could feel the damp sweat under my arms and the palms of my hands felt hot.

"You must be very happy," I said.

She looked at me curiously over the rim of her glass. "What brought that on?"

"Oh, I don't know. Big house. Private swimming pool. Beautiful grounds. Expensive car."

She pulled her legs up under her. "Can't we talk about something pleasant?" she wanted to know.

"Sure, but I'd think those things were."

"Never mind. Tell me about yourself."

"There isn't much to tell. I'm just a guy trying to make a living. You can't add it up to anything more than that."

"Did you do anything more about your loan at the bank?"

"I tried. I spoke to your husband but it did no good."

"I know," she said. "He told me about it. Of course he yelled when I happened to mention that I'd called you about the television."

"It's funny that he waited until now to get sore. I've been doing business with the bank ever since I started out and there's been no trouble until this week. They seemed happy to get my time payment accounts."

"That's because Ferris didn't know who you were before."

"I've never hidden my name."

"He thought you were one of the other Sampsons in town."

"That explains a little."

"You probably had to put your father's name on the application and when he saw it he realized who you were. Anyway, that night at dinner he was fuming. He said he'd bust you if it was the last thing he did."

I finished my beer.

"That's crazy," I said. "He's already had his revenge. How much more can he want?"

She smiled and got up to take my glass. "You don't know my husband."

"And I'm not holding my breath for the day I do!"

This time she brought back two cans of beer. While she fixed her own drink I just sat, quiet and feeling low. Condon could do a lot to me that I could do nothing about. You need money to fight money, and I didn't have his kind of dough. I could not understand why he had carried a grudge for all these years, but I knew some people were built that way. They kicked the neighbor's dog to get even for something the neighbor himself had done. It did not make sense.

Unexpectedly she said she wanted to dance. It was difficult on the thick rug, but with the kind of music she played on the hi-fi—slow and warm and somewhat on the dreamy side—you don't really dance. She kicked off her shoes, saying the heels bothered her. Barefoot and five feet five, she stood just high enough to bring her silky blond hair to my lips. The heady odor roused me again. She did not try to stay away from me. I could feel the heat of her skin through the thin dress. I touched the curve that flowed away from the small of her back to her hips. I felt the thrust of her breasts as they flattened out against me.

"Enough of that," she said finally. "Do you mind?"

"No," I said reluctantly.

"But you dance well."

"Thanks."

"And you seem a nice enough guy."

"Thanks again."

"Some men have to paw you."

She walked barefooted to the bar, moving like one of those girls you see in a stag movie, and I wanted to paw her, all right, wanted to do more than that.

"Maybe I shouldn't ask this," I said after she joined me on the sofa again. "Maybe I shouldn't bring it up at all."

She pulled up her legs again, swinging about to face me. Her dress was having more trouble with her breasts. She didn't seem to notice it—maybe she was just high. "You can ask but that doesn't mean you'll get an answer." Her eyes met mine steadily, never wavering.

"I was only thinking about a girl so young marrying a man your husband's age." I just had to know.

She was unmoved; no doubt she had heard the same question before.

"That's easy. Haven't you heard of a summer and winter romance?"

"Now and then," I admitted.

She got more drinks for us but when she resumed her seat she said it was the last of the beer. She said she had a combination cook and maid—I should have guessed that from the size of the house—and the woman would be home soon. I knew that I had better not be there when the woman came in.

"He bought me," she said, continuing the story of her husband. "He saw a pretty toy and he bought me. But perhaps you don't think I'm pretty?"

"I'd say beautiful. Beautiful—with a shape."

"He likes the shape."

"I'd think he would."

"If he'd only get his brain off business long enough to enjoy it." She laughed. "Now there I go getting conceited."

"You just said he bought you." I put my head back. The sight of her was driving me wild. "How? A guy could own the mint and not be able to buy a woman."

"Not even if she was down on her luck?"

"That might do it."

"I was down on mine." She paused. "But why am I telling you all this?"

I opened my eyes and reached down for the last of my beer. She now sat with one leg extended and the other pulled up. I took my time about getting the beer. What I saw of the inside of her thigh—and beyond—was better than the beer.

"I guess you just want to talk to somebody," I said as she put her leg down and I sat up. "People like to talk," I added, realizing how stupid it sounded.

"We met at a convention in Philadelphia."

"There's no place like a convention to meet. At least that's what I've heard. I've never been at one of them. I might go this year if I can afford it."

"A few of us girls were hired to mix with the men," she said. "We got paid so much for the job. If we felt like going any further with a man that was up to us. Some of the girls did and some didn't. I didn't. I was introduced to Ferris the first day and when the convention broke up I came back here with him. You can say what you want about being a model but it's a tough life. You never know where you are. For some of the assignments I was too big in the bust. That's strange, isn't it, when most men like that part of a woman best? Or," she corrected herself, "next to best."

She was just high enough on the booze to be frank and I go for a woman who is frank. Why conceal what almost everybody feels?

"You've got it made," I said.

She gave me a long look.

"I've got it made in hell." The look became more searching. "If I had my way, I'd get out of the hell."

"What's stopping you?"

She stood up and so did I. It was about time for the woman to arrive and I sensed that my hostess wanted me to leave.

"Things," she replied. "I'd rather not go into it now."

She walked with me to the door and there was only one way to tell her good night, to show her what I wanted from her the instant she was willing. It was like dancing with her again, almost, only this time my arms were hard around her, my mouth over her lips, the power of my body bending her to me.

"Come back again," she said when I released her. "I'll call and let you know when."

"Don't make it too long."

"I won't," she whispered.

I stepped outside and I moved toward the Ford that sat parked there in the moonlight. I'd forgotten the wrench again.

Now I would have to go back sooner or later—and some inner feeling told me that I should not, told me that her hell, whatever it was, would become mine if I did.

Frankly, I had enough of that already.

But I had not had enough of her.

Chapter 5

By five o'clock Monday morning I was at my repair bench. It sounds crazy, but I had several jobs to get out and many things to do before people were up and around. That's one trouble with working alone—you're like a paperhanger without a ladder. You get busy in back and then somebody opens the front door. Even if it's only for a donation for some organization—and those people are always coming in—it's time out from earning money.

I worked hard for about four hours, but I still was far from finished. So many unexpected things, like a broken extension cord—it works fine while you are hunting for the trouble, and then puts out the whole set when you turn around—keep you behind schedule.

Actually, I had tried twice to get somebody to help me but all I found were boys who had taken those worthless correspondence courses, and I did not have time to train a man. Naturally I had thought about Ben Stucker but I could not trust him. One experience in business with him had been enough. If he had cheated me before, he would cheat me again.

Still, I was glad when I answered a knock on the front door and found that it was Ben. He could not do much harm in an hour or two and I did not want to close the shop for what I had to do. A lot of service calls come after the weekend and it's a shame to miss them. About one service call in ten may mean the sale of a new unit. Since I needed money for what I had in mind, I could not afford to miss even one of these calls.

"You look rough," I said to Ben as I let him in. "If I didn't know better, I'd think you were back on the farm and that you'd just tumbled into some slop."

His clothes were dirty and he smelled of sweat. He had gone down so far he was never going to get up on his feet again. It was a crying shame. He had the talent, but he was too quick to grab a fast buck. I could not see why Kathy bothered herself with him.

"I said I'd work out that money," he explained. "It was kind of a lousy thing to do and I want to make it right."

"It's all bench work, Ben."

He shrugged.

"Who cares? You know me on the bench. Nothing much fools me any. I'd even say that I'm better than you are at it."

We walked toward the rear of the building.

"What's the use of being smart if you don't work at it?" I asked. "Anyway, we won't go into that. I just want some honest jobs and no gimmicks. Half of these people are poor and they can't afford the parts that you try to shove off on them. But why should I tell you that? You found it out the hard way."

He looked around the shop.

"New equipment, Hob? You're always keeping up, aren't you? Hook up a set, turn a dial and you've located your trouble. Neat."

"It isn't that simple, as you well know." I lit a smoke. "And I've got to get straightened out, or it may all go to pot. Maybe I'll be operating out of the city park from under a tent."

After I started him working, I told him I had to go out for a while. He said for me to take as long as I wanted, that he would just lock up when he was finished. I thought he would try to touch me for ten bucks or so but he did not. In fact, he said nothing at all about money. I could not understand it....

I drove out to C.S. Potter's. He knew about the loan refusal, of course, but I had not tried to deal with him on a personal basis. Now I thought I could persuade C.S. to sell the building to me on time—to take over the mortgage himself—if I talked hard and long enough. Sure, there were other stores to be had but the rents were higher and I liked it where I was. Figuring what I was saving on my living quarters, my rent was low. Besides, I got worried when I thought about my chances in another location.

For a man who owns a lot of property, C.S. Potter had an unimpressive house. The white paint was peeling and nobody had bothered to trim the hedge. That hedge must have been six feet high in some places. When I went up the front steps, I noticed there was a board missing. It was like all of his other property. He never did anything unless he had to. If one tenant moved out, there was always somebody else ready to move in. I had no way of knowing whether this was good business or bad, never having owned any real estate.

The bell would not work so I knocked on the door and waited. After a while I fumbled impatiently for a cigarette and found that I had left the pack behind. I am not sure how long I stood there but it must have been five minutes, at least long enough to wonder whether or not he was home.

He was.

"The hell," he said as he opened the door. He wore pants but no shirt. "You got something on your mind, Hob?"

I told him I did but that it would take a few minutes to find how worthwhile it was.

He let me in. The house smelled musty, the way a house smells when a man keeps it closed up most of the time and uses it only for sleeping. As I walked into the living room I noticed that he spent very little on furniture. What was there would have brought less than fifty dollars at auction.

We sat down and I tried to explain my proposition to him. The car, I told him, was paid for and I thought I could raise some money on that. If I put this with what I had in the bank I could make a good down payment on the building I occupied.

"Look at it this way," I said. "You'd have a six percent mortgage and that adds up to a nice income, doesn't it? What would you get if you converted the property into cash and put it into a savings account? Three or three-and-a-half percent? And if I grounded out—say by getting sick or something—you would still have the property."

I talked for quite a while, trying to convince him, but I guess he thought if I wasn't good enough for the bank I wasn't good enough for him. I did not go into the business about Condon. The matter was personal and I doubted that Potter would believe me, anyway. A man at a bank may not like you, but if you have shot square you can usually get credit. A bank makes money by lending money. But Condon was a breed all by himself.

"No, I won't do it," C.S. Potter said finally. "When I went into real estate, I thought it was hot stuff. But I'm so cold on the whole thing now that I want to get out of the business altogether. You might try for some private financing. There are people who loan out money."

"Who?"

"I don't know, exactly. Not in this town. But Ferris Condon might be one."

I left there feeling as low as the tops of my shoes. No one I knew had any ready cash and I felt that I could count out the other two banks. Since I had never done business with them, they had no reason to trust me. Of course, there were a couple of building-and-loan associations, but their job was to lend on homes, or so I had been informed.

If somebody reasonable bought Potter's building, I might still be all right, but if not, sooner or later, I would be out on the street.

I needed a drink, but it was too early and I passed it up.

For about an hour I looked at vacant stores. Only one interested me and even that interest disappeared when I learned the rent was two hundred a month. Since it had no place for me to live, it was just too much money. Had I been bigger and already established in the appliance field, I might have gone for it, but I was still growing and I did not want to swamp myself with payments.

"A hundred a month I could stand," I told the man.

"So who gives anything away?" the man sneered.

I walked out and got into the Ford. All the way back I thought about what the man had said. He was right. Nobody gave anything away—there was always a catch. There would have to be a catch somewhere if that blond ever did come across. And more trouble I did not need. I decided to get her television set back to her and call it quits.

When I returned to the shop, Ben was working on the bench. He had received three calls for service work and he had written down the names and addresses.

"One dame sounded like a dream," he said, grinning.

"She's probably a pig."

"Who cares as long as she's willing and she's alone?"

"Don't you ever think about anything else?"

"Sure. About once a day."

I told him about the color chassis, that I was not going to bother with it, and I asked him to run it out to the blond for me and bring back the set I had lent to her. He said that he did not mind, that one thing was about the same as another to him, and he left in a couple of minutes.

I felt better.

I was finished with the blond and I was pretty sure that my frustration and need for her would die a natural death.

The phone rang as I was sweeping out the display area. It was Kathy.

"Thanks for the check," she said.

"That's okay."

Then she told me that she was out for her morning coffee, that she had squared off at the real-estate office and that she had decided to keep her job there. I did not understand it, but I did not protest. It was her life.

A few minutes later the woman who had purchased the cheap imported radio came in and said it would not work. I could have reminded her that I had not guaranteed the thing but I simply gave her the other model and said nothing. I was that disgusted.

Ben was all smiles when he returned and I helped him in with the set.

"You see the blond when you were out there?" he asked me.

"Yeah, I saw her."

"Some number."

"She's pretty enough."

"Pretty? Hell, you should have seen her. You know these new rigs they sleep in now? They call them some kind of sleeping shirts, down to the knees with an initial at the top and just a pair of briefs underneath. No wonder you sent me out there. Any guy who had one foot out of the grave would sleep with that in a patch of briars."

"What did she say?" I asked casually.

"Nothing, but she acted sore."

"Tough."

"Too bad some woman was there. If she'd been alone, she'd have gone down on her back."

"I doubt it."

"No? You don't know me, Hob. She'd have gone down even if she'd said no. I'm that kind of a guy."

He still had not worked out his money, but I said nothing when he walked out. I did not care much. Just not having to see the blond had been worth the dough. Maybe I was not the smartest man in the world, but I could sense a dangerous situation. At least I thought I could.

About one o'clock a man came in. He had been saving for months for a television set and I made a neat sale of a console. Like so many sales, it was a time-payment thing but he had the third down, and the installments were not too high for him. I made out and signed the papers for the bank, and had him sign them. He said he could take the set with him because his apartment already had an aerial and a wire he could hook into. We put the set in the trunk of his car, leaving the top elevated, and I told him I would stop by in a couple of days to see what kind of reception he was getting. Generally, sets do need adjustments. A man on one side of the street may require nothing, but the fellow across the street can have problems that are worse than a hangover.

At two I closed for a few minutes and drove to the bank. Once I had a note from a man I did not waste time getting rid of it. I always needed the money to pay for a replacement. Some distributors have a "floor-plan"— where you pay only for what you sell—but I had never gone in for that. There is interest to consider, which can chew into profits. Besides, I took pride in looking around the display room and knowing that what I had there was mine.

Usually the bank just went through the motions and gave me the money promptly for the balance due. That day they did not. I had to go and see the same man I had seen about the mortgage.

"We can't continue to carry you," he said. He did not look at me when he said it. "You'll have to make some kind of arrangement with somebody else. I—well, I'm sorry but that's all I can tell you, Mr. Sampson."

He had not asked me to sit down, but I took a chair anyway. My legs were suddenly weak and I did not feel like standing.

"So he got me again?" I asked tightly. "He threw the knife and I got it in the back."

This time the man looked at me.

"I'd rather not discuss it."

"I think you should. I sell fairly and I've never had a customer who did-n't pay when his payment was due. Cars can be a greater risk. A man can ruin a car in a month. But people take care of their television sets."

A long silence hung between us. I sat there until he broke in.

"This is simply a matter of policy, Mr. Sampson. If you sell to someone who can handle a note on his own, we'll be glad to accept it. But we do have to consider the amount of paper you have outstanding. It's true that the payments come in but what if they did not? Could you cover the obligation?"

"Everybody wouldn't default. Use the same rule for almost any man in business and you'd ruin him." I paused. "Is that what Mr. Condon wants to do to me?"

"I suggested before that you talk to him."

"Which I did, but I could have accomplished as much if I'd talked to myself."

He was uncomfortable, not liking what I said, but he knew it was the truth. Condon, if his dislike for my father was so great, might have had some excuse for blocking my loan, but it was cruel and unfair of him to go this far.

"I'll manage," I said, and got to my feet. But I did not know how I was going to manage. "I'll get along."

"Frankly, I hope that you do."

"Yeah. Thanks."

I felt miserable. I could not keep selling television sets and financing them myself. It was like having a well with only a limited flow of water. Pump steadily and the well goes dry.

It was a foolish thing for me to do but I drove over to Condon's Lumber Yard again. I had had enough of him, too much. They would jail me if I slapped him around, but it would be worth it. At least I would get rid of my anger and he would be aware that there was somebody in town who was not afraid to fight back.

But I did not see him.

His secretary would not let me—unless I hit her first, and I could not bring myself to do that.

I left there in a rage.

A blind furious rage.

Chapter 6

I should have made some service calls that night but I did not. I was sore at the whole damned world. A person works hard and plans and then some character pulls the floor out from under him. That's the kind of thing that makes people fight wars or jump off bridges.

There wasn't much of anywhere to go, so I stopped off at the hotel where Ben had a room. It had no class as far as hotels go, but it had a bar that was lively. Some girls who made fair money hung out there and if one of them happened to like you there was an excellent chance you would not sleep alone. I had thought of seeing Kathy, but her father was probably in from the road, and even if he was out I knew just how it would end for us. It would end with her twisting body fighting to get closer to mine and afterward we would both be sorry, the fear of the possible consequences tormenting her and keeping me awake.

I was surprised to find Ben at the bar. He smelled fresh and clean, and the suit he was wearing appeared new and fairly expensive. He was not drinking his usual beer, but a highball.

"You hit a gold mine?" I asked him.

"Let's say I had a little luck."

I ordered a bottle of beer. I guess the hotel made more money from bottled beer or it was less trouble. They never had any on draft.

"Somebody buy your stock and equipment?" I inquired, still curious.

"Not yet. I was going to give you a proposition on that stuff."

"Sorry, but I wouldn't want to part with the cash."

"How come?"

"Because things are rough and getting worse."

"They shouldn't be."

"No, but they are."

He pushed his empty glass forward.

"If I could unload I'd blow this town," he declared. "As soon as I could. Tonight. Tomorrow. Even yesterday if that was possible."

"Maybe you do need a change."

"Nobody knows it more than me."

He did not talk to me very long. A couple of girls were at the end of the bar, both of them rather cute, and their roaming eyes said they were available. He had no difficulty getting in between them. He ordered a round of drinks right away. They switched from beer to hard liquor but that was nothing new. Many girls do that when they are not paying. The only thing new was his sudden prosperity.

I got sick of the bar after a while, and left. The beer had helped a little to kill the tension, but I was still burning inside and hating Ferris Condon's guts. I knew it was wrong. Nobody should hate another person. You should try to look at the situation from the other side, but I could not do it in this case. My father had done his job right, and Condon had been the crook.

I had several more drinks in another bar—somehow I needed what did not taste good to me—and then I bought a six-pack. I realized that it made no sense, that I would not have done it unless I had been drinking, but I headed for Fossard Street. The memory of Kathy in my arms kept coming back to me. I kept telling myself that if somebody was going to have it with her it might as well be me. If I gave her what she did not want, what no single girl wants, I would just have to marry her and make the best of it. Besides, I could think of a lot worse arrangements than that. I could think—well, why not be honest about it? I had reached a point where I did not care any more—where tomorrow was something to stay away from, when the only time that counted was now.

There was a light in the kitchen when I got there, none in the living room—if her father were home he was watching television—and I stomped up the back-porch steps, kicking over one of the milk bottles that always seemed to be standing around at the top of the steps. It made a terrible racket going down but it did not smash on the cement.

She came to the door right away, turning on the overhead light and looking outside.

"You and those bottles," she said and let me in.

"Yeah, I must be allergic to them."

She wore a plain robe, but on Kathy it looked good.

"I never know any more when you're coming," she said.

I ripped two cans of beer from the six-pack, found an opener in one of the drawers, punched holes in them, and put the remaining cans in the refrigerator.

"Do you mind?" I asked as I got out glasses.

"You know I don't, but my father might."

"He working?"

"He had a date of some sort."

"Well, you can't blame him for that. A man isn't meant to live alone."

"No, but I feel sorry for the woman."

"Why?"

"Because he wouldn't marry again and there's only one reason why he'd date her. She's a widow and I suppose they both miss what they were used to having."

"So who can hate them for that?"

"It's not decent."

She wanted to watch the news and we carried our beer into the living room, sitting there on the sofa where it had happened before. She was a bug on the news, but I couldn't see much sense to it. Somebody was always stirring up conditions in the world and somebody else was trying to calm things down. To me it was like a race with the horses going in opposite directions.

When the news was finished, she shut off the set and got fresh beer from the kitchen.

"Kept your old job, huh?" I said as she sat down again.

"Well, we got straightened out. I thought it was better. There's late work on the paper and I don't have that at the office."

"What about the guy who was bothering you?"

"He'll be all right."

"Yeah, sure."

She turned to look at me seriously.

"What's the matter, Hob? You sound as if you thought he got what he wanted from me."

"I wouldn't ask a question like that."

"You don't have to, but I'll answer it anyway. He didn't and he never will. There's been you and nobody else."

The next time I got the beer and that was the last of it.

"I saw Ben," I said, for no good reason. "He's in the money."

"In the money? I don't understand."

"You're not the only one. He was at the hotel bar and he was dressed sharp. He seemed to have cash to burn. I wish I did. They even cut off my credit at the bank."

Suddenly she leaned forward, holding the glass in her hands, her shoulders hunched.

"I think I'll go to bed," she said at last.

"Why?"

"I'm tired and—and upset."

"What about?"

"I don't know, Hob." She was plainly annoyed. "Can't a girl have a mood?"

"Yeah, but I thought...."

"Never mind what you thought." She got up from the sofa. "You can sit here if you want but you'll sit alone."

All I could do was leave. When I tried to kiss her good night she twisted her head at the last second and my mouth touched only her cheek. She had never been so cold before. I could not understand her.

I stumbled over the darn bottle again as I walked to the car and I kicked it off into the grass. They say you can lose a woman by sleeping with her and a friend by giving him money. I had committed both sins with Kathy.

There were places I could have gone, probably girls I could have picked up, but I abandoned the thought and drove toward the shop. I could not afford to blow my money anyway, and the idea of having a girl just for pleasure did not appeal to me. As much as it hurt, I was glad that Kathy had drawn the line. For her own good, she had acted wisely. Then, too, there was her father to consider. He could have had his fun early and walked in on us. That would have created a scene.

A car was parked in front of the shop and I parked behind it. I did not pay any attention to it when I walked past.

"Hello, chicken," someone said as I was fitting the key into the lock.

I paused for a moment, freezing. The voice belonged to a woman, a woman I knew.

Slowly, I turned.

It was the blond.

She came toward me, the white sheath curving down over her body, the click of her high heels sounding like pistol shots in the stillness of the night. She had a sensual roll to every movement. Although I could not see her face clearly I had the impression she was smiling.

"You're chicken," she said as she reached me. She was smiling, her head tilted as she looked up at me.

"So I couldn't do the job," I said thickly.

"Or you didn't want to do it?"

"Have it your way. You're the one who's telling me."

"Some creep you sent out there for your set. He smelled like a barn in hot weather."

"I was busy."

"Naturally. Oh, of course. Busy. Busy doing nothing."

She had an odor about her that was utterly feminine, an odor that reminded me of spring mint, the kind of mint that grows along mountain streams. I supposed it was perfume, but it was more exciting than others I had smelled.

"Your husband wouldn't think much of it if he knew you were here," I said. "He'd kick your cute little fanny all the way down the street."

"You think so? Just let him try it."

"He wouldn't only try it—he'd do it."

She shrugged. "Well, he can't know. He's playing cards."

I nodded, unable to see myself playing cards if I were married to her. All I could see was a bedroom with a soft light and her naked body stretched out on the bed, that smile of hers inviting me and her blond hair spilling out over the pillow.

"I hope he loses," I said. "I hope he loses his damned shirt."

"He won't. He doesn't play to lose. He never loses. He wins all the way down the line."

I pulled out cigarettes and lit two. I had the feeling that I ought to go inside and leave her but I did not. Her eyes put the fix on me just as a cat does with a bird; the bird goes crazy and tumbles from one limb to another until the cat snaps him up.

"Thanks," she said and filled her lungs with smoke, the front of her pushing forward as she did so. "I forgot mine and I was going wild waiting for you." She laughed. "Waited for you while you went bar crawling."

"Nobody told you to wait."

"Can't I do what I want?"

I looked past her and up the street.

"Not with another man," I replied.

She was suddenly and unreasonably furious. But it was a poor choice of words.

"Are you saying I'm anybody's woman?"

"No. Far from it."

"Well, don't. I'm supposed to be his woman and that is pretty hard to write off."

"So why bother with me?"

"That's simple. I was curious about you and the way you acted. I've got the money to pay for the work and you just won't do it. You should have heard Ferris curse at dinner because the set hadn't been repaired. He even tried to get somebody else but he didn't have any luck. He went storming out of the house but not before—"

"Before what?" I wanted to know as she hesitated.

"Before—oh, you know. Why does a man live with a woman?"

I realized what she meant and I hated his filthy insides. I could not accept the thought of his using her for his enjoyment. There was no honest cause for the instantaneous jealousy, unless it was what he had done to me. But the jealousy was there and it tugged at me like something alive and wiggling in my guts.

"He's ruined me," I said. "Or he's going to ruin me."

"Yes, he mentioned that at dinner. I tried to get to the bottom of it, but he just said you were no good."

"It's not me who's no good. It's he. Why should he hop on me for something my father did? It's no wonder his wife left him. What is he—some kind of a nut or something? He doesn't have a dime to gain from what he's doing—not a cent. Most men wouldn't waste their time."

But I knew better than that. I knew that proud men were capable of bitterness, that they waited their chance, then seized the advantage.

"Nobody knows him better than I do," she said. "And I couldn't tell you what kind of a man he is. I just know that he's rich and that he pays for what he gets from me. If he won't buy me the things I want, I sleep in one of the guest rooms. Sooner or later he buys them."

"That's the same as selling yourself."

"More than one woman does it that way. If the old man won't come across, he sleeps alone."

She was wrong but I did not think less of her for it. She had a miserable mate and she was using the only weapon she had. Obviously they were not on good terms, they were drawn and held together simply because each had what the other needed.

"I'd better go up," I said. "And you'd be smart to go home."

"What about my television set?"

"Try somebody else in the morning."

"Am I poison?" she asked.

"No. You're beautiful and that's the trouble."

Her laugh was low.

"You're scared, aren't you? You're scared of me."

"Let's just say that a fire isn't always easy to put out."

She flipped her cigarette into the gutter and moved all the way up to me, crowding me against the locked door. The fullness of her breasts pressed against my chest, and her tilted face was serious.

"You big lug, I like you," she breathed. "Can't you get that through your thick skull? What does a girl do about a man she really likes? Club him over the head? Take his hand and lead him to whatever they might find together. Is that...."

"Cut it out." My voice sounded as if it belonged to somebody else. It was strained and hoarse. "You're married and...."

"Shut up." Her body was hot as she pushed forward, her breath rushing out of her lungs. "I liked the looks of you when I saw you in the bar that night and when you came out to the house I liked you more. Then you kissed me, just as though you liked me too, and then this morning—this morning I wanted it to be you. I could have sent the woman to the store and Ferris was at the office. But, no, you wouldn't come. You sent out some smelly guy who raped me with his eyes and got a cheap thrill for himself. That's why I waited for you tonight. I want to know if there's anything between us or not."

Right then there was nothing between us. I could feel the sweep of her curves, the fullness of her thighs pressed to my legs. The sweat came down into my eyes, blinding me.

"Cripes," I said, fighting to control my natural instincts. "Do you know what we could do to each other, what it could mean?"

"Is such a thing unusual?"

"I don't know."

"It isn't. A young girl marries a man of sixty and she looks for more than just money, more than just a big home and a husband who can't always be a man. I'm only twenty-two, reaching my peak if you can believe what you read, and I need somebody, need him terribly. But, I need somebody who doesn't want me simply because of my body but wants me as a person. I can't talk with Ferris the way I can with a man close to my own age. Nearly forty years between us is a gulf we can't cross. I've tried and I can't. When I try, when I tell him, for instance that I don't want his child because he would never live to see it grow up, he's apt to beat me. He...."

"Huh?"

"Beat me. With his fists. Once he did it with a shoe and I couldn't get out of bed for two days. He didn't care. He didn't care how much I suffered."

My arms lifted from my sides and went around her.

"That lousy bastard," I said violently. "The dirty lousy bastard."

Gratefully, she clung to me.

"He's all that and more. Nobody knows. Nobody can understand. One night he's sweet, too sweet, syrupy sweet—then the next night he hauls off and slaps me in the face."

"No man has that right."

"Maybe not, but he takes it."

My mouth found her lips and lingered over them. They were more urgent than they had been before. Her lips parted, the tip of her tongue searching frantically.

"Leave him," I said. "Cut the rope and turn him adrift."

"I will, but not until I get what I want. Not until I have what I've earned. And not until I've helped you."

"Helped me?"

"Why not? I think I can. You'll need money and I think I can force it out of him."

I kissed her again.

"I don't want his money," I said.

She pulled back her head.

"Stop being so moral. Is there any reason not to take it? Look what he's done to you, stepping on you because you're trying to get along and he's a big shot. The old crumb. Strip, he tells me. Walk around the bedroom and let me see what you look like." With a swift movement she pulled my head down and kissed me hard on the mouth. "I'd much rather show you than show him. How about it?"

She was there in my arms, the surge of passion that went through her body demanding and insistent. Here I was, just a little guy with everything to lose—everything I had not already lost, that is.

"Not tonight," I said, forcing myself to refuse, knowing that after she was gone I would hunger for her.

With a vicious thrust she fought loose of my arms.

"I said you were chicken," she reminded me as she walked toward her car. "I guess I was right."

"Hey, now I—"

"Good night, jerk."

She tore off in a burst of screaming rubber. I turned away from my door. I knew I could not sleep now, that I would only lie in bed staring up at the dark ceiling, remembering my wild urges as her body had been pressed to mine and living with the realization that I could have had her.

I got in the Ford and drove toward Orchard Street. This was foolish but I knew there was a woman down there who could ease this torment in me. If it had to be for money there was no other way now. Something strange had happened to Kathy, something that had suddenly caused her to deny me, but my own actions with the blond were even stranger. Why, actually, had I denied her? I did not know. Yet I thought Kathy had been right, at least from her point of view, and by the same token I had been right to turn down Doris Condon.

But I needed relief.

The woman must have been asleep because she was yawning as she opened the door.

"What do you want?" she asked.

I walked past her into the apartment. "What do you think?" I snapped.

She laughed and closed the door.

"Come with me," she said. "Let's see whether or not it's a waste of time."

It wasn't.

Not one minute of that half hour was wasted.

I felt cheap as I left.

What had it proven?

Nothing, except that man is half animal.

Chapter 7

I woke up with the extension phone upstairs ringing and spoiling a wild dream about the blond. Blindly, I stumbled to the phone and picked it up. "Yeah?" I said.

"C.S. Potter," the old man answered. "Thought I'd tell you I'm selling the building and you can take it from there."

I looked out of the window. There was nothing to look at.

"Who bought it?"

"Ferris Condon. Sight unseen. He just called me."

I continued to look out of the window but there was still nothing to catch my eye. The year before a girl had lived over there in an apartment that was now vacant and she had been very careless about drawing her blinds. Not once had I intended watching her but a man can't help noticing a naked female. I had dated her twice and found out what she liked. It had not been television.

"Thanks," I told Mr. Potter. "I might as well hang myself with a strong rope from a high limb. Maybe I'll even set fire to the building and collect my insurance. That's quicker than a panic sale."

He laughed, wished me luck and hung up. I was not laughing but I did have to look at it logically. The building could be repaired and rented out for more money than I was paying. After all, it contained not only a store downstairs but an apartment above that. So Condon might very well be buying it as an investment. I certainly felt that he would not put out that much cash just to satisfy an old grudge. I was well aware that he had no use for me, but I figured he liked money too much not to look out for it. No explanation that I could devise made any sense, unless it was simply that he was trying to harm me.

The blond....

I wished now that I had taken her, that I had taken pleasure from what Condon owned, that I had not been a pig and gone down there to Orchard Street the night before. Orchard Street was no place for a decent man to go except, maybe, to fix a television set.

While I shaved and showered, I cursed, not just Condon alone but myself, too. I should have seen this coming, should have worked a little harder to prevent it. But how? A man can only do so much. There are twenty-four hours in a day and some of those hours are for sleep. Besides, I was not the only man in Hawley doing television repairs. There were two others who were pretty good, and a couple who were not.

I guess I thought about giving up the business but I was twenty-five and

I did not have the knack for anything else. Of course, there were other towns, but that meant starting all over again, and I could not see that. If I took that bigger store uptown and put in appliances, I would have to dig in the dirt for a while, but I might be able to make it. I had only one thing against selling appliances. I did not know how to service them, had no time and no way to learn. Hiring someone would be too great an expense. I expected the salesman to call that day and decided I would talk to him about it. I had heard there were some companies set up so that you could get repairs from them in an emergency, but I could not be sure.

Since I had made no service calls the night before, I did not have much work to do on the bench when I got downstairs and I just fooled around, struggling with a radio that wouldn't play and was in such terrible condition that it should have gone into the junk pile. But the people liked the radio, actually taking pride in the fact that it was so old. They kept it in their family room where their friends must have gotten a kick out of it. I finally gave up and put it aside. I just did not feel like doing anything.

I got three phone calls for service that morning, one a repeat from the day before and the woman was sore. I told her that I was up to my ears in things and that she would just have to take her turn. She said she would not and hung up. I scratched her name from the list.

During the noon hour a young fellow came in, a fellow of about nineteen. He picked out a television set he liked for his widowed mother and offered to buy it on time. The fellow worked steady in a local factory and had the down payment. Yet I could not complete the sale.

Exasperated, I just closed up shop and drove over to another bank to talk to them. I finally got in to see one of the officials and the man listened to me while I explained my situation and asked for the credit I needed.

"Who would co-sign the notes with you?" he asked me.

"There isn't anybody."

"You mean, you don't know some person who would help you?"

"No. I've been too busy working. I haven't made any friends who have that kind of money. But you can check with my present bank. They can tell you that I've never had one note that went sour. People like their television sets too much to lose them. They'll make their payments even when they go hungry."

However, I did not get very far with him. It was obvious that if the bank I had been doing business with was not interested in me, he wasn't either. He finally said he would look into it, and took my name and address. I was pretty sure that he would not. It was just a polite way of getting rid of me.

After that, I tried one of the finance companies but it was just about what I had expected. The fellow there said they would entertain applications from the people who bought from me. They charged an arm and a leg and if that were not enough to suit them, they took half of the leg that was left. In addition, he insisted that the chattel mortgage cover not only the television set but all the personal property a man had. It was the same no-down-payment gimmick that was used in big cities, especially on new cars, but I did not think the people in Hawley would go for it. Anyway I did not like the plan and I was so disgusted that I left.

The appliance salesman was waiting for me when I returned to the shop. I felt like talking to somebody and I unloaded my troubles on him. I suppose he was used to that sort of thing and he listened patiently, but even while he was listening he started closing his briefcase.

"It happens," he said when I had finished. "Happens to the best of us." Then he went on, "Your question about service on appliances is easy. We have a company man in the area, which takes that problem out of the picture. But we're a little premature in considering anything right now. What you say about your bank is probably true enough, but it's a reflection on your credit and my sales manager wouldn't be happy if I took an order from you. He could talk to the bank about you but they'd never tell him the real reason and he'd figure that you'd just screwed things up for yourself. That doesn't mean that I don't believe you, that this guy puts the blocks to you, because I do. I can only say that it's a hell of a way for a bank to operate. It's often true that in a small town one man can have too much power. One man can make you or break you and it looks like you are being broken. Still, I'll try to do what I can. I don't promise anything. With the floor plan you mentioned we have you post a bond and there might be difficulty getting one. You can see why we need a bond. A man might order a dozen refrigerators from us, sell them all, pay us nothing and we'd have to sue for our dough."

I did not feel any better after he left and I tried to think the whole affair through. I had never cheated anyone. I had done my best and now I needed money behind me. Where did I go for it?

The blond.

I shook my head. She had been sore at me the night before and she would be just as sore now. Anyhow, I did not see how she could get that much money. Condon was no fool. He might or might not be generous with her but in either case probably she had to account for every cent.

But I kept thinking of her.

I could see her running naked from the pool—see her in the red dress that showed the wet spots—see her at the bar in the living room, her cleavage deep and inviting, her breasts thrusting out against the material. I wanted her, no doubt about that. My need for her exceeded any need that I had ever felt before.

How wonderful it had been the previous night, with her body pressed to mine, the door hard behind me, my mouth feeling the passion of her lips, the white sheath straining over her breasts, all the female of her searching and craving for the one thing that was male.

Lovely....

And she was Condon's wife, a beautiful wife who had been bought with his money and who no longer wanted her marriage. Living with her would be constant excitement. Yes, living with her, giving her children—but how would I be able to pay the bills? Poverty, stark and real; she would not want that and neither would I.

She answered the phone when I called. She was cool and distant.

"I only try once," she said. "Once and I count you out."

"Sorry, but I was upset."

"You were chicken. Don't tell me you weren't. You were. A big guy and chicken all the way through. Why should I bother with you?"

"I was thinking about fixing your television," I lied. "Like driving into New York for the tube and doing what I should."

"Ferris already took care of that. He doesn't want you around and he'd smash the thing with his fist if you put it in."

I looked at the ceiling.

"That little bar where I first saw you," I said. "Think you can make it?"

"Why should I? You weren't much of a man last night." She laughed. "Man? I could have made out better with some school kid."

"All right," I shouted savagely. "Find yourself a school kid."

I slammed down the phone and cursed. Yet I had no cause to curse or to be sore. She had waited for me, taking a chance, probably a long chance, and I had not been a man. I had been afraid of her, more so than the first time.

After that disappointing call I prowled through the shop, looking at the display and wishing that I could sell everything for cash on the line. Was I weak? Maybe with her I was and yet I had to have her, had to know her, terribly and violently but also with a tenderness that I had never shown another woman. The night before she had offered herself, practically begged for the joy of being utterly female, and I had not had the guts to rise to the occasion.

Ben came in then with part of a six-pack of beer. I was not exactly glad to see Ben but the beer looked all right. We went out back and opened a couple of cans.

"That bitch," he said sourly. "The one I was with last night."

I decided that he had not had any fun with her.

"You can't always win," I told him. "Some of them never heard of the word yes."

He shook his head.

"Oh, she came across all right. I stoned myself on that liquor and she clipped me. Took everything I had except some change and a couple of dollars that she missed."

"Tough."

"How do you prove a thing like that?"

"I don't know. Her word is as good as yours."

"She was just drifting through town. We went to her room and this morning she was gone."

"Live and learn, Ben."

He leaned against the bench.

"How about ten?"

"No." I was firm about that.

"It ain't much," he protested.

I wanted the other can of beer but he got it before I did.

"You don't know the half of it, Ben. They stopped my credit at the bank, and now this building has been sold. I'm worse off than when I started out."

He did not ask any questions about it and I did not go into things any deeper. It was no concern of his and the money he had had was no affair of mine, either, but I did wonder about it. A man who is flat in the morning and flush at night has to have made a strike somewhere.

The phone rang and some woman wanted me to bring out a set for a demonstration right away, so I told Ben I was closing up. He went outside, climbed in his old truck and drove off. The woman had not said whether I should bring a table model or a console but I picked out a table model and loaded it into the station wagon. The set was a year old and I thought I could turn it into cash if I brought the price down far enough. Money in my pocket was better than having the investment sit in the shop.

Calls like that don't come in very often and most of them are pretty good. Once a set is in a person's house they are almost obligated to buy it from you. Oh, there are those who shop around, but the average buyer is inclined to be honest and show consideration.

When I reached the house, I carried the set up to the front door and the woman let me in. She was about forty, somewhat on the dumpy side and her faded wash dress was dirty. She explained that they had had a television but that her husband had dropped the thing while moving it. I could see that all the important tubes were smashed, and some of the major parts.

I hooked up the unit, showed her how well it worked, saw that she was pleased with the reception and I gave her the price in cash.

"I never pay cash," she said with determination. "You pay cash and then you can't get anybody to fix what you've bought if something goes wrong."

I tried to reason with her but it was hopeless. In disgust I unhooked the set and took it out to the car. Everybody was credit queer and if you could not extend it you were licked. Maybe I could have gone along with her, or should have, but I did not want to find myself with a lot of money outstanding and nothing coming in.

There was a drugstore in the next block and I stopped there to call Kathy at her office. She came on, her voice cheerful until she found out who it was. She turned down my invitation to dinner. She even said that it might be smart if I did not visit the house any more. When I asked why, she said she was busy and disconnected us.

Back outside, I sat in the car and turned it over in my mind. If I had wanted to be a hog, I would have gotten sore over that three hundred dollars I had given her, but it hardly seemed worthwhile. I could use the three hundred all right, but it was not enough to save me. The way I saw it nothing would do that. I had put some slim hopes on the blond; however, she had finished with me before anything could happen.

I considered driving over to see Condon but I knew that it would not do any good. There was nothing I could say that might have even the slightest chance of changing his attitude.

I rode down to the shop and put the television set in the window with a special price on it. Somebody might come along and be smart enough to grab a bargain.

After that I went to the newspaper office and arranged to have a display ad run as soon as possible. The ad man helped me with it and we headed up the ad: EARN DOLLARS WITH YOUR CASH. I featured some terrific buys for cash only and he said I ought to pull in business. I did not know whether or not I would but it was worth trying. If I could raise enough money to get established in a new location, Condon would be out of my hair and me out of his.

"You missed hiring a good girl," I said to the ad man for no good reason at all. "Too bad she changed her mind."

"A girl? We haven't needed a girl in months."

"Funny. I thought you did."

"You thought wrong. Once a girl comes with us she stays until she gets married or pregnant. Even then they come back. Conditions here are excellent."

It was something more for me to think about as I walked to my car. Why had Kathy lied? If she had lied about the job, wasn't it possible that she had also lied about her reason for wanting the money? I could not see just how the two fitted together, but the impression that they did fit was too strong for me to shake off.

Mulling it over, I had to admit that Kathy seemed thoroughly despicable.

She had known what three hundred dollars meant to me and yet she had taken it. Maybe she had lifted the money from the firm, and maybe the partner had had his fun with her. I had been the first, but I knew—or thought I knew—that I would not be the last. Awaken the average reluctant virgin to sex, and she quickly becomes its greatest fan.

When I was almost to Orchard Street I changed direction and headed for the little bar where I had first seen the blond.

Chapter 8

In the beginning my luck was as bad in the bar as it had been trying to sell that television set. Ben's truck was not parked out front but he was at the bar, trying to sell the suit of clothes he had been wearing the night before.

"I wish you were shorter," he said to me. "This suit is a steal."

I ordered beer for both of us.

"You nuts or something, Ben?"

"Sure. Over money."

"Why buy clothing one day and sell it the next?"

"I told you. It's because of that dame. She just about cleaned me."

I drank some of my beer.

"Where's your truck?"

"On South Street. Blew a tire, and I have no spare. Last week I sold the spare, wheel and all. How rotten can things get?"

"Let me know. You're finding out the hard way." Suddenly I had a desperate idea. "What about your folks?" I asked. "If you'd straighten up we could try it together again. We'd need money but they've got it, haven't they?"

He laughed. "I'm the black sheep, as black as midnight without the moon. The old man would laugh in my face if I so much as asked for a dime."

I finished my beer and had another. It had been a stupid thought, anyway. It would not work even if he could get the money. He would steal just as he always had.

Before he left he got a couple of bucks out of me—who could say no to a couple of bucks?—and he told me he was going to hit some other bars, offering the suit for whatever it would bring. No matter how much he got for it, the money would do him no good. The dough would only add up to a few drinks, a free-wheeling dame, and a flat wallet in the morning.

I was on my third or fourth beer when she came in.

She had on that same white sheath dress and she looked even better than she had that first time. How she stayed inside that beautiful rag I could not imagine. She pushed up and out in front and everything she had threatened to spill outside.

"Go ahead and say it," she told me as she sat down. "I'm crazy. Blame it on the lousy heat."

"The old man playing cards again?"

"Better yet. He's out of town looking at some lumber. Won't be back till tomorrow night."

"Picking up some more crap to sell the suckers?"

"So who cares? Nobody holds a gun to their heads."

I hoped she would limit herself to beer because of my money situation, but she wanted a stinger.

"He bought the building I'm in," I confided.

"He told me. He also told me that you'll have to move."

"Well, he's got the whip hand."

"What are you going to do?"

"Let's put it in another way. What can I do?"

Eying the juke box, she said she wanted to dance. I was more than willing.

She kicked off her high heels and danced with me in her stocking feet. The first number was fine, the way it should be, with our bodies not too close together and not too far apart. But during the next number, she came in tight and warm, her breasts hard against my chest. When I shoved her into a corner, my mouth crazy for her lips, she returned the kiss wildly, fiercely, and she did not care who saw us. Our hearts were beating madly as we drifted back to the bar.

We stayed until midnight and it was as if there were no other people in the world, only us. Unaware of anything save our own desires, we danced several times, clinging close, her body bending to mine, her mouth waiting to receive my kisses. Maybe I was getting even with Ferris Condon in some way, but there was more to it than that, far more. I saw her in a house or an apartment—a house would be better—I saw her stomach swollen out of shape, her breasts bigger and heavier because of the child she was carrying. My child. The child who would bear my name, who would grow up a better man than I was or ever would be. Some of what I felt must have been in my eyes because her kisses were tender, yielding, and she stood up on her toes as I crushed her to me. Her breath came in rushes, an animal sound in her throat.

"We've got to get out of here," I said. "If we don't I'll go mad and kill the bartender so we can be alone."

"We can go out to my place. The woman is staying with her daughter for the night."

"My apartment would be safer."

We had to take both cars and I let her lead. As I drove, Kathy came back into mind. Kathy had not leveled with me, had not been honest. Her need for the money confused me. No matter how I added it up, it did not come out right. If she had taken money from the firm, or if she had not given in to the flesh-seeking partner, they would not have kept her, I reasoned. Then there had been the lie about the job in the newspaper office. Any way I looked at it, I came out of the deal hanging to the short end of the

stick. I did not like to be taken for a sucker by somebody I had trusted—
and loved.

Scowling, I followed the car in front of me. Doris would help me bury
every hurt I had ever known. She was so full of love that nothing else
would matter. The three hundred bucks was a loss but I would get over it.
Maybe Kathy liked Ben Stucker enough to go to the sofa with him. All
right, to hell with it. To hell with Kathy and to hell with Ben. There was
something between them that I did not know about, perhaps would never
know. I could not have cared less as I parked in front of the shop and got
out of the car.

She was first to the door.

"You got anything to drink?" she asked as I took out my key.

"No beer."

"I don't want any beer."

The door swung open.

"I might have a bottle of rye," I said. "Somebody gave it to me last Christmas when I fixed a set but I don't know what I did with it."

She waited at the bottom of the stairs while I switched on the light.

"Probably some woman killed it for you."

"There's been no woman up there."

"Don't hand me that. You're human, aren't you?"

I remembered the girl from across the alley.

"All right," I said. "A couple of times. But they weren't women, not your
kind. Just women. And I think there was only one. She was some sort of a
nut."

We went up the stairs to the apartment. When I flicked on the switch
in the living room I was ashamed of the place. It was adequate for a working guy, somebody trying to get along and save, but it was no place to
bring a beautiful girl. All the furniture had been bought used and whoev-
er had used it had not taken care of the stuff. There was one end of the
sofa that was downright dangerous. If you sat on that end, you got the
sharp end of a spring where you did not want it.

"What a dump," she said, looking around. Then she laughed. "But it's not
the first time I've been in one."

"And it won't be the last."

"Won't it? I'd never go back to something like this." She threw her pocketbook on a chair. "Believe me, I've seen it all, Hob. I saw it the same as this
and worse. Worse when I was a kid. Nobody worked and everybody drank.
I'd go out at night and come in and anything could be going on. Two to a
bed. Three to a bed. As many people as could get into one bed and all after
the little pound of flesh." She yawned. "Why don't you sell air condition-
ers? You could use one up here."

I kissed the back of her neck, and then I started looking for that bottle of rye. I had trouble finding it. The kitchen yielded nothing except a box of dry cereal, so I tried the closet. I saw that the girl who had been so willing had left some of her personal things behind and I pushed them out of sight where I had left them in the closet. Next came a fishing pole that I no longer used and a box of tackle that had been upset. Finally, I reached the bottle and wiped the dust from it with an old shirt.

"Cheap junk," I told her. "This won't match the proof of what you've been drinking."

She was examining some photographs that I had hanging in the living room and she stopped in front of one of my mother. "She's pretty," Doris said.

"Yes. My mother was always a pretty woman. Even the last time I saw her she looked twenty years younger than her age and she still had her shape."

Doris glanced at me, smiling.

"What about my shape?"

"Yours? Hell, yours is the most."

I went out to the kitchen, opened the bottle and got down a couple of glasses. There were some ice cubes in the refrigerator and I added a few of those. I wanted the rye about as much as I wanted Condon in my hair but when you're looking forward to something like Doris, you'll drink poison.

She was seated on the sofa when I returned to the living room. I sat down close to her.

"This is sort of silly," she said.

"Maybe."

"I knew you'd be at that bar and I told myself I wasn't going after you, but I did. If you had fixed our television the way you were supposed to, I might have stayed home."

"People do what they want to do."

"Always?"

"Pretty generally."

She laughed softly.

"Just what do you want to do, Hob?"

"I think our minds met on that before, or you wouldn't be here."

She sipped her drink and the sheath was up high on her legs, above her knees. Her knees were rounded and smooth under the nylons with none of the ugliness that some girls have. She had kicked off her shoes and she sat there curling her toes into the rug.

"He's got you in a bad fix," she said. "Hasn't he?"

"Yeah. Very."

"You have to do something."

"What I do is up to you."

"Me?"

I leaned toward her.

"Yes, you. You said I was chicken but I'm like the guy who goes to a race track and doesn't bet. You can't win so why be a sucker? Maybe your husband doesn't own the whole town but he's got the influence and the money. I'm going to sell what I've got and I'm going to go somewhere else. This morning I was determined to fight but I can see how hopeless that would be. He's doing this to me because he couldn't buy my father. He—oh, to hell with the guy. I know my field and I can make a living but I want you along. Our first kiss wasn't an accident. It was one of those things bound to happen. So you take it from there. You quit the big slob and we go it together."

She finished her drink. "Do you realize what you're asking me to do?"

"Absolutely. It won't be easy at the start. We'll have to watch our dimes and hang on to the dollars but I'll get a few thousand out of my stock and we won't starve. My mother said they needed a good television man where she lives. I've never been to California but it should be pretty nice, living there. My father has everything tied up in mutual funds but I guess they're security at a bank and he ought to be able to help us. We'll open a small shop and grow as we can. We're young and we've got time."

She thought about it for a moment.

"Get me another drink," she said. "And that is lousy rye. They should be shot for selling it."

I finished my own drink and got two more. I took a long while doing it. I knew what I was asking her to do, what I meant for her to give up. Even though I lived to be a hundred I would never have the kind of money Ferris Condon had.

"You've got to be sensible about this," she said when I returned to her. She was sitting up, her eyes wide and blue, her hair hanging like a golden cloud around her face. "What if we did do that? I've got no objection to California but only to the future. You'd have me pregnant in a couple of months—don't say you wouldn't because you would—and there'd be a kid. After the kid there'd be bills, perhaps more kids, and we'd go to our graves still struggling."

"It wouldn't be as bad as that," I protested.

"But it would, Hob, and you have to see that. I—I could be terribly in love with you, more than I should be, or I wouldn't sit here with you, but Ferris is my man and when I leave him, I intend to take my share."

"You won't get it."

"I will."

"How?"

"There are ways."

"Only divorce, and if you're the guilty party, which you would be, he wouldn't have to give you anything."

"Hob, I said there were ways." She sounded annoyed.

"Then you tell me."

"No, not now."

"When?"

"I have to think about it. He—did you know that he was going to run for mayor?"

"I didn't, but it doesn't surprise me."

"Not on any regular ticket because he's never been active in politics and he wouldn't be able to get the endorsement. So he'll run alone and he thinks he's got a good chance. He's got some important people behind him, also outside of politics, but the paper won't get the news for a week or so. Every plan I have hangs on that."

I nursed my drink.

"He has to have everything," I said.

"Yes, and he usually gets what he wants. Maybe he missed with your father, but he caught up with you."

"And he got you," I pointed out. "He saw you and he got you. Sixty years old and he owns your body."

"You're wrong. He doesn't own it. He just uses it."

I put my arm around her shoulders.

"Who does own it, Doris?"

She gave me a kiss on the mouth. "If you don't know, just keep on guessing."

I upset my drink as my mouth crushed down over her lips. I heard her glass go, too, but I did not care about the rug. My hand moved down inside the front of her dress and I felt the naked swell under my palm, the gathering hardness at the center of her breast. She twisted toward me, forcing my hand to leave her, and her lips parted, some strange and wonderful sound coming from deep in her throat. Her hands went to my hair, her fingers digging in, her teeth suddenly biting furiously at my lower lip. I tasted blood, and my arms crushed her to me. She cried out and clung to me, biting again, hurting.

Seconds later she was out of my arms, her face flushed. Standing in front of me she began working at the dress. She lifted it, her legs sensual pillars of flesh under the stockings. The dress went higher, her body anxious to free itself, and soon she was wearing only a garter belt and stockings.

"Unhook them," she said.

But I did not. I tried, my hands fumbling, and then, rocked by the naked beauty of her, I could not wait.

I didn't even take her into the bedroom.

It happened right there, her lips more furious than before, her moans echoing against the walls of the room, everything she possessed mine to take, the man of me hers to receive.

"This is the best," I groaned.

And it was.

Later, she lay in my arms, smiling up at me with a tenderness that brought tears to my eyes.

"You may have to do something for me," she said.

"Anything."

She lifted her lips to my mouth.

"Are you sure, Hob?"

"Yes."

"No matter what it is?"

"Anything," I said again.

She stayed with me a couple of hours longer.

We did not talk much.

There was only one thing we wanted to do.

As often as possible.

Chapter 9

I should have gone down to open up the shop next morning but I continued to lie there on the bed. It was not that I was lazy or tired or anything like that. I was thinking.

About Doris Condon.

With the warmth of her body pressed to mine she had asked me if I would do something for her. The promise was made and now I wondered what it meant. I thought I knew. She wanted his money, or as much of it as she could get, and there was only one way in which this would be possible.

He had to be dead.

It is not pleasant to think about killing a man. But I hated Condon. The money did not really enter into it. It was simply a fringe benefit.

I thought about my father—what Condon had tried to do to him. I thought about what Condon had succeeded in doing to me. And then I thought about Doris—how he had bought her and used her—and my hatred grew strong.

I knew I would be taking a long chance if I put him in the grave, a hell of a long chance. They knew at the bank what Condon had done to me and the police would eventually come upon that bit of information. Even the way Condon had treated my father was motive enough. Men have murdered for less. For a woman. In the heat of anger. For a lousy dime.

I got up from the bed, walked into the living room, almost stumbled over one of the glasses lying on the floor, and continued on through the kitchen. I did not want the rye, but I took some anyway. The liquor burned going down. I put the bottle aside.

No, I could not do it. Killing him not only went against my every instinct, my moral scruples; it did not even make sense. Too many facts pointed in my direction and I would never get away with it. There was only one answer. She should hire somebody, if that was what she wanted done. Hiring a man to murder another man is not as simple as hiring one to fix a car or a television set. The man has to be right, has to need the money.

Who needed money?

Well, Ben did. But, of course, Ben would always need money. There was no guarantee that he would not keep coming back for more. Still, he was a logical choice. You don't find killers for hire in a small town and if you go to a big city you don't know where to look for one. It is a dangerous game and you have to be careful.

A half hour later I went down to open up the shop. The mail had already arrived—an ad for a magazine, an offer from one of those gyp insurance companies and a letter from Condon's Lumber Company. The letter was pretty much what I had expected. He was buying the building, and I had thirty days to get out. I threw the letter away. In thirty days, more than that would happen.

I had planned on seeing Doris that night, but at noon she called and said that Condon was staying in for the evening.

"Cripes," I said. "You're mine, honey."

She laughed.

"Right now it's sort of a joint ownership, isn't it? I'm yours and he thinks I'm his."

"Aw, tell him you're going to the movies."

"No. Let's not risk it. We'll have years ahead of us."

"Starting when?"

"Soon. Beautiful years for just the two of us and what we create together."

"I'll wait," I said. "But I won't like it."

I walked around the shop after she had hung up. I hated Condon's guts, thinking of him being with her, of taking his pleasure from her body because he had the power and she was helpless.

I do not know what time the girl came in but I recognized her right away. She had been with Ben the night he had tried to borrow money from me. She was just a kid, nicely developed for her age.

"You're Hob Sampson," she said. It wasn't a question. It was a statement.

"I am."

She wore a snug dress and she looked full in the stomach but I didn't think anything of it.

"I'm Sharon Bellows and you're Ben's friend." Another statement.

"I've always thought so."

She leaned against one of the television sets. "Friend enough to help him out?"

I dug for a cigarette.

"Hell, I knew he'd sell that suit and blow his money. I suppose he got into trouble and he's in jail?"

"Not yet he isn't in jail but he will be unless something is done."

"Look," I said patiently. "Ben has his problems and I have mine."

"But not the kind I've got."

"Where do you come into the picture?"

"I'm not even seventeen. I won't be seventeen until December." She smiled. "That's a terrible month for a birthday. It's too close to Christmas and you never get the presents that you should." She lost her smile. "I've got a present right now that I wish I didn't have. Ben's present."

"I follow you." I was quite sure that I did.

"Ben has talked a lot about you and I didn't know of anybody else. I— my folks told me he was too old for me, but I didn't believe them. He said he liked me a whole lot and it didn't seem wrong. I know other girls who go all the way and nothing ever happened to them. I tried to get him to— well, be careful, but he said it was okay."

"I can't help you," I said. "I only fix radios and television sets. I can't stop a girl from having a baby."

She put her hands down over her stomach, obviously terribly aware of the life inside her.

"There's a woman who can—but she wants three hundred dollars. I talked to her with Ben and she won't take any less."

"You're a fool," I told her. "Girls sometimes die from that."

She nodded thoughtfully.

"I know. But what can I do? As soon as I begin to show, my parents will kill me, anyway. Having a baby means the end of school, the end of everything. Even if Ben would marry me I wouldn't have him. I know what he is now. But he should do what he can."

"He had money the other night," I said. "A new suit of clothes and money to burn."

"Did he?"

"Yes. I saw him."

"I thought he was lying. He said somebody got the money away from him."

"I guess that's true."

She frowned and bit at her lower lip. My own lip was sore from the previous night. Doris had been a tigress, demanding and violent in her passion.

"He said he was getting the money for me. He gave me his word—and now he's broke. Even his truck can't be driven. I had to think of somebody, something. The fault is mine as much as his but if my parents knew they'd charge him with rape."

I looked away from her tragic face, from the tears in her eyes. I believed in the girl's honesty but I did not believe in Ben. I did not believe he would ever repay me. And I did not believe in abortion. You can be low, even think of killing another man, but deliberately taking the life of an unborn child is just about the bottom of the ladder.

"I'm sorry," I said. "But I can't do anything for you. This is Ben's mess. It isn't mine. It's his—and yours."

"I'll get a job and pay you back. I used to work after school until I met him. It wouldn't be much every week, maybe five dollars."

"I don't understand," I said, now looking at her again. "Almost everybody I meet wants three hundred dollars. It must be a disease that's going around."

Her hands were still over her stomach.

"Afterward I'd be good to you. You'd just have to be—"

"I'm not crazy, honey. I like girls as much as the next man, probably better, but when I can't find one over eighteen, I'll give up in a hurry."

She tried again, talking and crying, but I remained firm, and finally she left. I felt sorry for her, but what did you say to a girl like that? What could you do? It was just one of those things and Ben and she would have to make the best of it.

By three, I was feeling pretty good. A bargain-seeker had seen my sign in the window and had bought the television set for cash.

"Deliver it tonight," he said.

"You know I will."

"What about an antenna?"

"Seventy dollars, give or take a few bucks."

"Too much. How do the little ones work?"

"Not bad. It depends. I'll throw one in and we'll give it a whirl. You may have to fool with it from time to time to get the reception that you want but that's no chore."

He paid in cash and I put the money in my pocket. Figuring the length of time I had had the set and what I had sold it for I had lost money on it. But today it did not worry me. When I was not busy I loaded the set into the back of the station wagon, wrapping it in a blanket so that the cabinet would not get scratched. I was just closing the car door when Ben came along.

"I sold the suit," he said. "For twenty bucks."

"And most likely drank up the money."

He scratched his head.

"Well, I was going to get a used tire but who sells tires at night? Nobody. So I found a nice quiet bar. Yeah, the dough is gone. I should cry. Some of the dames have cars. The one last night did. Her husband's car. He's turning out glass in some factory and she's getting what he can't give her on the back seat."

We walked inside the shop.

"I wish you'd keep your women away from me," I said.

"My women?"

"Yeah. For instance the girl you got pregnant. That kid."

"She been here? How come?"

"Hell, Ben, she had to go somewhere. Maybe what she wants to have done isn't right but you'd better get with it, no matter what she asks. She can burn you."

He cursed savagely.

"The little bitch, she promised not to do anything or say anything. I told her I had the money and that I got taken. What more does she expect of me?"

"You're nuts, Ben. You see a girl and you have to get her down on the flat of her back. Fine, but sometimes there's a price. You can't ask the girl to pay it alone."

Ben fooled with the knobs on one of the television sets.

"She can't prove anything."

"She doesn't have to prove. All she has to do is say. People must have seen you with her and your reputation isn't spotless."

He looked unhappy. He knew that I had told him the truth, that the girl could destroy him.

"I'd do anything to get out of this," he said. "I had the money but I went nuts with it. I bought that suit and I needed it like I need another head. Fifty bucks it cost and I wore it one night. Sometimes I think I'm not even human."

I thought about it. He had to have money, not just for the girl but also for himself. If I had him kill Condon I would have Condon's wife and she would get his money. Cute—and deadly.

"Perhaps I'll have something for you later," I said. "Something real big."

"Swell."

"But don't go out and buy beer on the chance."

"No, but if I tell the girl it may calm her down. You're right about her spelling trouble."

I gave him a couple of bucks, just to keep him happy, and he left. The couple of bucks wouldn't take him far.

As always, there was work to be done and I did a little of it. But I was not concentrating and I knew the reason for that. The memory of the night before was tight in my belly, the lust for the blond a powerful thing, and, on top of this, my hate for Condon was growing as fast as my lust for his wife. So he was going to be the mayor of Hawley. Yeah, he would become mayor all right—the mayor of his own private hell. He would get a bullet in the guts, and how much would his money buy for him after that?

Cursing and muttering to myself, I heated up my soldering gun.

I worked through until six and then closed up the shop. Just as I was locking the door the phone rang and I let it ring. When you service television sets, people call you at any hour expecting you to be sitting beside the phone just waiting.

The phone had stopped buzzing by the time I got upstairs and I showered and changed. When I walked through the living room I looked at the sofa, remembered what I had known there with Doris, and I hated Condon all the more. The phone rang again and I picked it up.

"Hob, this is Kathy."

"Yes, Kathy?"

"I—Hob, I'm sorry I was abrupt with you when I spoke with you from the office."

"It's okay."

"Thanks. Most men would be angry."

"There's nothing to be angry about."

"It's just that—well, I'm not myself."

"So?"

"I—oh, I don't know."

She hung up and I stood there holding the phone. What had gotten into her, anyway? She had called me and she had not said a thing really. Slowly, I replaced the phone, wondering about her.

Once, I would have asked her what was bothering her, what had made her change so drastically.

But the day for asking her had gone.

The blond was a new day, a fresh beginning.

Chapter 10

My ad broke in the paper the next day, but if anybody tried to get into the shop that afternoon, I did not know about it. I was busy upstairs. Busy with the blond, just as busy as I had been with her the first time.

Finally, I got up from the bed and stood there looking down at her. She was stretched out naked, her hair a mess where I had pawed it with my hands, her lips parted in a warm smile of love.

"Crazy thing for you to come down here," I said. I was having some trouble breathing. "Real gone."

"Aren't you glad?"

"Sure, I'm glad. But what about your husband?"

"He's at the office."

"And if he goes home?"

"He won't, not until five. He's working on his announcement for the paper. I was careful, Hob. I left my car in the next block." She laughed and lifted her hands to her swollen breasts. "I thought you were going to die right there when I walked in on you."

I got my cigarettes and lit two, then handed her one. She grabbed my hand and kissed the back of it before she accepted the cigarette. I liked that and grinned at her through the smoke.

"What happens after the announcement?" I asked. "You keep saying that we're holding up for that. I've come to the point where I've got to know what's going on. It doesn't bother me when I'm loving you but afterward it does."

She rolled over and sat on the edge of the bed. I studied her legs. They were beautiful legs, just as the rest of her was beautiful. Oh, yes, there was a blue spot on one thigh where she said Condon had pinched her. The blue spot made me see red.

"You may not love me when I tell you," she said. "But that's why I came to you this afternoon. You do have to know and, I hope, understand."

"I'll always love you," I said.

"Will you?" It was a plea.

"You've got my word. I don't want anybody except you. I wanted you when we met and I want you more now."

"But when I tell you—" She paused.

"I'm used to shocks. Run a hundred and ten volts through me and I light up."

"Be serious, Hob."

"All right." Under the surface I was deadly serious. I had a fairly good idea

of what she was leading up to. Condon in his grave. "I haven't been playing games, Doris."

"You haven't, but I have. With him. An old and rotten game."

"Go on." I could not get my hand to stop shaking.

"You know how I met him. I didn't hide anything about that but there's
something I did hide. From you. From everybody. Ferris and I are the only
two who know."

"Know what?"

She patted the bed.

"Sit beside me, Hob. Hold me, honey. It'll be easier if you do."

I sat down next to her and slid my left arm around her, below the shoulders, the palm of my hand cupped over one breast.

"Give it to me straight," I said.

"People call me Mrs. Condon."

"Of course. Why shouldn't they?"

She took a deep breath, pushing out against my hand. "Because.
Because—well, because I'm not Mrs. Condon."

My fingers closed and they must have hurt her. She let out a sharp cry.
I was stunned. "What the hell are you saying?"

She moved in closer to me.

"I'm saying what I said before, that it's an old game and a rotten one. I—
things weren't good when I met him. If a girl works a convention, she's
supposed to let herself be used for one purpose and I never would. But he
didn't ask for anything out of the way and he seemed all right. He said he
was divorced from his wife, that she'd run off with a younger man—I
know now why any woman would run away from him—and he asked me
to become his wife. It—Hob, it wasn't right but what could I do? It was a
chance and I'd never had one before. He had money and I guess I thought
of outliving him and getting it. That was wrong too, but I won't apologize
for it."

"We all do things that are wrong," I said.

"That's sweet of you. I—anyway, I told you he didn't ask for anything but
that's only partly true. As soon as I said I'd marry him, he did ask and I
slept with him that night. The next day he said he had to return home
because of business, that he couldn't take the time for marriage just then
but that I could live with him and use his name. Of course I was a little
sick about it but I had gone that far and I decided not to turn back."

"So you've been his mistress ever since?"

"That's a nasty way of putting it."

"Sorry."

"I suppose it's true. His mistress. No rights, legally. Just to be used when
he wanted to use me."

I crushed out my cigarette and kissed her hard on the mouth. It was tough to know the truth but I respected her honesty. And I loved her. I had not given my love lightly and something like that, bad as it might be, could not destroy what I felt for her.

"So it's simple," I said. "We sell out what I have and move to California. There's nothing to keep us here, no reason for us to stay. We'll—"

But she was shaking her head and I knew that she meant no, that this was not the way it was going to be.

"Hob, be reasonable. Be patient. He lied to me and he's got to pay for that. He's ruined you and that's another thing he has to pay for. Whatever we can get out of him belongs to us."

"You won't get a cent," I said.

"Honey, you can't see the woods for the trees. Before this, a scandal wouldn't hurt him much, but once he's running for mayor, he can't afford bad publicity. He'll pay fifty thousand or more to prevent having his name covered with mud—I know he will."

I looked down at her legs, thinking. Probably she was smarter than I was. Condon had dug a hole for himself and she could bury him in it. And he did owe the money to her. He had ruined me. It seemed as if we had earned whatever we could get.

"You asked me to do something for you," I reminded her.

She removed my arms and lay back on the bed.

"Oh, that. I—why did I say it? I don't know. A woman loves a man, wants him to love her, and any woman could have said the same thing. I—honey, I haven't got much more time. Please."

And then I was with her again but these were the greatest of all moments since the serpent told Adam why Eve had been created. I knew now that she was mine, that there were no marriage strings to cut, that the road ahead was clear and bright for us.

She left shortly before five, our parting kiss a kiss of fire, and I got dressed. Being alone and knowing the facts, I started considering that fifty thousand dollars she had mentioned. That kind of money could mean a lot to us, really get us started off with a big splash. We could have a home and a business and not worry too much about credit. The kids could come along and I would be able to support them. Besides, I would be near my folks and I would like that. They were getting older, and nobody could say what might happen to them.

There was a man waiting for me downstairs in front of the shop and he had his Irish or Dutch or something up, because the door had been locked.

"No wonder you're having a sale," he said. "When you don't stay open, you can't make any money. Fellow, you'd have to have a sale."

"I was busy."

"It must have been important."

"Yeah. I was taking care of something that wouldn't keep."

Once inside, he calmed down considerably and he bought a set. He tried to trade in the model he had and it took me a while to explain to him that I could not afford to give an allowance at such a low price. I guess he was satisfied and I made arrangements to deliver the set the next day.

I stayed open that evening, just as I had promised in the ad, and I got a fairly big play. By eight-thirty, I had lost count of the number of sets sold, but I was pleased. I was also pleased when Ben Stucker came in, and that was unusual.

"I read your ad," he said. "You must have slipped your clutch. I know what these things cost and you aren't making a dollar."

"Who cares? I'm clearing town."

"For where?"

"California."

"Need a passenger?"

"Hardly. I'm not going alone."

He bummed a cigarette.

"Kathy, huh."

"No, not Kathy."

"Some man?"

"Forget I said anything."

"Kathy's going to be hurt, Hob."

"I doubt it."

Another customer came in and I took care of him. It was a quick sale on a portable and he took the set with him. I slid the cash into my pocket and rejoined Ben. It was plain that something was bothering him, and I came to the instant conclusion that it was money.

"I'll put a tire on your truck and you can work for me tomorrow," I said. "You can bet your last cent, which you probably haven't got, that I'm not going to deliver all this stuff by myself. Besides, I can't deliver and keep the shop open. You'll get paid for it."

"Fine."

"Just fine, Ben? I thought you'd be glad."

"Oh, sure. Naturally. A buck is a buck."

"Thanks." I was slightly irritated by his lack of interest. Nobody came in after that and we just stood around smoking. He had very little to say, but I could tell that he was worried.

"That girl Sharon won't leave me alone," he said finally.

"Why should she? It's your trouble as much as hers. She isn't getting a stomach on her because she ate too many dried apples."

"You could bail me out, Hob. You took in a lot of money tonight."

"Yes, and I'm keeping it."

"You mail me your address when you get to California and I'll send it to you."

"I'd die if I held my breath waiting for it."

He frowned. "You're probably right," he admitted. "I guess I'm just no good."

"Well, why don't you do something about it? Stop feeling sorry for yourself and drinking so much and getting into more jams. Go to the girl's parents and square it for the girl. Marry her if it's necessary. But whatever it is, cut out horsing around."

He thought about it.

"Maybe now is a good time to start, Hob."

"The sooner the better."

"If you'll listen I can straighten it out between you and Kathy. She's a nice kid and she loves you. The bad part is I talked her into something and I feel like a stinker because of it."

"Skip it about Kathy," I said. "If you've got a yen for her, don't let me stop you."

"Knock that business off, Hob. There's nothing between Kathy and me except friendship, just a nice girl helping a dumb guy—and maybe the friendship is gone now. She did me a favor and I let her down. I let her down worse than I ever let anybody down, even worse than I let you down when we were in business together. She—hell, she didn't know. I fed her a line and I put on the weeps. I thought she had the money, had it saved, and I told her that I'd dated this young girl, that the girl was holding me up for three hundred bucks because of her age. I didn't tell her that the girl was pregnant. But you know Kathy. She believes everybody. When I found out that she didn't have the money, I tried you and after you turned me down I really cried a river. I said I had an insurance policy that I could cash in but it would take me a few days. So she got that check from you—how I don't know—and she cashed it for me." He paused. "It would have been all right, Hob, except that I didn't do with the money what I should have done. I went nuts with it and I got rolled. You take it from there but I feel better for having told you."

My fists closed, growing big and tight, the muscles of my shoulders throwing power down into my arms. Red anger swept over me, faded for a moment and then swept over me again. I had not trusted him but I had trusted her and she had turned out to be a cheat.

"I ought to belt you," I said savagely. "I ought to tear your head off your neck."

His eyes widened. There was no fear in them, simply acceptance.

"I've got it coming, Hob. I wouldn't fight back none. Give it to me if you want to. I know that you're the only guy for Kathy, that she's broken up because I went off my rocker and lied to her."

My right fist started upward but I checked the swing and I did not hit him. I could not hit a man who would not defend himself. Anyway, it was pointless. I blamed her more than I did him. For that one session on her sofa I had paid three hundred bucks. It had been an expensive night.

"Let's close up," I said and turned away from him. "I've had enough of this place for one day."

He followed me outside and I locked the door.

"You still want me tomorrow, Hob?"

"Yeah, sure."

"That's nice of you. I mean it."

"Drop it. Here's thirty bucks for a tire. You get here as soon as you can."

"I won't drink it up. Honest."

"Just do that, and I'll bust your skull."

He walked off up the street, and I got into the Ford. I knew where I was going and what must be done. I wanted Kathy to know I had learned of her little trick and just how I felt about it.

Only the kitchen light was on when I arrived at her house and that meant her father was not at home. It did not matter to me. It would not have mattered if I had found him sitting on the front porch with a loaded shotgun aimed at my middle.

I missed the bottles going up the back steps and I did not knock before I stepped inside. She was just leaving the refrigerator with a can of beer and she let out a scream. She wore nothing except a net bra and a pair of briefs.

I had not hit Ben. But I walked over to Kathy and slapped her hard across the face. She screamed again. I came to my senses and looked down at my hand, trying to convince myself that I had not used it, and then at the red finger marks on her cheek.

"Bitch," I said and I meant that. "Lying bitch."

She glared at me for a moment and then walked to the table.

"You found out," she said wearily. "I tried to tell you and I couldn't." She sat down. "There's beer if you want it."

"I don't. I only came here to tell you what I think."

"And beat me up?"

"Well, I shouldn't have done that." I sat down opposite her. "No, I shouldn't have done that. What I've got to say will hurt you more." I reached for a cigarette. "I called you a lying bitch and that's what you are. You made up that story about the money at the office and I fell for it."

She shook her head and her eyes filled with tears.

"I thought it was right," she said. "I was trying to be human, to help him when nobody else would. But it wasn't right. As soon as I'd given him the money, I was so miserable I couldn't look at you, couldn't think straight." She held up a can of beer. "Why am I drinking this? Because I want it? No. Because it helps and if I drink enough of it, I don't even try to think."

I decided maybe I would have a beer and I got one.

"Do you know what the money was for, Kathy?"

"Some girl was threatening him. He said she was under age and that he had once driven over to New Jersey with her. I guess that's serious and although he was foolish he claimed that he wanted just one more chance to settle down and be decent. I—"

"That isn't the way it was," I told her. "The girl is under age, all right, but the money was for an abortion."

The side of her face that I had not struck turned white.

"How horrible," she whispered.

"Yeah. Horrible and criminal. And you were helping him."

"I didn't know. I—Hob, I trusted him. But I've been trying to get a loan from a finance company and when I do, I'll return your money. I lied to you, yes, but I wouldn't cheat you. I've learned my lesson. Really, I have."

I got fresh beer for us and then I saw she had not touched the first can.

"How many times has he slept with you?" I shot at her.

Tears came to her eyes. "Never, Hob," she said.

"How can I believe that?"

"You can if you trust me."

"Give me one good reason for trusting you."

She shook her head. "Honestly, there's never been anybody except you. I don't want anybody else. I want your love, Hob—and now I've ripped it all apart."

"After my stock is sold out, I'm leaving town," I told her.

"I thought you might." Her eyes lingered upon my face. "Where are you going?"

"California."

"Your folks are out there."

"Yes."

She looked down at her bra. I could see her skin through the net.

"Take me with you," she said.

I did not think about the money just then. I thought of what we had meant to each other, that it was finished. "I can't, Kathy."

"I'd want marriage but if you'd rather not I'd still be willing. Later on...."

"I can't."

"Why not?" It was a quiet, desperate plea.

I shrugged. She had to know sooner or later. There was nothing to hide. "Somebody else is going," I said.

She looked away from me, her lower lip trembling.

"A girl?"

"Yes."

Now her eyes were back on my face. A terrible, lonely sadness was in them.

"And that night in the living room you—"

"Look, Kathy. It happened. I couldn't stop myself. I tried and I couldn't. As for the money—well, I'm not sore about that now. I suppose you did what you felt had to be done. About that night—again it was just something that happened. There you were—and things just got out of control. You can't stop a storm and you can't always stop what two people want to do together."

Her mouth twisted bitterly.

"Is she better than I was, Hob?"

"I don't want to talk about it."

"Or have you treated her with more respect?"

"Shut up." I went to get another can of beer.

"Sure. Shut up. Forget the nights and the months and the kisses. Of course. Shut up. Forget. How easy for you to say. But what about me? What do I tell the next man if there is a next one? That it was wonderful and that he'd better be as good?"

I sat down again.

"Get rid of your beer," I said.

She got rid of it all right. She threw the whole business in my face. But I did not do anything to her, did not even try. I just got out my handkerchief and mopped up what I could.

"I'm sorry," she said thickly. "Hob, I'm sorry."

"Thanks for nothing."

"There was no cause for that."

"No, and that's the truth."

"But—Hob, I can't lose you and stay sane!"

I felt sorry for her just then. She was a good enough kid.

"Well," I said and stopped. Then, "Hell."

She sipped some of the beer she poured out of the new can.

"Are you sure, Hob? About this girl?"

"Very."

"Do I know her?"

"Maybe. Maybe not."

"Nice shape?"

"Terrific."

"Better than mine?"

"Cut it out." I did not know why she was torturing herself. I had intended to blister her but not this much. "I won't answer any more questions," I added. "This is stupid and we both know it."

She smiled and stood up, shoving the chair back so fast that it toppled over. I did not understand what she was going to do, so I was not prepared for it. Her motion was quick as she reached behind her, unhooked the bra and then slid the straps down over her arms. She wasn't Doris but she was there in that kitchen, the love she had for me curving her lips, and the twin peaks jutting forward proudly.

"I ask only one last thing of you," she said softly. "And you know what it is. I—please, Hob."

It wasn't just the beer she had thrown at me that made me damp then. I was sweating.

"Don't be foolish," I told her. "You'll hate me tomorrow and I'll hate myself."

"No, please. Just tonight. Make tonight the kind of night it would be if you loved me. Then I'll have the memory of you."

My head throbbed and the beer tasted flat. "Your father," I said.

"On the road." She stood there half naked and lovely. "There's nobody else here, only the two of us. And tonight. Tonight is ours. It belongs to us. We'll say that it's my wedding night without a ring, that soon you'll be gone and that it won't happen like this for either one of us again."

"You're asking for trouble."

"I can take all the trouble you give me."

"Like Ben's girl?"

"Right now I don't care."

I cannot be certain just how I was able to force myself to leave her, but I did. This time I didn't miss the bottles and they scattered all over the cement with a crash.

Five minutes later I was sitting in a bar, drinking.

All that was going on was enough to make a saint take to drink.

It was enough to make a guy like me drown himself in the stuff.

Chapter 11

Ben did not show up the next morning until about eleven. I had decided he had gone on a drunk, but he claimed to have had difficulty getting a tire. We made up a delivery list and talked about this and that, but I did not say anything to him about seeing Kathy or slapping her in the face. In fact, I was making a determined effort not to think about her at all, to sell myself on the idea that she did not really exist. Both attempts were complete flops.

"Won't take you long to clean out," Ben said. "Then you buzz off for California."

"Yeah, they can have this town. It's had me."

"What about Kathy? She have you, too?"

"Say, I'm paying you to work and not make speeches."

At two I closed up for a few minutes and walked down to a stand to pick up a copy of the paper. I expected big headlines about Condon running for mayor but there was nothing at all. I was not too surprised. His copy might have gone in late and might be held for the next day. Small-town papers are not as fast as the big city dailies, not even with important items like this, and if they feel like sitting on a story for a week, they do it. Of course, that isn't always the case but it was in Hawley. Everybody complained about the lousy paper but everybody bought it.

It was hot that afternoon and the heat killed off some of the business. But since most of the men worked during the day, I anticipated my biggest play in the evening. I had no desire to stay open such long hours but what could I do? The sale was on and the fat was in the fire.

During a lull, I counted up what money I had taken in. It disgusted me. All that profit shot because one man had carried a grudge so many years. Yet at least I would come out clean, owing nothing, and Doris would hit him for a wad.

Doris.

The blond.

And California.

As for big, burly, ugly Ferris Condon—well, I had to forget about him. No good could come of the violence that I had wanted to turn loose on him, for the sake of my father and Doris. I would have to help Doris bank the money he gave her and feel satisfied with that as a settlement. It was not his blood but it was his money and I doubted that he would miss the blood I could spill as much as the money. Yes, the money would do.

Ben came back for a couple of more sets, griping about the heat and saying that he could use a beer. I told him to leave the beer alone and put up with the heat.

"How much do I get for today, Hob?"

"Twenty-five bucks."

"Aw, get with it, huh? I'm using my truck."

"So? I bought you a tire, didn't I?"

"Yeah, I guess you did. Sorry."

"And you can work tomorrow. Maybe I can keep you on until I close up."

"Can use it. Thanks."

Kathy stopped at the shop about five while Ben was still out. She was not smiling but she was not unfriendly, either.

"Here's your money," she said and handed it to me. "They gave me the loan."

"If you need it—"

"I don't. I—Hob—about last night I went completely out of my mind. I'm sorry."

She walked to the door, turned and stood there for a moment.

"Kathy—"

"Don't say it, Hob. Don't say you're sorry. Let me say it. If—if you ever need me, you know where I am. I'm not blaming you for anything." She swung around, her back to me. "But please remember, Hob, when you walk in the rain you get wet."

"What's that supposed to mean?"

"If you don't know, let's just skip it."

She went out, and I wadded the bills in my fist. My sympathy was with her, all the way, a sympathy the more acute because of the love I realized she felt for me. But I could not help what I was doing, and she knew it.

I did not need Ben that night and let him off as soon as he returned. I gave him his pay, thinking that he would go out and throw it away on some woman. I guess I could have parted with the three hundred Kathy had repaid, but I decided not to. If I gave him that kind of money, he would not give it to Sharon; he would go on a bender. Besides, I hated the idea of financing an abortion. And it was probably too late for one, anyway.

But as it happened, Sharon herself came to see me later that evening. She talked to me, when I was not busy with a customer. She did not exactly beg for money, although she mentioned her need for it. Most of her remarks were about her family and how strict they had tried to be with her and all that.

"I get good marks in school," she said. "Even when I wasn't studying, wasting my time with Ben, I was right up there near the top. I—funny, isn't it?—I wanted to be a teacher but now I can't be anything. Everybody will know. I bought a girdle but it won't hide my condition much longer. Hide it? Pretty soon I won't be able to get the damned thing on. They say you shouldn't wear anything tight when you're this way, should you?"

"How would I know?" I wished that she would leave, that she would stay away from me. It wasn't right for her to hang around the shop. People might suspect what was the matter with her and get ideas about me. "Why don't you run along?"

"Where can I look for Ben?"

"In any bar where there's a dame. If there's no women at the bar you won't find Ben. He likes his drinks but he wants his fun, too."

"How right you are," she said. "Fun. The creep."

After she left, business was slow. I looked over the display room and there was still a lot of stuff in stock. It worried me. The faster I got out of town, the better I would like it.

At nine the phone rang. I prayed that it was not a service call. A service call I did not need. If Ben could get himself organized, he could take over my considerable list of clients and maybe do quite well for himself.

But it was not a service call.

It was Doris.

"Honey, I've got to see you," she said.

"Things didn't go right?"

"Hardly. It was like dropping eggs on a brick pavement."

"Well—"

"After he's asleep. He's half drunk and it shouldn't be long, now. Leave your door unlocked." She laughed. "And make the bed. I hate a wrinkled sheet."

"You bet," I said.

I closed up immediately after that and went out for a couple of six-packs. When I got back to the apartment, I made the bed and had a beer, stripping out of my shirt before I did either one. In between sips of the beer I removed my shoes and socks. Then I sat down to wait.

It was midnight when she arrived in the red dress that made her bigger where a woman was meant to be big.

"Drunken fool," she laughed, smelling the beer.

"Yeah, I had a few."

Her lips were fine under my mouth, wet and hot and parting under the pressure. She responded for a few moments and then pulled away.

"You should see him," she said. "He's stoned."

She followed me into the kitchen where I got a beer for her and another one for myself.

"The story about him running for mayor didn't break in the paper," I said.

"And it won't."

"Come again?"

"It won't. He's changed his mind. There's something about a public housing development that may be built and he wouldn't be able to bid on it if he were mayor."

I handed her the beer and kissed her again, letting my free hand go to the front of the dress and holding her there. There was no bra underneath. Just woman.

Raw flesh, tilted and pulsing.

"There goes our fifty grand," I said. "No scandal, no money."

She didn't say anything until we were in the living room and seated on the sofa.

"I went after him anyway, Hob. I tore into him. Of course, I hadn't seen the paper before that, and I didn't know until afterward that he wasn't running."

"A trap," I concluded. "He wouldn't give you a dollar, I bet."

"He gave me more than that."

She held out her left hand. She had worn a wedding ring right along but I had never seen the diamond. It was huge, the kind movie stars go whacky over.

"We can always sell it," I said. "That thing must be worth many thousands."

She leaned over and kissed me on the cheek.

"Honey, you don't understand me. He blew his stack but then he asked me to marry him. Right away. Quietly, so that nobody would know the difference. He said—well, he said I was too good to lose."

"You can't do it," I protested. "You don't love the guy."

"No, that's true. I don't love him. I love you, Hob."

"Then that settles it. Move out on him. I'll take another week to sell out the store and if I don't get rid of everything, I'll close out the sets below wholesale to some other television dealer. The ring is yours. He can't touch that. When we get to California, we can borrow on it if it's needed or maybe I'll go to work for somebody else. Sometimes I think that would be more sensible. A little fellow has only half a chance in business today. Everything has to be big or it doesn't count. With fifty thousand I could have gotten fairly big but on what we'll have I may not be able to."

She went to the kitchen for more beer, her hips swaying under the dress, and the hunger for her started clawing at my insides again. I did not care about Condon or his stinking money. I cared about her. Only her.

"You talked about being sensible," she said, coming back to sit down beside me. "All right, let's be just that—sensible. How much could you make a week if you worked for somebody else?"

"I don't know. They say wages are high in California."

"Would it be a hundred a week?"

"It ought to be better than that."

"Well, whatever it would be, won't we want more? For ourselves? For the kids we're going to have?"

"Everyone wants more."

"Then we have to ask ourselves how much we want."

"I doubt if there's a limit."

Thoughtfully, I lit cigarettes for us but she did not want hers and I put it out.

"We'll make out," I said. "If you don't like the idea of me working for somebody else, I can try a business again. There's always a risk, but if the town is what my mother says it is, I should do pretty good. If you were willing, you could help some—modeling or something."

"In California? With all those beautiful girls out there? I wouldn't have a chance."

"You're more beautiful than anybody."

She laughed. "Wouldn't I look kind of silly trying to model after you get me big?"

"We can plan our family."

"Can we?" She laughed again.

"We don't have to get to the top all at once," I told her. "We'll belong to each other and I think both of us want that more than anything else. Money is important, but not without love. Money won't buy love or health. People with millions try to buy those things every day and fail. I can't promise you that we'll be rich or that we won't have bills, but I can promise you my love."

"I know that." She ran one hand up and down my leg. "You're the kind of a guy that loves all of the way or not at all. We fit because I'm that type of a girl—with you. Not with him. Never before with anybody else."

I turned my head to look into her eyes. The blue seemed to be deeper, warmer.

"We can leave by the middle of next week," I said.

Her face became serious.

"You may have to leave alone."

"No, not that. You have to be with me."

She was silent for a moment.

"You hate his guts, don't you, Hob?"

"Naturally. He's grabbed my business away from me and he's used you. Either one would be enough for hate but he's doubled the whole thing."

"He's a very wealthy man."

"Why shouldn't he be? He's taken everybody who ever had anything to do with him."

Again she was silent.

"Hob," she said at last. "Hob, listen to me. If I marry him—it's no worse than what I've been doing—and if he died I'd get everything he owns. We would get it—his insurance, his business and his cash."

I stiffened, sensing danger, the same danger that I had sensed before. Of course, I had thought some about killing him but I had been able to bury those thoughts until this moment. Or at least I had thought I had buried them. Only I had not. Each day, deep down, the violent need to destroy him had been growing. Perhaps it had stopped a little when I had learned that she was not really married to him, but the hate had not stopped. For what other reason—although I had not fully realized it at the time—had I resumed my past friendship with Ben? Of course, I needed help during the sale but there were other men I could have hired. Some unconscious force had been guiding me, bringing me to this night of decision.

"He may live twenty years," I said, avoiding the issue.

Her hand moved up to my arm and squeezed it.

"Honey, he won't live ten seconds if somebody puts a bullet through his head."

"Yeah." My voice sounded strange in my own ears. "Yeah, I guess you're right. Ten seconds? Not even one second."

"You know what I'm saying, don't you?"

"I'd be an idiot if I didn't."

"He's made bad friends. He plays cards and he wins. Some of the men can't afford to lose. Or it could be made to look like a prowler. I could report a prowler to the police ahead of time, so it would seem logical afterward."

My cigarette had gone out and I lit another one while she went for some more beer. She only brought in one can, a can for me, and this time she lay down on the sofa, putting her head in my lap. With a lingering smile she took the cigarette from me and ran my hand down inside the front of her dress, placing it over her right breast and still smiling up at me through the smoke.

"Yours," she said. "They belong to you. He may get his hands on them but they aren't his. Yours, Hob. Always and forever yours."

I stroked her and drank some of the beer. My stomach revolted against it and I put the can aside.

"I couldn't do it," I said.

I felt her body go rigid, then relax. Her breast rose with a sudden thrust.

"Not for me? Not for us?"

"I'd be insane if I did it."

"Who would know? Nobody."

"Yes, they would. The police. Give them credit for being smart. They are. And I'm loaded with motives. The police would uncover them all. I can't hide what he's done to me. The reasons are enough for an angry man to kill."

She thought about that and while she did she moved my hand to the opposite breast.

"I could say you were repairing my television set at the time he was killed."

I weighed that.

"No good," I said. "When we get married the plan will become too obvious. Any fool would be able to see through it."

She frowned. "I suppose you're right," she admitted. "What do you suggest?"

"Simple. Forget the whole thing."

"Don't you want me?"

"Hell, you know I do."

She guided my hand down to her flat stomach. "Then it has to be on my terms. I'm not settling for less than all."

I considered the situation. Yes, I wanted her. I had to have her. If I did not kill him, his blood would not actually be on my hands. Also, there would be his wealth and we would never have to worry about money again.

"Somebody else has to do it, and even then I'd need an alibi," I said. "But with somebody other than you. That would be too dangerous."

"Do you know of anybody?"

"Yes." I was thinking of Kathy as an alibi.

"You wouldn't be able to kill him yourself and be safe?"

"No."

"So who would do it?"

My hand returned to her breasts, going from one to the other.

"I guess I can arrange it."

"With whom?"

"Never mind. It's okay. This guy will do anything."

It was hot in the apartment and she must have felt it. She reached down and pulled the hem of her dress up high on her thighs. They were rich, shapely, and she was not wearing stockings.

"Have it done in front of the house. That would fit in with my prowler report to the police."

"Yeah, we could do that. Might have you tied up and really jazz the works."

The cigarette had burned down and I took it from her, crushing out the thing in an ash tray. "We're leaving town in the morning so we can get married in a hurry. Sit it out for about a week and then give him the blast," she said huskily.

Her skin was soft to my touch, the centers of her breasts angry torches of fire.

"I wish it didn't have to be this way. Your marrying him, sleeping with him."

"It won't be the first time I've slept with him."

"It's odd," I said and kissed her on the mouth. "I don't even know your last name, what it is right now."

"It's Larkin. I'm not proud of it. We had so much poverty when I was a kid that even the neighbor's garbage can—" She stopped abruptly. "Oh, the hell with it. A month from now we'll need somebody to count our money for us."

We did not talk about Condon after that, or what we were going to do to him. In fact, we hardly talked at all. Her passion was blazing like a furnace out of control and I was no better.

She never did find out that night whether or not I had made the bed.

The sofa was too handy. And our needs were too great.

"One for the road," she begged, the last time around.

She got her wish.

Chapter 12

The next morning I got up early, but I did not open the shop right away. Instead, I walked aimlessly through the streets. The desires of the night before had cooled and a sense of horror at what Doris and I were planning had set in. I felt that somewhere along the way this whole affair had gone terribly wrong, that in some manner my own guts would spill out onto the ground before I was finished. And yet, how could that be? I would be protected, and the man who does the killing cannot talk without seating himself in the electric chair.

Worried?

Sure.

In love with the blond Doris?

Yes, awfully in love, so much in love that it was about the only thing that made sense. The two of us. Money to spend. A wonderfully bright life ahead of us and that bastard of a Condon planted in the ground.

Why, I asked myself, should I have the slightest hesitation about having him killed? He was no good and never had been. He had damaged first my father and now me. Add Doris to this combination and it was explosive. More than that, it was murder.

The idea of taking a life, even Condon's life, sickened me, appalled me. Even with my size and strength I have never been a violent man. Of course, I get mad, but as a general rule I try to refrain from reverting to the solution of a savage. I had considered hitting Ben there in the shop and I had slapped Kathy the same night but they were isolated instances stemming from frustration and hurt.

Still, as Doris had said, there was no other way. It had to be. For myself I might not go through with it, but for her I would. He had promised her marriage and until now he had given her nothing that she could not have received from any man.

I told myself that I had to see that it was done.

For her.

I opened the shop at nine-thirty and picked out the sets that had to be delivered. I still had not sold a beautiful four-hundred-dollar console that I had knocked down to three hundred and twenty-five bucks. The set was one of the best in the shop but the buyers had gone for the gimmicks. It was not my fault. I could not help that.

Ben came in and it was apparent that he had been walking. His shirt was soaked with sweat.

"Blew another tire," he said. "Out on some country road last night. Then when I tried to get off the road the hunk of iron slid down into a ditch. Thought I could use your Ford."

I did not want him driving the station wagon. He would make the deliveries all right but then he would cruise around and if he got half tanked, he might try to cut down a tree with the front bumper.

"No," I said. "I'll do it. You stay here and try to get some sales. Just help me load."

"Okay, Hob."

He looked out at the street.

"Crazy deal last night," he started, a little nervously. "That girl—you know the one—comes to the hotel and I had to talk to her. So she isn't old enough to be in the bar and she didn't want to go up to my room. What would you do? I get a couple of quarts of beer and buzz her out into the country. She won't drink the beer, just keeps yelling at me. Then the tire blows and the ditch comes next. She wouldn't even let me get a cab or walk her home. I don't know how she got back to her house. She only said for me to get the loot she needs, otherwise she cuts the ground out from under me." He grunted, "I'm telling you, Hob, if I had the money I'd square with her and leave this town behind."

I did not say much as we loaded the station wagon. He was playing into my hands, partly because of his own foolishness, and it would be simple, I thought, to get him to put Condon in an undertaking parlor. That was why I did not offer to buy another tire for him. I wanted him busted and down with nobody to turn to except me—so I could put a gun in his hand.

I won't say that I like delivering television sets but it's all part of the business. My first stop was a sweetheart. The old set had been moved already and all I had to do was plug the new one in. But neither the next delivery nor the one after that were easy. I guess the woman in the third house thought I should even sweep the floor. Was it my fault that she never shifted her stuff around and that she had dust all over?

Although I did my work and I joked with a couple of the customers, I really was not thinking about what I was doing. I was thinking of Doris, of her marrying Condon today, of the big mess following his murder. Just why he had not married her before but was doing it now, I did not know. Since he was not running for public office, he could stand almost any kind of a scandal and the scandal was as much hers as it was his. That part I had to be fair about. She had been living with him in sin. Still, I didn't think any the less of her for it. That, in itself, was rather strange, not thinking less of her for what she had done. Had it been Kathy Bolton, I would have been bitter and hurt and that was another thing which was strange. I was going to marry the blond when she was free, not Kathy, and yet I felt something for Kathy that I did not for Doris.

The thing bothering me most, though, was that I could not seem to change the course of the events now that they had been set in motion. There would be the police. They would question me, and I would have to lie, to thrust a nice girl into the middle of notoriety, meaning Kathy. Then Doris would be tied up settling the estate. There would be the wait until we could marry in safety. Unless....

I stopped off at a drugstore and called the Condon house on the chance that they had not left town yet. Suddenly I did not want them to leave, did not want her to go through any kind of ceremony with him. What we had said to each other last night had seemed to make sense at the time, but now it did not. I did hate his guts. Doris had been right about that. But now I wondered if I could live on his money and ever be happy, even if I did have Doris, besides.

The maid answered and said that they were not home, that they had gone out of town, that she did not expect them until the next day. Was there a message?

I hung up and bought a pack of cigarettes from the man behind the counter. Message? No, there was no message. Doris was going ahead with her plan. I had to do my part now. And then her wonderful body would belong to me. It was a high price I would be paying, but as I left the drugstore I came to the conclusion that perhaps the price was not too high, that lots of people did what they did not want to do—to get what they had to have.

Sharon, the girl Ben had in trouble, was just leaving the shop when I drove up, but she did not speak to me, merely nodded and hurried down the street. Her face seemed brighter, as though the clouds had been rolled back and she could see the sun.

As soon as I entered the shop, I saw that the big console was gone. I felt good about that and wiped the sweat from my forehead.

"See you got rid of it," I said to Ben.

"Of what?"

"The console."

"Yeah, a guy took it out on trial."

"Trial? What trial? This is a close-out sale."

"Well, that thing was a dog."

"You get the man's name?" I said wearily.

"Sure. It's written down."

We got a couple of people after that, but they were just looking. Ben stayed until five. Then I told him to take off and come in early the next morning. He asked for money but he did not get it. He was not sore, just disappointed.

"I've got to get that truck off the road," he said.

"We'll take care of it tomorrow. We'll line up a used tire maybe and I'll pull you out of the ditch."

"Why not tonight?"

"Because I've got other plans."

"With Kathy? Have fun. She's all right, that girl. She won't give unless she means it."

"Shut up."

I closed at eight. That console had me worried. I wanted to put over the sale of the set and with a guy hooking it up himself, he could do a lot of things wrong. I decided to pay a visit.

The man lived on John Street. None of the houses on John Street were new but the people who lived in them were reliable. For the most part they were in the middle income group, not poor and not rich. The house in front of which I stopped was in excellent condition. As I went up the steps, I could hear the television going, but it was turned down as soon as I rang the bell.

"Just checking on the set," I said to the man when he opened the door. "I wasn't there when you took it out but the shop belongs to me. Want to make sure she's clicking as she should."

"You don't have to check. The set is swell."

"Then you want to buy it?"

He frowned.

"Buy it? Look, fellow, I did buy it. He came down to three hundred and I paid in cash."

I did not like what I was beginning to think. At least, I did not like it at the moment.

"Have you got a receipt?"

"Say, what is this? Sure I've got a receipt."

He dug into his pocket and came out with one. My receipts are not numbered—I get them in the five and dime—so I would not have noticed at the shop that one was missing. The receipt was solid, with Ben's signature at the bottom and the imprint of my rubber stamp at the top.

"Sorry," I said and went down the steps in one jump.

Naturally, I looked for Ben that night, at his hotel and in some of the bars. I was upset. Three hundred was more than enough to take Ben out of town. I was not anxious for him to leave so soon. There was a little matter of murder I wanted to take care of first.

I did not find Ben, but I got myself half loaded in the attempt. I even danced with one of the girls in a bar but when she told me she was only seventeen I did not dance with her again. She said it was okay, that she knew what she was doing, but I suggested that she get smart and put her fanny down in front of some soda fountain.

It was midnight before I returned to my apartment and I went straight to bed. I was tired, and concerned about Doris. As I lay in the darkness and thought of Condon pawing her, his big body meshed with hers, I swore.

At two the phone rang. It was Doris.

"We're in a motel," she said, laughing. "He isn't near the man you are. He's asleep."

I looked down at my bare feet, aroused by the mere sound of her voice.

"Level with me," I said. "Did you marry the slob?"

"But what else?"

"I was hoping you hadn't."

"Why?"

"Because now we have to do it."

She laughed again, low and sultry, the kind of a laugh a woman gives when she feels something for a man.

"Yes, we have to do it, but right now I'd rather be doing something else. With you."

"Hurry home," I told her.

"Like a big bird chasing a little bird."

After that I stretched out on the bed again.

An hour later I drifted off to sleep.

I had a dream.

About a court trial.

And I was guilty.

Chapter 13

A policeman was waiting for me when I opened up the shop the next morning. He asked if I was the owner and I told him that I was.

"I guess my car is parked too far out from the curb," I said. "I wasn't in such hot shape last night."

"Car?" He scratched his head. "I'm not interested in any car. I'm interested in a girl."

"What girl?"

He showed me a card.

"This yours?" he wanted to know.

"Yes, it's mine."

"We found it in the girl's pocketbook."

"Plenty of people have them, people I don't know. I hand them out and they're on the counter where they can be picked up. Anyway, what's this about a girl?"

"Sharon Bellows. School kid."

"You've got me."

"Somebody found her in the park last night. She'd had an abortion, a brutal job, and she was bleeding to death. They got her to the hospital and she lived just long enough to give us the name of the woman. We nabbed the woman all right and she had the three hundred dollars the girl paid her. She didn't name any man but if some man did take her there or put up the money, we want to talk to him. Your card was in her pocketbook so the chief said to call on you."

I knew now that Ben had not left town, had not had the funds to do it, and I also knew where the three hundred dollars from the sale of the console had gone. He had given it to the girl and she had bought her death with it.

"Sorry, but I can't help you," I said. "I'm not saying that she's never been in here but I am saying that this is news to me."

He did not stay very long—the girl having the card did not prove anything—and I did some work that I had been putting off, thinking of the girl as I did it. It seemed a shame that she had died so young and for such a foolish reason. Better that she had had the baby and put it out for adoption. She could have started over again. Other girls did and some of them turned out pretty well.

I said nothing about the girl or the money when Ben came in. I could understand how this was working to my advantage—he was digging a deep hole for himself. I doubted very strongly that the police could do anything to him about the girl, but I could plaster him hard over the money. A thing like that might send him to jail.

"A lousy night," he said.

"Why?"

"No money."

That was another lever I could use on him. How he would take the girl's death I did not know but it was a fair bet that he would not want to stay around Hawley and if I toyed with him enough, he would reach the point where he would shoot his own mother for a bundle of cash.

He worked on the bench while I made a couple of sales. At noon we closed up, leaving a sign on the door, and drove over to a junk yard to get an extra wheel and tire for his truck. I paid the man and Ben directed me out into the country. Somebody had stolen his tools out of the back and he cursed like a maniac.

It took us about thirty minutes to get the truck out of the ditch and, using my jack, to change the wheel. He did most of the work and he was pretty dirty when he finished.

"I'll stop off at the hotel and freshen up," he said. "I can't go back to the shop looking this way."

"Okay, but don't spend all afternoon."

"Where could I spend it? And on what?"

I got a few customers after opening up the shop again and one man offered me five dollars for the portable radio that would not work.

"You could fix it for a few extra," he said.

"Not me. I don't even know where I could get the parts."

"Then I don't want it."

Ben's face was white when he came in. I wasn't busy just then and he shook his head as he came over to me.

"Sweet Jesus," he said, continuing to shake his head. "Oh, sweet Jesus, I saw the paper and that girl got the works."

"What girl?" As if I did not know.

"Sharon, the one who was chasing me. She tried to get rid of the kid and the abortionist bungled the job. She's dead!"

"Tough. Real tough. Poor kid."

"Where does that leave me?"

"How would I know?"

"Her people will figure I knocked her up." He frowned. "Or maybe they won't. I only went to her house a few times, twice to work on their television, and they have no way of knowing."

"Where did she get the money?"

He could not look me in the eye.

"I don't know," he said. "Maybe she put out for a few bucks."

"She seemed like a nice kid," I said, trying to draw him out.

"Yeah, but don't they all? The minute a girl says yes, she isn't so nice." He was looking at me now. "I was afraid of her because she was so young but she kept asking for what she got. I'd pick her up after school sometimes and we'd go down to the shop. I'd close the door to the back room, where I used to stay when I couldn't pay my hotel bill, and she'd take off her clothes without even being told. It was crazy for me to fool with her but she was good."

I found a cloth and wiped off the top of one of the sets.

"Ben, you didn't play square with her. She was just a little stupid about some things and you could have helped her. Now you can't. Nobody can help her."

"I hope they railroad that woman."

"What about you?"

"They can't do anything to me, can they? I wasn't with her and I didn't take her there. For all I know the baby could have belonged to somebody else. As long as she went the limit with me I think she must have had other guys." He put his hand on his forehead and it came away all covered with sweat. "Aw, I'm just saying that. There wasn't anybody else."

I got a customer just then, and Ben stood by quietly. It was plain that he was worried, more worried than he was willing to admit. And certainly, he felt guilty. He wasn't one to feel that way but of course he had never had any of his girl friends die.

The customer did not buy and I returned to Ben. I had the fork to stick into him right then but I decided to wait. If I talked to him about the killing, his conscience might get the best of him and he would not do it.

"What would you do with a couple of thousand bucks?" was all I asked.

"Are you kidding? Where would I get that kind of money?"

"Search me, but supposing you had it?"

He gave that some thought.

"I'd get out of town," he said finally. "I've messed it up around here—but good—and a couple of thousand would stake me. You couldn't get into business with that but I don't want my own business again. For somebody who can budget himself it's swell, but you know how I am with money."

"I figured you might straighten up some with your people and go back to the farm."

"Bull. Plain bull, Hob. Who wants to live on a farm? I don't. I look at a cow and I get sick at my stomach. Anyhow, I don't see any reason for it. I know my trade and there's a living in it. I don't have to get up in the morning at five to start work and it isn't a deal where you can't get a day off now and then. On a farm you're never finished. In this racket you can call your shots."

"I thought you might take over for me when I shove off," I said, feeding him a dream.

"You'd want payment."

"Maybe not. Once I lock that front door the last time, I'm through. You could catch up on your rent in your old building and take over my service calls. We're reaching a point where you wouldn't have to keep a big stock of sets any more. None of the other men in town serviced the way I did and there's money in that."

We talked about it some, about how he could get along and what he could do, but he wasn't really interested. He was a desperate man—all he wanted to do was run. That was fine. Now all I had to do was to keep him desperate, make him willing to go through with a crime that I could not take care of myself.

"You aren't very busy," he said, a few minutes after four.

"I don't see any business."

"How about me taking off the rest of the day?"

"Sure. Go ahead."

"I could use twenty."

"Will you settle for ten?"

"Why not? I'll take what I can get." He grinned. "I know why you don't want me to have all of it. You think I'll blow—and maybe I would. So I'll ride out the sale with you. What have I got to lose?"

He took the ten and left. He would not get far on that, perhaps one or two bars, making it with some woman who came free, and in the morning he would show up.

I stayed open until nine, turning a couple of sales, and although I thought of calling Condon's house, I knew that I should not. He would not be out playing cards so soon after marrying her. It made me sore to think about what they might be doing together—almost as if I were her husband, knowing that she was with another man.

As soon as I had closed, I went upstairs to shower and change. If I were going to use Kathy for an alibi, I ought to start seeing her again and not make it for just that one fatal night. I decided to do a little looking ahead because, otherwise, on the one night that I needed her she might not be available. Of course, I would have to lie to her to establish the situation, but I could not hurt her any more than I had already. Most likely Condon would stay close to his home for the next few nights and I would not be able to meet Doris, anyway. All we had to do was one unwise thing and all our plans would fall apart.

On the way over to Fossard Street I bought two six-packs of beer and hoped that her old man was out on the road. It was a good bet that he was. Usually, he made a trip every other day, but some of the men who worked with him liked to go fishing or take it easy during the hot weather and he often took their turns. All of this added up to big pay, but I could not understand why he was killing himself with so much work, not to mention the in-between-time visits to his woman. In a few years he would be able to retire on a good pension and he did not have any mortgage to pay. What he had was security to a modest degree. I laughed. What I would have with the blond would be so much security that I would not know what to do with it. Sure, having Condon killed was bothering me more and more, even though I tried not to admit it. But if I wanted Doris, and the security that went with her, it had to be done.

I drove slowly toward Fossard Street. It struck me as being a little strange that there were so many things about Doris that I did not know. Yet I did not dwell on that. I knew what I was after and what I was going to get. I was after her. I was determined to get her for my own. I guess she could have been a dancer in a peep show and it would not have mattered. The memory of her body moving against mine, of the furious way that she kissed, of the loveliness of her legs, was all that I had to have to stir me. Sex? No, I did not think so, not just sex alone. We were ideally mated but that was only a part of it. There was that look in her eyes, a look of longing; there was the way she walked and talked; there were the things she wanted out of life, things that I wanted myself. On only one point did we differ. She had to have money, Condon's money, and while I knew money was necessary to everybody, it was not that important to me. I had two arms and two legs and I could make a living for us. No, the money was not thrusting me into this. I was in it because of my love for her and my hate for Condon. Add the two together, and it was like throwing a match into a drum of gasoline.

There was no light in the living room of the Bolton home and I carried the beer around to the back. The usual bottles got in the way and I cursed her old man for putting them out there.

I knocked this time and she came to the kitchen door. She was wearing a dress, a yellow dress with a zipper down the front, and the fabric roamed over her curves like some affectionate hand.

"You didn't phone me," she said, somewhat annoyed but she let me in anyway.

"Since when do I have to call you?"

"Since you found somebody else."

I turned toward the door. I didn't have to stay. There was that girl on Orchard Street and I might be able to use her if she wasn't too afraid of the law. But any girl who sells herself cannot be trusted. It had to be a decent girl.

"So long," I said. "Hello and so long."

She grabbed one of my arms.

"No, Hob. It's just that—well, it's all changed for us, isn't it?"

"Not as much as you think," I lied.

Her hand squeezed my arm.

"Did you have a fight with her?"

"Maybe."

She walked to the refrigerator and opened it.

"Put the beer away," she said, laughing. It was obvious that she was pleased. "All except a couple of cans. I haven't been drinking but I could use one now."

I shoved the beer into the refrigerator, opened two cans and we sat down at the kitchen table. She left room for me at her side, but I did not sit there. With her thinking that I had quarreled with the other girl, just one thing was bound to happen between us and I did not think I had to go that far. Using Kathy as an alibi was one thing, but using her as a woman was quite different. Call it respect or whatever you want. I simply did not want to cheapen her.

"Your father out?" I asked.

"Not working. With that woman."

"You can't blame him for having a little fun."

She looked down at her beer.

"He may marry her, Hob. He says that he doesn't love her the way he did my mother but that they're both lonely and that they don't want to grow old alone." She glanced up from her beer. "It's an awful thing to say, but I just wouldn't want to be in the same house with her. I say it's awful, and unfair, because I hardly know the woman. Still it would be their lives, you see, without any real place for me."

"I guess I know what you mean."

"And it's time I had somebody of my own, something to work for. You exist in a void, just going from day to day, and it isn't any good. I'm young but I want my babies while I'm young. I want to grow up with them, to be close and as much a friend as a mother. My mother gave her life for me and while I'm scared of the same thing happening to me, maybe, it's not going to stop me."

"You read the papers," I said. "There's one girl who won't have any kids."

"Ben must feel terrible."

"He doesn't feel so hot. It seemed to get at him where nothing else has."

"You can't hold him completely responsible. The girl is the one who had the baby inside of her. He may have started the life, the two of them together, but she was carrying it. She's the one who decided, no matter what he may have said."

We had another beer and we talked some, mostly about our own relationship. She did not know how she was, if I had done anything to her or not there on the sofa, and she did not seem to care. She was convinced that I had returned to her, that everything was all right. I felt like a lousy heel and I tried to drown the feeling with the beer. It was just as impossible as trying to drown a horse in a bucket of water.

"There's one thing I haven't told you," she said. "I was keeping it for a surprise."

"Oh?"

"Well, you know my father. You know how he is, working almost all the time. It's been that way since I was born, first to pay a woman to take care of me and then because it had become a habit. Anyway, he's made money, and all these years he's been having twenty percent of his pay put into government bonds. When I needed that three hundred dollars I couldn't go to him, because I was afraid to tell him the truth, but that has nothing to do with you. And we've talked about you, talked about you a lot. You had this thing in your mind about a television cable to homes to prevent the pictures from jumping when a car goes by. He's seen it here and other places and he's discussed the idea with a number of people. They think it's terrific, just as you did. There's hardly anybody who wouldn't sign up."

She hesitated and I got some more beer from the refrigerator.

"I don't follow you," I said. "You lost me back there when he started buying bonds."

She laughed, a bright, sincere laugh.

"The bonds pay pretty good but he'd like a better investment. He thought he could post them as security with the bank, get a loan for you, have part of the business for himself—only a small part. Then everybody would be happy and make money."

I lit a cigarette. This was a situation made to order but I could not take advantage of it. Soon Condon would be dead, and Kathy would know the truth about my relationship with the blond. It was too late to start anything like that.

"It has to be gone into," I said. "Things have to be cleared with the utility company about using the poles and I suppose there are federal agencies that have to give permission. But it's nice of him. I didn't realize he thought that much of me."

"He's looking out for himself, too."

"Sure. Who doesn't?"

We drank most of the beer and when I kissed her before I left, her lips told me silently that it did not have to stop with a kiss.

"Not until it's legal," I said.

She clung to me.

"You're sweet, Hob. You're a sweet guy and I'm terribly happy that you're back with me again. It's right for both of us."

Once I was away from her, driving back to my apartment, I felt sick. Already I felt like a criminal.

It was a hot night and I showered, getting rid of the beer sweat. Just as I was drying off, somebody knocked on the door. Wrapping the towel around me I went to answer it, thinking that it was Ben and that he needed more money.

"Don't ever lock it," Doris said. She handed me a couple of bottles of liquor and smiled. "I can't tell when I can get away from him. Once he's asleep it's all right, but I have to wait for that."

When I kissed her, hanging on to the towel with one hand, I could tell that she had been drinking. It figured. She probably had to drink to put up with the big slob.

She opened the liquor while I put on a pair of shorts. She looked stunning in black, her blond hair falling to her shoulders.

"What have you done?" she asked me when we were seated on the sofa.

I told her what I had done, all the way from Ben to Kathy. She nodded her head as I spoke and drank thoughtfully.

"Saturday night," she said when I had finished.

"That soon?"

"The sooner the better. He's got a card game on for that night and he may not have another one for a week."

"I thought he played a lot."

"He likes something else better. He can't do much at his age but he certainly tries."

"The stinking crumb."

"Say it again."

"The stinking, rotten crumb!"

"All right." She reached for one of the bottles, splashing liquor into her glass. "Set it for eleven. The game will be breaking up by then, and I can call him and get him to come home. I'll report a prowler to the police on Thursday night and I'll use this as an excuse. But don't have the man tie me up. They'd look for a rape if he did and I wouldn't be able to get to the phone. There are some bushes by the side of the house and the man can hide in them. Ferris uses the front door and the man can cut him down right there."

She kept drinking, much more than I did, as we went over the details. I would be with Kathy, Doris would report the killing, and we would meet in secret for a while. The plan appeared to be solid but we covered it several times to make sure. I smoked nervously, wondering if we would be able to get away with it, speculating on what would happen if they trapped us. Then the question came up about the gun and since buying one would be too obvious, we decided to use one that Condon had in his collection. Nobody would miss it and Ben would not be exposed to danger by making a purchase.

Doris got pretty drunk and I had to carry her into the bedroom. She was not much help when I undressed her, but I thought she would come around when I started to make love to her. Looking down at her as she lay there on the bed I turned into a mass of trembling desire.

Then I saw a couple of things that I did not want on her. His rings—the diamond, and the wedding band. I wanted her completely naked, wearing nothing that belonged to him.

I had some trouble with the rings but I finally got them off and put them on the stand at the head of the bed where I kept my clock. She was too drunk to protest, to know what I was doing.

In one thing I was wrong. She hardly knew it when I possessed her, responding only feebly and without passion. It was far from satisfactory but I excused her for that.

Later, I sat on the edge of the bed and because I had nothing else to do, I looked at the rings. I did not know anything about diamonds but this one seemed to be a corker, one of those rocks that many a girl would give herself for—as often as necessary.

The wedding ring might have been cheap or expensive. I was not concerned about that. It was the inscription on the inside that got me. As I read it, I found myself wondering about her. The date inside was not a recent one. It went back to about the time she should have married him—the time he had brought her home after that convention.

But I put the rings aside and tried to forget the whole thing.

It took me until five in the morning to get her sobered up enough to go home.

"How come that old date on the inside of your wedding ring?" I asked her at the door.

For just a moment she appeared to be confused.

"Oh, that. It was his idea."

We kissed and she departed.

I did not go to sleep right away.

Something was bothering me.

Chapter 14

Convincing Ben was not the easiest thing in the world to do, but the two thousand dollars cinched it. He was willing to do almost anything to get that much.

"There'll be a stink," he said. "He's a big man in town."

"Let it stink. Nobody can pin anything on anybody. The prowler gimmick will throw them off."

"And the gun?"

"You get it from her. But don't eject the shell right there. If the bullet goes through his head they won't know what kind of a gun to look for."

"When do I get the money?"

"As soon as he's dead."

"What about some in advance?"

"And have you take off? To hell with that."

He hedged some more, but I had too many clubs over his head and he needed the money too much to refuse. I made it plain about the money he had taken from the sale of the console, leaving no doubt in his mind that I would go to the police. He did not want that and then the business about the girl had him upset, too.

"You worked this neat," he said finally, giving up entirely.

"Sorry, Ben, but you dug the hole yourself. You did it with the girl and my money and if you want anything at all, this is the only way."

He lit a cigarette.

"Maybe it won't be so bad. I don't know the bastard, but you must be pretty strong on this woman to go off the deep end."

"She's the greatest."

"When should I get the gun?"

"You can pick it up now," I told him. "Then get back here and make a couple of deliveries."

He went out and I hoped that I would not get any customers. I was too upset to bother with them.

This was Friday and I had not seen Doris since that last night in my apartment. Of course, I had been stopping over to visit Kathy, setting up the deal, but all I did was drink beer and I guess I was pretty poor company.

The display room looked bare. The sale had gone over well and I had only a few sets left. All in all, I should have felt all right. But I did not. That inscription on the inside of her wedding ring chewed at my stomach, creating a doubt that should not have existed.

It did not seem to me that he would have had the ring inscribed that way, that....

Well, what if she had married him in Philly? What difference did it make?

Obviously, it made a lot of difference because if she had lied about that one thing, there might have been other lies. And if she had been married to him all this time, what reason was there for hiding the fact. Then there was that business of her calling me to fix their television set when she knew that Condon hated my guts. However, maybe she had tried others and they either could not or would not do the work. Still, it was a point on the minus side of the chart. I had not considered it prior to this but I did now. If she had not been married to him, why had she risked making him angry with her?

I had a set in the shop that had been dropped off for repairs and I tried to do something with it. I could not. I was in love and I was confused, not because of my love for her but because of all the things that seemed to head out into different directions.

Somehow, I found myself at the phone, talking with Western Union, sending a wire to Philly and asking if there had ever been a marriage between Doris Larkin and Ferris Condon. I told them to wire me collect, that the information was urgently required.

I felt like a skunk when I replaced the phone. As long as I loved her I should place complete faith in her, a powerful faith that allowed no doubts, no questions. Still....

I went back to work on the set. The guy who owned it was a baseball nut and I had promised him fast service. If he missed one game, he would quit me. I shoved the set aside, disgusted. What did I care? With Condon dead there would be thousands and thousands of dollars at my disposal. I would not have to test television tubes or run my rear into the ground. She would feed me money while we were waiting for marriage and if I had to get a job, that would be all right.

Ben was gone about two hours, longer than necessary, and he was all smiles when he came into the back room where I sat smoking and brooding.

"Anybody would kill for that number," he said. "They should put bumpers on the front of cars like she's got."

"Shut up. What about the gun?"

"It's in the truck."

"Just don't miss."

"I won't. I wasn't brought up on a farm for nothing. I could get a wood-chuck at a hundred yards. She gave me soft-point bullets and I'll notch them. They blow apart when you do that. You won't be able to find his head afterwards."

"So I guess we're set."

"You are but I'm not. You get the woman and all I'll have is two thousand bucks. How far can I go on that?"

"It depends."

"A few dames could cost me that in a month."

"Forget the females, Ben."

"You aren't."

"That's not the same."

"No, and I'll bet that blond isn't the same as the others. I know the type. You take care of them and then they're after you again. The kid was the same. Sharon. She never wanted to quit."

I put him to work on the set, told him to snap the lock on the way out at five, and then I climbed the stairs to my apartment. I entered the bathroom to shower but had to throw up first. My nerves were shot. And I was even sicker than I knew. Sick in the heart and sick in the head.

The water was hot, but I shivered under the needle spray. The murder was set now and all I had to do was wait. Waiting was the worst part. Once it was done, nobody could change it. But then there would be more waiting, a reasonable period between his death and our marriage. It would take her a few weeks to clear up the estate and I would have to be patient.

As soon as I had showered, I changed into fresh clothes and had a drink from one of the bottles Doris had brought. But it would not stay down. When I thought of Condon with his head blasted off, nausea took hold of me. Hate pushed through my blood but the hate was not enough to stop the way I felt. You can ruin a man with money and he can come back somehow, but when you destroy him with a gun he is wiped out forever.

I did not check the shop before driving over to Fossard Street. I had given Kathy money for a steak, and we were going to have a quiet dinner together. When her father wasn't working he was with his woman and he seldom came home any more. He claimed he slept on her sofa, but I figured that was the biggest lie of the century.

She had the steak on when I got there and I kissed her lightly. It was another hot day with the stove throwing out more heat and she was in her shorts and halter. I sat at the table while she worked, staring at her bare legs and I was surprised that I had not realized before how excellent they were, not quite as full as Doris Condon's legs but with smooth lines that would last for years.

"Don't talk so much," she said to me.

"Sorry."

"You never say anything lately. It's as if your body is here but your mind is somewhere else."

"Well, I'm tired."

"Tired? You used to be tired before, but you had a line of chatter a yard long." She opened the broiler to look at the steak. "You don't have to bother with me if you don't want to."

"Oh, cut it out."

A few minutes later we ate and everything was fine. But I could not eat much. I told her it was the weather. She was right. My mind was somewhere else and occupied with many different things. Just when I decided that I had the whole mess sorted out, it became a bigger mess than ever. It was like looking at a puzzle, knowing there was something perfectly simple that would solve it, but not being able to see what it was.

After we ate, we did the dishes and because of the heat, I suggested a ride.

"Swell," she said. "Up along the river. It's always cooler near the river."

The river running through the outskirts of Hawley is not big and it did not feel any cooler down on the little beach than in Kathy's kitchen. There are a few fish in the river, mostly trout and bass, stocked by the state in the spring, but if you can catch one you ought to have your name put up on some sort of honor roll.

We sat on the sand, watching the shadows moving in across the water and slapping at the bugs. They were not the kind of bugs that bite much, but they buzz around your ears and drive you half nuts.

"There's something wrong with you," Kathy said.

"No, nothing."

"Don't lie to me. You've had your chances and you wouldn't take them."

"We've got years ahead of us."

"Most men don't want to wait, do they?"

"Who said I wanted to wait? It's just sense."

Darkness, once it started, came swiftly, but it seemed to get hotter.

"We could swim," she said.

"In what?"

"In the river, silly. Who needs to wear anything?"

I said it was idiotic but after a while we began to undress. She had some trouble with her halter and I had to help her with that. As the halter dropped to the sand I pushed aside all the reservation I had had about her and placed my hands upon her naked breasts. They rose to me and she pulled my head down so she could kiss me on the mouth. It was not the way Doris kissed or the way Kathy had ever kissed me before. She was not a savage about it but gentle and soft, a good girl who wanted to belong to her man.

"We were going swimming," I reminded her.

"And stumble over the rocks?"

"Well, it was your suggestion."

"Somebody has to have a suggestion, Hob."

I told myself that it was pointless, but I suppose Custer told himself the same thing during the last stand. There are things you have to do and you cannot stop yourself from doing them.

I knew I could not stop with her.

Not until an hour had passed.

"I hope you did," she said as she lay there in my arms, her emotions drained of all need.

"You hope I did what?"

"You know. Yours and mine. What every girl wants from the man she loves."

I turned my head and blinked back the tears.

Girls cry. A man cries too, sometimes.

Chapter 15

I tried to make a change in my plans the next day, tried to set up the girl on Orchard Street for an alibi instead of Kathy. But I learned that the girl had left town for a few days, so that was out.

Ben worked with me in the shop but we did not have much to say to each other. We both knew what the night would bring and we avoided the subject.

Shortly after noon Doris called. She told me that she had set it up with the police on the prowler thing. She thought Ben was a good choice, that he would go through with it and that our real worries were about over. I told her I guessed they were and rang off, far from being convinced that you can have a man killed and not have to worry about it. When you are on the other side of the fence you like to think that the police are inefficient and careless, but when you look at their records, you know they are far from being that. A town such as Hawley barely pays its policemen a living, so they aren't in the profession for the money. It is pride with them, pride in doing a job well.

We closed the shop at two. The pressure was just too much for us and we both needed a drink, Ben because he would fire the gun and me because I had placed it in his hands.

"Hot," Ben said as we walked to the bar down the street.

"Yeah."

"This will be a night we won't forget."

"Aw, it's like shooting a mad dog."

"For you. You don't have to do it. You pay out the money, or she does, and you get with her." His steps slowed. "But you're in this as deep as I am, Hob, and don't forget it. Once you've hired a killer, you're as guilty as he is. Besides, you forced me. You rode me into this thing. Women I'll take any day of the week, ugly or otherwise, but killing a guy is a little out of my line."

"You know what happens if you don't do it."

"I know. Stop telling me."

We found a booth in the place and we sat there, taking turns getting beer from the bar. Nobody could hear us and we talked about it some more, deciding that the gun should be thrown in the river and thinking about what Ben was going to do following the crime. He was all for leaving town the next minute but I pointed out that it might not be wise, that we should keep on working in the shop just as if nothing had happened, that the sale would go on and we would sit tight.

"Kathy is going to catch this right square in the face," he said.

"Don't you think I know? But what can I do?"

"You should have married her. You were nuts about her and she's crazy over you. Then this blond comes along...."

"Drop it, Ben."

"No. I won't drop it. When it comes right down to the facts, you fit the blond better. You're using Kathy and she's helpless and innocent. You don't care about that, do you? And look what you're doing to me. I'm no killer but you're making me one. Granted I'm a louse, that I never amounted to anything, but even after I've pulled the trigger on the gun, I'll be a better man than you are."

I finally got tired of the whole thing and I told him to beat it and leave me alone. He asked for money but I wouldn't give him any.

"You'd better have the two grand," he said.

"I've got it. I haven't been selling those television sets for marbles. See me in the morning and you'll collect."

I sat there for a long time after he had gone. There seemed to be something that I had forgotten, that had started and had not yet been completed. I could not figure out what it might be, but the thought kept nagging at me.

At five I picked up my car and drove over to Fossard Street. Kathy's father was romancing his woman, so we ate alone. When she went in to answer the phone, I threw my food into the garbage can. I did not want it. I couldn't even drink the beer she had poured for me.

"There's a good movie," she said as we washed the dishes.

"Okay."

I paced the floor while she changed. A movie was just what I needed. I did not have to watch what was on the screen, or talk. I could sit there and try not to think.

The movie program turned out to be a double feature which would not let out until almost twelve o'clock. That should be alibi enough for me. Condon would be dead by then.

We were well into the second movie when I realized what had been disturbing me.

"I'll be right back," I told Kathy, jumping up.

She smiled, thinking that the men's room had a customer, and I tore out of the theater.

The Western Union office was in the next block and I got there just before eleven when they were scheduled to close. The girl behind the counter was helpful but I had to pay for the telegram before she would give it to me.

"They tried to deliver it this afternoon, but you weren't around," she said.

I opened the telegram right there and read it.

I knew now that Doris had been lying. She had married Condon on the date inscribed inside her wedding ring.

I raced from the office in the direction of the Ford. I was convinced at last that this had to be stopped, that if she had lied about her marriage, she must have lied about too many other things. Then there was the business about Condon's suddenly buying my building—a thing I had never been able to understand. The trouble at the bank was easily understood because he had been striking back at my father through me. That had cost him nothing, but the building had. The purchase of the building, like so many others things, did not make sense.

I chose the shortest route to Neversink Drive and rammed the gas down to the floorboards. My mind raced like the motor. How did I ever get into this mess? And the picture of Condon with his brain scattered over the steps of his own front porch haunted me. And my best friend, Ben, standing there with cruelly filed bullets—a paid killer. Ben was right. I could not push this off on him. If it had already happened....

Too late I realized that I had taken the road by the drive-in movie. It was just letting out, and for nearly a mile I drove bumper to bumper with the kids trying to keep on playing in the car, and the women who were so big with child that they were ashamed to go to a regular movie, and the usual throng of couples young and old who used the drive-in as a necking place.

Desperate, I decided to risk it and pass some cars—knowing I could kill myself doing it. I swung out and pushed down the accelerator as far as it would go.

As luck would have it the next three cars were strung out and I could just barely duck in between them as another car came toward me on the two-lane road. The near collision left me shaken. I stayed in lane for a moment, afraid to make another long run for it. Just then a car in the lineup passed me at racing-car speed, coming from as far back as I had. I decided to try it again—goaded strangely by Doris. "Chicken," she had said. "You're chicken." I guess I was—anyone who would hire a man to shoot another down was chicken-hearted, was yellow as a lemon.

All together it took maybe four minutes to get through that traffic, but it seemed more like four months. My stomach was knotted and my eyes hurt. It was as though I had been on a month's bender—come to think of it, that's just what it was—a month's bender. Why hadn't I seen it before? Why couldn't I see that a woman like Doris would treat me just as she treated Condon? Here I was, putting out all I had—including two grand from the sale of my stock—to kill her husband. For what?

I felt as if my whole gut convulsed when I saw the Caddie drive into the lane just as I turned into Neversink Drive. I was going to be just late enough to be unable to stop it—just late enough to see it—

Why I did not come into the driveway with my horn blowing I don't know. All I could think of was getting to Condon before he passed those evergreen shrubs where Ben was hiding. He was getting out of the Caddie and walking across the grass to the lighted porch as I turned in.

I skidded to a stop and was out of the car and running toward Condon before I realized that my voice was hollering, "Duck! Duck!"

Condon turned around right on the porch—a perfect target.

I jumped him just as I heard the shot.

For an instant I thought I was too late; Condon was under me and covered with blood. He had struggled free by the time I realized the blood was mine.

Then I heard Ben scream in disgust and revulsion, "Oh, Jesus—God!"

And then Doris shouted, "Ben, Ben—shoot him! Shoot the son of a bitch!"

Condon, in a stunned voice, yelled, "What the hell is going on here?"

I could see Ben standing there half-concealed in the evergreens—standing with the gun in his hand, looking wild-eyed.

He dropped the gun, and Doris and Condon both jumped for it. Condon scooped it up.

"What a pair of dung-heads," Doris shouted, hysterically. "Chicken, what are you doing here? Chicken! Chicken!" Condon was holding her, keeping her from hitting me. "Oh, screw it all!" she cried as she broke down into convulsive weeping.

I could hear Ben calling to me, "Hob, Hob, are you hurt bad? Hob, you all right?"

I felt his hand touch my back.

He tore my shirt and stuffed it tight under my arm. "Somebody get a doctor, quick!"

I could feel nothing in my left arm, and I was too weak to move. But I was not too weak to speak....

I remember saying, half laughing, "The hell with a doctor. Get the cops—"

I just have the cable system these days but it's more than enough to keep me busy managing it. I have two men working outside and a girl in the office. My left arm is almost useless but the doctors claim that it will get better in time. There is no point in being bitter. A bad arm is a small price to pay when the top price for murder is the chair.

You can say that I was lucky but it's what I did for Condon that night that brought me the luck.

He came to see me at the hospital the following day. I told him the whole story, how everything had come to a head and how I had not found it in my guts to go through with it or have it done.

He thought for a while. "I cut you off at the bank because of something that should have been left in the past," he said to me. "But the building's different. I bought it because Doris said you tried to molest her, but she couldn't prove it. I didn't want a scandal, but I decided to stamp you out for good."

"Why did you change your mind about running for mayor?"

"I never did decide to run. I had often been encouraged to do so, but the idea did not appeal to me and I turned down the nomination."

The piecing together we did that day was only a prelude to the trial. It was there that Doris Condon's whole sordid tale came out. Her cold-blooded plan to get at Condon's money became completely obvious.

The court was lenient to me, maybe too lenient, because of what I did for Condon that night. My sentence was suspended. Of course, you never really get away with anything and I am on probation for the next two years.

Ben was not so fortunate. He is doing time, along with Doris, and when he gets out of prison—if he is interested after what I did to him—I will give him a job. He may have changed. As for Doris, I would not give her the right time of day, but I do have to admit that without me she might not have gone to such desperate lengths. She wrote to me once but I did not answer. Since then, I have not heard from her.

Kathy's father wanted to get into the business with me but relatives and money don't mix, in my opinion. So I am going it alone, with Condon's cooperation at the bank. I won't say that he is friendly with me but his close brush with death brought out some of the fairness in him, killed the hate, and he manages to get along with me when we meet. That's more than I can say for Kathy's stepmother. The woman tries to boss everybody and we don't go over there very often.

Nights I'm tired, but I'm never too tired for Kathy.

Never too tired for the wonders of her body, always happy to lie beside her afterward and enjoy the warmth and the goodness of her.

I cannot ask for more.

I would be insane if I did.

Out of the whole sorry affair, this day of sanity came for me.

The End

Afterword:
Themes and Motifs in Orrie Hitt's Fiction, or Obsessions of the Shabby Shakespeare of Sleaze
by Michael Hemmingson

The Curse of the Prolific

In his brief career (1953-1970) as, per the label I choose, the Shabby Shakespeare of Sleaze paperbacks, Orrie Hitt published 148 books under his name and the nom de plum Nicky Weaver, as lesbian author Kay Addams, and in collaboration writing as Roger Normandie, Charles Vern, and Fred Martin. He'd held many jobs before becoming a professional writer, jobs that, with precise detail, his characters also do: hotel desk manager, insurance salesman, frozen food distributor, food buyer for restaurants and grocery stores, radio DJ, bartender, TV and electronics repairman, and general handyman Jack of All Trades on farms and resorts.

In this Stark House Press omnibus, two of his best books have been reprinted: both are first-person narratives, both have to do with the hero falling for a femme fatale who talks him into committing a murder with the promise of riches and all the sex he can take. *Cheaters* is centered around a waterfront bar in a corrupt small town where a dirty cop runs the prostitution trade in an area calked The Dells, and also coerces "protection" money from area business. *Dial "M" for Man* is an obvious cash-in on the Hitchcock film, *Dial M for Murder,* but doesn't share any themes with the Hitchcock classic, other than crime; the hero also gets seduced by a vivacious vixen who wants her wealthy husband dead so she can gain control of his bank accounts and cash a big life insurance check. Hitt was best when writing in the first person, which isn't to say his third-person narratives are lacking, there are some fine gems there as well, but using the "I," we get into the psychology of why Hitt's heroes do the crazy, vain, and stupid things they do.

Hitt was quite prolific, as Brian Ritt (the last name is coincidental) describes him in the front matter of this book: cranking out a novel every two weeks (during his halcyon days) on an old typewriter on the kitchen table, slugging down iced-coffee to keep the energy up, and smoking a constant chain of cigarettes. Prolific authors historically tend to burn out psychically and physically (from Balzac to Barry Malzberg); some who started young can keep it up into their autumnal years (Lawrence Block, Dean Koontz) and some recover from burn-out and return to writing, albeit at a slower, refined pace (Robert Silverberg). Orrie Hitt fell into the first category, his imagination and stamina coming to a stand still by 1964, and instead of 20-plus titles a year, he dwindled down to three or four, then one, and these books are incoherent in plot and repetitive of themes and characters: the curse of the prolific author. The prolific also tend to have pet themes and motifs—let's consider them. The test after this afterword will be multiple choice and count for 1/3 of your grade in Vintage Paperback History and Studies. So takes notes....

The Plots and Themes

Major plots in Hitt's novels are money scams large and small (insurance, door-to-door, mail order catalogs, nude photos); James Cain-esque situations of a man falling for a young woman married to an older rich guy and they scheme his murder and the hero becomes a patsy (*Cheaters, Dial "M" for Man, Two of a Kind*); the young woman, between the ages of seventeen and twenty-three, who struggles to survive in the misogynic 1950s and, with little education, has only one asset worth money: her body, either as a model, prostitute, or stag film actress (*Campus Tramp, Four Women, Trapped!*)—some of them are not victims, however, and are clever and strong: the heroines of *She Got What She Wanted* and *Sheba* use their womanly wares to get ahead in sales, auto and housing improvements, and while the men in their lives believe she has fallen for their games of prowess, she later proves that she's the manipulator, using sex as a method of empowerment in an era where women's roles in the workplace were relegated to girl Fridays and hash slingers.

Hitt examines the lives of prostitutes and call girls and how they fell into that life, coming from abusive homes, turned out by stepfathers or bad boyfriends (*Trailer Tramp, Nude Doll, Naked Model, Girl of the Streets, Call South 3300: Ask for Molly!, Party Doll, Tawny*); there are also the strippers, who either keep the boss of the club happy or hook on the side (*Torrid Wench, Libby Sin, Strip Alley, Burlesque Girl*); and then there are the young women who, for financial needs and emergencies, become models for the nudie picture racket, sometimes by force or blackmail (*The Promoter, Leased, Girl's Dormitory, Sin Doll, Wayward Girl*). Then there is the plight of the transient farm hand that is just trying to keep food in his belly (*Dirt Farm, Violent Sinners, Love Thief*), post-Depression products of quiet desperation.

Other examinations in sexual deviance are his peeping tom volumes, either as main focus (*The Peeper, Peeping Tom, I Prowl by Night, Lust Prowl, Unnatural Urge*) or sub-plot (*Warped Woman, Panda Bear Passion*). Were these books written for a popular theme in sleaze paperbacks? Or did Hitt have certain insight into the nature of voyeurism, as his peeper books go into great psychological detail: a glimpse of a naked woman as a boy, an obsession with birth marks. It was common practice for paperback publishers to take note of trends in subject matter and plots, and request their writers to crank some more out about, say, wife-swapping and cheating in suburbia (*Suburban Sin, Sexurbia County, Never Cheat Alone, Suburban Interlude*), trampy swamp and hill girls (*Ellie's Shack, Pleasure Ground, Ex-Virgin, Wild Lovers, Sins of the Flesh*), summer beach resort shenanigans (*Hot Blood, Summer of Sin, Private Club*), evil cheating wives (*The Lady is a Lush, Bad Wife, Frigid Wife*), juvenile delinquents (*Wild Oats, The Cavern, Girl of the Streets, Torrid Teens*) nudists resorts (*Nudist Camp, Naked Flesh, My Wild Nights with Nine Nudists!*) and lesbiana (*Virgins No More, Lucy, Queer Patterns, Three Strange Women, Warped Desire, The Strangest Sin, My Secret Perversions*).

Repetitive sub-plots emerge: the salesmen who sell anything from pots and pans, frozen food, fake diplomas, bogus small town historical books, magazine subscriptions, weather vanes and roofs; the out-of-work heels quickly get jobs as hotel desk clerks, cooks, bartenders, and driving instructors. With *Dial "M" for Man*, the hero is unique: a TV repairman. In *Lonely Flesh* (aka *Lola*), the hero operates food distribution and grocery store management; in *Ladies Man* and *Women's Ward*, the hero is a DJ at a small radio station, and in *As Bad As They Come*, the hero runs a mail order catalog business; but often these heroes and anti-heroes sell insurance (*I'll Call Every Monday, Shabby Street, Tramp Wife*), write ad copy (*Rotten to the Core, Tell Them Anything*), work at hotels (*Hotel Women, Hotel Girl, Summer Hotel, Hotel Hostess*) or are small businessmen (*Lonely Flesh, Dial "M" for Man, Twin Beds*) struggling to pay employees and tuck away a little profit.

Leitmotifs

Hitt's heroes always tend to be large, muscular men six foot one to six foot six, with red hair; hard labor men who juggle multiple sex partners at the same time without guilt or remorse. A psychiatrist might have a lot to say about the projected alter ego, as Hitt was five-foot-five, stocky, balding, and a devoted family man with a wife and three children. In general, his heroes eventually fall for the "good girl" of his various lovers, after screwing something up with the law or with morality, and they see the light, marry the girl, live happily ever after—this was, of course, a requirement of formula fiction at the time, the necessity of redemption from sin, but the texts read a genuine optimism in Hitt's rationale, that there can be happy endings in shabby, criminal lives, that redemption and forgiveness is always possible.

His heroines tend to have at least thirty-eight inch busts, sometimes forty or forty-two, with nineteen-inch stomachs and thirty-six-inch hips, the ideal Marilyn Monroe female form that was popular with American men in the 1950s and early 1960s. The women are jilted wives, cheating wives, secretaries sleeping with the boss, the ambitious young woman not yet ready to marry, the modestly talented actress or singer who gets roped into nude modeling and prostitution, the impoverished woman who finds herself nude modeling and hooking, the naive girlfriend of a bastard who ropes her into nude modeling and sex for pay, and the gaudy hill girl.

One common Hitt heroine, or villainess, is the younger woman who is married to a rich older man, or lives with a rich relative (*The Widow*), who offers herself to the hero and talks him into a murder plot where he will become the patsy—this is the classic James M. Cain scenario often borrowed by writers of vintage noir fiction (e.g. Gil Brewer's *The Vengeful Virgin*); in Hitt's hands, he transcended mere Cain imitation, adding in unique knowledge of employment and economics from his personal life.

Pen Names

Nicky Weaver is the narrator of Orrie Hitt's first novel, *I'll Call Every Monday* and later becomes a pen name for two tough guy private eye books, *Love, Blood and Tears* and *Love Them and Leave Them*. *Monday* ends with Nicky Weaver disillusioned about the insurance business, feeling like the fool for having fallen in the trap the evil wife set up for him and her older husband; he sets his sights on the road, not knowing where he's going. Weaver shows up in the 1961 novel, *Ladies Man*, working as a radio DJ and ad salesman. He briefly mentions events from *Monday* and if the reader is not familiar with the first book, Weaver's ruminations mean nothing. Here, Weaver uses his salesman's prowess to boost a small radio with a higher share of a local market, thus attracting more advertisers and higher rates. Again, he falls in a murder trap to take over the station that was inherited by a woman who doesn't know much about radio. He commits the murder and the end finds him in jail.

He pops up again, however, as the narrator of two private eye novels from Kozy Books, published under Weaver's byline. Is this the same Nicky Weaver? There is no mention of the events from the other two books— did he get acquitted of murder and turn his skills to the gumshoe biz? This incarnation of Weaver is a Mike Hammer-esque, Sheldon Scott-type hardboiled two-fisted tough guy, sans the wise cracks but containing a serious number of wise guy cracked heads. Like a Philip Marlowe case, the narrative is hard to follow, loosely plotted.

The first Kay Addams novel was *Queer Patterns*, a lesbian affair published by Beacon. The book went through several printings and was popular, so Kay Addams continued her sleaze career about "the third sex" sin with *Lucy, Three Strange Women, Warped Desire, The Strangest Sin*, all with Beacon. With Novel Books, Ms. Addams tells the true story about how she became a lesbian and a writer, "as told to" Orrie Hitt, who gets post-modernly self-reflexive by having himself appear as a character: Addams expects a six-foot-plus tall muscular man based on Hitt's heroes and is disappointed to find that he is short and balding. The five Addams "memoirs," starting with *The Autobiography of Kay Addams* and ending with *Cherry*, are all very short books, each around 30,000 words, and pick up where the previous title left off; these titles generally deal with Addams' struggles between lesbian or straight sexual orientation, with "the third street" winning out, unlike the Beacon titles where, for marketing reasons, all lesbian books ended with the heroine choosing the heterosexual life of marriage and family, or ending up in jail or broken for her sins of the flesh: moral tales that depicted lesbian sex as, yes, titillating but also a decrepit crime with a heavy price.

Roger Normandie and Charles Vern were pen names he used when he collaborated with another writer; there's no record of who that writer is but based on author's notes at the front of the books, it is most likely Joe Weiss. Weiss had collaborated on many books with Jack Woodford, who made a fortune writing trashy cheesecake softcore sex novels in the 1950s and 60s, then hired young writers to develop outlines into full books (still a common practice today). Hitt did this once with Woodford. The result was *Leased*, published in hardcover by Woodford's own company and reprinted in paperback as *Trapped* by Beacon (without Woodford's co-byline). Both the Normandie and Vern books are uneven, one can tell where Hitt leaves off and the other author comes in, using a completely different writing style and also tossing in a great deal of spanking and light S/M scenes. This sort of jumbled text is also present in two Beacon titles: *Hot Cargo* and *Add Flesh to the Fire*, both about gun smuggling in Florida with pronounced Hemingway influence (*To Have and Have Not*)— I contend these were also co-authored but only Hitt's byline was used. Two of the Normandies were reprinted by Kozy Books under different titles, and none of the Vern books went to paperback, although their mix of lesbianism and S/M is fascinating; *Mr. Hot Rod* is set among racing car enthusiasts and *The Wheel of Passion* is set in a carnival, containing the same exact plot (a young woman inheriting her father's carney) from *Carnival Girl* and *Carnival Honey*.

I also contend that a Midwood novel published in 1959, *Hired Lover* by Fred Martin, is Orrie Hitt writing with someone else, again probably Joe

Weiss (*Unnatural Urge* "as told to" Hitt by one Joe Black is a clue). Again, the writing style switches back and forth between what is obviously Hitt's and then someone else's. That book is not listed in the bibliography at the back of this book; however, a number of readers who know Hitt well also see Hitt's hand in *Hired Lover*.

The Publishers

Hitts' first two novels were published in hardcover in 1953: *I'll Call Every Monday* (an insurance scam and murder plot along the lines of Cain's *Double Indemnity*) and *Love in the Arctic*, set in Iceland, based on Hitt's personal experience working in an Icelandic hotel. He was paid a $250 advance for each title, after a lot of rejection letters from the mainstream publishers in New York. *Monday* was picked up by Avon Books for paprback; *Love in the Arctic* is one of those curious obscure novels.

Hitt had a decade long relationship with Beacon Books, a company that released almost half of his oeuvre. Universal Publishing, which issued a number of general interest magazines, published racy novels in large folio format under Uni-Books. In 1954, Uni published Hitt's *Cabin Fever,* and months later launched its Beacon Books imprint with Hitt as star author with *She Got What She Wanted* and *Shabby Street*, both 90,000-word, fat paperbacks; by 1957, Beacon switched to the more common 50,000-word book length. Hitt did not publish any books in 1955 and 1956, except for the Woodford collaboration, but he was most likely writing them, such as five in 1957 from Key Publishing, under the Normandie and Vern pennames. From 1957-9, Beacon published a whirlwind of Hitt titles, almost one each month, and continued to do so until 1963.

Hitt titles proved popular and no newsstand or drugstore counter were without several of his books for sale at all times. His early Beacons are ambitious and some of his best: *Pushover* is about a unique scam using Roosevelt's Federal Writers Project that put destitute authors and college professors to work; *The Promoter* is about a freelance journalist who searches for a runaway girl and gets entangled with the Syndicate; *Woman Hunt* is about a man deviously plotting the murder of his wife so he can be with another woman; *Rotten to the Core* is about a clever but doomed scam of a question-and-answer game show on TV; *Sheba* is about a young woman who succeeds at selling cars, a vocation typically held by men; *The Sucker* is about designing racing car engines; *Dolls and Dues* is about a labor union boss' loves and violence.

Remaining with Beacon, Hitt started to sell manuscripts to Midwood Books in 1959, publishing a dozen titles through 1962, beginning with *Affair with Lucy*. Other Midwoods dealt with teen prostitution (*Girl of the Streets*), mail order catalogs (*As Bad As They Come*), and soap opera-like lives of medical professionals (*A Doctor and His Mistress*).

In 1959, Kozy Books reprinted the Roger Normandie novel *Race for Lust* (with a Nazi spies in Hollywood sub-plot) as *Run for Cover,* and a number of original Hitt titles from 1960-2, with themes of mail order business (*Bold Affair*), night clubs (*Love Slave*), white trash hill folk (*Pleasure Ground*) and even the African Congo (*Dark Passions*).

Fly-by-night paperback company Chariot, later New Chariot Library, published a handful of books of lesser quality, possibly manuscripts that Beacon or Midwood passed on. These were about dancers (*Libby Sin*), models (*Passion Street*), airline stewardesses (*Passion Hostess*), a small town lesbian doctor (*Bed Crazy*), and sultry nurses (*Man's Nurse*).

Hitt was approached by Novel Books, an off-shoot of a cheesecake magazine publisher in Chicago, and told he did not have to adhere to genre formula and could expand his ideas in the shorter form of 30-40,000 word books. His Novel novels often take side steps to pontificate on politics: the pros and cons of labor unions (*Shocking Mistress!*), the conservatives of America who wanted to ban books such as his (*Warped Woman*), the welfare state (*Easy Women*), the very rich who exploit poor workers (*Man-Hungry Female, Abnormal Norma*) and political mis-use of the media (*An American Sodom*). There were also the Kay Addams memoirs. Novel had tried an experiment in unique book sizes with the Vest-Pocket imprint; the first boxed set featured two Hitt short novels that, despite the novelty, are not his best work: *Carnival Sins* and *Playpet* (about women in the public relations field). This boxed set is hard to find and fetches a price of $400-800 with collectors.

A shady practice of Novel Books (and their other imprint, Merit Books, which were hardboiled crime titles), one Hitt apparently did not approve of, was the re-issuing of books every year under different titles: *Warped Woman* is also *Wilma's Wants* and *Taboo Thrills*, and *Easy Women* is *Inflamed Dames!, Love Seekers* and *Jenkins' Lovers*. Hitt was aware that his fans felt ripped off thinking they were buying a new book from him, when in fact it was a re-packaged title from the previous year or two.

Hitt had one-title shots with a number of small companies: a gay novel, *Male Lover,* with Gaslight Books—while the idea of Hitt creating a homosexual six-foot-two hunk hero (and ex-football star) is intriguing, the story is hard to follow with too many flashbacks. This is also the case with *While the City Sins* from Ember Books (a William Hamling imprint at Greenleaf), and the rare, much-sought-after *Panda Bear Passion* from PEC Books (an offshoot of Greenleaf, created by former Greenleaf regional booksellers) that is known among collectors as "the Holy Grail" of hard-to-find Hitt titles; the cover shows a naked woman on a bed looking lustfully at a stuffed panda bear doll. Saber Books published *Love Princess* about an incestuous relationship between a teen girl and her stepfather, a topic far too taboo at the time for Beacon or Midwood. Unfortunately, as with all Saber Books, the binding easily comes loose and the font is so tiny you need a magnifying glass or else risk tragic eyestrain. Finally, his last published book, *Nude Model*, from McFadden, with a plain cover, no art, was yet another foray into the sad life of a woman who can only make money by letting herself be photographed in the raw.

A handful of titles from Lancer Books' Domino imprint covered old territory, peeping toms and nude models, except for *The Color of Lust,* which concerned racial issues (the hero is black and sleeping with white women, including his boss) and the trucking industry, with some political rants tossed in that make it read like a Novel Books title.

Beacon became Softcover Library in 1965 and reprinted many of Hitt's Beacon titles with new, racier photo covers featuring photos of naked women, and, because of certain landmark court cases in censorship and obscenity allowing publishers to entertain more explicit sex scenes, curious pages and paragraphs were inserted into these reprints, completely out of character with the tone of the book, to give the title a more seedier appeal. Softcover originals such as *Gang-Up* and *The Sex Pros* are poorly written and incoherent, containing explicit sex scenes Hitt did not write.

The Downward Spiral

By 1964, the quality of Hitt's books took a serious decline, but whether this was from burn out or illness is uncertain.

And then he vanished.

Just like that... as was the case of many paperback genre writers: there today, remaindered tomorrow. His health issues and the changes in publishing and the marketplace for sex books were major factors, of course; seems it was simply his time to fade away, obscure and remembered only by a handful of fans who passed his books around, something that is still true today. With the publication of this omnibus, it is our intention and hope that a revival of Hitt's work will occur-like any prolific author, his novels are a hodgepodge of the good, the bad, and the ugly... toss in twenty or so gold bars of excellent and ambitious aspiration, well, you've got yourself some lost American classics of the paperback's salad days to hold and behold.

MICHAEL HEMMINGSON
SAN DIEGO, CALIFORNIA

Orrie Hitt Bibliography
(all paperbacks unless noted)

Love in the Arctic (Red Lantern hb, 1953)

I'll Call Every Monday (Red Lantern hb, 1953; Beacon, 1954)

She Got What She Wanted (Beacon, 1954)

Shabby Street (Beacon, 1954)

Cabin Fever (Uni-Book, 1954)

Leased w/Jack Woodford (Signature hb, 1954; revised by Hitt & retitled Trapped)

Trapped (Beacon, 1958)

Unfaithful Wives (Beacon, 1956)

The Sucker (Beacon, 1957)

Nudist Camp (Beacon, 1957)

Pushover (Beacon, 1957)

The Promoter (Beacon, 1957)

Ladies' Man (Beacon, 1957)

Dolls and Dues (Beacon, 1957)

Trailer Tramp (Beacon, 1957)

Teaser (Woodford hb, 1956; Beacon, 1957)

Devil in the Flesh (Valentine hb, 1957; Kozy, 1957, as Sins of Flesh)

Ellie's Shack (Beacon, 1958)

Suburban Wife (Beacon, 1958)

Summer Hotel (Beacon, 1958)

Wild Oats (Beacon, 1958)

Affairs of a Beauty Queen (Beacon, 1958)

Call South 3300: Ask for Molly! (Beacon, 1958)

Burlesque Girl (Beacon, 1958)

Girl's Dormitory (Beacon, 1958)

Woman Hunt (Beacon, 1958)

Hot Cargo (Beacon, 1958)

The Cheat (Beacon, 1958)

Rotten to the Core (Beacon, 1958)

Love Princess (Saber, 1958)

Hotel Women (Vantage hb, 1958)

Hotel Confidential (Vantage hb, 1958)

Sheba (Beacon, 1959)

The Widow (Beacon, 1959)

Add Flesh to the Fire (Beacon, 1959)

Private Club (Beacon, 1959)

Carnival Girl (Beacon, 1959)

The Peeper (Beacon, 1959; Softcover Library, 1973, as Twisted Passion)

Too Hot to Handle (Beacon, 1959)

Sin Doll (Beacon, 1959; Softcover Library UK, 1973, as The Excesses of Cherry)

Tawny (Beacon, 1959; Softcover Library, 1964, as Lovers by Night)

Ex-Virgin (Beacon, 1959)

Suburban Sin (Beacon, 1959)

Affair With Lucy (Midwood, 1959; Midwood, 1961, as Married Mistress)

Girl of the Streets (Midwood, 1959)

Summer Romance (Midwood, 1959)

As Bad as They Come (Midwood, 1959; Midwood, 1962, as Mail Order Sex)

Hotel Woman (Valentine hb, 1959; Kozy, 1960, as Hotel Hostess)

Wayward Girl (Beacon, 1960)

The Torrid Teens (Beacon, 1960)

From Door to Door (Beacon, 1960)

Motel Girls (Beacon, 1960)

Tell Them Anything (Beacon, 1960)

Call Me Bad (Beacon, 1960)

Untamed Lust (Beacon, 1960)

Never Cheat Alone (Beacon, 1960)

The Lady is a Lush (Beacon, 1960)

Sexurbia County (Beacon, 1960)
Tramp Wife (Chariot , 1960)
Hotel Girl (Chariot, 1960)
Lonely Flesh (Chariot, 1960;
  reprinted 1963 as Lola)
Suburban Interlude (Kozy, 1960)
The Cheaters (Midwood, 1960)
A Doctor and His Mistress
  (Midwood, 1960)
Two of a Kind (Midwood, 1960)
I Prowl by Night (Beacon, 1961)
Dirt Farm (Beacon, 1961)
Summer of Sin (Beacon, 1961)
Four Women (Beacon, 1961)
The Love Season (Beacon, 1961)
Frigid Wife (Beacon, 1961)
Virgins No More (Beacon, 1961)
Party Doll (Chariot, 1961; reprinted
  1963 as Strange Longing)
Man's Nurse (Chariot, 1961)
Hot Blood (Chariot, 1961)
Diploma Dolls (Kozy, 1961)
Dark Passions (Kozy, 1961)
Twisted Lovers (Kozy, 1961)
Suburban Trap (Kozy, 1961)
Pleasure Ground (Kozy, 1961)
Carnival Honey (Kozy, 1961)
Wild Lovers (Kozy, 1961)
Easy Women! (Novel, 1961; reprinted
  1963 as Inflamed Dames, 1964 as
  Love Seekers, 1965 as Jenkins'
  Lovers)
Shocking Mistress! (Novel, 1961)
Peeping Tom (Wisdom House, 1961)
Love Thief (Beacon, 1962)
Dial "M" for Man (Beacon, 1962)
Torrid Cheat (Chariot, 1962)
Twin Beds (Chariot, 1962)
Naked Model (Chariot, 1962)
Libby Sin (Chariot, 1962)
Passion Street (Chariot, 1962)
Bad Wife (Chariot, 1962)
Passion Hostess (Chariot, 1962)
Bold Affair (Kozy, 1962)

Campus Tramp (Kozy, 1962)
The Naked Flesh (Kozy, 1962)
Violent Sinners (Kozy, 1962)
Love Slave (Kozy, 1962)
Frustrated Females! (Novel, 1962;
  reprinted 1963 as I Need a Man!)
Warped Woman (Novel, 1962;
  reprinted 1963 as Taboo Thrills,
  1964 as Wilma's Wants)
Abnormal Norma (Novel, 1962)
Bed Crazy (Novel, 1962; reprinted as
  Perverted Doctors)
Man-Hungry Female (Novel, 1962;
  reprinted 1964 as More! More!
  More!)
Carnival Sin/Playpet (Vest-Pocket,
  1962)
Torrid Wench (Kozy, 1963)
Strip Alley (Kozy, 1963)
Nude Doll (Kozy, 1963)
Loose Women (Lancer Domino,
  1963)
An American Sodom (Novel, 1963)
Male Lover (Gaslight, 1964)
Passion Pool (Lancer Domino, 1964)
The Color of Lust (Lancer Domino,
  1964)
The Passion Hunters (Lancer
  Domino, 1964; Domino, 1966 as
  This Wild Desire)
Lust Prowl (Lancer Domino, 1964)
The Love Seekers (Novel, 1964)
The Tavern (Softcover Library, 1966)
Woman's Ward (Beacon, 1966)
While the City Sins (Ember Library,
  1967)
The Sex Pros (Beacon, 1968)
Panda Bear Passion (P.E.C., 1968)
Nude Model (MacFadden, 1970)

As by Kay Addams
Queer Patterns (Beacon, 1959)
Lucy (Beacon, 1960)
Three Strange Women (Beacon, 1960)
Warped Desire (Beacon, 1960; UK as Night of Desire, 1975)
The Strangest Sin (Beacon, 1961)
Autobiography of Kay Addams (Novel, 1962)
My Secret Perversions (Novel, 1962; reprinted as Hidden Hungers)
My Wild Nights With Nine Nudists! (Novel, 1963; reprinted as Nocturnal Nudists)
My Two Strangest Lovers (Novel, 1963; reprinted 1964 as Beyond Love)
Cherry (Novel, 1963)

As by Joe Black (*as told to Hitt*)
Unnatural Urge (Midwood, 1962)
As by Roger Normandie (co-authored with Joe Weiss)
Run for Cover (Key hb, 1957; as Race With Lust, Kozy, 1959)
Web of Evil (Key hb, 1957)
The Lion's Den (Key hb, 1957; as Tormented Passions, Kozy, 1959)
As by Charles Verne (co-authored with Joe Weiss)
Mr. Hot Rod (Key hb, 1957)
The Wheel of Passion (Key hb, 1957)

As by Nicky Weaver
Love, Blood and Tears (Kozy, 1963)
Love or Kill Them All (Kozy, 1963)